Esta

BOOK EIGHT

A STAND-ALONE
NOVEL

ALSO BY BRYCE GIBBY

The Princess of Selgovae and the High King

His Majesty and the Prince of Lothian

The Captain and the Dark Queen

The Red Dragon and the Crown of Saxnôt

Knights of the Argoat

The Young Knight of Selgovae

Cwen

Esta

Eșta

A NOVEL

BRYCE GIBBY

ISBN: 9798992326710

First Edition

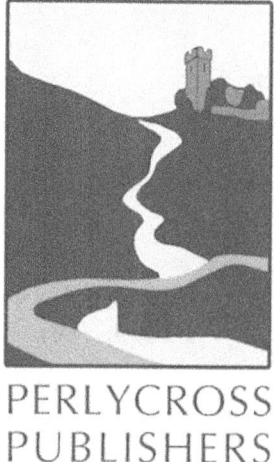

PERLYCROSS
PUBLISHERS
Wilmington, Delaware

"The Perle, as it !ows on the north of the Churchyard, the bridge two or three hundred yards below, the vale, and the hills which shape it, are comprised in the parish of Perlycross."
R.D. Blackmore

CONTENTS

Notes Regarding the Series

A Tetralogy of Tales includes the following works:

    Book One: *The Princess of Selgovae and the High King*

    Book Two: *His Majesty and the Prince of Lothian*

    Book Three: *The Captain and the Dark Queen*

    Book Four: *The Red Dragon and the Crown of Saxnôt*

Three sequels were added to the series. The expanded series is named *The Annals of the Heroic*. The additional works are:

    Book Five: *The Knights of the Argoat*, a stand-alone novel

    Book Six: *The Young Knight of Selgovae*, a stand-alone novel

    Book Seven: *Cwen*, a stand-alone novel

Three additional sequels were added to the series. The expanded series is named *The Decalogy of Antiquities*. The additional works are:

    Book Eight: *Esta,* a stand-alone novel

    Book Nine: *Cinnia and The Witch of Systrafoss,* a stand-alone novel

Book Ten: *The Castle of Caer Sidi,* a stand-alone novel

Books One and Two are a set, as are books Three and Four. Books Five, Six, Seven, Eight, Nine, and Ten are stand-alone works that continue the storyline of the previous books.

Genua

Pisae
Labro
Cemenelum
Papulino
Narbonensis
Massilia
Isola
d'Elba
Cosa
Dianae
Rome
Jaca
Ostia

Barcino

N
W   E
S

Esta's First Voyage

Hadrian's Travels from Rome
through Gaul, Germania, Britannia
and Hispania
(dashed line)

Esta's Journey from
Londinium to the Woods
(dotted line)

PART ONE

CHAPTER 1
WHERE THE SUN RISES

"How is life timeless? How? Raven locks soon grow white and then grow not at all."

La menina[1]

---

1. Occitan for grandmother, the language spoken anciently in Southern Gaul.

Esta and Naomi, a sudden storm

The late day was warm and clear with no hint of foreboding. The Mediterranean Sea ebbed peacefully, blending hazily with the blue sky of the horizon. Esta and Naomi were delightedly gathering mussels from the stony bay. A gentle breeze began to stir when a black cloud appeared in the distance, as if conjured by a sorcerer. The two maidens were shocked by the suddenness of a gale that darkened skies, ripped at their hair and clothes, sending the waters about them frothing as if tossed in a wicked cauldron. Astounded, they hastened towards higher ground when they were caught by the surge, waves higher than their heads. Naomi was luckily dropped by a briny hand upon soft sand, but Esta was flung against a sharp outcrop. When the wave rolled momentarily seaward, Naomi saw her friend prostrate on the rocks, her head bleeding copiously.

~

When Esta was very young, she asked her mother, "La maire mama,[2] how did I get my name?"

"That is a strange question for such a young maid!" she answered. "Your name is your name. Why do you ask?"

The girl of nine answered happily, "In our village there are many demoiselles and mesdames. Two that are called Michela, three Zita, Raimonda and Catarina, and even more known by Ivona, Camila, Celina, Rosalina and Marta." She laughed, "Shall I go on, for I can name them all? Yet, I alone am Esta!"

Her dame chided, "How does such a waif as you know these things and why do you care? Does it help you spin, or weave? No! 'Tis

---

2. Mother in Occitan.

3

your sire's doing. He says you are bright and pays good silver for you to learn ciphers and numbers."

"Oh mama," Esta chirped, "did not Apollo say we should 'Always learn.' And why do you scowl like an owl!" This she said so happily that the frown upon her mother's face vanished. The girl continued, "You know it gives me much joy to twine thread or to help at the loom, and never am I long at my lessons. Do I not do all you ask?"

"Ah yes, yes," answered the dame, now smiling herself, "and more." She quit the work of her hands and sat down beside her fair child. "Well, among our people Esta means 'star.' This fits you well! But 'twas your sire that gave you the name, borrowed, he said, from Italia and in that language, it means 'from the east.'"

The maid cocked her head to the side, which she always did when puzzled. At such times her little nose scrunched, her brow furrowed and her lips pouted delightfully, an expressive manner that was hers alone. "From the east?" she asked. "I've seen naught but the vales and hills hereabouts, though I long to see distant kingdoms— like those spoken of in the codices or the place where Naomi, the Jewess, used to live."

"Nay, you'd not like that!" exclaimed her mother. "Wars plague all lands but ours. For our ports are the southern gates of Gaul and the might of Rome protects us well. We live quietly and many come from far away to dwell here peaceably, saying they are led to our shore."

Again, Esta cocked her head. "Why is there fighting out there but not here?"

"Hmmm," she said thinking. "It seems our land is blessed with those who, though feeling deeply, allow others to have deep feelings of their own. We live not in the great heat or the frigid cold. The land yields bountifully and provides for us deliciously. Why should we fight? We trade abundantly, and as for pirates and thieves, the legionnaires drive them from us. Though we often disagree with each other, seldom is blood spilt among us. No, la filha,[3] be content to live and labor in Occitania.[4] Now help me an hour more, then, if Naomi, or another of your friends can go with you, you may run down to the stony clefts of the sea and fetch us a good basket of mussels. Lo paire papa[5] will surely be pleased!"

Esta exclaimed, "Oh thank you mama. Let us serve him only the shells, and see what he says!"

"You may do such a thing and have a good laugh, but I will not! Take a leather cloth to pry them free, lest your hands be cut, and beware the tide!"

Esta was the youngest of ten children and lived with her family in Massilia[6] in the Narbonensis region of Gaul. Her mother was a Celtic-Greek, while her father was a Roman,[7] formerly a Legionary, who, having served his sixteen years, left the army with considerable wealth and settled in the "Province"[8] with others of his class.

---

3. Occitan for daughter.

4. Occitania: Lower region of Gaul, what is now Southern France, known later as the Kingdom of Languedoc, where the language of Occ was spoken.

5. Father in Occitan.

6. Massilia, now Marseille, France, was first a Greek colony founded in 600 BC and was a primary port of the ancient world. Pytheas led an expedition from Massilia to Britannia, Iceland, the Shetland Islands and Norway in 330 BC. Later Massilia came under Roman rule enjoying peace and relative freedom.

7. "The Province, now Narbonensis, was planted with settlements of retired Roman soldiers; it soon became a land of city-states and was comparable to Italy in its way of life." https://www.britannica.com/place/France/The-Roman-conquest, 2022

8. Provence was the first Roman province outside of Italia, called by the Romans "Provencia Romana." http://www.lifeinprovence.com/p_past.html, 2022

The City of Massilia

Her older brothers were married, as were two sisters. While the mesdames lived with their husband's families, her brothers, their wives and children lived in their father's house, along with their grandmother. Within the courtyard of their domus[9] was a small lodging for their slaves. These were well treated and considered part of her sire's household. Their mutual livelihood was derived from a beautiful olive grove of 280 jugers[10] of land, oxen, asses, olive presses and a large flock of sheep to dung the grove and provide wool.

Though picturesque, with a lovely atrium and portico, their tiled villà was of modest size for so large a family. In fact, Esta shared a single room with three sisters and all four shared one bed! As she was the youngest, she was consigned to sleep length wise at the feet of her siblings. This she did, however, only when the weather was cold. Otherwise, she slept on a small balcony that overlooked the western grove. Nonetheless, the maidens seldom argued and loved each other kindly.

---

9. Domus: a Roman house.

10. Juger, a Roman measurement of land. 280 jugers would be approximately 180 acres.

Esta's childhood villa

Esta's mother was a Hellenized Celt, a devotee of Apollo and the Delphic maxims, while her father was a passive follower of the Roman pantheon. He seldom spoke to Esta of his faith, for his personal beliefs were often in conflict with the popular opinions of those who believed in the gods of Rome.

La maire mama daily taught her family the essential principles of their faith which greatly influenced all of her children, but especially Esta. Apollo was said to be the divine son of Zeus, the King of the Gods and the AllFather. Apollo was known as the God of the Sun and Light, the Healing One, the Averter of evil, the Prophetic Deity and was also the god of knowledge, music, poetry, beauty, order, archery, and agriculture.

Overlooking Lacydon Bay, which was the natural port of Massilia, rose the ancient Temple of Apollo. As at Delphi, there was inscribed at its base these apothegms:

> *"Know thyself. Nothing in excess. Surety brings ruin.*
> *Follow God. Respect your parents. Be defeated by*
> *justice. Know by learning. Be thyself. Desire marriage.*
> *Honor the hearth. Control yourself and temper. Honor*
> *forethought. Swear not. Embrace friendship. Get*
> *wisdom. Praise good. Do not find fault. Praise virtue.*
> *Practice justice. Shun evil. Be fair of speech. Look after*
> *your own. Despise insolence. Regard suppliants. Give.*
> *Fear deceit. Be Holy. Pray. Endure hardships word-*
> *lessly. Honor generosity. Envy not. Hope. Despise*
> *slander. Gain possessions justly. Speak plainly. Be*
> *content with what you have. Listen and observe.*
> *Work. Despise strife. Detest disgrace. Control your*
> *tongue. Be just. Be kind. Be courteous. Act decisively.*
> *Repent. Control your eye. Give timely counsel. Guard*
> *friendship. Be grateful. Keep confidences. Dissolve*

enmities. Accept old age. Do not boast. Always learn.
Do not fight an absent foe. Respect the old and
instruct the young. Do not trust riches. Crown your
ancestors. Be willing to die for your country. Share
burdens. Do not wrong the dead."

Often Mama would take her children to the temple, sometimes to hear a priestly oracle or listen to the musicians but always to study the maxims. She expected her children to recite these until all were committed to memory; this that they should internally craft an honorable compass to guide them through life. When they errored, she would ask which they had transgressed and what precept should be used to right the wrong.

Once she said to Esta, "What is the foundation of Apollo's Temple?"

"I know not the name of the stone, but it must be very strong to support pillars so grand!"

La maire mama corrected her. "Nay la filha, the true foundation of the sanctuary are Apollo's dictums and will long outlast man-hewn stones. All edifices, no matter how grand, at last fall to ruin, but truth is eternal!"

"Ah," said Esta, "truth *is* heavier than stone! When I try to carry all his words in my head it hurts from the weight of them!"

HER WORK FINISHED; Esta hurried down the lane that led from her father's grove to the ramparts surrounding the old Greek colony of Massilia. She soon crossed the Agora,[11] a large park of fountains,

---

11. "Agora, in ancient Greek cities, an open space that served as a meeting ground for various activities of the citizens." https://www.britannica.com/topic/agora, 2022

statues, and monuments, tributes to heroes long dead, where august men gathered to argue and old women to gossip.

"Esta," cried out the white-haired patriarch of a venerable clan, "Do not rush by in such a hurry! Come and sit with us and help me make my point. Sebastian is as dense as a lifeless crow!" Seated about the aged man were three others, who a moment before were speaking rapidly with raised voices and angry grimaces. Yet now, all four grinned pleasantly with inviting countenances.

"Yes, come and sit," said his friend. "Senator Aléxandros is sadly suffering from delirare mentem![12]

The maid slowed her pace and let loose her own oration, "Oh, I see that Cicero from Arpinum is debating our very own Pytheas from Massilia!" Esta stopped and bowed deeply. Then quickly resuming her stance, exclaimed, "Men of repute, I think it unwise for a poor maiden, unlearned and awkward as I, to place herself between the powers of Rome and Greece! Nay! 'Tis best I quit your company before the battle begins! I am off to gather mussels and have no time to tend wounds that surely must follow this heated banter!"

The distinguished quaternion broke into uncontrollable laughter as Esta dashed away as quick as a hart. Nearby dames who had stopped their prattling that they might hear the girl's rejoinder, tittered amusedly. One said, "She is but nine, for so she tells me; yet Esta speaks with the wit and manner of a scholar of years!"

"Yes!" said another. "And she is so good and kind. Mark what I say, Esta shall be a grand lady one day!"

---

12. Delirare mentem, Latin for demented mind.

Bazar of Massilia

Soon she was through the Bazar of Massilia, where Naomi's father, Eitan, sold everything from leather bottles to gemmed ornaments. Together the girls made their way past the quay of the port and beyond the marshes to the rocky inlets. They saw but one man along the shore, a Galatian, a veteran fisherman, regarded as a barbarian by the aristocrats of Massilia. The Galatian was gathering his nets from a day's hard work and beaching his skiff. Neither he nor they called out a greeting, for he was a silent man, wrinkled, weathered and very sad. The older children of the village said he was Charon, the ferryman of Hades. The truth was, the mariner was the sole survivor of a terrible shipwreck and had no friends or family. He sold his fish wordlessly at the market through the agency of a strange woman that some said was once his betrothed, though never were they seen together, save when he brought her fishes.

The late day was warm and clear, with no hint of foreboding. The Mediterranean Sea ebbed peacefully, blending hazily with the blue sky of the horizon. Esta and Naomi were delightedly gathering mussels from the stony bay.

A gentle breeze began to stir when a black cloud appeared in the distance, as if conjured by a sorcerer. The two maidens were shocked by the suddenness a gale that darkened skies, ripped at their hair and clothes, sending the waters about them frothing as if tossed in a wicked cauldron. Astounded, they hastened towards higher ground when they were caught by a surge, waves higher than their heads. Naomi was luckily dropped by a briny hand upon soft sand, but Esta was flung against a sharp outcrop. When the wave rolled momentarily seaward, Naomi saw her friend prostrate on the rocks, her head bleeding copiously.

Naomi screamed for help as she tried to lift Esta to safety, for another breaker fell upon them. So deep was the swell that the two maidens were lifted from the rocks and carried out by the riptide with such force that Naomi lost hold of her dear friend's senseless hand. With great effort the Jewess made her way landward fearing that at any moment she too would be dashed upon the crags, for more often she tumbled below the surface than swam upon it, gulping more water than air.

Suddenly the maid was seized powerfully and lifted free of the awful surge. Naomi was quickly carried to shore and laid safely upon a natural seawall, high above the swell, by as yet an unseen deliverer, for his strong arm was about her waist, her back to his chest. In an instant she was alone, for the man was returning to the howling waves.

Through the mists the exhausted girl saw the desolate form of Esta, face down in the foaming white of an eddy, four rods or more distant. She cried aloud, "Father, let her not die! She cannot! There is none like her. Please, please, I beg of thee, let Esta live!" In the gloom she saw the strong man make his way through the whitecapped straits and twice his tall silhouette vanished beneath the salty flood. Yet, somehow, he found his footing and soon had hold of the unconscious child. Steadily he pressed for the shore and soon was in clear view. To her astonishment it was the Galatian who carried Esta.

When the waters were about his thighs he began running to a stretch of sand above the tide's flow. Quickly, but gently, he laid the maiden upon her back, tilting her head back so that her mouth drew open. Then with his palms he pressed successively upon her stomach until water spurted from her mouth. Then as it was written of the seer, he blew air into her mouth until she began to breathe once again.[13] Still Esta was insensible and so it was that Naomi guided the old mariner, who carried the bleeding child to the villa in

---

13. 2 Kings 4:32 And when Elisha was come into the house, behold, the child was dead . . . And he went up. . . and put his mouth upon his mouth, and his eyes upon his eyes, and his hands upon his hands: and he stretched himself upon the child; and the flesh of the child waxed warm . . . and the child opened his eyes.

the olive grove. Without a word of explanation to her mother, the man disappeared into the darkness of the stormy night.

Esta's father was gone when they came, for he was out searching for his daughter. Yet his sorrow was turned to joy when he came again to his own house. Naomi told all that had happened and stayed until the morning and the end of the tempest.

Esta awoke a day later, but in delirium, suffering more from the blow to her head than from her near drowning. Gradually she returned to her senses. Her grandmother was watching over the child one day when she opened her eyes and spoke coherently, saying, "La menina, He told me: 'Life is timeless.'"

"Oh Esta," the grandmother replied, "you speak! Who told you this? Have you dreamed a dream?"

The injured maid answered, "The Burning One said this to me."

"Oh child, for days you've been right here with only your family about you. That you speak is enough, even if there is no sense in what you say! How is life timeless? How? Raven locks soon grow white and then grow not at all."

The old woman called out to others in the household. When her sire was come, the grandam repeated Esta's words. He then dismissed those gathered about her bed, including her mama, saying, "I will sit with her for a while. Please return to your work."

When alone he said, "Esta, what did you mean, 'the Burning One?'"

"Papa," she answered weakly, "He spoke with such love, such kindness!"

"Did he call to you while you were in the sea?"

"But I wasn't in the sea!" she replied with confidence.

"Where were you?" he asked.

"Far away," she said assuredly, "where the sun rises, in a place of brilliant light. But nothing was so bright as was He!"

"Esta," said the humble sire, "well did I name you! Now you

know that Massilia is not where you began. All of us are strangers here. Now you know that you *were* before you were here. You were *sent* and *preserved* for great purpose! And you will *be* when many think you are not. I, even your father, know little of these things and have never seen that which you've seen. Speak carefully of that which you know, for sacred knowledge must be quietly cherished. Sleep now and recover, but do not forget!"

CHAPTER 2
THE GALATIAN

Neither did I much good or bad an' lived a sailor obed'nt t' capt'n. Ashore in Massilia, I courted a maiden but loved her not enough t' give w'ht she most want'd, t' be daily wit me—for I loved more t' sea an' far off places. Years passed an' stole away our lives. Then came t' tempest nigh unto t' Pillars of Hercules, break'n masts first an' then hull upon teethy rocks. All kill'd, 'cept me. An' why was I left t' live?

Maros

Naomi asked, "Can Esta come play with me in the grove?"

"Not yet, but soon," answered the sick girl's mother. "She is resting on her balcony. Go to her for you are dearer to Esta than her own sisters!"

The two girls looked out upon the grove. Naomi said to her friend, "I hope you are well before the harvest!"

"Of course, I shall be!" Esta replied,

Esta as a child

"We'll climb to the highest branches and pick olives that no one else can reach! And when papa is near and not looking our way, we'll throw olives at him!"

"Yes!" exclaimed Naomi, "until he begs our mercy!"

Esta became very quiet and Naomi supposed her friend was in those sudden spasms of pain that often came upon her. Never did she complain at such times, but ceased speaking instantly, fighting an inward battle that left her face pale. Naomi knew most of Apollo's maxims, for Esta often practiced reciting them to her. How well did her friend observe "Endure hardships wordlessly!"

Naomi loved the maxims, though she was a Christian. Her Jewish grandmother had learned of Christ from a woman named Martha and her brother, Lazarus. Naomi said they left Jerusalem because of persecution and sailed to the south of Gaul, with others of their faith.[1] The grandam was about Naomi's age when her family welcomed Martha into their home and gladly accepted her teachings.

---

1. This journey is detailed in the Rabanus manuscript, entitled *The Life of Saint Mary Magdalene and of Her Sister Saint Martha*, in the library of the Magdalen College of the University of Oxford.

Naomi as a child

Many years had passed since then, yet far greater were the followers of Apollo and Artemis in Massilia than those who followed Christ. Still, Christians lived peacefully in the region, whereas in other nations they were continually harassed.

Perhaps this was due to the similarities of values of the Christians and the disciples of Apollo and Artemis. The adages of Apollo clearly were virtuous, as has been said. So also were the attributes of Artemis. Plato, in the dialogue of Cratylus, stated that "Artemis is the defender of chastity, virginity and faithfulness."[2] While Aeschylus taught, "May pure Artemis look upon this band of unwed maidens in compassion, and may marriage never come through Aphrodite's compulsion."[3] Thus, though the prominent religions of Massilia might be called pagan, yet they were of a far higher order than those who believed in the carnal gods of the pantheon and were more closely allied with the precepts taught by Christianity.

As Esta and Naomi sat upon the balcony overlooking the beautiful grove of olive trees, Esta's silence was not caused by pain, but by her thoughts. After a time, she questioned Naomi, saying, "I remember looking up at a great wave that rose high above our heads and then crashed thunderously upon us! For an instant I felt smothered in swirling mirk, then all was still to me. What next I experienced I will someday tell you, but please tell me again what you saw and did."

Naomi related once more how she tried to save her friend, for she saw that Esta was insensible and her head was bleeding badly; then the pitiless whitecaps tore her away as she screamed for help. Excitedly, Naomi told again how the Galatian saved them. "Ah, I thought

---

2. Ruth Marie Leger, *Artemis and Her Cult*, University of Birmingham, April 2015, p. 40, https://core.ac.uk/download/pdf/33528589.pdf, 2022

3. Ruth Marie Leger, *Artemis and Her Cult*, University of Birmingham, April 2015, p. 40, https://core.ac.uk/download/pdf/33528589.pdf, 2022

him so old! Yet his strength was greater than the sea and soon he placed me safe, beyond reach of the swollen breakers!"

"Will you show me the place?"

"Oh yes!"

"And then?"

"I saw him rush back into the dreadful waves, for we saw you! I thought you dead! Somehow you were afloat upon your stomach, your face buried in the deep tide! How I prayed for you! Then you disappeared below a foaming crest and I thought you lost, swept beyond sight! But he found you and, fighting against a great roller, brought you ashore and laid you on your back on a stretch of sand. Still, you would have died, but he forced water out of you and blew air into you. When your shallow breaths were your own, he carried you here, following me. He said not a word! No sooner than we came to your portico than he turned himself about and was gone!"

"Naomi, how was it that the Galatian heard you above the storm?"

"I've wondered the same thing! But he must have, for he came!"

In a fortnight Esta was able to leave her room and balcony to join her family for meals in the courtyard of the portico. A week later she was well enough to walk with Naomi in the olive grove. Afterwards, she spoke with her father, saying, "Papa, have you spoken with the Galatian?"

"Nay," he said. "Twice I have walked down to Lacydon Bay and looked for him, for I must thank him heartily for saving your life. But I could not find him!"

"Oh," she replied, "I hope he is alright, for there is no one to know if he fell sick! Perhaps when he rescued us, he took ill!"

"Have no worries child. His boat was gone, so he was only at sea."

"Could I go down with Naomi?" Esta asked. "He has a shack in the marshes and sometimes his skiff is beached there in a reedy inlet. We've seen it in our play."

"Well, that I didn't know. But you're not well enough to walk that distance yet," her father replied. Then seeing her disappointment, added, "But I'll tell you what we could do: How would you and Naomi like to ride in the olive cart, and I'll walk at your side, leading the donkey? We could go down this very eve, when likely his sailing is done for the day!"

Esta answered excitedly, "Oh yes! Thank you, papa! I can't wait to tell Naomi!" She was not long in doing so, for her friend came to see her every day.

The sun was an hour from its setting when the father and two girls came to the small lodging in the marshes. As Esta had said, his small sailing boat was pulled ashore nearby. The Galatian apologized for his dress, manner and habitation, saying, "I never thought t'at some'n would come here for t' see me, an' I speak'n so corse like, an me old vestments are not fit, an I've not chairs in my little house, save one. Non'less, I've caught good fish t'day an' a fire is go'n."

Esta's father answered with a broad smile, "We'd love to eat with you and can do so from the back of the cart." In only a few minutes the Galatian laid before his guests savory cooked fish on a clean plank of wood.

Esta said cheerfully, "This is the best meal I've had since I was hurt! Now I've two things to thank you for. Not only did you save my life, but I thought I'd lost my passion for food! This is so delicious! And I feel so ashamed, for we don't even know your name. Please tell us so we know who it is we thank!"

"Yes," said her father, "I can't believe that I've seen you about the market or at the shore for so many years and have never thought . . . never known anything about you. I've only heard you called the Galatian. You must please forgive! Never did I think that I would owe you a debt that I could not repay. Esta and perhaps Naomi too would be gone from us if it were not for you!"

"Nay," said the old man. "I'm known by another. 'Tis Charon, an' fitt'n it 'tis, for I've been so many years n' a lonesome hell. But never did these two maids call me by t'at cursed name an' many a smile they gave me. Ah, but I'm Maros."[4]

The Galatian was standing close by the cart where Esta sat upon the side board. Instantly, she reached out and put her arms about his waist and embraced him, thinking naught of pressing her fine garments against his tattered and salt-laced clothes, saying, "Oh Maros, how can I thank you for my very life?"

To which her sire added, "You could have lost your own in that tempest, no matter how accustomed you're are to storm and strife! Thank you Maros, you are welcome always in my villa, to eat with us and sleep in our home. If you ever tire of the sea, you have a place in my groves to help me husband the olives."

"Yes, yes," cried Esta, "you are now part of la familha and must no more live a solitary life!"

Naomi also embraced him, tightly, as he had held her when lifting her slight form from the surging waters. The aged mariner had not felt arms about him for many, many years and he wept.

There was silence for a time, which at last was broken by the sire who had been thinking earnestly. "Maros, your lodge and skiff will do fine without you for a while. This very night I would that you should return with us. I have a suit of clothes that will be a good fit for you and my wife will set before you fresh fruits and cheese, for I suppose you've not had such fare for a time. Then we will make for you a soft bed. In the morning I will show you my groves!"

---

4. Māros, a Slavic word meaning "sea." https://www.ancestry.com/name-origin?surname=maros

The Olive Grove

The man of the sea was astounded with all that had been said and could say nothing in response. Hence, Esta exclaimed, "Ah, Maros, papa's groves are truly enchanted. We can't wait for you to see them. Please come!" The young maiden tugged on his hand so that he could hardly resist as she pulled him down to sit on the back of the olive cart next to her and Naomi.

The father again led the donkey, while one old man and two young girls rode from the marshes to the beautiful villa. It was a joyful, warm night. The lamp and fire lights of Massilia shone brightly ahead. Naomi, who had been quiet, suddenly asked, "Maros, I have seen you take your fish to a woman in the market, a seller. Is she your sister?"

The question would not have been asked by someone older, for it might have been hurtful to him. Nonetheless, he answered politely, "Nay, that be Eponi, for when young her hair t'was black as ebony pearl!"

LATER IN THE EVENING, by the hearth of the portico, Esta's parents sat with Maros alone, for the maidens had gone to sleep on Esta's balcony. Whenever Naomi stayed late, she always stayed until the morrow.

The mother asked Maros, "Esta told me that the woman in the market who sells your fishes is named Eponi. I'm sorry that I didn't know her name! Is she your betrothed?"

"Once," was his simply answer.

The sire then said, "Why did you never marry her? You are a good man and she is no doubt a good woman and never has married another, for she has been alone at the market for as many years as I can remember."

"What could I do," he said sorrowfully, "take her t' such a place as is mine in t' marshes? Nay, an Eponi would not abide alone whilst I was seaward."

In so few words he had told so sad a story that Esta's mother's eyes became wet. She asked that he tell her more.

Maros answered, "You say t'at I'm good. Well, neither did I much good or bad an' lived a sailor obed'nt t' capt'n. Ashore in Massilia, I courted Eponi but loved her not enough t' give w'ht she most want'd, t' be daily wit me—for I loved more t' sea an' far off places. Years passed an' stole away our lives. Then came t' tempest nigh unto t' Pillars of Hercules, break'n masts first an' then hull upon teethy rocks. All kill'd, 'cept me. An' why was I left t' live?"

The father answered assuredly, "I will tell you why you were left to live! Without you our cherished daughter would now lie still in the cold earth! She who is the brightest star in Massilia and who has such a hold on my heart, that if she should have died, I would be a broken man! Now here is what we will do. We shall build on to the east side of the courtyard and make for you a home in my domus. Never shall you want! Neither for sustenance, clothes or honorable labor, which will never be exacting and fitted to your desires and health. You shall live among us, not as my servant, but as our lo pairegrand!"[5]

"Ah, yes!" exclaimed Esta's mother as she caught hold of the wonderful intent of her good husband, "and you must make haste to your beloved and tell Eponi that you have found your familha, and that at last she and you are to be wed! No more will she toil in the market but will spin at my side and talk with la menina of the days when they were maidens and all of life was before them! Tell her that her day of honor will come quickly, for your lodging will be raised before the harvest is over. Ah, think of it! We shall celebrate the end

---

5. Lo pairegrand: grandfather in Occitan.

of the season of the olives and your marriage on the same wondrous day, together with our familha and all of our friends of Massilia!"

FIVE YEARS PASSED in happiness for Esta's family. The olive trees produced more abundantly than ever before, in large measure due to the care given the trees by Maros, who proved himself a better husbandman than the good fisherman he had been in former years, for now he was contented and labored in love. He rose every day before sunrise and could be heard singing with his rich Galatian voice, which seemed to delight even the songbirds who flocked about the groves and harmonized with the old man in ever increasing numbers.

Later in the morning, as other family members and servants came to labor with him, they could not help but be enthralled by his melodious mirth and would lend their voices to his. Additionally, Maros introduced vineyards to the groves, a custom observed in his native land. The vines thrived, adding aromatic beauty to the Eden surrounding the villa and nearly doubled the families gain, so succulent were its grapes.

When the sun was high, Eponi, with the house servants, brought the mid-day repast to the vineyards and groves. They too would lift their angelic voices, joining the others, making the meal a daily celebration. When she was not at her lessons, or helping her mother spin, Esta, accompanied always by Naomi, ran to help Maros or Eponi. They too would sing! The young maidens' sweet and pure tones were like the distinctive compositions of the Citril Finch, rising hauntingly with ascending trills and beautiful flourishes.

Never did Esta's sire allow hunting in his woodlands, which hence became a safe haven for red deer, grey fox and the marten, all of whom adopted a benign aspect of friendly appreciation for their paradisical abode.

"They eat but little of our bounty," said the sire, "and they add such joy to our eyes!"

Garden of Music and Life

The wondrous qualities of his villa, groves, vineyards and forest were not lost on his neighbors and the townspeople of Massilia. They loved to come and buy oil and wine, walk the verdant paths, see the happy workers and hear their songs. When it was time to harvest the grape and the olive, more were they who came to help for the pleasure of it than those who belonged to the domus of Esta's sire. His dominion became known as "O Xardín da Música e da Vida de Massilia," or Massilia's Garden of Music and Life, spoken in the Galatian tongue in honor of old Maros, who was beloved by everyone.

CHAPTER 3
THE INCREDIBLE PASSAGE

"You speak far beyond our years, as if you were already a great lady, a prophetess."

Naomi

W hat is impossible? Is the possible only what we know from our own experience? Of course not. Often, we believe in what others say. Naomi had never been to Africa, yet Eitan, her father, had been to far off Carthage and told of its wonders. Nobody doubted his stories and all who came to his store loved to hear him speak of that most important center of trade on the Mediterranean Sea, especially his own daughter.

Children readily believe what adults call fantasies of imagination. Is this infantile gullibility or do they have recent veiled memories of experiences far more astounding than anything they encounter in the first few years of "real life?" Is this why little ones gladly accept the fantastic? If they could better speak their minds, would they say sardonically, "Of course what you tell me is wonderful, but don't you remember the amazing odyssey of your birth and what happened before? Now that was truly amazing! So, you see, your tale, though marvelous, is far less astonishing than what I went through to get here! Of course, you experienced the same thing, but sadly have forgotten everything!"

Also, is their puerile mind indeed more capable of seeing the truth of life, especially in the small and delicate miracles of creation, delighting more joyfully in flowers, brooklets, and the small creatures of the forest than their elders?

There is an actual phenomenon, a marvel, a "rapid forgetting" of our earliest memories that is common to all of us.[1] Most learn to speak when they are two and well understand the daily occurrences in life and interactions with friends and family. But can they remember those daily episodes when older? No. Some may be able to recall a vague reminiscence from when they were three or four. However, most memories build with time and coalesce into clarity later in life. Some believe this is a result of a still developing brain, an unproven theory. Rather, is there an aperture of forgetfulness that is secured over our minds at birth and slowly closes until it admits but a pin prick of recollection thereafter? When the orifice closes, does it block out the first years of mortality along with former, truly awe-inspiring, memories?

---

1. "Infantile amnesia, the inability of adults to recollect early episodic memories, is associated with the rapid forgetting that occurs in childhood." From The Journal of Neuroscience, https://www.ncbi.nlm.nih.gov/pmc/articles/PMC5473198/, 2022

AT FOURTEEN YEARS OF AGE, Esta had grown into a remarkable young woman of renown wit, tempered by exceptional grace. Massilia had for centuries been a celebrated center of education in the civilized Mediterranean world and was considered a safer, more conservative seat of learning than the great cities of the Empire.[2] As Esta's father recognized her apparently native genius, he used his growing wealth to provide the maiden with every erudite opportunity that Massilia offered. Her primary tutor, Eutropius, the foremost scholar of Massilia, declared that Esta could no longer be taught by him, but gladly would he learn by her! Amazingly, she had become fluent in Greek, Latin, Gaulish, Galatian, Occitan, Iberian, Euskara, and several Celtic tongues. Therefore, at such a young age, Esta was the most notable linguist of Massilia![3] Additionally, she understood the principles of mathematics as taught by Archimedes and could identify most of the constellations of the night sky. She loved the theatre, especially comedy, and could recite many lines of popular plays. So much so that this became the sport of the learned men who argued with each other in the Agora.

---

2. "Many Roman nobles preferred sending their sons to Massilia for their education —a Greek town, planted far away from the vices and luxuries of the East." J. P. Mahaffy, M.A., Old Greek Education, Harper & Brothers, 1882, p. 138, https://www.

gutenberg.org/files/65058/65058-h/65058-h.htm, 2022

3. Although such accolades are extraordinary, especially by today's expectations of teenagers, in ages past there are examples of greatness in the young. The Lady Jane Grey in her mid-teens was considered famously renowned for her education and was a talented linguist. http://conorbyrnex.blogspot.com/2014/01/the-lady-jane-grey-

construct.html, 2002

Young Esta

One summer's eve, Esta and Naomi were walking through that pleasant park and stopped to admire statues of the pantheon, exquisitely sculpted by the famous Phidias of Athens. Presently they admired the colossal effigy of Zeus when Aléxandros, seeing the two demoiselles, abruptly broke off his conversation with his fellows and spoke a line from Aristophanes' play "Knights," looking directly at Esta.

"Ah there, Nicias, A statue?" recounted Aléxandros, "What kind of statue? Do you really believe that there are gods?"

Smiling the maiden replied to Aléxandros, "Why yes Demosthenes, of course I do!"

Acting the part of Demosthenes, Aléxandros questioned further, "What sort of evidence have you got for that?"

Esta recited Nicias' lines perfectly, saying "Well, I'm someone the gods clearly do not like. Does that not count as confirmation?"[4]

The group of men laughed uproariously and one of their number slapped Aléxandros on the back as he said triumphantly, "I told you that you could not best Esta, the Wonder of Massilia! Now pay me the drachm forthrightly and without complaint, for our champion did not miss a word!"

"Too soon," answered Aléxandros, "she must understand the point Aristophanes is making. So, Esta, what does Nicias mean?"

"Ah that is really too easy," said Esta smiling wide. "Surely next time you will make it harder! He means his misery expressly proves there must be gods, else he would fare far better!"

Aléxandros immediately put his hand in his purse and withdrew the forfeited drachm while his friends laughed all the more. A distinguished man of their number, another senator of the City-State of Massilia, said to his friends as the girls walked away, "Never have we

---

4. Lines from Aristophanes, *Knights*, Translated by Ian Johnston, Vancouver Island University, Nanaimo, British Columbia, Canadas, 2010

seen such a one as Esta! We have known wonderful priestesses of Artemis, divine oracles, yet none approaches the Maiden of the Olive Grove. I tell you, she is enchanted, magical! How can one know as she knows! Easily Esta matches wits with even Aléxandros, the wisest among us. But he was not always so! It took him a lifetime of learning! Can you remember when we were young, how foolish *he* was?"

Aléxandros retorted, "Ha! Did not all of you follow me then? Yes! I admit I was Magister Stultorum."[5]

"Agreed!" answered the senator, "we *were* Discipuli autem Stulti."[6]

"Esta," Naomi said when they were beyond the hearing of the men, "How do you do it?"

"Oh, I spend too much time at the theatre. It is a simple thing to recall such lines!"

"No more than do I, for never do we attend apart. Yet I, who have attained the same fourteen years, cannot remember so well as you. And it is not just recitation, but it seems you grasp every truth that you are taught with such firmness that never do you let it go! How do you do it?"

"Hmmm," Esta answered, "It is not *my* doing."

"Whatever do you mean?"

"Let us walk down to the sea wall where Maros saved our lives and I will tell you that which I promised five years past."

There were in the bay a goodly number of ships, as was customary for the port. From one of these a rowboat had just come

---

5. Latin, Master of Fools.
6. Latin, Disciples of the Fool.

ashore. Yet the two demoiselles noticed it did not tie off at the quay. Rather the rowers ran their boat up on the beach in the precarious shelter of a whisp of sand amid towering rocks. "Those men are not familiar with our tides," said Naomi, "else they would never do that. If they do not return before nightfall their skiff will be splinters!"

Esta replied, "I think they are sailors true and will be ashore for only an hour or two—see how they make haste! Surely our tides are the same as theirs."

The sea was tranquil, a light breeze blowing. The maidens slipped off their sandals and loosed their tresses, which fell comfortably upon their shoulders and backs. Between the rocky crags the soft, warm sand felt soothing and invited play. Esta chased a retreating wave and screamed with delight as the water splashed her so thoroughly that her lower gown clung to her slight form. "Too cold to swim today!" she exclaimed.

"Come, let us walk inland of the sea wall and dry you off!" said Naomi. "Anyway, we came to talk, not to dally with the waves, or have you forgotten your promise?"

"Nay," said Esta suddenly in a subdued voice. "But it is hard for me, because I have only spoke a little of this one time. Only my sire believed me, but he cautioned me, saying 'sacred knowledge must be quietly cherished.' I also have wanted to do as Apollo commands: 'guard our friendship, never boast and keep confidences!'"

"Esta, our friendship cannot be shaken, and though your ken is far greater than mine, always are you humble! As for keeping confidences, we tell each other everything, do we not? Whose confidence do your regard above mine?"

"Heaven's," she answered.

"Whatever do you mean?" inquired Naomi.

"Do you remember how I told you that I saw the towering wave above us?" Naomi nodded assent. "It felt like the mighty hand of death fell upon me. Then came the suffocating convulsions of my drowning, followed by remarkable stillness! What came thereafter I experienced alone. When I came back, I wanted to tell you where I had been, but it was so incredible! I thought you, even though you are my dear friend, would think I was struck in the head so severely that my senses were gone from me—that I was mad!"

Naomi did not understand and asked, "What do you mean, when you came back? You were never gone! I saw you face down in the sea. I saw the good Maros revive you and carry you home. I came to you daily and never did you go anywhere!"

"But I did!"

Naomi looked intently at Esta, "Though often you jest, never do you lie. Know this, there is a feeling of surety and peace about us. I will believe your words."

"That day, it was so beautifully strange," said Esta, "for an instant only was I near and heard you pray."

Naomi exclaimed, "That I did! Never did I tell you this thing, for though we are the dearest of friends, still we are not of the same . . . of the same belief in God!"

"Naomi, perhaps we are! It is hard to explain in words what happened to me. I tell you this, it was *real, a real journey!*"

"A journey? Where did you go? How did you go for you never left my sight? I don't doubt you, Esta, it is impossible that I should, but I do not understand."

"Well, I will try and tell you where I went, though I can't tell you its' name, for that is not allowed, but I will describe things as best I can. After the stillness, I became aware that I was to *go* and suddenly *I knew the way.* How this happened I do not understand, save that I remembered! I had come down the path nine years before. It was not as if I tread on a road. Nonetheless, I traversed a great passageway and did so in an instant. Afterwards, I knew I'd come far, and I knew the place that I returned to, a brilliant abode of arcadian splendor! Not only was this a swift journey, but I felt my mind quickened immeasurably in the process, for I was able to perceive everything about me!"

"Where were you?"

"In the center place, the core of all glory, of all creation. I saw familiar faces and villas, gardens and beautiful fountains. I wanted to run where I knew I had run before. I wanted to converse with every kind face I saw and knew and loved. I had so many questions! And I *knew* I would comprehend the answers as soon as they were given. Yet somehow, I perceived that there was not time—or rather it was not yet time to receive such a fullness of joy. I said aloud, 'If so, why am I here?' It was then I saw the most noble and kind man, the greatest of the hosts of glory, whose very form was brighter than any of the great suns of the heavens. There was about me or perhaps in me that which was most holy, for though he burned with omnipotent power, yet was I not consumed."

Naomi was awe-struck and silent. Esta continued, "A thought came powerfully into my mind, yet it was but a whisper: 'Life is timeless!'

"Suddenly, I felt myself breathing. All about me was blurred and there was great pain. I was then only partially aware of my surroundings but could not open my eyes. In that moment I wanted to tell everyone of the incredible passage. Later I was able to tell the truth given me to La menina. She told me it was foolishness and was only a consequence of delirium. Glad I was that my father believed in the few words I'd spoken and counseled me aright.

"Nonetheless, as I recovered, I knew I'd been given a great gift. Not only was a portion of the gift that of renewed life—but *everything* was part of that gift! You, my family, the olive grove, the vineyard, my labors, my tutors, my purpose, *my mission*. What my father had told me was true and I knew it. I did not spring into existence when I was born of my mother. I was before. You were before! Once I had *seen* this truth and knew it surely, everything I did took on new

41

vitality. This is not something I can claim as my own achievement. Nay! I was given this knowledge of heaven and with it came a quickened mind. So you see, it is not my doing."

Naomi asked kindly, "Did the Burning One say his name—tell you who he was?"

"Nay, I have thought on this hence. I thought in times past that perhaps he is the AllFather or Apollo, his son. Then, as seasons came and went, and you told me more of your beliefs, I have thought, with a peaceful feeling, that mayhap he is *your* Lord. As there was nothing of the pantheon in that holy place, I have come to think that the gods of Greece and Rome, regardless of the virtues that are attributed to the greatest or the evils that are ascribed to the worst—they are all but shades and corruptions of that which really is. They are what a blinded world receives when people desire mysticisms in the stead of truth."

Naomi replied, "You speak far beyond our years, as if you were already a great lady, a prophetess."

"That I am not!" Esta replied emphatically. "I am but a maiden. Though I learn more quickly than do others, still I know I have but little knowledge. Having seen the majesty of our home and the glories of the heavens, I truly understand how very little ken there is in all the ways of man! Yet I thirst to know all I can glean while I walk a stranger on this small field of creation. I want to learn, Naomi, all you can tell me—teach me, for I feel in matters of the heart you are my superior."

The two maidens left the seashore and returned to Massilia by way of the old aqueduct, which, though decaying, was an easy footpath for it was level and traversed a good distance into the city. "Esta," said Naomi, "your father is so good to you!"

"Why yes, he is," she answered. "Your sire is also a kind man. I am much beholding to him, for often he allows you to leave his business in the bazar, to come with me—to be my companion!"

Naomi replied, "He likes you. He loves you! So does everyone! But as for my coming to you, very soon that will end."

Esta caught Naomi's arm and stopped immediately. "Whatever do you mean? Why?"

"A man who is twice my age, a trader, like my sire, is arranging to take me as his wife."

"Oh no, Naomi! He must not be one of your choosing, for never have you told me of this."

"My father told me of the betrothal only this very day. I ran from his shop crying. I don't even know this man who will be my husband! Oh, I have heard your sire say that he has turned down many offers for your hand, because he wants you to continue your studies, to better the genius of your mind. He even speaks of sending you to Athens and Rome! Ah, that my life would be as yours will be!"

Esta was quiet, for she could not bear to think of what this would mean to Naomi—and to herself. Then she spoke resolutely, "I have a plan. When my father talked to me of the great cities and the scholars who should teach me, I meant to ask you if your sire would permit you to come with me. This now must happen immediately. My father will do this for me—for us! He will speak to Eitan, your sire, and say, 'I am sending Esta, the Wonder of Massilia to learn at the feet of the masters of learning. But I cannot send a maiden so young without a companion and no one will suit such a purpose but your own Naomi! Of course, I will pay you in oil and wine, more than you might receive as a Sponsa Pretium,[7] or Bride Price. Yet this shall only be payment for certain years, and still she will be your daughter and will return to Massilia by her eighteenth year!"

Naomi exclaimed joyfully, "Oh, Esta, will he do it? I think it will work!"

---

7. Sponsa Pretium, Bride Price in Latin—like a dowry but paid for the bride by the bridegroom or his father.

"Yes!" said her friend. "Think of the days we will have together—in Athens and Rome!"

Naomi

The two girls approached the old aqueduct bridge, a place where care must be taken as it was narrow and certain of its stones were made loose by many wandering roots.

MOST COASTAL TOWNS and cities of the Mediterranean were set back from the shore a league[8] or more. This was to provide a buffer of security. Pirates and thieves of the era were mainly seafaring men, for land routes were not as abundant as the open ways of the ocean. Yet robbers would not readily plunder a town where escape was difficult and the way back to their ship too distant. However, Massilia was a port city and the gateway to Gaul. Numerous roads led from Massilia to the many kingdoms of the continent. Yet it was under the protection of the Roman Empire and few were the raiders that dared to accost its citizens, though the city lay near the bay.

THERE WERE GATHERED at the ends of the aqueduct bridge a number of people. A host was assembled atop the stairs of a near wall, looking and gesturing towards the bridge, while below the span several women and children stood talking. "This is most unusual," said Esta.

"Has someone fallen?" mused her friend.

---

8. A league is considered to be approximately 3 miles.

The Aqueduct Bridge in Massilia

"If so," said Esta as she peered over the side of the ancient conduit, "they have been carried away."

As they drew near, a woman who stood at the end of the span looked up and saw the maidens. Immediately she ran to them and caught hold of Esta with trembling hands, exclaiming, "Oh my dear! You do not know, do you!"

"Know what?" said Esta with alarm.

"Your father and mother were on this narrow passage robbed but a short while ago!"

"Robbed?" cried Esta. "Where have they gone?"

"Oh, my dear," said the woman, now crying herself. "The thieves are murderers, for your sire tried to fight them off and both he and your dame were thrown off the bridge!"

CHAPTER 4
NAOMI

"Esta, you have no mission from the gods, save to follow the customs of Massilia."

The Eldest

Her elder brother looked up from the parchment of accounts and said regretfully, "Esta, do you know what is the biggest expenditure of the groves and vineyards?"

The maiden did not want to talk about silver. It had only been a week since her papa and mama were killed and she was numb from the inconceivable loss. Nonetheless, she answered politely, "No, I'm sorry. Papa did not speak of such things to me, nor did mama if she knew. However, now that the villa, the groves and vineyards, the servants and all else is yours to govern I can understand why such things would be foremost in your mind."

It was the custom of Massilia that the first-born son inherited the majority of his sire's property so that grand estates would not be broken up on the deaths of their owners—which also contributed to the stability of the city-state. The eldest then had the responsibility to care for his sire's domus, now his, and all who resided there, kin, citizen or slave. Married daughters seldom received an inheritance, for they, by rite, had joined another domus and were to be cared for by their husband's family.

Esta's father's will was in accord with this custom. The villa, lands, and all that pertained to the household, grove, vineyard and their care became the property of his first-born son. His other sons received an equal portion of his silver and gold, save for a small sum given to Esta. This resulted in an unforeseen consequence as it severely restricted the amount of ready coin the eldest had on hand to operate his holdings for several harvests to come. Hence, it was likely he would have to borrow from the money changers, who were notorious in Massilia for high usury—unless . . .

At the time of his death, all of the daughters, with the exception of young Esta, were married and were, therefore, excluded from his will, save for certain personal effects they received from their deceased mother. To Esta their father willed an amount of silver that was equal to one fourth of the value given to each son. This also resulted in another unanticipated result. Esta's parents were in the vigor of life when they were murdered. Her sire had felt the keen responsibility to cultivate Esta's extraordinary intelligence and had spent significant funds on her, securing the best tutors in the land. He believed that he would live many years beyond the age of her majority and would continue to advance her opportunities, including the aforesaid journeys to the great seats of learning. But he had tragically been slain and though he left behind a great legacy, and not in property only, the reality of his untimely passing intensely changed the maiden's prospects.

"I'm sorry to have to tell you this, Esta, my beloved sister, but it is you!"

"It is me?" she answered with uncertainty. "What is me?"

Her older brother explained, "You are the greatest cost! Papa gave your tutors a sum greater than any other outlay of funds required to produce our oil and wine. I did not know of this until now and am left breathless at the sum! How he hoped to send you to Athens and Rome and still operate the groves and vineyards is beyond my imaginings!

"Then all is changed," Esta answered quietly.

"All *is* changed!" the eldest replied emphatically. "I have already notified your tutors that their hire is terminated."

"What?" exclaimed the maiden. "Do not I have a say in this matter? After all, I was willed a fair amount of coin!"

He answered, "At the rate papa was paying, what is given you would be spent within a season. Also, you have not reached the age of your majority—and so I will look after your inheritance until then."

A thought came into Esta's mind, "He will spend your money on his domus! Demand it be given to a lender in Massilia and then you will have increase at least!" The girl cocked her head to one side, considering the thought, which did not seem as if it were her own.

She said aloud, "How strange!" for Esta did not know that thoughts could be placed in her mind by unseen adversaries.

"Strange?" her brother retorted. "There is nothing unusual about what must be, for it is the custom of our land."

Esta countered, "I did not know it was customary for the eldest to keep inheritances for one as old as I, for many maidens of fourteen years are already married!"

"Exactly! And I say you otherwise misunderstand! You are not the only one with wit and sometimes you do not see the way when it is right at your feet! I do not say that it is customary to keep an inheritance, such as yours, for very long, provided the heiress becomes joined to another domus—which *is* according to custom. There is no cause for you to remain here. In fact, quite the opposite. Did you not know that you, my own sister, are the most sought after maiden in Massilia?"

Esta was growing angry, despite her internal resolve to never lose control of her emotions, for she desired to be governed in these situations by the maxim *"Control yourself and temper."*

Nonetheless, she exclaimed with raised voice, "Marriage? You want to marry me off? That is how you propose that I should keep my inheritance? That is what you say 'must be?'"

"Calm yourself," he replied. "Not a single suitor has asked for your inheritance as a dowry! Rather, it is they who pledge fortunes, as Sponsa Pretium to our sire's domus for the hand of 'The Maiden of Massilia!' Think of our household, of old Maros and Eponi! Think of la menina, of your brothers who still labor with us, of our good slaves! There are not sufficient monies left me—I who must see to their bread and shelter, without such an endowment. Think of yourself! Think of the life you will lead in the domus of a rich and powerful man! A man of your choice, even the great Aléxandros has asked for you! Lastly, is it not a command of Apollos that you should 'desire marriage?'"

Accusations flashed in Esta's mind, but she did not speak them, for the very thought of such a betrayal shook every sense of her being. And again, these strange thoughts felt like words whispered from another. Rather, the maiden looked steadily into her brother's eyes and was silent.

"Well," he said at last, impatient and uncomfortable with her gaze, "You cannot answer my arguments, for they are sound. Think on the matter for a day or so. Whose wife will you become? But say nothing to anyone. For I, as your guardian, must set the price and see that it is paid. Still, most likely, the choice will be yours in the end, for I think all of your suiters will pay fairly, for they are men of means and renown."

Now, totally in control of herself, Esta said evenly, "It is interesting, dear brother, how you speak of my marriage as benefiting *our* sire's domus and *our* household, when it is now *your* domus and *your* household. Of course, I desire marriage, but not for years to come! How readily you have dismissed the mission given me of heaven, that you might profit *now*. Your domus is a rich inheritance, a treasure, which you did not buy. It cost papa all that he had when he quit the legion and all of his labor thereafter. Then when Maros joined himself to papa's domus, vineyards were added to groves, and wealth multiplied. True, you labored with your brothers, but in exchange you were given the means of life, for yourself, your wife and children and lived secure and well fed. Then papa and mama died, a most peculiar and horrible death, and suddenly most all that his life produced is now yours, and yet that is not enough! You want my life's labors as well! You think my learning comes with ease, that I speak many tongues naturally? You who can only speak Occitan well and a smattering of other tongues? Heaven enlightens only that which we labor strenuously to put into our minds. Our father believed there was great purpose in my mission!"

"Your mission?" he scoffed. "You have a mission of heaven, do you? Did Artemis, or perhaps even the great Apollo speak to you and give you a quest?" Esta was silent, believing she had spoken too much and regretted belittling his intelligence. "You have no answer for me," he continued, "for you have no mission from the gods, save to follow the customs of Massilia and marry. You speak as if I should pity your circumstance, you who will become the foremost woman of one of the great domus' of our land! What is the labor of a mind compared to my bleeding sweat? I knew that it was I myself who labored many years for your ease! Now it is only right that I, who am now master of this domus, receive your Sponsa Pretium!"

53

Esta was almost bewildered. "You say it was *you* who provided for my learning? Did you not just tell me that you knew nothing of the great cost of my tutors until after papa died? Now I see clearly that you begrudged the expense of magnifying my gifts of knowledge before papa was murdered and feared the great cost of my future travels."

"You put your own meaning behind my words," he said with a twitching eye. "I fear nothing. There will be no voyages to Athens and Rome for you, Esta. You will do as I say. And you speak too highly of the old fisherman, for it was *I* who caused vineyards to be grown. Also understand, that without the monies I must obtain for your hand, the mendicant Galatian and his wife must, of necessity, be turned back to their seaside hovel."

Suddenly, Esta was flooded with emotions, "I owe Maros my life! Papa promised Maros that he would always be with us!"

The brother smiled, "That he shall, provided you do as I say."

THE TWO MAIDENS sat on the sea wall, watching the cresting waves. "

"Naomi, what shall we do?" Already Esta had told her friend that she too must be wed, and soon. She had learned that her brother, as her guardian, indeed had authority to legally barter her life away. He had the power to effect a marriage or even to arrange for "the acquisition of a concubine from the maidens of his domus," the law said, though gratefully he had not threatened Esta with so deplorable a state.

"Naomi answered, "I think I can do nothing, but submit to the will of my father. But you, the foremost demoiselle of our city, can surely appeal to the justice of the Senate of Massilia with words such as only you can propose and convince them to forego the custom of our land!"

"Nay," said Esta, "how can I appeal to the senate when six of their number would have me for wife? There are others of great power, men of wealth, and not from Massilia only, who want me. All have forgotten my erudition. I have become but sport; each man courts not me, but my brother and already give *him* gifts to win *his* favor. It will not be as my brother said, a man of my choosing, but he who pays the most will obtain the prize, for that is all I am to him. The only reason why I am not now a married woman is that the bids keep getting higher!"

As there seemed to be no solution, Esta turned the conversation. "Naomi," she said, "It was your grandmother who learned of the Galilean Messiah from those who came from Jerusalem, is it not so?"

"Yes," answered Naomi.

"And it was here, in Massilia?"

"Again, you are right."

"But your people are also from Jerusalem?"

Naomi saw the question that was in Esta's mind, and said, "Grandmother's family, with others, fled from the Holy City when Titus destroyed Jerusalem and the great temple of the Jews. It is said they lived beyond the walls of the city, near the sea, and barely escaped with their lives. I think this was before Titus became Emperor. I don't know how it was they were so fortunate as to find safety in Massilia, save that her father, like mine, was a merchant and somehow found passage for his own."

"Was this then about the time the first Christians also fled Jerusalem?" Esta asked.

"Nay," Naomi said, "our family fled a score of years after that. They had been settled in Massilia for many seasons when the goodly Martha, then an old woman, came to their home. Grandmother, then yet a maiden, said it was this that so impressed her dame, that someone so aged would travel about unwearyingly. She said that when the saintly woman, bowed and gray, spoke of Him who saves us that her visage was radiant and an indescribable warmth filled their small house. Many times my father told me this story, just as his mother had told him."

Destruction of the Temple in Jerusalem by Francesco Hayez, 1867

"That is a beautiful story," said Esta, "save for their flight from Jerusalem, which must have been dreadful. Can you tell me more of this?"

"Nay, grandmother was said to never speak of it; it was so terrible! Although she was only a child when her family was forced to flee, the memory of it haunted her dreams all of her life. Oh, she was so grateful to find peace in Massilia and to learn of new truths in this ancient city."

"Was she always happy here?" asked Esta.

"Very happy. After a time, her father betrothed her to distant kinsman who also had survived the destruction of the Holy City. So they shared common memories of the unspeakable. After their marriage, he slowly saw the truth in her family's beliefs and so they eventually shared the same convictions. She bore many children; my father was the youngest."

"How did your papa become a traveling merchant?"

"I guess he inherited his trade and for a while worked with his sire. Of course, he grew up here, a Christian, and never experienced the persecutions his parents suffered. He was not content just to buy and sell in Massilia, but wanted to sail to distant ports. When he was of age, his father sent him out, as he desired."

"What an adventure!" Esta exclaimed. "Did he love it?"

"Oh yes! You have heard many of his stories!" Naomi said. "But he learned that many people hated Christians. In other places it is not like Massilia. And so he learned to be careful if he wanted to stay alive."

"It was that bad for him?"

Naomi replied, "He does not speak of these things to others. When he was in Alexandria, a city of magnificence, he was taken, bound and cast into the prison house, all because he was heard speaking of our Lord. There he almost died. In truth, wane and feeble, he lost his senses and was set out to die in a field beyond the prison gate. A maiden, half his age and also a Jew, found him and with her brother carried him to their small house. It was she who saved his life!"

"Oh Naomi!" Esta replied, "that is so tender! Did he grow to love her?"

"Yes, oh yes! While he was ill, he only spoke of his faith to her, for her sire hated Christians, and so he was very careful. Later, papa asked him if they could be wed and promised to give his daughter a comfortable life, explaining that he was a merchant from Massilia. Her sire was suspicious and said, 'How is it then that you came into my house destitute and nigh unto death, with no one but my maiden to give you life? It is likely you know the feel of shackles, for so spoke the wounds about your ankles and wrists! I have not cast you hence because you are of the House of Israel, like us. But beware! Now that you are near recovered, get you far from here, lest I repent of the mercy we've shown you!"

"Oh no!" exclaimed Esta. "What did he do?"

"That very day, while her sire was about his business, he fled with the maiden to the Port of Alexandria. There he was blessed to find a merchant ship that knew him. Before the sun set, they sailed from the shores of North Africa."

"Oh, it is wonderful!" said Esta.

"It gets even better, but never tell this story to anyone, for father kept it a secret from all, even his own family! He spoke of it to me only after I pressed him for years, begging to learn more about my mother!"

Esta replied, "It is a beautiful love story and I cannot see how it could 'get better.'"

"Oh, it does! Heaven smiled on them, for there was a Rabbi aboard the ship. He saw them and guessed the truth of their escape. Yet, he did *not* find fault with their actions, but said, 'Not all great unions are of custom. If you will promise faithfulness, to be true to the one God and each other, I will bind you, here and now!'"

"And then?"

"My father returned to Massilia with a beautiful bride! Oh, how his family loved her and they were so happy! Yet, in travail, she died giving me birth! His own family had believed his lie, that she was given to him in Alexandria by her sire. No one knew that he had stolen his wife. Condemning himself for her death, for he believed it was his just punishment for what he had done, he mourned the loss of her and never has his heart healed. Only when I begged him to tell me of my own mother did he finally relent.

"Then he said to me, 'Naomi, there are truths inscribed on the codices and there are truths that are preserved in the traditions of our people. To violate either is to transgress. Nothing is so vital as the binding of a woman to her husband. Live a true Christian but always uphold the customs of our race regarding the rites of marriage. Never,' he said, 'could I marry again, but have lived since *only for you.* Know this, my daughter, when the time comes, I will only bind you to a worthy man, one who will give you joy.'

"When first he told me this, I was grief stricken for my mother's sake and for his. I resolved then to be a faithful daughter and obey his will. Now my heart is in conflict, for us both! Deep down I feel it is not right that either of us are wed—not now, not yet!"

Esta, said quietly, "Then what are we to do? Always, my friend, you are my exemplar and I must hear your counsel."

Naomi answered, "Oh, I can say naught but this: there is *nothing* for us to do, save to obey, I to my sire and you to your guardian. After all, we are but maidens of age to marry, yet not of age to decide our own fate. Also, you could never allow old Maros to be cast out! If only your parents had not been killed! Then could we have traveled to Athens and Rome and returned to Massilia, having reached our majority and could have followed both custom and the feelings of our hearts!"

CHAPTER 5

THE NECKLACE

"His sire is Cain."

Esta

∿

Corpulent and jocular, the nobleman from Jaca laughed raucously, "I did not travel by cart from my citadel to the Ebro River, by boat to Barcino[1] and by ship to Massilia to quarrel over nothings! For two centuries my house has forged the coins of Rome![2] To you what is a hoard of silver is but a trifling bag to me! I am not here, Master of the Villa, to contend for the Maiden of Massilia! Ha! Rather, I shall arrange to *emptio virgo sine certamine!* Ha!" His gaze passed from the eldest son to Esta as he said, "You see,

---

1. Roman Barcino is known today as Barcelona.
2. Talbert, R., (2000). (ed.) Barrington Atlas of the Greek and Roman World. Princeton University Press. Map 25, E3.

fair demoiselle, I am truly a scholar and will yet teach you to understand such words!"

Esta replied with a dismissive wave of her hand, "So you intend
to 'purchase the virgin without a fight,' do you!" She glanced at her
guardian as she said, "My brother knows I am not a slave to be
vendidit ad auction."[3] The man flushed with embarrassment and was
about to submit a vain apology when Esta asked, "Lord of Jaca, what
price do you bid? You cannot say, 'A thousand pieces of silver more
than anyone else,' because my brother is too shrewd to disclose what
others will pay for me!"

The guest was not accustomed to be humbled by word or
gesture. It was apparent to the elder brother that his sister had
offended the rich suitor. Quickly he said, "Esta's wit must yet be
tempered by an august hand, such as yours, most gracious
grandes."[4] The compliment immediately had the desired effect.
Seeing this, he continued, "Although you may disagree with the
manner of my sister, the truth of her words does strike at the arrow's
point, does it not?"

"Ha!" replied the man, a smile again furrowing his obese cheeks.
He raised a finger and his servant left the room. "This is exactly what
I intended, and in fact meant by . . . by that obdurate expression. You
shall see that I speak with intent that cannot be misunderstood!
While we wait, another flask would do me well!"

Esta was silent, while her brother spoke genially with the
pompous and foolish man. At length the servant returned, together
with five strong men with swords at their sides and bearing heavy
burdens corded from their shoulders. These caskets were placed at

---

3. Sold at auction.
4. The title grandes meant the great ones, those who were at the pinnacle of the
ranks of the rich and powerful.

the feet of the eldest son, while the servant opened each coffer one by one.

Triumphantly, the Lord of Jaca declared, "Two talents! Twelve thousand drachmas![5] Ah," he laughed heartily, looking at the astonished face of her brother, "There is no more need for you to haggle with senators and merchants! Soon this treasure will be yours!" Then, moving his eyes only, for it was difficult to move his body, he said, "Now Esta, even your composure is markedly altered. Have no fear, Maiden of Massilia. Soon you will be the greatest noblewoman of Jaca, esteemed as a queen and of far greater worth than the silver and gold you now see laid before your brother."

Seeing his host speechless, he continued, "My guards shall watch over this invaluable Sponsa Pretium and I shall remain your visitant until the rites are accomplished, here in Massilia! Have no fears, Esta, how I love ceremony! The wedding will be splendid, glorious, regal! You shall be the envy of every demoiselle and mesdames in your great city, before, shall we say, seven days are spent?"

Esta remained silent. Seeing her crestfallen countenance, her brother replied, "Mmh, my lord. There is much preparation required for a great wedding in our country. Methinks Esta is overwhelmed by this sudden magnificence, which has surely exceeded *her* every expectation. Let us be realistic. Shall we say ten days?"

"Ha!" came the immediate answer. "Of course!"

No longer was the villa a peaceful home, serene and orderly. The Lord of Jaca occupied the room where Esta's parents had so recently

---

5. "Hellenistic mercenaries were commonly paid one drachma for every day of service, which was a good salary in the post-rer (III) days. 6,000 drachma made a talent." https://simple.wikipedia.org/wiki/Talent_(measurement), 2022

slept. The servants were tented, while his soldiers guarded the Sponsa Pretium, or the bride price, in their small apartments. The groves and the vineyards were neglected, as slaves made frantic preparations for a ceremony dictated, not by the customs of Massilia, but by the commands of the wealthy nobleman of Hispania. Overnight the news of the instant betrothal and ridiculously short engagement spread throughout Massilia, much to the consternation of the formerly expectant men of the city.

"Esta, Naomi," cried Senator Aléxandros as they walked through the Agora and past the familiar meeting place in the beautiful garden, "who are these giants that trail you?"

"Ah," she answered dejectedly, "my Jacaian guardsmen. It seems that when I am without, I may never be without them!"

"But why?" countered Aléxandros, "never are maidens accosted in our land and you of all people are safe here in Massilia!"

Naomi answered, "The Lord of Jaca commands it! He fears his lady's capture and subsequent demands of ransom!"

"A quick game, dear Esta," he answered only half in jest. "What maxims of Apollo are relevant to this extremity?"

"Yes, yes!" said his companions, eager to relive the pleasant contests of recent days. Their spirits needed lifting, for with the announcement of Esta's betrothal, it seemed a colorless and dank stratus had enveloped the whole of Massilia.

Esta was silent and Naomi, wishing to unburden her friend from the friendly inquisition, said, "I too have learned, I think, every saying of the son of Zeus. Mmh, 'Desire marriage' and 'Be defeated by justice!'"

Aléxandros placed his strong arm on the maiden's shoulder and said graciously, "For one so young and a Christian, you answer understandably. Nonetheless, those axioms cannot apply to Esta. This proposed marriage cannot be desired, by her or anyone of sound mind—neither is it just, nor should Esta ever be defeated!"

With his hand still kindly on Naomi's arm, he addressed the betrothed demoiselle, "I am thinking of four edicts of the god that you must obey. What are they?"

Esta was silent, as were they all. Then she raised her eyes and met those of the senator and answered, "'Despise insolence! Fear deceit! Hope! Do not trust riches!"

Although Esta said these words with conviction, the friends of Aléxandros exclaimed, "Excellent, most excellent! Another round of wit, if you please!

"Esta, the illustrious Aesop spoke of a fox and a bramble. Tell us the tale with application to your affairs."

The Maiden of Massilia replied, "There was a Fox who was fiercely pursued by dogs, He thought there was no way for him to survive, except he should attempt to leap through a bramble hedge. Alas, his feet were torn by thorns and he fell headlong, bruising his head badly. In his stupor he began licking his bleeding paws while cursing the Bramble for its unkind treatment. 'What is this?' answered the Bramble, 'softly and carefully you should speak to me! You should know better than to lay hold of one whose nature it is to lay hold of others!'"[6] Esta gave no more explanation than this: "My elder brother thinks himself a fox."

When they were apart, Esta said to Naomi, "Oh, my friend, nothing seems to sooth my mind—not the fountains or the bustling streets of our city."

"And those . . . what did Aléxandros call them?" said Naomi.

"Giants!" answered Esta.

"Yes, those ever-present lumbering, hulking giants! They hear every word we say. Turn and see! I but called them ogres and there are laughing at my dismay!"

A sudden thought came into Esta's mind and her face bright-

---

6. https://fablesofaesop.com/the-fox-and-the-bramble.html, 2022

ened. "Trees!" she exclaimed. "When nothing seems right there is only one thing to do!"

"Yes, oh yes!" Naomi rejoined. "Let's run to the olive grove and climb the tallest tree!"

That the guards were men of athleticism was proven, for the easily kept pace with the maidens and soon found themselves in the shade of the grove. Suddenly Esta turned about and commanded in their own tongue, "Stay you at least two rod's distance from us. We will always be within your sight, but you cannot accompany us into the boughs, for we will ascend quite high and the limbs will not accommodate your weight."

Naomi added, but in the common tongue of Massilia, "It would be quite unseemly, would it not, for great soldiers to be seen scampering up behind us!"

The captain of the guard understood her well, but protested, saying to Esta, "Gran doncella, you cannot be serious! I thought you jesting when you spoke of this in the Agora! This is dangerous sport! What if you fall?"

"Ha!" Esta replied. "You will fall unawares on your own sword before we would fall from these boughs. Your master did not forbid us from climbing trees!"

"Never would he have thought to do so!"

"Then it is not in your power to forbid me. You may keep your eyes on our movements from a distance!"

Old Maros greeted the two demoiselles as they entered the grove, "Ah, 'ta angels is come! Well said you, 'n years past, t'at 'dis place is n'chanted!" Then drawing close he whispered, "'Ta magic will vanish when y'er gone! Ah, how quick life is chang'd! Oh 'tat I could sail you both far 'way. I still know 'ta sea, but my skiff is na''more worthy to ply 'ta deep!" The maidens embraced their benefactor and told him unabashedly of their love. Taken aback, he said, "Now I knows you aren't in 'ta groves jus' 'ta see me, but surely have come fer climb'n!"

Soon they were at the base of the tallest tree in the grove. Beneath their frocks they wore a type of pantalettes, which provided all the decency required, in the present setting, to tie their gowns about their waists that they might easily climb the gnarled limbs. High in the tree, happily Naomi said to Esta, "Look how everything is plainly before us. We can see afar! The villa appears once again peaceful. Far beyond, the ramparts and port appear flawless and the sea—well, the sea is *perfect* and forever!"

"That is why we climb this living soul," said Esta. Think of the ages this tree has seen! Papa told me it was old when the first Greeks from Phocaea came here in centuries past. Oh, that this sage could speak, impart its wisdom to me, for no being can live so long without *knowing*. Ah Naomi, there must be a way! If it cannot be seen from this great height, where can it be seen?"

The two girls laid side by side in the crook of a branch and were as comfortable as if they were in their own soft beds. Neither spoke for a time. Suddenly Esta started, exclaiming, "Naomi, I have been so distraught at my own misfortune that I have scarcely given thought to yours! Nothing has changed for you since we spoke of your betrothal. Remember our plan!"

"Yes," she answered, "and I think it would have saved me. I did not tell you this before, but my father is in that same state that your elder brother *thinks* he is in."

"What do you mean?"

"Your brother possesses great wealth, but *thinks* himself desperate for lack of coin and has made you his unlikely but highly profitable benefactor. My sire is in hard circumstances, for he provided the monies for a merchant voyage. Upon the ships return, his wealth would have been greatly magnified. He ventured far more than ever he did before. The ship has not been heard of since it sailed and its expected return is far past. He admits sorrowfully that my marriage will redeem his trade. Still, my betrothed is a good man and my case is far better than your own."

"So, our plan would have truly saved you from this early marriage?"

"Yes," Naomi replied.

"Well, I have another! Listen! From my mother I inherited a necklace. It is a very colorful piece that she would wear on festive days. When my sire was a captain of Rome, he was principal in the capture of a rich city and was given this necklace as reward from his general—my sire said it was from the treasury of the king of the land! Yet I didn't think its worth too great, for my brother did not object to my receiving it when mama's gifts were read to us. Still, it must be of some value. Yes, it must be for I *feel* led to do as I propose. Let us take the necklace of many colors to your sire. Surely, he will know its value and it may be of sufficient worth to satisfy his straits."

"Oh Esta, but how could you part with such a legacy?"

"The gems mean far less to me than do you, my dearest sister. And have you forgotten that my betrothed promises me jewels without end? Let us get down from these oracular boughs, fetch the necklace and hasten covertly to show them to your father! I will tell him that all that I have is *his* if he will grant unto you the space of four years more of maidenhood. When that time is ended, you will obediently enter into godly marriage with a love of *your* choosing, *but only with his consent*. When that time is come, he will receive another Sponsa Pretium, one that will bless him well into his old age!"

Before nightfall, Esta and Naomi left the villa with the precious necklace hidden on Esta's person. With their guards dutifully following, they made their way into the town of Massilia to Naomi's home. As they drew near, Esta commanded her guards, "For you to enter this house would violate our customs, for it is forbidden that men-of-arms come within, especially if they are of foreign birth, save they leave their weapons without. I know this you cannot do. Therefore, put a man to guard each corner of this place. It is small. I cannot leave without your knowing and no other person may enter without your leave." The captain acquiesced and ordered his men to surround the cottage and guard it faithfully.

After the maidens supped with the good merchant, Naomi said, "Sire, you have betrothed me to a man of means. Know that I will be obedient to you always. Yet you must see that I am aggrieved because of it."

"Oh, my Naomi!" he said. "This I know and have suffered because I see your heart is not satisfied in this thing. Still, I feel that all will yet be well. You know our state. I am truly your sire and tell you there is no other way. Your marriage is honorable. Fear not, love will follow honor."

Then he turned towards Esta and said, "You, our dear friend, I love you as if you were truly the sister of my own maiden. What joy you have brought into our lives! Never could my daughter have a truer friend than the Maiden of Massilia! How I mourn your state! I knew well your sire and never, no never would he have done what his eldest son is now doing to you! Ah, that he should marry you to The Infidel of Jaca! You the wonder of his villa, nay, the wonder of our land! That you are being sold for gold makes me ashamed of myself! Is that not what I also do?" So saying the father wept.

Esta put her hand upon his trembling hand. "Nay, *my* father," she said. "My brother did not arrange a betrothal with such as one as you have found for Naomi, and he will not provide rites for me according to the traditions of Massilia! Yet, tell me, could you honorably break Naomi's troth if another way was shown you?"

Startled, he looked up, "If I returned the pledge he gave me, which I yet have, saying that I fear this early betrothal is too unsettling for Naomi—that I fear for her health, her life, which truly I do!

Then could the agreement be breached." He paused, as if a distant light shed a single beam upon his darkness and cried noiselessly with resolute understanding, "Ah, I see! Yes, this is what I must do, though I lose this house and am cast into debtor's prison and must leave Naomi to your care! Tell me, surely she could accompany you to Jaca and wait upon you?"

Esta spoke quietly, fearing she should be heard from without, saying, "Sire, there is another way!" She withdrew from its hiding place the necklace and laid it upon the table. "This was given my father in the wars. He gave it to my mother and now it is my inheritance. I know that some of the stones are carnelian and jasper and onyx. Yet there are many other stones of delightful colors. I know not its value, but believe it might at least be equal to the Sponsa Pretium you would receive for Naomi. Is it not so? Grant unto your daughter four years more of maidenhood and then grant her the privilege of choosing a husband suitable in every way to your judgement. Do this and this necklace is yours!"

Eitan was stupefied as he carefully lifted the necklace to examine it more closely by lamplight. He exclaimed, "Ah, I do not believe my eyes! Emeralds, diamonds, rubies, sapphires, garnets, jet, topaz, amber—pearls and opals from Persia, lapis lazuli and, as you say, the least of these are beautiful stones of carnelian, jasper and onyx! Esta, do you know this necklace was worn by a great queen! Not only would it buy the four years you ask, but would also buy *you* a fine ship and the labor of its crew, and with trade would provide the means of life for you and yours for *years* to come!"

Esta excitedly, but softly asked, "This hope was whispered to me while I rested upon the branches of the great olive tree in my father's grove! Will you arrange this quietly and quickly, as I've not much time? Would you speak with Maros and tell him that he must be our captain, that his leaving of the villa must be secret, that he is to take his good wife with us! You also must come and ply your trade as

Maros plies the sea. We sail first for Athens and then to other great cities, and lastly to the city of Rome, where I will yet learn and fulfil that which my father dreamed for me!"

Tears filled Naomi's eyes, for such a thing was beyond her hope. The goodly father answered, "Yes, yes! But we must beware! Not only will your brother be roused to murderous anger, but so will the Lord of Jaca, and his reach is long!"

Esta replied, "Already my brother was stirred to such an evil wrath! He is not the seed of my father, for his sire is Cain—this much I have learned from the codices of your faith. We must *all* be wary, for our lives depend upon it! I thank you, for if we do not succeed, then surely I will perish in the Hell of Jaca!"

Naomi was yet more astonished. "Your brother is like unto he who first took human life, the slayer of Abel?"

"Ah, Naomi, always do you think the best of everyone, even those who fear not the Powers of Heaven. Did you not find it strange when we saw the men quit their small vessel apart from the quay and hasten to the city? When was the last time you heard of robbers in Massilia, in defiance of the soldiers of Rome? What great wealth could these bandits have taken from my father on the old aqueduct bridge? On his person there was nothing of sufficient worth for them to risk such a brazen assault! And why did they contend unto death and why did they murder my mother along with my sire? My brother knew that my father's wealth would pass to him should he and mama be slain, as would also the Sponsa Pretium if I were wed before my majority, for he knew he could profit by me! How he reveled in his sin when the Jackal of Jaca laid the treasure of a king at his feet, for then his plan seemed realized—and such was far beyond his imaginings! And now heaven ordains that we undo the spoils of blood!"

Esta

CHAPTER 6
THE CALLERS

"When all in the villa are asleep, you must, with upmost care, leave your room and disappear into the night."

Eitan

When next Esta accompanied Naomi to her house in Massilia, they met not only the merchant but old Maros as well. The maidens embraced the aged mariner and spoke quietly so that her guards would not hear their conversation. As customary, the men-at-arms waited without and did not know that Maros was within. "'Tis well," Maros said, "ta masters see naught amiss. 'Tay slap each o'ter's back an' pay no mind 'ta me if'n I be in 'ta grove, 'ta vineyard or take leave 'ta Massilia!"

To her brother and the nobleman of Jaca, it seemed Esta was warming to their scheme. At first, she was silent or worse. The reports of the guards told of the disdainful discourse between Esta and Aléxandros and other signs of the bride's displeasure. But then Esta began to engage those she met happily and turned every scornful comment aside, saying things such as, "Oh do not suggest that I dispute the inevitable! Did not Apollo say we should despise slander, strife and enmity? Jaca cannot be too far distant from Massilia, for if my husband made the journey, it certainly—ha!—cannot be strenuous!"

The guards told how she sought out merchants in the Bazar to buy attire and goods for herself and her attendants, relaying these exact words: "I will take certain maidens with me and several tutors! Jaca shall become a New Massilia." They said she paid no mind as to the cost of her purchases, saying "my husband, the Lord of Jaca and the Empire's Treasurer, shall pay all!" Then turning to her guards, exclaimed, "Pay the merchants and if you have not enough, send word to your master and return quickly with silver!" She instructed the sellers to hold her goods until she called for them, taking no immediate benefits. This pleased the bridegroom immensely for he felt his riches had won over Esta's heart. Still, he had her constantly watched, but it seemed to no purpose, for she only went to the Bazar, to the Agora, and to Naomi's house.

In the privacy of Eitan's house in Massilia, Naomi's sire explained that he had indeed purchased a boat, five rods in length, suitable to his trade so that it attracted little attention. Although it was not a large merchant ship, it nonetheless would accommodate their captain, his wife, six sailors to work the sheets and oars, the two maidens and a maid servant. The hold was of sufficient size to be a true vessel of trade. Eitan was making haste to supply the boat and purchase the needed crew. He had arranged to buy slaves as his sailors as this would help ensure their loyalty, especially as he was known as a fair master to the few men he commanded.

Maros said to Esta, "Eitan has told me all an' gladly will I be yer capt'n, fer I've not forgot 'ta sea, though my hairs are white. An' happy I am fer yer sakes if'n ye escape yer brother and Jaca! But know this, 'tis real danger we do! The boat ya have, though much grander than my ol' skiff is not a warship, as might be sent a'gn us! I've sailed on large merchant ships armed 'ta fiercely fight an' such also Jaca might hire."

"Esta answered, "Oh, good captain, we know our way will be perilous, but it is our only way of hope!"

The Galatian shrugged in understanding, but continued, "An' Athens be too far off, being fifty days or more at sea frum Massilia! That be a great journey, save we drop anchor in many a port betwixt here and there. No, 'tis best we sail first for Genua,[1] three, maybe four days sail'n. We'll put ashore with ya below an' out of sight an' Eitan can work his trade. Then sail hence fer Ostia, the Port of Rome, only four days more at sea. Was not Rome where ya also wanted t' go?"

Esta replied, "I want to put a great distance between my enemies and myself. That is why I desire to flee to Athens, then return to Rome later when circumstances would be safer."

"'Tis not safe t' be long at sea!" he answered, "Well, we'll make Ostia first, then consider more." He paused, then said, "Ah, how can this be done? Now, this I do most willingly, fer I am old. Non'less, yer young an' well favored. 'Tis true ya'd be truly safe only if ya had guards a'plenty. Could be yer death or worse!"

---

1. Genua, known today as Genoa.

Eitan purchased a boat for their escape

Eitan then advised, "Maros, speak none of that, for God protects who He lifts. Esta, we have made ready a skiff, like unto that which Maros had in former days and have made repairs to his old shack, where the skiff will be beached. On the morrow Maros will tell your brother that he is taking his wife and returning to his nets, for he will say that he has made ready his old lodging and boat—that he cannot bear to witness the sale of such a bride as you. Little will your brother care about Maros' departure and may truly be glad to be rid of him. He will then take Eponi to the hovel in the marshes. In the light of day, Maros will go a fishing *with* his wife. I will take leave of Massilia noticeably on the day after the morrow. Before my leaving, I will come to your villa with Naomi and tell your brother that as you have asked for my daughter as your companion, I shall willingly give her to you, for I would rather offend Naomi's betrothed than the new Lady of Jaca. Nonetheless, I will tell him that I am leaving Massilia forthwith, as her betrothed is angry with me and I have trading to do in Barcelona. Naomi shall stay and we shall sail southwest, out of sight of the quay and bide our time, withdrawing safely if we come within sight of another ship. Your marriage is planned for three days after our leaving. Your actions during this time must be beyond suspicion."

Esta and Naomi listened eagerly, Eitan continued, "Now this is what you must do. As your brother will feast with his guests on the night before the wedding, see to it that all are served much wine. Nonetheless, you will not partake saying you are not accustomed to such delights. Then insist that you must rest with the setting of the sun, explaining that the festivities that are planned for the day of the rite must not be marred by a weary bride! Command that the villa be a place of quiet repose that you might sleep restfully and awake refreshed for the joyous wedding. Then, when all in the villa are asleep, you must, with upmost care, leave your room, by way of the balcony, and disappear into the night. Maros and Eponi will be waiting for you at his old lodging in the marshes. The four of you will leave in his skiff and we will meet you just beyond sight of Massilia. You will see our lamps."

Esta asked, "Will not our enemies see what has been done when they find we are gone, as also is Maros?"

Naomi's father answered, "They will suspect, it is true. But we shall mar the skiff with blood and break its feeble bulwarks. Then send it adrift where it will surely be found near the port. Nonetheless, regardless of their suspicions, of Maros, of myself or why blood was found in his skiff, we shall be sailing east, for Genua, and it will take them a day or two more before they will set to sea, and *whither* shall they sail not knowing where we have gone? We have a chance!"

The following morning Esta supped with her brother and her betrothed, as she had been asked to forego her usual excursions with Naomi. To their mutual surprise she answered that she would be overjoyed for the occasion, adding, "My Lord of Jaca, you are like a king to me and I dare not approach Your Majesty without your invitation. Oh, I have been so eager to hear all about your greatness, your blood line, and why Rome for generations has entrusted the striking of silver to your sires, and now to you! Please, you must tell me all!" Esta prattled on, "And oh, you must tell me of the customary delicacies of Jaca! Your sumptuous fare must be rich indeed, for your girth is so, so *noble,* and I too aspire to be plump!"

With this her brother's brow furrowed, growing hot, but his anger soon abated, for the rotund grunter was absolutely delighted with Esta's banter, for he was a man of extreme appetites. "Oh indeed, I shall make you . . . Mmh, well rounded!" and he laughed raucously so that his belly undulated unbelievably. "You, my dear, shall not be known only as the Lady of Jaca, but as the Pearl of the Pyrenees! Ha! for is not that gem the roundest of jewels!"

He had just started expounding his illustrious history when a servant carefully interrupted the meal, saying, "Master Maros desires but a moment."

"Send him away!" said the heir of the villa. "Can't you see I am engaged!"

"As you wish, but he is leaving the groves this very day," the servant said sadly.

"Leaving? Have him enter at once!"

Maros came into the room, not with the difference he had always showed Esta's father, but almost livid. Seeing Esta he said frankly, "How t's such a one, beloved by all Massilia, play 'ta co'quet, bow'n to riches? Never would yer sire believe it."

Her brother could scarcely comprehend Esta's manner and answer, for she was not abashed in the least, but smiled condescendingly and said, "My dear Galatian, when the sea tempest blows do you fight or run with the wind? Times change, fortunes change and I am being carried by a gale to Jaca. You can't be happy here without me, can you now! Come with us to Hispania and grow old in ease!"

"Nay, Nay! Nor will I stay hereabouts! Rather, I'll take Ep wit' me back to my old lodg'n, fer I've fixed it up and made my skiff seaworthy. I'll not stay and see ya shamed!"

Again, this pleased the Jacaian, for he chuckled at the unfolding drama. Yet the brother lashed out, "Leave my villa at once and do not return!"

The next day the trio was again enjoying the morning repast in the courtyard when the servant announced Eitan and Naomi were without. Esta quickly spoke, saying, "Oh yes, admit them at once for I have so missed Naomi's company!" Then, when they were come, Esta said, "You must sup with us and hear the great deeds of my betrothed, for truly he has had wonderous adventures!"

Eitan answered, "Thank you noble Lady of Jaca!" then he bowed deeply to the man and then, much to the brother's astonishment, to him also. "I cannot stay, for I must make the tide. Surely you know that Esta desires Naomi to attend her in Jaca, yet I pledged my daughter to a man of means before this. As you expected, I'm sure, I will not offend Jaca and therefore broke the betrothal, making an enemy of a friend. Hence, I now leave Naomi with her mistress and as I have trade in Barcelona, I think now is a propitious time to quit Massilia."

Hearing this, the Lord of Jaca exclaimed to the brother, "Ah, see how the fury you expected bellows against others and not against us! This good merchant will not risk an infraction with the treasurer of Rome! He looked closely at Naomi and said to the maiden, "Come child, we shall see to your every need." With this, Naomi went immediately to Esta's side as her father hastily left the villa with apparent emotion.

An hour more was required to satisfy the eager hunger of the Jacaian lord. No sooner were the plates cleared from the table when the man fell asleep right where he sat.

Esta said to her brother and friend, "We must not leave our lord's side without his giving us leave. Let us speak quietly and enjoy this time, for soon Naomi and I shall be gone from this, my old home. Brother, do I now please you?"

"Why, yes!" he answered. "Never did I think to have won you over to the right cause so . . ."

"So easily?" she finished his sentence, then continued. "This will ensure that our father's villa will prosper and you and all of those whom I love will live well!"

He looked directly at Esta and said, "Somehow, I feel this is all pretense, that you are making a joke of me in so finely crafted a way that you think you have duped me! Is it so?" Esta was silent. He then asked, "Convince me, dear sister. Tell me what changed your thinking—your actions? You acted, at the first, disgracefully!"

She answered with firmness, "I disgraced you?" Then Esta smiled and softened, saying, "Well, I guess I did act insolent for a short time.

I hope I have made that up to you, dear brother. Your question is a good one. It was a maxim of Apollo that changed my thinking. Did he not command, 'Crown your ancestors. Do not wrong the dead!' This I do knowing that our sire's eyes are upon us, they are fixed mightily on me—on you! We cannot wrong him without terrible consequences. We must do as you say and Apollo commands us to 'detest disgrace!' And why, because nothing is removed from the all-seeing eye of God who grants our own dead that they also know of our deeds! Have you forgotten that papa and mama's blood was shed in murder? Can I then murder their memory? Nay, I will do what is right, though the way is long and difficult."

For two hours more, the elder brother, Esta and Naomi conversed, Esta directing the conversation to a time long ago when the days passed in the villa and groves in idyllic delight. When she spoke of their mama and papa and the wonderful life they had given their family, the brother became pensive and only said, "You were raised much differently than was I. Papa expected much of me. He bid my rise each day before the sun and always I toiled ceaselessly!"

"Come now," said Naomi, "Never did your sire require more of you than himself. And think of the harvest feasts when the season was done. I remember seeing you dance with your wife as your children played joyfully. I remember your smiles and laughter! How happy you were then! Now, after all the wealth you've gained, your countenance is despairing, you are anxious and there seems no happiness in your heart." As she said this, he hung his head.

Thinking to try a last attempt to thwart his miserable plan and recall him to his senses, Naomi added evenly, "It is not too late to unwind the cock of the catapult before you send your sister hurling like ballista fodder to Jaca! Still, you have power to do right from this moment on! Do not a greater wrong than what you have already done!"

Esta was stunned by Naomi's words, for she had not thought her quiet friend capable of such a rebuke. Nor did she think any good would come from reprimanding her fallen brother. He was also taken aback by the soft-spoken demoiselle and, for a moment, was silent.

But then his face began to flush as he rose menacingly to his feet. Loudly he stammered, "Naomi, of what bloody deed do you accuse . . . what wrong have I done? What I have taken . . . what is passed to me is only my right!"

He might have said more, but was silenced by the Jacaian. His angry denunciation had awakened the podgy nobleman from his stupor. "Enough!" he exclaimed, "Hold your tongue. Why accost the gentle girl?"

Esta interjected, "Surely Naomi knows not what to think or say. Has she not just sadly bid adieu to her sire? Lord of Jaca, excuse us please, for I must prepare—we must prepare ourselves for the night's festivities. This is the eve before our wedding. Hence command gaiety and serve wine abundantly, only do not ask that I partake of intoxicants. I am not accustomed to spirits as they make me ill. Also, please command that *all* retire early. The villa is by no means large and as I am already apprehensive, for never have I done that which I am about to do, the noise of much laughter will not fail to disturb me. In the morning I desire that you also are well slept and eager for the wedding rites." Esta appeared to be exuberantly happy as she added, "When the sun has risen but two hours, I would that you seek for a bride who is likewise refreshed and is ecstatic for the next adventure of her life!"

This pleased the Lord of Jaca immensely. Smiling he said, "Take your leave and return not until the nuptial feast begins. All shall be as you have asked, for always it is my will to please you! Our guests will dine on sumptuous fare and make merry for only three or four hours. Hah! If then there is one who so much as sneezes I will have him thrown from the sea cliff. You shall sleep undisturbed!"

Esta and Naomi bowed prettily and quit their company. When they were gone, the brother said, "Do not be so taken by Esta. If she was as allied to this thing as she appears, Naomi would not have spoken as she did!"

The big man chortled, "You think Esta lies?"

"No," the brother replied, "only what did she actually say to you?"

"Hmm," he murmured in response, "either you worry too much or I too little."

Never had Massilia seen such a wedding feast as was given that night. The lower floor of the villa, the courtyard, and even a near grove was set with tables, chairs, rich decorations and lit by a thousand torches. The finest musicians of the city played, their melodies filling the warm night with exquisite airs. The fare was delicious and bounteous. Fine ales and rare wines were served in abundance. In addition to family and friends, Sebastian and other senators of Massilia attended. Nonetheless, Aléxandros was obviously absent, as were many of his close associates. Esta was radiant and even Naomi appeared to be caught up in the regal spectacle of the evening, causing the Jacaian to whisper gaily to the elder brother, "See, all is as it should be!"

Nonetheless, an hour before midnight the last carriage left the villa for Massilia. In thirty minutes more, the entire domus and grounds were still and somnolent. Only two maidens rested in the bridal chamber, waiting entirely awake. An hour more passed before they quietly made their way to the balcony dressed for travel as commoners. They traversed the lattice work, descending deftly and silently. Reaching the ground Esta and Naomi listened attentively, making sure all was yet still before carefully continuing to the olive groves. From there, they planned on taking a circuitous route to the marshes to meet up with Maros and Eponi.

As they rounded the corner of the villa, a man stepped from the shadows. He raised his hand, signaling others and immediately Jacaian guards emerged from concealment, surrounding the maidens. The man was her elder brother. He laughed, saying, "It is as I thought! Fleeing, are you?"

Esta answered, confidently, "Fleeing? To where? Nay, we only decided to once more climb the olive trees, for never can we do so again. You know we have done as much many times before on a star lit night!"

"Indeed," said the brother. "Then we shall escort you there and await your pleasure as you frolic among the boughs. Know only that we shall also escort you back to your chamber when you have done with your fun. And to be certain of your safety, guards, especially qualified for the task, for they are eunuchs, shall stand watch at your door and on the balcony."

Esta replied, "As you have taken the joy out of our lark, I have no desire now for the groves, only we shall return the way we came. As no guard shall pass through my room, those you post on the balcony must also ascend up the frail lattice work, or stand guard below it." Without waiting for his reply, the two girls swiftly turned about, ran to the lattice and disappeared up and into the shadows of the elevated portico.

Within the chamber the demoiselles could hear guards take their position outside the door, but heard no clamor on the small terrace. Esta ventured outside and looking down saw them below. There was nothing more for them to do. Eitan's carefully crafted plan had failed.

"What shall you do?" asked Naomi, now in tears.

Esta replied resolutely, "We were so close! If only we had turned to the left and not the right. How could he have known?"

Her friend answered, "It was I! I put your brother ill at ease with my foolish words. Always I say things that I wished I could recall the moment they are spoken! Because of me he no doubt surrounded the villa with Jacaian guards. It would have made no difference which way we went! Our capture was assured. But *now*, what shall you do?"

Esta was quiet for a long while. At length she said, "We must hope, and as you say, pray inwardly until the very last. Yet I know not what to hope for, as I can see no way out of this dire quandary—hence, as I cannot even imagine an escape, how can I supplicate heaven?"

The Christian girl answered, "I have read where Paul said:

> *'The Spirit also helpeth our infirmities: for we know not
> what we should pray for as we ought: but the Spirit
> itself maketh intercession for us with groanings which
> cannot be uttered.'"*[2]

"Oh, Naomi," Esta cried, "of course, we cannot see the beginning or the end of the things as does the AllFather. Our plight is not ours alone! We must hope for something better . . . better than we can imagine and put our trust in Him. We shall play the parts we've been given, but never doubt in our deliverance."

Naomi asked, "And if you find yourself given by your brother to the Jacaian and the moment comes for you to speak the vow, what shall you say?"

Esta smiled, answering resolutely, "Before a hundred witnesses, I shall simply say, 'No!'"

"Oh, my dear friend," said Naomi, "surely they will have thought of that. If you cannot be fairly purchased, he will steal you away, perhaps at that moment or later, according to his cunning. Likely he will make a pretense of wounded feeling. Then it will be said, after you are gone, that you repented of your foolishness and willingly left with him."

---

2. Romans 8:26

To this, Esta could say nothing. The night passed slowly and little more was said. At dawn, sadly and solemnly Naomi helped maid servants dress Esta for the "inevitable mockery." At the appointed hour, with Naomi's hand in hers, the Maiden of Massilia descended the flight of stairs to the main floor of the villa. The invited wedding guests together with Esta's family awaited in the courtyard where the ceremony would be performed. Nonetheless, the Lord of Jaca and the Master of the Domus were talking jovially near the hearth when they heard footfalls on the steps.

"Ah," never have you looked more beautiful," said the bridegroom. I am sorry your brother disturbed your outing last night. Hah! Have no fear, there are trees a plenty within the walls of the Fortress of Jaca! Though I would ask that you also climb these at night as it would be unseemly for my queen to be seen acting so childishly!" As the bride made no reply, he added, "I see you are resolved, my dear. That is good. You see, you are mine, my very own possession. Come then, let me see you smile, as you did yesterday and tell more of your love for, how did you say it? Ah, yes, your 'next adventure!'"

Her brother was silent and determined to remain so until the deed was done, and the treasure his and this nightmare ended, for he loathed the fat buyer of his sister. At that moment a servant entered and said, "Sire, you have a demanding caller. Senator Aléxandros says he must see you before you take a step into the courtyard. He is accompanied by a host of soldiers!"

The Jacaian exclaimed, "Senator Aléxandros? Was he not one of many suitors? Did he not shun last night's festivities? The audacity! Surely, he must know at last that he is defeated?"

Her brother assured him, for he hoped the game was already won, "Nay! Perhaps this is business of a different sort. He may have come bearing gifts! Or, as I am late in filling his orders, having been much distracted with your affairs and as my oil and wine are the best in Massilia, well," he muttered on, "he buys much from me. Not everyone buzzes around my sister bee. I must see to Aléxandros!"

"Indeed, you shall!" thundered a voice, for the senator was already entering the vestibule.

The brother replied, "Senator. Welcome, we have but a moment. As you can see, Esta's wedding rite is about to begin. Perhaps we can talk after?"

Aléxandros strode over to where Esta and Naomi stood, both with confused looks upon their faces. As he bowed to Esta, he said quietly to her, "Fear not, all will be settled soon."

He turned about, glanced briefly and disgustedly at the ponderously fat man from Hispania, then faced Esta's brother, saying, "Master of the villa, did you know that I was confederate with your father?"

"What do you mean?" the brother answered.

The Jacaian said with a broad smile, "Ah, it is plain to see that this man *is* buzzing still about my queen. Perhaps he will claim that your father already promised Esta to him! Well, the sire is dead and so are his benumbed assurances! Well, I do not fear one senator of the Assembly of Massilia, when I am the Treasurer of Rome! Speak on and lay your claim!"

Aléxandros replied with disdain, "You sir are not so eminent as you claim, for they are many who strike coins for Rome, nearly as many as there are mines! Now your stroke misses the anvil entirely. Nay, I speak of a day last year when I spoke with Esta's sire about her gifts and heard of him that which he desired for her! Hence, I composed a letter which enumerated every divine attribute of the Maiden of Massilia. This was sent abroad, much to Esta's fame, for it was sent, for surety's sake, by several couriers. These were also commissioned to proclaim the excellence of her name, as they journeyed, that her reputation might proceed my tidings. Perhaps, even you, most illustrious Canis Aureus,[3] heard of her because of my epistle!"

"What did you call me?" said the offended man. "Speak plainly and watch your words, lest I bring the might of Rome down upon your skinny neck!"

"Rome you say?" said Aléxandros. "Might you mean Emperor Hadrian? Well, as the gods ordain, I bear this command of Rome, sealed by Hadrian's signet. Please, be so good as to read it aloud so that Esta might hear her name spoken in so astounding a missive. This epistle arrived but an hour agone."

The eldest took the parchment with a shaking hand, and read:

To Aléxandros,

Having been gone from Rome to Greece, I recently returned and belatedly, but joyfully, received your epistle.

Long has it been since we played as soldiers in the domus of Acilius Attianus, my guardian. How the gods have dealt with two boastful boys of days dreamed and not lived, for so seems the past to me. You a Senator of Massilia and I the Emperor of Rome. What do you think old Acilius thinks now of his two tormentors?

As for the Maiden of Massilia, it shall be as you ask and her father desires. Your praise of Esta is great! I must meet her at once and play your Game of the Agora. You know I advance the wisdom and culture of the Greeks throughout the Empire. I am rightly known as foremost, not in power only, but in erudition. If then, this young Esta can best me in the Agora Contest she

---

3. Golden Jackal.

shall not only be taught here and in Athens, if there be anything she can yet learn, but there shall be built in Massilia a great School of Philosophy, and Rome shall bear the cost. It seems we must nurture your city if it is to bear more fruit like unto this young goddess you extol.

A trireme and a century of guards will be at anchor in the Port of Massilia, awaiting you and your charge. Esta may bring with her any of her family and attendants, as she desires.

Hadrian, Emperor of the Empire of Rome.

CHAPTER 7
NECROPOLIS

"Δεν μπορείς να κοιτάξεις πίσω σου, γιατί όταν γυρίζεις αυτό που είναι ακόμα μπροστά σου, αυτό που φαινόταν έχει φύγει. Ούτε μπορείτε να κοιτάξετε πολύ μπροστά, γιατί αυτό που είναι δεν έχει έρθει ακόμα."

"You cannot look behind, for when you turn that which is, is yet before you and that which was from view is gone. Neither can you look far ahead, for that which is, is not yet come."

Greek inscription on the gate of the Necropolis

Emperor Hadrian was rarely in Rome for he continually traveled the length and breadth of the Empire. Although a skilled military commander and as such was quick to subdue rebellions, he was gifted with the ability to govern his realms with extraordinary reconciliatory skills. He allowed, and even fostered, local autonomy, allowing conquered peoples a high degree of self-government and religious tolerance, so long as each and every land regarded the preeminence of Rome. When this was challenged, he met opposition with a firm hand.

Jerusalem had been garrisoned by the 10th Legion since its destruction by Titus in 70 A.D. Nonetheless, many Jews returned to the Holy City, attempting to reclaim their homeland in defiance of Rome. Hadrian gave Jerusalem a new name, that of Aelia Capitolina, and in other respects began to passively Romanize the ancient city. It was then that a charismatic Jewish leader emerged from the ruins of the old and wasted Jerusalem, a man who declared himself to be the promised messiah, foreordained, he said, to establish the independent military Kingdom of Judah. His name was Simon Bar-Kokhba.[1] After initial success against the garrison of Aelia Capitolina, Kokhba's revolt spread over a significant portion of the Province of Judea.

The reaction of Rome was lethal. Emperor Hadrian sent General Sextus Julius Severus to conquer the Jewish rebels with an army of six legions. Severus destroyed some fifty fortresses and hundreds of villages, depopulating the remnants of those who had survived Titus. Hadrian went so far as to rename the region, calling it Syria Palaestina, and subsequently prohibited the return of Israelites to the ruined city.

When the Emperor traveled by sea, he often sailed in a mighty Deceres, a massive warship equipped with eight hundred rowers, five hundred men-of-war and one hundred soldiers of his Imperial Guard. Hadrian's great warship was accompanied by Quinquereme escorts, as if leading a miliary offensive—even if not at war.

Tertullian wrote that Hadrian was "an explorer of all curiosities." Cassius Dio said of Hadrian, "He personally viewed and investigated

---

1. His last name is written with variations, including Ben Koziva, Bar Kozevah, and Bar Koziba ("a pun on the Hebrew word for liar").

"It was likely changed to Bar-Kokhba during the revolt, as a reference to a verse in the Bible referring to the Messiah as a star *(kokhav)*." https://www.jewishvirtualli brary.org/shimon-bar-kokhba, 2022 absolutely everything." While Historia Augusta states that Hadrian was "so fond of travel, that he wished to inform himself in person about all that he had read concerning all parts of the world."[2]

Thus, in his rule, Hadrian journeyed from Ostia Roma to Gaul, Germania, Britannia, Hispania, Egypt, Arabia, Greece, Palaestina, Mesopotamia, Armenia, Asia, Dacia, Macedonia, Thracia, Assyria, and Belgica. He dwelt for a time in many cities—unleashing his army of engineers, architects, artists and craftsmen, making vast improvements to roads, building temples, aqueducts, civic centers, theatres and public baths, from Sparta to Londinium.[3]

Durant said of him, "When Hadrian left Athens it was a cleaner, more prosperous, and more beautiful city than ever before in its history . . . No other man ever built so plentifully, no other ruler so directly . . . he could leave the capital for five years and trust his subordinates to carry on, like a good manager, he had organized and trained an almost automatic government . . . the lust for travel was in his blood and [he had] so much of the world to rebuild."[4]

Before he attained the throne, Attianus and Trajan infused in young Publius Aelius Hadrianus a love of Greek literature and he became accomplished in every discipline of Hellenic culture, including mathematics, music, painting, sculpting, drama, poetry and, of course, warfare.

The emperor Trajan gave Hadrian his niece, Vibia Sabina, to wife. Although she at first traveled a great deal with her husband, they did

---

2. https://www.worldhistory.org/article/1892/hadrians-travels/, 2022
3. A more complete list: Sparta, Athens, Ephesus, Patara, Tarsus, Antioch, Cappadocia, Palmyra, Pelusium, Alexandria, Dyrrhachium, Syracusae, Aleria, Caralis, Carthago, Lambaesis, Caesarea, Trapezus, Nicomedia, Byzantium, Thracia, Troesmis, Ilium, Pergamon, Smyrna, Troesmis, Viminacium, Singadunum, Aquileia, Ravenna, Agusta Vindelicorum, Mogonticacum, Colonia Agrippina, Durocortorum Lutetia, Londinium, Eboracum (to supervise the building of Hadrian's Wall in Britannia), Tarraco, Carthago Nova, Legio, Bracara, and eventually Massilia.
4. Will Durant, *Caesar and Christ*, Simon and Schuster, New York, 1972, pp 418, 420.

not find happiness in each other, so great was his interest in the concerns of the Empire. "He showed her every favor and courtesy, and gave her every kindness but affection."[5] Time passed and no children blessed their union. Then in the city of Bithynia, Hadrian met an accomplished young man in his teenage years, named Antinous, who was very intelligent, lithe and energetic. The young Greek was made page to Hadrian and the historian wrote "the childless Emperor loved him as a heaven-sent son."[6] Horrifically, when Antinous was but eighteen years of age, he drowned in the Nile. Spartianus wrote that Hadrian grieved inconsolably over the death of Antinous. The Emperor had a temple built on the shore where the lad died and there buried him with every regal honor.

Hadrian was strikingly tall and athletic, extremely strong and vigorous, curly haired and charismatic. Although he diligently studied philosophy, especially Epictetus, and "encouraged the national faith," he was superstitious and dabbled in magic, necromancy and astrology. Yet he "laughed at oracles," believing his destiny and Rome's could not be altered by their mutterings.

He was a most unusual monarch, for, said Durant, "He visited the sick, helped the unfortunate . . . orphans and widows, and was a generous patron to artists, writers, and philosophers . . . A man of peace, he knew the arts of war and was resolved that his pacific temper should neither weaken his armies nor misguide his enemies. ...While visiting the camps, there he lived the life of the soldiers, eating their fare, never using a vehicle, walking with full equipment twenty miles on a march and showing such endurance that no one could have guessed that he was at heart a scholar . . . It delighted

---

5. Will Durant, Caesar and Christ, Simon and Schuster, New York, 1972, p. 414.
6. Will Durant, Caesar and Christ, Simon and Schuster, New York, 1972, p. 419.

him to gather scholars and thinkers about him, to puzzle them with questions and laugh at their contradictions and disputes."[7]

This then, was the man who invited Esta to visit him in the capital of the empire, the personal friend of Aléxandros, the most powerful king in the civilized world.

The transport sent to fetch Esta was a Roman Trireme, a type of ship that had sailed in the Greek and Roman navies for the better part of a millennia, but updated with many improvements, including a seated pavilion on its deck. Its beam was well over a rod in width and its overall length was nine rods. The warship was fitted with two sails, the aft sheet being much larger than the fore and was further powered by a veritable army of rowers—having one hundred and seventy oarsmen working three banks of oars! Additionally, there were eighty men-of-war aboard, Esta's guards. The formidable escort sent to Massilia to grant Aléxandros' request plainly dominated the port and was clearly visible from the terrace of the villa.

After her brother had finished reading the remarkable letter, Aléxandros' said to its hearers, "How wonderful that the imperial decree should arrive in time to prevent the tragedy! Look now to the Port of Massilia and see the Trireme, while just beyond this portico stands four score of the emperor's guard! Unworthy and miserable son of my noble friend, your scheme to sell Esta to this flatulent ass is hereby thwarted, unless the maiden herself tells me now that this mock of a marriage is truly her desire. Esta, what say you?"

Esta ran immediately to Aléxandros' outstretched arms, and embracing the senator cried aloud, "I would not have spoken those vows, but rousing whatever helps could be gathered of my friends, for my own brother was my betrayer, I covertly obtained a small ship, to be captained by old Maros and supplied by Eitan, the good sire of Naomi, my dearest friend. This wedding morn would have

---

7. Will Durant, Caesar and Christ, Simon and Schuster, New York, 1972, pp. 415, 417.

95

found us gone, already far from Massilia had not my brother discovered Naomi and myself last night, even as we were about to flee. Please, good Aléxandros, send word to the marshes, to Maros, telling him of this—and he will, by use of his skiff, fetch back Eitan! Still, I would that those, my truest friends, sail with us to Rome. As for these who would sell and buy one who had not yet reached her majority, leave them to their own conceits, but obtain from the senate of Massilia a decree that no more is my brother my guardian, but you, dear Aléxandros."

"It shall be as you desire," answered Aléxandros. He looked disdainfully on the silent and abashed miscreants. "And I shall not leave you for a moment here unattended. Gather for Naomi and yourself that which you desire to take and come with me now to the city." In a half hours' time, the two maidens were gone from the villa without a word passing between Esta and her brother. Still Esta embraced her grandmother and others of her family as she bid them a lasting farewell. As none of these had conspired with the brother, all were glad indeed for Esta's turn of fortune, for they had come to despise the noble of Jaca and were angry with the eldest. La menina had even put a malediccion, or curse upon his name.

A week later, Esta and Naomi, Eitan, Maros, Eponi and Aléxandros were all gathered at an inn near the gardens of Agora, under the protection of the Roman guard. All were overjoyed and excited with future prospects. Esta thanked each of her friends for all they had done, and were willing to do, to save her from such an end. Eitan had secured a buyer for his ship and crew, so there were no impediments for their leaving for Rome. Fortuitously in this, the astute merchant turned a profit and was able to redeem Esta's beautiful necklace, in addition to a sizeable increase of his own fortunes. Maros had never dreamed of the chance to sail on a warship and was truly euphoric to return to the sea on such a galley. Eponi said her life had been one of hardship and disappointment, until the good sire had given Maros and her a home in his villa. How she had loved Esta's parents and their goodness! Then had come the woe of their deaths and the horrible attempt of the brother to sell Esta to Jaca! How grateful she was that this was no more, and now she would voyage to Rome! Could anything be more wonderful? Naomi, who had stood resolutely at Esta's side through it all and had faced her own trials, said only that her prayers had been answered; the blessings given were far greater than anything she had supposed might be granted of heaven.

It was late evening when Aléxandros walked Esta and Naomi to their room. There was no one else about when Esta spoke quietly to the senator, saying, "Our kind friend, there is one thing more I must tell you about my brother."

"Say on," said Aléxandros.

"I fear he is guilty of far greater a crime than the intended Sponsa Pretium. I believe it was he who hired my sire's murderers."

He answered, "We also think he hired the assassins. The senate has covertly sent agents abroad to find these killers and if possible, find proofs. Not only was your father our good friend, but his oil and wine were important Massiliote trade. There can be no sense made of his killing, save the motive of your brother's gain. It may take a great while, but the truth of the matter will be found out."

"Thank you," she said. "I felt you must already know this thing, for the deed was so apparent that it could not be veiled! And what of the Jacal of Jaca?"

"He has not left the villa and we have seen his dogs about Massilia. Do not be frightened, but they are even now very near this inn! Nonetheless, you are well guarded and all is made ready. On the morrow we sail for Rome."

The Trireme was not designed to remain at sea overnight, but would put ashore each evening to refresh stores and accommodate the rest and refreshment of crew, marinus,[8] and passengers. Still, as the ship could easily make thirty leagues a day and as many as forty-five leagues in favorable conditions, the voyage from Massilia to Ostia, Rome, would only be from four to six days. Overnight stays were usually propitious, for port towns greatly profited from royal vessels and always went to great lengths to provide regal hospitality.

The first stop would be the Port of Cemenelum.[9] Founded by colonists from Massilia in the fourth century before Christ, the city was first known as Nikaia after Nike, the Greek god of victory. The walled oppidum[10] was a fortressed metropolis, not as great as Massilia, but still of considerable size and beautifully situated above sandy beaches overlooked from magnificent villas.

In the clear and mild dawn, Aléxandros led Esta and her small company, surrounded by a century of guardsmen, from the inn to the quay. Boarding the ship, the senator introduced Esta to the Trierach, the captain of the Trireme. The Trierach bowed to her and said, "Illustrious Maiden of Massilia, we are sent by the emperor to conduct you safely to His presence. We shall only sail when the weather is clement and within sight of land, as our swift warship is not designed for rough seas. Hence, you will find this passage most pleasant. The winds blow from the west. Therefore, we shall be in Cemenelum before the sun sinks midway from its zenith."

Esta replied, smiling widely, "Never have I been beyond the mountains that lie close about Massilia! And to think that before this day is spent, I shall set foot in Cemenelum! It is a wonder! Good Trierach, these are my dearest friends," and she gestured to each,

---

8. Marinus, Roman marines.

9. The ruins of the baths and the amphitheater of Cemenelum can be found on a hill above the present day city of Nice. http://www.roamintheempire.com/index.php/2020/01/15/cemenelum/, 2022

10. Roman town, normally fortified.

"Naomi, Eitan, her sire, Eponi and her husband Maros. I have something to ask of you."

"Please say on," he replied.

"Maros is a seafaring man of many years. Might he sit by your side as you direct the helmsmen of your ship?"

The Trierach grasped the arm of the old sailor and said energetically, "I thought you had the look of brine and sheets about you! Welcome captain to my ship! You shall soon see how such a grand vessel is easily controlled. See here," and he pointed to the two steering oars. "The helmsman stands before me on the half-deck, and by use of the arms attached to the steering oars can direct both at the same time. Why then, with the aid of the rowers, I can command the ship's course to be reversed in less than a minute's time!"

Maros was amazed and exclaimed, "T'woud of thought it should t'ke a half hour fer such a vessel of length to turn 'bout!"

"Nay," said the Trierach. "Now come with me and see how we get underway and leave your wife to sit in the shade of the pavilion with her friends."

As the two seamen quit their company, Eponi said, "Never has Maros been so happy as he is this day!"

Soon the waters of the Mediterranean Sea were cut by the Trireme, as one hundred and seventy oars pulled in perfect cadence while its two sails were filled with a fresh westerly breeze. Esta exclaimed to Alexandros and Naomi, "It feels as if we are soaring above the waves as steadily as a gliding eagle along the cliffs of Massilia! And look back, the port is already gone from sight!"

Already old Eponi was fast asleep. Some of the guardsmen stood, relishing the voyage, while others sat, nearly shoulder to shoulder, for there was not much room on deck for so many men. It was more crowded yet below deck, where the rowers sat and pulled oars.

Nonetheless, the Trireme was light upon the waters, with a draft of only three feet.

Naomi said, "How strange it all is! But eight days back we planned on rowing to father's boat in Maros' old skiff, and that in the middle of the night. Now here we are, guests of Emperor Hadrian, aboard a great warship. I scarce can take it in. And we move so swiftly! Has anyone ever moved with greater speed?"

Esta thought of the inexplicable voyage she took when she was drowned, but said nothing.

Cemenelum was similar to Massilia, yet more ornate and flowered with many small gardens. Their ship was met with carts and they were conveyed up the cobbled road to the center of the town where they were given quarters in the finest inn of the oppidum. There they dined sumptuously and rested in comfort. Nonetheless, they were guarded continually and for good cause. Esta's fame had preceded her coming and it seemed that everyone wanted to see her. Indeed, there were many who lined the way to the inn and shouted praises to "the Emperor's Scholar," or to "the Maiden of Massilia," or "the Marvel of Massilia." Some attempted to approach her while she ate, but were prevented from doing so by the guards. In truth, Esta was given more deference than was shown the senator.

This mattered not to Aléxandros. Still, there was one thing that did disturb him. When they were conveyed to the Port of Cemenelum for their departure, there was a ship in the bay that was not there the night before—a ship of Hispania. Yet, as no mischief had befallen them and as he felt confident in the Roman forces at hand, the senator laid the concern aside.

Once again, the day was bright and the winds at their backs. Before the sun was three hours from setting, the Trireme arrived at the great Port of Genua,[11] where more than two score ships were

---

11. Genoa.

anchored. As always, the guests of Hadrian were well attended. Now they were securely in Italia and the change in culture delighted Esta and Naomi. In the company of four guards, for the maidens would have no more, they toured the quaint streets of the oppidum, the shops and gardens, while Eitan looked for opportunities to trade.

On the third day they reached Pisae,[12] just as a storm began to blow a tempest. The foul weather continued for three days more and so they remained in the Roman colony, waiting for the skies to clear.

On the morning of the fourth day, the Trierach said to the Galatian, who had become a good friend and a mentor of sorts to the Roman captain, "What say you, Maros? The clouds are still low on the mountains, but the western sky is unfettered. The winds are from the northwest—perfect for our voyage. Chances are, if it picks up, we can make Ostia before the day is done!"

"An' 'f not?" Maros asked.

"Of course, we'll sail close to the coast. There are many suitable beaches to run ashore, but more importantly there are three great ports between Pisae and Ostia. Labro,[13] Populino[14] at the straits and Cosa,[15] where Emperor Domitian built his sumptuous villas! More likely than not, we'll spend the night in Cosa, which would prove a delight for the maidens and Ep. Then it will be an easy run from Cosa to Ostia on the morrow."

The old sailor studied the sky. At length he replied, "You're 't capt'n an' ya know 't Trir'me far better than me—though I've larn'd much of yer ship since we pushed off frum Massilia! Non'less, 't sky is a'worry. See 'ta clouds, a red an' slowly curl'n over 't mountains? 'T winds about 't change an blow frum 't east. Best stay 'n Pisae."

---

12. Pisa.
13. Livorno.
14. Piombino.
15. Orbetello.

"Nay, my friend. If it is as you say, we shall at least make Labro or perhaps Populino afore the weather turns." To this Maros said nothing, though he had sailed many more years than the much younger Roman.

Hence, the Trireme was soon again out to sea. The northwest winds did become stronger and the warship moved more swiftly through the Tyrrhenian Sea than ever they had sailed since leaving the Port of Massilia. "Ah," said the Trierach as he slapped Maros on the back, "what did I tell you? If we can keep this pace, we must indeed reach our home port of Ostia before the setting of the sun!"

However, Maros hardly heard what the captain said for his eyes were fixed on the darkening eastern sky. Seeing this, the Trierach said, "Certain it is that a squall shall be born o're the mountains there. Nonetheless, the winds are strong out of the northwest and such will keep the storm at bay. Still, to ensure safe passage, we'll steer more to the west and stay beyond its reach!"

Maros replied steadily, for never did he allow himself to appear anxious, for he was a veteran of both the sea and life, "T' do as ya say, we must leave t' lee of t' coast an' 't safety it gives."

"Only for an hour or so," replied the Trierach.

The great Trireme skimmed over the white tossed waves driven by an ever-increasing wind. Esta and Naomi were thrilled with this new adventure, while Aléxandros, Eitan and Eponi were becoming quite concerned. The senator quit his seat beneath the pavilion on the foredeck and made his way carefully past the crowded deck of guardsmen to speak with the Trierach. By the time he reached the commander's chair at the stern of the ship, the entire sky was thick with lowering, billowing clouds.

Above the sounds of wind and waves, Aléxandros yelled, "Trierach, why are we not safe in some inlet. This is not what you foretold in Massilia!"

The captain's face was like granite and neither he nor Maros displayed the least fear. He answered with a loud voice, "Weather's tuned suddenly foul. Clouds will soon touch the sea! How then shall I see to guide us if now we turn in, for fog will blanket the shore? We must outrun the gale and put in when we can. Now senator, quickly return to our charges and be bound with them!"

So saying, the Trierach shouted orders for the rowers to pull with their might and for certain of the guardsmen to take rope and tie their passengers securely to the mast on the open middeck. Others aided the rowers and bailed the hull. Esta held Naomi's hand tightly as the merchant's daughter prayed for safety.

Soon the warship began to pitch and roll, for having no keel of depth the tempestuous waters began to pummel the vulnerable Trireme. Still the Trierach did not lower the sails, which billowed full, for as yet the strong oaken masts held fast. Maros knew that such a mighty gale could devastate any ship, but especially one with so shallow a draft. He was amazed at the skill of the Trierach and the helmsman, as they steered the flying behemoth with great agility, so that few waves swept over the bulwarks and even the greatest waves had not yet capsized the warship.

Immense banks of clouds shrouded the heaving brine. At times the eye could see no more than a few rods, then a howling burst would lift the vaporous cloak so that looming waves were seen a furlong away. Still the captain flew his sails, believing he must out-distance the storm. Without his knowing, for the Romans possessed no compass and relied on landmarks, the sun and the stars to navigate, the gale shifted mightily from the northwest to the east, blowing Sirocco winds born over the Sahara Desert. Flying at hurricane speeds, these winds rip across the ocean, paying no heed to subcurrents.

An hour more passed and finally the Trierach was forced to lower sails, for the foremast cracked with a loud snap! Nonetheless, it did not fall and was quickly lashed secure by expert seamen. In the next moment the Trireme rolled violently with a rogue wave allied to a tremendous gust of wind. For an instant it seemed as if the ship would overturn, for the oars on the high side of the Trireme were lifted entirely above the frothing sea, floundering in the air, while the lower edge of the ship was buried in the jet-black deep. Cries were heard as men were swept overboard by the powerful surge. These were forever lost! For only an instant were the frantic men seen in the melee of the wild, cresting seascape. The strongest swimmers among them could in no way close upon the leaping warship or fight long against Neptune's suffocating hold. Nonetheless and providentially, the warship righted itself, claiming no more lives!

Now the Trireme was driven west, southwest with the surface current, moving nearly as fast as the whitecaps and was kept abeam the waves by the labor of the rowers. Never had Maros or the Trierach seen such a marvel and both veterans of the sea were moved beyond expression that they were yet afloat. Of this they said nothing and their looks did not betray their thoughts. Then, through the mists they espied land, jutting out here and there. Surely, the captain yelled, they had overshot Labro and were now in the straits of Populino. In this he was mistaken, for the land they saw was the Isola d'Elba.[16] The Trierach did not attempt to turn in, fearing the roughness of the sea but skillfully steered clear of every cleft that rose dagger-like from tempestuous waters.

In such a precarious way they continued for three hours more. Slowly the winds began to abate and the sea began to calm. The sun, though mostly obscured, could be seen sufficiently to ascertain directions. The passengers were allowed to return to the more spacious foredeck. The chairs that were stoutly affixed to the ship were still solidly in place, but the Pavilion was in shreds. The sighted land was gone from view, but ahead another shoreline was seen. Yet

---

16. Island of Elba

as they drew near, sailing south, the land lay *not* larboard, as would the coast of Italia, but was starboard of their ship. As the skies continued to clear it became obvious that the landmass was an island of considerable size. They rowed down the desolate and mountainous coast for a great while, sails yet lowered, looking for a safe harbor, but all was rugged and rocky coastline. Then, just as the sun was about to set, Maros cried out, "Look'e thar! We have come 't Corsica an' b'fore us is Aleria."

"Ah yes," exclaimed the Trierach happily, "*Dianæ Portus!* Amazing! We have crossed the Tyrrhenian Sea and shall soon take our rest in the safest harbor of Corsica. Maros, as you know Aleria you also know we shall certainly have the aid of Roman shipbuilders, for Aleria is a great colony of craftsmen."

Soon they drew along the shore of the blessed bay, for many there were aboard who thought they must perish as surely as did their shipmates. After Esta and her company were lifted aground, much to their amazement, the ship's crew of some two hundred and forty men *lifted the Trireme from the shallows* and set it upon drydock timbers. The Trierach said to Esta, "The guardsmen will see you to the inn that overlooks the Gardens of the Necropolis. I must stay and oversee repairs to my ship. Ah," he said looking on the ship by torchlight, "the foremast will need doublers, a new pavilion built and the ship dried out. Perhaps more. However, it will soon be sea worthy again. Then, when the weather is propitious and the winds blow from the west, we shall sail to Ostia without further delay. The distance is easterly but forty leagues across open sea."

The Trierach made no mention of what he alone had noticed, for the bay was of considerable length and in the gathering night, he steered well clear of an anchored ship of Hispania. Whither it was the same vessel they had seen in the Port of Cemenelum, he could not say. The captain determined to covertly make inquiries before he said anything to his guests.

He was weary and the maidens felt sorry for him and the loss of those who were lost at sea. They, along with Naomi's sire, the senator, Eponi and Maros were also wet and exhausted. The guardsmen helped the men but *carried* Eponi and the maidens to the garden inn. Their personal equipage, which had been stowed securely beneath the middeck. was also taken to the inn, to be washed of brine and dried. Baths of warm water were drawn in each of their rooms and robes provided. Later, they supped together on a terrace overlooking Dianæ Portus. The food was delicious and they conversed quietly and genially, rehearsing the miraculous events of the day.

Naomi said, "In the moonlight I can see the lovely gardens of the Necropolis, but I confess I know not the meaning of the word!"

Esta answered, "Necropolis is Latin, of course, and literally means 'The City of the Dead.'"

CHAPTER 8
NYX

"Nyx, child of Khaos, alone she spawns sleep and death, the very substance of night, veiling the light of Aither, the shining blue of heaven."[1]

Esta's eldest brother remonstrated, "Know you not that because of you the groves and vineyards have been hopelessly neglected—spoiled! And now you tell me that all you promised is forfeit?"

The Jacaian laughed, "How can I pay a bride-price when there is no bride? And what of the cost of all that Esta bought in Massilia? Should not that be your debt?" The brother hung his head in despair. "Now then, we are friends, though it appears we are bested!"

"Yes, bested!" the brother moaned.

"Ah, how easy you are conquered! More wine!" A servant filled his glass. "A question! Do you fear the gods?"

---

1.   https://www.theoi.com/Protogenos/Nyx.html, 2022

He rattled a response, "Nay, but what is that to you that you should ask me such a thing when I am in such a state?"

"Ha!" the Espaniard jested, "is not the Emperor of Rome but a god? Then fear him not!"

The brother was incredulous, "Hadrian is the mightiest man alive. At his command thirty legions of men-at-arms obey! Of course I fear him, and so do you! You, who boasted continually that you possessed the strength of Rome and yet when Aléxandros read Hadrian's epistle, you were as submissive as a lamb!"

"Ah, that! Well, at that moment his guardsmen were in number greater than my own. I only say that *we* may yet obtain that which *we* desire! For now, more than ever before, I must *possess* Esta! And why should I not! She is only a weak maiden and cannot always be surrounded with legionary!" He was quiet for a moment, then said, "Did you hear how she spoke to the senator, to me? Such magnificent disdain! Esta is a wonder, a marvel! There is none like her in the Empire and *she is mine!*"

"You are mad!"

"Ha! Do not think so, lest your ruin be as sure as your dribbling self-pity. Take courage man! Remain my confederate and you will yet be given the promised riches!"

Hearing this the brother took evil again to his heart. "Then I am with you yet. Nonetheless, I need ..."

"You need a little silver in the meantime, do you?" From under a fold in his copious vestments he withdrew a bag as large as the span of his hand, ladened with coin. "Come, take this. It is too heavy to toss."

As quickly as a dog retrieves meat from his master's hand, the brother fetched the bag, asking as he did so, "What would you have me do?"

"The thing must be done aright. The Trireme must sail along the coast, for such a vessel is always at risk in deep waters. My ship may sail into the heart of the Mediterranean. Hence, we shall sail only so far as Cemenelum, the nearest likely port for the royal warship. Even there we shall watch for a chance to steal her quietly away. Then, if we fail to get the prize, we shall sail for Rome, stopping only in Dianæ Portus of Aleria, Corsica. In Ostia there are many ships of Hispania. Hence no notice will be given mine."

"We? I am to come with you? What can *I* do?" said the brother.

The Jacaian answered, "Never should we trail Esta but from afar, for she must not know anything of our business until it is done. Any spy would know her when close to her person. But you, dear brother, know her ways, her movements—you can follow her anywhere from a great distance. You shall be my spy! With the silver I've paid, your villa is well funded for a time!"

The brother was still puzzled. "So we shall look for a chance to take Esta. But when she is missed, surely they will think of you—of me! Our houses are well known. Certainly, they will come for us and kill us!"

"Ha!" said the Jacaian. "Have you no ken? There are many ways such a simple thing is resolved. Likely we will take Esta in the great capital city, where its very size is a cloak! Why then go to Cemenelum at all, for the chance of taking her there is very small?" The brother could not answer, and so the Espaniard continued, "It is this. Many of the maidens of Cemenelum are Celtic Greeks, as is Esta. Therefore, it should not be difficult to find in Cemenelum a demoiselle that we shall take with us, of similar height and features."

"Lord of Jaca," exclaimed the brother, "you speak like a fool. First, if you want such a maiden, why not take her from Massilia? But no matter, how can such a one take the place of Esta, for there is no one like her—that can speak or act as she does, and there is no maiden fool enough to try!"

Exasperated, the Jacaian replied, "Ah, you are as stupid as dung!

A maiden stolen in Massilia would cause a clamor and who here abouts would not be searched out? But if taken quickly and stole away on my ship from Cemenelum—well it is an easy thing I have done before from other ports! As for the maiden impersonating Esta, that is also an easy thing. You will furnish us with clothes Esta has left behind and these shall adorn the bloodied demoiselle, bludgeoned *almost* beyond recognition. When *she* is found, no one will look more for my lovely Esta. My palace in Jaca shall then be her gilded prison and you shall be paid riches beyond that which you were already shown. Also, I have no intention of sending agents throughout Cemenelum to find such a victim, for they would blunder in finding the right match for Esta and their Hispanic accents would be suspicious. You, however, shall not fail to both find the girl and entice her into our net!"

Aboard the Jacaian's ship, the two murderers sailed from Massilia to Cemenelum soon after the Trireme departed from the same port. The Hispanic vessel, though not nearly as swift as the Trireme, was built for deep water and sailed further from shore, her captain setting their course by the stars and the occasional lights along the coast when night came. Long before morning dawned, they dropped anchor in Cemenelum and saw that the Jacaian had rightfully predicted this port as the first stop of the Trireme.

Early the next day, Esta's brother hastened to search out the taverns, shops and bakeries to find a maiden suitable for their treacherous plans, careful not to be seen by Esta or her friends. As he was about to buy a light meal of baked cheese and honey from a bakery, he met a poor maid of Esta's height, well-favored of form, as was his sister. Most remarkably, her hair was dark auburn, again like Esta's though somewhat disheveled. Her face was not as finely proportioned as hers, nor was she as clean, for she was wet with perspiration. The matron of the thermopolia continually berated the unfortunate girl and though she was a Celtic Greek, and likely free born, her station was lowly indeed.

The brother waited for the few customers to leave before he approached her. Then he said to the young maiden in hushed tones, "Not a dame or demoiselle of my villa is so ill treated as you!" The girl sighed, but said nothing in response. "Your dame treats you like a slave!"

She answered downheartedly, "She is not my mama, for she is dead and my sire, a seaman, has long been gone at sea."

"Have you no other kin?"

"I have an aunt in Gallia Narbonensis, but I have no way of going to her and so this is my lot. What can I get you to eat?"

"I came for baked cheese and honey. But seeing you in this distress, when I hold the key to your happiness—well, I have lost my desire to eat!"

"You hold the key?" The maiden looked at Esta's brother with doubtful eyes. Yet he spoke her tongue and was of her race. He was dressed as a man of means and seemed quite sincere. "I don't understand."

He replied carefully, "If you look to the harbor, you will see a great ship of Hispania. Its owner is a buyer of *my goods,* for I have a fine villa, olive groves and vineyards in Massilia and what I barter he desires above all else!" The brother was careful not to disclose that the merchandise he intended on selling was in truth his own sister. Nonetheless, all of what he said was true and therefore rolled easily off his lips. With feigned concern he added, "I cannot leave such a one as you to lead this life of near servitude!"

She asked hesitantly, "I still cannot understand—are you saying that you will help me? Why?"

"Oh," he answered as if distraught, "You, dear maiden, are so much like my own sister, who is gone from us!" He reached out and tenderly touched a stray strand of her hair. "It is a strange thing, my meeting you, as if I were sent of Artemis. I know little about the goddess, for I am only a seller of oil and wine."

"Sent of Artemis? Please, please, what do you mean?" she implored.

"Can you tell me by what name you are called?"

Michela

"Michela," she said simply.

"Michela, it is this!" he answered, "This will I do if you will let me. The ship of Hispania will only be at anchor a few hours more before we sail. Nonetheless, if you would change your fortunes, then do as Apollo commands and act decisively. For, if you will, you may sail with us. I will see to it that you are well fed and clothed, as if you were my own la sòrre." He spoke "sister" in the Occitan tongue, for he knew that would endear him more to her. "When we return to Massilia," he lied for the first time, "we shall seek out la tanta, for Gallia Narbonensis is not far from my home!" Again, he gave the Occitan words for "your aunt," for he saw that he was winning her heart.

Esta's brother and Michela were aboard the ship of Hispania an hour later, for the maiden had but few possessions to gather. The Jacaian could not believe their good fortune, for a better substitute for Esta could not have been found. What was more, he was amazed with the brother, for Michela had willingly followed him aboard, excited beyond description for future hopes. He explained the unfortunate condition in which he had found her, the promise given the maiden and how she reminded him of Esta. The jackal smiled knowingly as he prattled on and on. "My dear young demoiselle, you indeed look very much like the sister of my dear friend, but yet there are distinctions in your features that are decidedly your own. Mmh, I think when you have laved off the grim of your former labors and put on new clothes, you may prove quite lovely! Ah, show your guest to the little cabin in the stern. It will be a bit snug, but all your own and may be securely locked at night. I will have a tub of water warmed and ready for you soon and have Esta's, ah, poor Esta! —I will have her clothes brought to you. I will also have our cook bring delicacies to your room so that you can sup as you ready yourself. Take your leisure for there is nothing for you to do but enjoy the day, which shall be entirely spent at sea. Alas, we shall not sail to Massilia for a time, for there are wonderous ports for us to visit and you will see great sights—mostly from the ship, however. For you cannot risk going ashore without your new friend and he has much work to do for me, if he is to procure, then sell me that which I must possess! As for myself, I spend most of my time, at sea, or in port, in my luxurious cabin, which you may visit whenever you like."

Michela looked about, somewhat worried that she saw no women on board, but only sailors making preparations to get the ship underway. The girl took the hand of the brother in hers, which gave her a measure of reassurance, and said to the ship's owner, "I cannot thank you enough for your kindness. I will willingly work to pay my way, and have learned cookery. That I can do! Your cook will find me good at what I do."

"Nonsense, my dear! Enough! Ha! For now, I will be your guardian, and as long as I am, you shall not do common labor for the rest of your life!"

The Trireme had already sailed from Cemenelum when the ship of Hispania sailed for Corsica. There the Lord of Jaca planned to learn all he could of Hadrian's court in Rome, for there was much commerce between Ostia Portus and Dianæ Portus and questions in a foreign port would seem less suspicious. While the Trireme stopped at Genua and Pisae, the Jacaian sailed directly for Corsica. When the Sirocco winds began to howl, the Hispanic ship was nearly to Aleria and made Dianæ Portus before the storm became furious. Much later when the Trireme rowed into Dianæ Portus, the Jacaian was much more surprised to see the Roman galley than the Trierach was to see again a ship of Hispania, for the Jacaian believed the Trireme would certainly follow the coast all the way to Rome. He was, of course, delighted with this unexpected turn and retired to his bed but half asleep, for his schemes filled his dreams.

As for Michela, the voyage to Corsica were to her the most wonderful days of her life. Although she possessed a happy disposition, continually loveless servitude had nearly killed the inborn hopes of her heart. Yet when Esta's brother spoke kindly of delivering the maiden to her aunt in Gallia Narbonensis with no untoward obligations, she was hesitant only for a moment, for something deep within her soul stirred it to acquiescence. Then when she was given the promised clothes, so rich and beautiful, and her old tattered dress was discarded, and she bathed in warm water, something she had never done before and was given delectable food made by another, solely for her, she was overcome with gratitude and fond emotions for Esta's brother. However, Michela was never at ease in the presence of the Jacaian and took pains never to be alone with him.

Despite the physical resemblance to his sister, the brother was surprised to find how much he enjoyed the company of Michela. He had always envied Esta and the attentions given her by their parents. Although much younger than he, yet she had grown to become much more popular in Massilia. In the city, he was not called by his given name, nor even as his father's son, but was most often referred to as "Esta's brother." This was true even after he had his mama and papa killed by confederate bandits. When the noble of Jaca offered to pay a fortune to purchase his sister, he secretly cherished the notion of Esta being carried away and completely out of his life. How different was Michela! He savored her admiration of him. Always she was thanking him for . . . for everything! She knew so little and begged him to tell her about the ship, the sea—tell her of Massilia, of his villa, groves, vineyards and of himself! The brother only became less loquacious when she asked about Esta and what had become of her. This was a subject he disdained and so Michela quickly learned not to speak of her, thinking his silence was a result of a sad death and his broken heart.

The brother had spent a delightful evening speaking with the maiden of Cemenelum when he was summoned to the owner's cabin alone. The noble of Jaca said when he had shut the door behind him, "It is beyond my expectations!"

"What is?" asked the brother.

"Everything! First that you have so entirely seduced Michela without even bedding her! The maid trusts you explicitly which makes thing so much easier. Secondly, as the two of you were gazing upon the lights of Aleria from larboard, I sat looking out upon Dianæ Portus starboard. And what did I see? Ah, it takes my breath away! The Trireme! Yes, Esta's Trireme! How is it here? A mystery! I saw her upon the deck with the others." The brother was silent. "Now this you must do. Although the Trireme is likely in Dianæ Portus to be repaired, for it must certainly have come close to destruction in the great storm, yet we cannot long remain in this harbor without becoming known to Aléxandros, Maros, or the ship's captain. Hence, steal away now into Aleria and covertly find our prize! If you find her alone, perhaps in her room or in a garden, slap your hand over her mouth and bind it! Carry her noiselessly away. There is but a sliver of a moon. Darkness will cover the deed! No one must know! If this you do, we shall send you back to whatever place you found Esta, with one of my guards, bearing the body of Michela—for when I *see* Esta, Michela's eyes will no longer *see!* Ha!" He paused his rant, then said, "If still Esta is well guarded, simply return and we shall quit this port of Ostia before dawn and at our leisure make a better plan in Rome where her guards will surely be fewer."

Supping from a terrace overlooking the Garden of Necropolis, Esta dined with her friends. Among the flowered crypts were white sculptures of the gods dimly seen in the faint moonlight. Said Aléxandros, "We have talked enough about the amazing events of our voyage. Let us talk philosophy with Esta as our sure guide."

Esta laughed, "I have not the look or bearing of a logician, most noble senator. While you have the ken, countenance and character of a Socrates! You must lead out!"

He smiled and said playfully, but most woefully, "What you mean to say is that you are very, very young, while I am as old as Parmenides!"

"Not at all," she answered rightly, although no one understood her meaning. "You are as ageless as truth."

Aléxandros smiled again and put forth a riddle. "Construct a statement that if true is false and if false is true." There followed much laughter, trial and error, from Eponi, Eitan, and Naomi. Maros seemed withdrawn, as if his mind was still on the adventures of the day. Esta said nothing until the senator spoke again to her, "Why is it you do not venture a guess? Have I at last bested the Maiden of Massilia?"

She answered curtly, "I am lying."

To which Naomi said cheerfully, "But as yet you've said nothing! How then," she laughed, "did you tell us a lie?"

Aléxandros replied enthusiastically, "Ha! Do you not see Esta answered the riddle without a misstep! If 'I am lying' is true, then it is false, and if it is false then it is true!"[2]

When the laughter subsided, Naomi said, "I am amongst trusted friends who I believe only wish me well." Her father gave her a stern look of warning. Nonetheless, she continued, "You may know that I understand but little of the Pantheon, for I worship but One. There must be purpose, but I only see perplexity in many gods. Also, it seems to my mind that learned Greeks and Romans speak much about the gods but believe little, while their countrymen without letters speak less about the gods but believe more! If we are to speak of philosophy, can you help me understand?"

---

2. https://www.britannica.com/list/8-philosophical-puzzles-and-paradoxes, 2022

Her father interjected, "Naomi, we needn't trouble our friends about religio or our obligations to the heavens, lest qualms beyond ken should cause offense." This he said, for Christians were then persecuted and sometimes killed for denying the gods.

Aléxandros answered reassuringly, "Have no fear Eitan, for Naomi's question shall not bring reprisals from a senator of Massilia. Rather, it is a good question and deserves an eloquent answer." He looked at Esta, "I have often seen you at the temples of Apollo and Artemis. I know you have been taught even by oracles. Speak then to Naomi of the gods!"

Esta did not hesitate. "There are many beliefs in common with Religio Romana and Grecian Piety. Sometimes a god is known by different names. Greeks call the king of gods, Zeus, while he is known to the Romans as Jupiter. In like manner Poseidon in Greece is Neptune in Italia, as Cronus is Saturn, Ares is Mars, and Aphrodite is Venus and so on. But there are also differences; the Greek faith holds that the life of gods is unattainable for mortals. Whereas, the Romans, like Christians, believe that mortals can aspire to become God-like. Is not the Emperor considered a god?"

At this, Aléxandros raised an eyebrow, saying, "A god should not be self-proclaimed. Esta, please continue."

She added, "The Greeks consider their gods to have human form, as do most Christians who understand they are created in the image of their God. Whereas the Romans simply call the gods *nurmna*, or spirits."[3]

All listened in rapt attention to the young maiden as she expounded the reverence given to divinities, "Common beliefs are further shared by many lands. The Greek, the Roman, the Galatian, and the Christian, all believe that the planets and stars are living

---

3. Will Durant, *Caesar and Christ*, Simon and Schuster, New York, 1972, p. 207, Kindle edition, 2022.

beings, as is also the earth, the sky, trees, rivers, seas, animals and so on—all are endowed with *mind* and *life*. Christian writing states that God speaks and the winds and elements obey him, for they have intelligence and *know* his voice. The codices state that so do the heavens, which were created by Him, know Him and obey Him. The Romans and Greeks believe that not only are these *knowing* and *living* but they are deities with godly powers. Now to my understanding, for I am not an oracle, there is beauty in much of this, for it binds us to the spiritual world where every aspect of existence has importance."

Aléxandros, most particularly, was mesmerized by the wisdom of the Maiden of Massilia. "Please," he said, "tells us how this is so."

Esta explained, "Always there should be a fire on the family hearth, for this is the goddess Vesta, the endurance, warmth and love of the family that must never be extinguished. Always must the Fire of Vesta be kindled and tended. Di Penates, the dii familiars, are the household deities, the Di Manes, or Kindly Shades, our male forebears whose grim death masks look down from our walls and warn us of evil. We must honor the papa of the domus, the Genius, for he has the godly power to beget, and the mama, the Juno, who possesses the miraculous creative power to bear. The god Janus stands invisible over the threshold of the domus, a two-faced god, watching that which is without and that which is within the home, watching every leaving and every coming; not of the domus only, but Janus watches over the nation as well, for the nation is the totality of its homes and every home is a nation. The 'Gates of Janus' in Rome. are closed in times of peace and opened in times of war.

"The earth is Tellus or Terra Mater, the Mother Earth, whose soil is in all. Yet there are so many—thousands of life forms that are considered to be gods! Pomona for our orchards, Ceres for crops, Vulcan for making fire, and so on."

Naomi queried, "With so many gods, how is it possible to know, much less, to venerate them all?"

Esta answered, "It is as simple as recognizing all of the wonders that surround us! Many ancient gods of Greece are honored by Rome, such as Apollo, the god of Light and Artemis, his sister who guards the chastity of virgins. Is it not a natural thing to both see and understand the warmth and light of the Daystar and the beauty of womanhood undefiled? The religio of the gods sanctifies all aspects of our lives, ennobles our craft, and provides purpose and direction in war and peace. The tiller of fields believes in the gods more, perhaps, than the citizen of a great city, for he relies on timely rain and fair winds. Nonetheless, when the battle grows sore, the general prays for victory just as sincerely as the farmer."

Naomi asked openly, "I admit, that is the beauty of such beliefs! What then of the carnality and brutality of certain Greek and Roman gods?"

Esta answered, "Should not a god, especially the king of gods, be able to curse as well as bless? But I think your question, Naomi, is of a different type."

Naomi replied, "Yes, it is. How can true deities exhibit debauchery?"

Esta thought for a moment, then explained, "Mmh, I think the history of the gods would be very different if the chronicles were scribed by their own hands. Nonetheless, we have it only from mortal oracles. If the holy scribe is just and interprets revelations aright, and if these are given of true beings and not usurpers feigning godhood, then we may trust the chronicler. But often wizards decrypt meaning from something like a solitary clap of thunder or from the entrails of a sacrifice, and according to their allegiance these conjurers attempt to prophecy that which *another* desires."

"What do you mean?" said Naomi.

Esta answered, "Some stories of the gods are meant to justify the carnal nature of men of power, for if the gods are said to behave jealously, lustfully, maliciously, then kings and rulers may rationalize their own wickedness. When in truth, *reign* is taken from the word *regere*, which means to rule, direct, keep straight, guide in a straight line,[4] to lead aright, or in other words to lead *righteously*. Hence, neither a true god or a true king has lasting authority to lead wrongly. Perhaps the truth is that there are good spirits and there are evil spirits. These are ageless beings, who have knowledge beyond the sight of man, some much more than others. Hence, in this sense all such may be said to be supernatural and may claim to be gods. So then we must scrutinize and choose who it is we follow and what attributes we wish to emulate. The Phoenician goddess Ashtoreth is worshiped by the Greeks as Astarte, and by the Romans as Venus, and she instills in her devotees sexual desire, whither married or not. While the Greek goddess Artemis, who is known by the Romans as Diana, guards the chastity of young women and watches over mothers in childbirth and is said to help care for their children. Hence one should choose carefully who they emulate!"

Aléxandros interposed, saying, "Esta, have you considered whether the unseen beings of power are of different orders or races?"

Esta quietly thought for a time before she answered. Then said, "There *must* be a difference between the embodied and the unembodied presences and even Rome must admit that not all gods are spirits. When they pronounce the emperor to be a god, has he not a physical form? Do we not traverse the very body of Tellus, the earth? What of the sun, planets and stars worshiped by Rome? Are they not celestial bodies? Yet these must be of a very different godly race than the AllFather. For if he is our Father and we his children, which I believe is certain, then we must be *of* His lineage, and as the Christian believes, must be *in* His image."

---

4. https://www.etymonline.com/word/reign, 2023

Enthusiastically, Naomi responded, "Yes, yes! Please continue."

Esta replied, "Spirit beings cannot be denied, for there are *many* testimonies of credible men and women who say they have seen spirits and even conversed with them. Others will admit there are times when their presence is felt, though the ghosts remain unseen. It seems to me also that spirits can speak to our thoughts, both to bless or tempt. Hence, we must be diligent and again distinguish good promptings from malevolent provocations. There is much more that I could say," and Esta thought of the Burning One, "but that is sufficient for now. Naomi, my friend, think on these things."

Aléxandros exclaimed, "Never, no never have I heard such a narrative of the gods! Often it is asked, 'Do you believe in the gods?' And the person is left to wonder how to answer, for as the gods represent every form of life and as life surrounds us, we must admit belief! Yet when that person considers certain frightening or implausible legends of the gods and their doings, then he doubts *within* even if he professes *outwardly* to believe. Oh, that all could hear, dear Esta, the answers you have given Naomi—and not her only but all of us! Who among us can challenge the veracity of your sayings!"

As they were retiring to their rooms, Eitan asked Naomi if she would remain, for there were things he must tell her. When alone, he spoke of the persecution of their people, and of that which he himself had witnessed! Only in Massilia was their liberality in diverse thinking. "Aléxandros is of Massilia, but we are no longer in that fair city and you must not speak as you did tonight. Do not openly speak of the One, lest you be the cause of your own death and of mine. How hated we are, you cannot imagine!" Then, although fatigued, the loving father and the obedient daughter conversed until they heard the horrific cry.

When Esta went to her room, she did not feel weary. She felt joyful and lit from within. It seemed she had taught her friends more than she knew—that her words exceeded that which she had learned from her studies. Somehow, she felt truths were given her even as she spoke.

There was a staired balcony off her room. Although the door into her room was guarded by two sentries, she was surprised that no soldier stood by the rear balcony. Yet she thought there must be guards without. At first Esta only intended to look upon the night sky from her terrace—until she saw the gate of the Necropolis. A lighted torch was affixed to an outward wall. This she took in her hand and extended it as far as she could reach beyond the waist-high wall of the elevated portico, attempting to read the inscription of the gate. Nonetheless, the rays of torchlight fell well short of the garden entrance, which was illuminated only by a wane moon and starlight.

Esta felt impulsively and inwardly drawn toward the Necropolis, yet she knew better than to venture alone beyond the safety of her room. How often, when one meets with folly, do they afterwards consider the presentiments they ignored? For a few minutes she stood on the balcony, enjoying the quietude and trying to understand why it was the silent park seemed to beckon her. A thought came into her mind that on the morrow, with Naomi, Aléxandros and an armed escort, she might venture out among the terraced crypts and discover the reason for this uncanny attraction. On the heels of this came a whispered challenge, "You are far now from danger, far from the intrigues of Massilia, are you not? Dangers are past and how can you sleep, wondering? The night is quiet, warm and safe, and the Necropolis is right there, just beyond your torch-light! Why if you heard anything amiss, could you not, in but a few steps, run back? Of course, all is well and why fear foolishly? You think best when you are alone and surely you have much to consider! What words are inscribed above the gate? Perhaps they are the key to this mystery."

Esta struggled to read the first line of the inscription, and interpreted the words haltingly, "'You cannot look behind . . .' Why?" she asked herself.

Mustering courage she then soliloquized, "Often Naomi and I quit my room on the darkest of nights and ran bravely through the groves! I am fleet of foot and can outthink any foe!" Then she mused, "Wait, that is not true! I am not so wise that I am above the cunning of the evil one. Where did that thought come from?" Nonetheless, Esta slowly made her way to the head of the stairs that led down to the garden and began a careful descent.

As she stepped upon the grass, the quiet voice within her spoke a single command, "Wait!"

She rebutted the directive as if it were her own, saying quietly aloud, "Why should I wait, for there is something about this place I must learn. As I am alone, there is no one to hinder or hurt!" She made her way effortlessly to the gate and raising her torch read:

> "Δεν μπορείς να κοιτάξεις πίσω σου, γιατί
> όταν γυρίζεις αυτό που είναι ακόμα
> μπροστά σου, αυτό που φαινόταν έχει
> φύγει. Ούτε μπορείτε να κοιτάξετε πολύ
> μπροστά, γιατί αυτό που είναι δεν έχει
> έρθει ακόμα."

For her own understanding, Esta translated the Greek inscription, saying:

> *"You cannot look behind, for when you turn that which is*
> *is yet before you and that which was from view is*
> *gone. Neither can you look far ahead, for that which*
> *is is not yet come."*

Esta said to herself, "Meaning—the past and future, though both vital, are not more important than the present, for all we do is in the *now* of our existence." Although these words were pregnant with meaning, Esta was convinced that this was not the reason for the keen curiosity she felt about the place. She stifled the inner voice that prompted her again to return to her room, for the demoiselle had looked into the heart of the cemetery and saw the beauty of the statues and the tombs beyond. Being inclined to the spiritual, for great was the *feeling* of the place, she continued into the City of the Dead, wondering that there were no guards about. Had Esta been more observant she would have seen, in the night-shade beneath her balcony, two sleeping Romans, for they had been given wine laced heavily with the powder of valerian root.

As Esta quietly passed from monument to monument, her torch casting firelight about her, she sensed that she was being watched. Indeed, this was so and by the same man who had given the guards the tainted, but delicious wine. Yet the night was warm and beautiful, so different from the hellish storm of but a day past and as she had silenced the warning voice by her disobedience, the maiden proceeded into the bowels of the Necropolis without further hinderance.

Esta came across the sculpture of a beautiful woman. Strangely the inscription at its base was written in Celtic and read: "Fionn màthair mòran," which interpreted means "Fionn, mother of many." There came into her heart the desire of nurturing a host of children as this Fionn had done. She wondered who this woman had been, a Celt in Corsica! Had she given birth to many? Was she a mother to orphans? That she was of a wealthy family was certain, for the monument of her grave was expertly sculpted. Indeed, the marble was so well fashioned that the statue seemed to her as living flesh, white and pure!

In the midst of this amazement, Esta suddenly felt the pang of a garrote snap about her face. She wrenched mightily, attempting to free herself, thinking the assassin had missed her neck, for a garrote is used to strangle a person with more force than using bare hands. Nonetheless, quicker than thought, the rope, over which was wound thick cloth, was forced into her mouth, gagging the maiden with such violence as to nearly render her unconscious. As Esta's strength faded, she slumped into the arms of her attacker, who tied a knot at the back of her head so that the horrid restraint would hold fast. He lifted her roughly over his shoulder, so that she hung from her waist as he swiftly ran through the garden of the Necropolis.

The torch had fallen from Esta's hand in the assault and the man did not fetch it again, for he was desirous of making a quick escape from Aleria. Twice he stumbled in the gloom of night, but he did not fall or lose his burden. Yet just as he neared the gate, he was struck at the back of his legs by a large staff and he fell hard upon the grass. The rescuer immediately found the rope tied about Esta's face and pulled it over the top of her head. Though painful, this allowed her to breath freely and she heard herself scream. Though her vision was yet blurred, she saw her attacker and her savior, fighting desperately. In the dimness of night, Esta could not see who it was that had captured her, nor who it was that was fighting to save her. She struggled to her feet that she might assist her champion, who even then was suffering defeat, for the assailant vehemently struck him repeatedly with a rock he had laid hold of.

Nonetheless, Esta had been so viciously attacked that she could not lend help and wavering fell again to the ground. Still, she saw many torch bearers, for the guards and her friends had heard Esta's piercing scream and were running from the inn towards her. The aggressor saw this too and knowing he must save his own life, fled into the abyss of darkness. Although pursued by Roman guards, he was not seized.

Esta wept as the torchlight revealed her protector as old Maros, bloodied and unconscious. Both were lifted and carried to the inn.

Still the maiden was not altogether mindful as she drifted in and out of awareness. Yet she saw Naomi, Eitan, Eponi and Aléxandros. He was leaning over Maros, who had opened his eyes as he tried to speak. The maiden heard the old seamen angrily utter three words. Hoarsely he said, "'Twas her brother!"

All through the night Maros struggled for life, fired by a solitary purpose. When the morning came, he was lucid and asked if he might hastily see Esta, for he must soon die. Esta had somewhat recovered, although her nose and mouth were sorely discolored and her throat was swollen from her strenuous struggle to breathe through the folds of the garrote. Naomi helped her to the chamber where Maros was laid. There she found Eponi by his bedside, holding his hand in hers as she cried tenderly.

When Maros' eyes met Esta's, he smiled and motioned for her to come closer. She carefully embraced the bruised and broken man, as her tears fell upon his cheeks. "Now then," he said, mustering strength, "'tis good t'at this be me end. Think not t'at I've lost me senses, for though I'm a dying, yet 'tis sure t'at what I tell ya is true! Last night, Ep soon fell fast asleep, non'less *I saw a spirit*, such as ya spoke of. A soft light fill'd t' room an there stood a beautiful woman in a'flow'n gown. Said she, 'Save my daughter' an she pointed towards t' garden. I jumped 't my feet an no sooner done than t' spirit turned an flew into t' night." Maros coughed and was quiet for a moment, then said, "I oby'ed, not know'n what I should do, but look'n down I saw a torch fall frum its bearer's hand. So's I grabbed me staff an run t' gate. 'Twas then we fought!"

He coughed again, closing his eyes, resting, for in so few words he had told her all. As Esta stayed at his side, together with Eponi, his life's love, and Naomi, who also loved him dearly, she thought of this good man who had twice saved her life. In both of these traumatic events, there was manifest preternatural powers, instructive and redemptive. Although Esta knew she had been first to receive a spiritual impression last eve, she shuddered with the realization that she had not *listened* to the admonition. Rather she succumbed to another presence, one allied to the evil designs of her brother! Oh, the cost of her ill-fated action! If only she had returned to her guarded chamber! Maros would yet be sleeping at the side of his beloved and would not now be stricken nigh to death! Esta chastened herself severely, thinking it is one thing to blunder innocently but to ignore forewarning was inexcusable! Never would she do so again, if only Maros could live!

Then Esta thought of the angel who had come to Maros and the words spoken: "Save my daughter!" Who was she, this spirit being who had the appearance of a mortal woman, for she wore "a'flow'n gown?" Was she her own deceased mama? Or rather a la reire-menina, her mama's mama from long ago?

It struck Esta forcefully that this spirit had lived on this isle—that was certain, for her grave was in the Necropolis! Ah, what was that that had come into her mind—the angel lived in Aleria and was buried in the Garden of the Dead? Could it really be that Nyx, the goddess of *this* night, was the ghost of Fionn? In her heart, Esta prayed, "Please, Father, let Maros return to health and to the arms of Eponi! Help me to come to an understanding of all that has happened this night!"

Nyx with symbolic wings

CHAPTER 9
ROME

Friendship, the least jealous of the loves . . .

One half of the century of legionary had left the inn of Aleria soon after the attack on Esta and Maros. Although they ran swiftly to Dianæ Portus, they did not overtake her assailant. So quick were the guardsmen in their pursuit that they had not heard of Maros' telling Aléxandros the identity of his killer. The other Legionary also took no rest but surrounded the inn, save for two couriers. The first speedily hailed the commander of Roman forces in Aleria with news that a kidnapper had made an attempt to capture the emperor's charge. The second ran to the Trierach bearing the same tidings. The captain of the Trireme immediately looked towards the ship of Hispania, which had been anchored in the bay at some distance from the drydock. But he saw only the blackness of the night. Nonetheless, he cursed himself, for he knew it must be the same vessel he had seen in the ports of Massilia and Cemenelum.

There were no warships in Dianæ Portus at that time, save his Trireme. Nonetheless, there were a number of troop transports, known as Navis Lusoria,[1] at the quay. These carried thirty soldier-oarsmen and a single mast. It took more than an hour for the Trierach to find his half century of men, for the bay was large and they were searching in darkness for the fugitive. Yet with these he appropriated a Navis Lusoria and carefully combed the bay of Dianæ Portus. They found not the Hispanic ship and when first light was come, they saw it was gone from the harbor.

Hence, he allowed his men to take their rest in shifts while others gave aid to the shipwrights. These craftsmen were commanded to speedily repair and dry his Trireme and work on no other vessel. Meanwhile, the Roman commander of Aleria had soldiers search about and sent several Navis Lusoria beyond the bay, but without success.

When the morning was bright, the sun rising high in a perfect sky, Eponi felt the hand of her husband grow cold. Yet she would not release it until the young Naomi put her arms around the aged wife and embracing her, said, "Oh, for so long you have been vital in my life, since your great Maros saved us from a watery death. You came to live at the villa with him, which was my second home. Always you cared for us, just two little girls at the first. You were like another grandmother, always praising and never scolding. Oh Eponi, how I love you! How I grieve with you. Yet know this, one day soon you will see Maros again and somehow, someday, you will be with him always. *I believe that love outlasts life*—at least this life. For never are we truly gone. The spirit of your husband lives and loves you yet."

---

1. A Navis Lusoria was extremely nimble on the water. The name literally meant a dancing ship.

Then for a long time they wept together. At last Naomi said, "Come grandmother. You must rest for then you will feel him nearer." For several hours all of Esta's friends slept.

They were awakened by a courier who told them they must make haste for Dianæ Portus. The Trireme would soon be ready to sail and departure was urgent. Not understanding, yet they were obedient and bore the injured Esta upon a litter, as they also carried the body of Maros, for Eponi would have him buried at sea.

The Trireme was already afloat when they arrived at the quay, with rowers in their stations. The guardsmen helped their charges aboard, giving the upmost care to Esta, placing her upon a secure bed, safe on the middeck and then took their places along the sides of the galley. Aléxandros said nothing to the stern faced Trierach, who shouted commands with fierce intent, until they were in the open sea. Then the senator asked, "Captain, I thought we should take rest a while longer in Aleria and allow Esta to recover before leaving Dianæ Portus, thinking also more time would be required to make your repairs."

The Trierach replied with a grim smile, "Look at the cloudless sky! Feel the fair westerly wind upon your face! See our sheets filled and the strong rowers at their oars! Ah, this day we may cross the deep water of the Tyrrhenian Sea with agility and unmatched speed! Scores of laborers worked their skill upon my ship, through the dark hours and yet more when the sun rose! See how my Trireme flies towards Ostia Portus! Yet before you see the Bay of the Emperor, *you will see the power of Rome!*"

Aléxandros did not understand these words until later in the day. He observed that rowers were often relieved by soldiers, each taking their turn, that the galley's incredible pace did not slacken. Then he saw before them the growing image of the ship of Hispania. The Trireme's speed was much greater, even though the Jacaian's vessel was at full sail.

The Trierach shouted, **"By Jupiter and Mars, I have found our prey!** *BATTLE STATIONS! RAMING SPEED!"* Quickly the legionary placed Esta's friends about her bed on the open middeck and ordered that they hold fast. Then most took up spears and swords, while the remainder laid hold of grappling hooks.

From his position, the senator, standing against orders, could see the thrilling and incredible sight that was unfolding to his view! The closure with the ship of Hispania was like a warhorse closing on a fleeing foot soldier! Then Aléxandros saw the thick Jackal looking down in astonishment from the rear deck of his ship, the elder brother at his side, their eyes wide with absolute terror, their eyes fixed on the rostrum, the massive bronze ram jutting well to the fore of the painted prow of the Trireme! On either side of the bow made rigid with great beams of hardened oak, artisans had fashioned great eyes. This, with the ramming arm, turned the visage of the vessel into that of a hellish monster intent on devouring its kill.

Neither of the two murderers ran to the fore of their ship. Yet they were cravens and did not hold their stance in bravery. They were both simply frozen with fear!

The ram did well its work, gutting asunder the stern, like an assassin's knife plunged into a great belly. The wrenching sound was horrific, as timbers were torn asunder. Upon impact, the elder brother fell backwards, but the Jacaian was struck in his own swollen gut by a large splinter, forced upward from the demolition of his deck. High he rose on the death faggot, writhing like a wounded hare upon a child's wooden spear.

Grappling hooks were thrown as the ship of Hispania swung wide from the force of the blow, the great rostrum breaking free, leaving a gaping hole in the stern, as the sides of the two ships were pulled together. Surely the Jacaian's ship would sink, but not before the Legionary boarded the doomed vessel and reaped total destruction upon its crew, for the order had been given that none should be spared.

The elder brother, uninjured by his fall, seeing a mighty Roman rush towards him with drawn sword, stretched out his arms, crying for mercy, even as his head was lifted from off his shoulders.

Quick work was made of the business of war. Large bags of silver and gold were taken from the owner's cabin, along with other plunder easily seized. When all but three legionary had left the doomed ship, pitch was thrown about and set afire by torches. When the last man was about to jump to the Trireme, he heard a faint scream of a maiden. Though he had but little time to search, he followed the pathetic shrieks to a small cabin, engulfed in smoke but not yet in flames. With the butt of his sword, he broke off the lock of the stout door. Swiftly he carried the swooning maiden across the fiery deck, then threw her bodily into the waiting arms of his fellows upon the Trireme.

This done the man quit the sinking vessel. Grappling lines were cut, rowers pulled and from a distance of many rods, voices were lifted in a great shout as the burning ship slipped beneath the waves. Not a single Roman had been wounded, save for burns the gallant rescuer had suffered about his legs.

When Esta saw the saved maiden, dressed in her own vestments, she was greatly perplexed. Aléxandros was not confused, for then he understood the scheme of the dead men. Yet Esta, seeing the girl was greatly frightened and fatigued, for she had tried desperately to free herself from the slight chamber. Also, Michela had inadvertently learned the true intent of the Jacaian, for when the elder brother had boarded the ship after the foiled kidnapping and told how they were hotly pursued, the fat man screamed derisive epithets at the brother. He, in an angry heat, had shown some residue of empathy, and had withstood the words of the Jacaian, saying, "You shall *not* kill Michela! We must find another way!" For saying this he was struck to the ground; the escape had sapped his strength and he could not defend himself. Then the Jacaian ordered Michela to be locked in her cabin and commanded anchors raised for a swift but silent departure. Hence, the maiden was exhausted as she stood at the side of Esta's bed, sadly uncertain as to her fate.

Esta asked nothing of Michela but her name. Then said, "Please, my sister, rest with me upon my bed. We shall sleep for a time and gain strength. I know not your sorrowful story, but I feel our lives were somehow bound by the ill doings of my own brother. Say nothing, but lay your head upon my shoulder and know that we will let no more harm come to you."

Sometime later, the body of Maros was lowered into his beloved Mediterranean Sea, with Eponi, Naomi, Aléxandros and the Trierach looking on. Said the Captain, "No greater seaman was ever aboard my Trireme. He knew the wind and waves as a son of Neptune and read danger in the skies when I was blind to perils that would nearly take my ship! Though aged, he was strong and in saving the emperor's charge, he saved my own, for surely Hadrian, the Just, would have had me slain at her loss! Yet you, my greatest friend, are avenged!"

AN HOUR before dusk the Trireme entered the magnificent man-made bay of Ostia Portus, but five leagues overland from Rome! Soon the travelers rested comfortably in the Imperial Inn, their voyage complete, their enemies vanquished, while the century of Legionary stood guard without. As they supped, Michela told her story. Esta could hardly believe how cruel her brother had become, all for the sake of money he did not need. Before he hired the assassins to kill their mama and papa, he lived a secure and wonderful life in the most beautiful villa in Massilia. How he should have cherished raising his family in his sire's domus until a natural death would have given him far more than he wickedly stole. Although, as a murderer he could never find true joy in his ill-gotten inheritance, yet the magnificent properties that he received at so great a cost of life were debt free and all he lacked was ready coin, which a few seasons of diligent labor would have easily provided.

Nonetheless, once he valued silver and gold above all else, including familial ties, it was inevitable that he should attempt to sell his sister! When that failed, how easily did he conspire with the Jacaian to entice poor Michela away from Cemenelum with the intent of later killing her! Esta looked at Michela and thought to herself that the plan might have worked! They were nearly the same age, the same complexion, the same height and form, the same hair color, even her nose was like her own! Had it not been for Maros, poor Michela would have been found dead in the Necropolis of Aleria and she would have been forced to sail to the port of Barcino, and thence to Jaca, a captive slave! How grateful she was that, at the end, her brother showed a glimmer of compassion, for he had pled for Michela's life.

Now he was dead, as were his evil plans. Aléxandros would send word to Massilia disclosing his infamy. The villa, groves and vineyards would pass to the next oldest of her brothers. Because of his crimes, the senator said, his widow and her children would be sent to her sire's domus, for such a murderer cannot leave a legacy of property. Hence, unless her own family was charitable, they would be beggars in Massilia. Had he, Esta thought, ever considered how his sins must be answered upon the heads of his innocent wife and children? This was something she must weigh in her mind, for it troubled her.

In the morning, the Trierach called on Esta and her company. He explained that her guardsmen would continue with her to Rome on the morrow. For their comfort, he had arranged a carpentum for them, an elegant four wheeled carriage with leather strap suspension, spacious and richly decorated.

With great delight he further explained that they had taken a great treasure in gold and silver from the Hispanic ship, spoils of the very short war-at-sea with the Jacaian. Such was in his power, save for that which was due the state. The remainder, an amount greater than ever he had seen, was his to distribute to his soldiers, rowers and whoever else he felt deserving. To Aléxandros, Eitan, Eponi and Esta he gave equal shares of silver, but none to Naomi, as she was yet in her sire's care. To Michela he gave a token only, yet it was more than she had ever possessed!

When this was done, Esta spoke to the senator apart from the others, saying, "Aléxandros, when you send your courier to Massilia with news of my brother's death, give him also my silver." She placed her bag in his hand. "Tell him this legacy survived his death lawfully and is left to her and her children."

Aléxandros replied, "Was their ever one such as you? Shall I not have him say how it was lawfully given and who is the giver of the gift?"

"Nay," said Esta and she quickly withdrew to the company of Naomi and Michela.

The maidens, yet guarded, took leave of Aléxandros, Eitan and the grieving Eponi to walk the gardens and byways of Ostia, one of the first colonies established in Italia by the old Romans. Horreum[2] and shops were abundant, for trade flourished in the busy port established in the ostium or the mouth of the River Tiberis. The city was richly adorned with decorative brickwork and intricate mosaics. The aroma of freshly baked bread and the fragrance of blossoms mixed with the scent of a gentle sea breeze. The amphitheater was ornate and larger than its equivalent in Massilia. So also was the

---

2. Warehouses

Agora with its multitude of sculptures of Roman, Greek and Persian heroes and gods. Such a leisurely stroll was a new experience for Michela, who was excited with everything she saw. Yet her enthusiasm was matched by Esta and Naomi, for they were all young and loved sharing the adventure.

Hadrian's Rome

When the maidens returned to the Imperial Inn later in the day, they were greeted by Eitan. Naomi's father had also spent the day in the bustling port city. With introductions given him by the Trierach and with a portion of the riches recently obtained, Eitan had struck bargains with tradesmen of two merchant ships, the first bound for Massilia and the second for Narbonensis. The kindly sire said to Michela, "It seems Providence has blessed you with a way home to your aunt. If that is still your desire you may sail to Narbonensis in four days' time as my representative. The captain of the ship will warrant your safety."

Although this was the very hope that had enticed her away from Cemenelum, Michela was taken aback. Never before had she *friends*. Naomi and Esta had always known the power of this great affection, one of the most potent aspects of their lives. True friendship, the least jealous of the loves, is never exclusive and rests chiefly on a foundation of shared interests and seeking of truths. This was why, in one sense, Maros and Aléxandros, though not of their age or sex, were their dear friends. Now Michela had been instantly admitted into their sisterhood, perhaps at the first out of sympathy. Yet quickly Naomi and Esta learned that Michela possessed substance and deep feeling, hungry for their guidance and companionship. She also possessed a natural grace, which of course needed refinement, for never was she schooled by a kindly dame. Though only in their presence for a few days, Michela unconsciously emulated her new friends and because they were *worthy* she was lifted almost effortlessly.

Michela, not knowing how she should answer, looked at Eitan silently. Esta placed her hand on Michela's arm and said, "We know how much you wanted to find your la tanta,[3] but that was before we found you! Nonetheless, Naomi's father has done you a great service;

---

3. Aunt

the *choice* is yours to make. How wonderful is that word, for it takes the bondage out of being. Sail to Narbonensis and you will yet be dear to us, always! Yet rather I would that you come with us and share our grand adventure!"

Michela looked at Esta with tears in her eyes and said, "But you go to the emperor! The invitation was to you alone and how should I know what to say and how to act at Court?"

Naomi answered, "True, he summoned Esta to Rome. I also was not invited, directly, that is. He said for her to bring whoever she desired to bring. Hence, here I am and you as well. I also cannot speak like Esta. Often when she is asked great questions, I remain silent! It is easy to be quiet and quiet can be rewarded. Esta, is it not so! How many times have the great ones of the Angora said, 'Naomi is so wise!'"

"Oh, that is true," laughed Esta. "And all the while she says nothing, only looks upon them with knowing eyes! What say you, Michela? Shall you sail aboard an old ship to Narbonensis or ride with us in a splendid carpentum to Rome?"

With glistening eyes, Michela said, "The way I've been chattering today, you must think I have no power to hold my tongue! But I promise, I will be like Naomi and will soon be known as the wisest maiden in Italia!" She turned to Eitan and said, "Thank you! I did not believe I would ever be able to make such a choice as this. I will go with my friends and someday," she prophesied, "I will return to Narbonensis, find my family and they will see that I have much to give." She paused, then continued, "Ah, never have I rode in a carpentum!"

Esta and Naomi replied in unison, "Neither have we!"

The River Tiberis

THE ROAD from Ostia to Rome paralleled the River Tiberis. Aléxandros, Eitan, Eponi, Michela, Naomi and Esta were exuberant as they rode in the expansive carriage, enjoying the beauty of the day-long journey. Aléxandros, the only one of their number who knew the way, for he had been to Rome many times, pointed out vistas of interest and history. Yet nothing could have prepared them for the sight of the city of over a million inhabitants and its seven magnificent hills! Upon Capitoline Hill, the highest of these, towered the great Temple of Jupiter, overlooking a sea of marbled edifices, including the Forum and Basilicas, the Pantheon, the Therma or the Imperial Baths, the Colosseum with seating for 50,000, the incredible Circus Maximus, designed for 150,000 seated spectators—and their new home, the old Imperial Palace of Rome. At the gates of the city, they stepped down from the carpentum and where seated on several lectica, as horses and carriages were not allowed within the city during the day. These lectica were Roman litters, elaborately decorated with overhead canopies and curtains, which could be opened or closed, according to the patrons' desires. By means of supporting poles, either four or eight tall men, the lecticarii[4] or litter-bearers, carried the lectica upon their shoulders and over the heads of the crowd. Again, this was a new luxury for the maidens as they were carried swiftly to the Imperial Palace.

Here they were greeted by the prefect and their guardsmen were relieved by the Praetorian Guard, the personal troops of Hadrian. Eponi and the maidens were shown to exquisite adjoining chambers, lighted by garden atriums with flowing fountains and opulent furnishings, while the Senator and merchant were given fine accommodations, though more spartan in décor.

Refreshments were provided and Esta was told the Emperor would summon her in three days' time.

---

4. http://vroma.org/vromans/araia/litter.html, 2022

The Colosseum

CHAPTER 10
ARRIAN

"Think of God more often than thou breathest."

Epictetus

E sta said smiling, "Michela, when we were eleven, Naomi said
to me, 'If Neptune's moods change the sea, so that whenever he is angry the waves are furious and when he is happy
there is great calm, both of which are deadly to the sailor, how is he
to be worshipped?'

"'I see your question,' I said. 'Mmh, how do you make such a god
just a little angry, so that his winds are just right? Too much and a
ship is sunk. Too little and its sails hang loose and the ship is
stranded! I don't know. We must ask Sebastian or Aléxandros.'"

"Naomi was not done with me, but said, 'But then, how does
Neptune huff and puff at all? Is not Aeolus the god of winds?'"

Michela laughed at this, saying, "I love how Naomi thinks! How did you answer her?"

Esta replied, "I said to Naomi, 'There are many wind-gods. There's Boreas, the North Wind and Notus, the South Wind and Eurus, the East Wind and Zephyrus, the West Wind, and Skeiron, god of the Northwest Wind and Leuconotus, the south-southwest wind and . . .'

"'Enough!' said Naomi. 'Suppose Neptune wants only to blow gently from here to there?'

"I said, 'Then all he needs do is summon Aura, the Breeze.'

"Naomi asked, 'And she can blow in any direction?'

"'I suppose so,' I said. 'As long as she stays gentle, for if Aura blows hard, she is no longer herself!'"

"Naomi thought on this and then said, 'Can Aura, mild and kind as she is—can Aura push aside dangerous Eurus or cold Boreas?'

"I answered her, 'I believe she does! What a thought! Often a mild breeze in truth supplants a gale!'

"Naomi, who is far wiser than I, then said, 'Then Aura, who surely must be a lesser god, for I have never seen her monument— then Aura must be greater than all the winds and even greater than Neptune himself—for where Aura *is* the others cannot come. Yet she is caring, for *a breeze* can still fill the sails of a ship and, without danger, send it to a far port!'"

Michela said, "Aura must only think herself a lesser god, for she must also be humble. Did you ever get an answer to Naomi's first question?"

Esta replied, "We did ask Sebastian and the others with him in the Angora. Aléxandros said one thing, Sebastian another and when we left a full hour later, the men were still hotly debating the matter."

Michela laughed as Esta continued, "I learned a great truth from my dear friend that day. I decided to strive to emulate Aura, to do as

Apollo says, to be courteous and not envy boisterous blowhards. That is what we first saw in you, our friend. You are Aura. You want to be up and doing, yet softly, without aggression. You, Michela, leave peace in your wake."

The two maidens sat by the side of a beautiful fountain. After hearing this compliment, Michela said nothing but looked intently at her reflection in the pool, thinking how much she desired to be worthy of Esta's esteem. At that moment, Naomi came running towards them excitedly and exclaimed nearly out of breath, "Haste! The Prefect Marcius himself waits on the portico with father and Aléxandros and says that Emperor Hadrian will see Esta and her company! *Now!*"

Michela said to Esta as she swiftly arose, "See how Naomi ran to us, from the south, I think. Notus?"

"Huh?" said Naomi.

"Most definitely she is the southern tempest," answered Esta as the two maidens laughed. She continued, "It is nothing, Naomi. We are ready. Come my friends. Remember the protocol we've been taught. Yet, do not dismay if you make an error," Esta giggled, "only do not point it out!"

The maidens found Marcius and Aléxandros conversing warmly, for they knew each other, while Eitan politely nodded assent to whatever it was they discussed. Eponi had excused herself, staying in her room. Seeing their approach, the prefect immediately left off speaking with his old friend and said to Esta, "The Emperor keenly anticipates seeing you, most erudite maiden, for the Trierarch of your Trireme and the Captain of your Legionary Guards has told him of your remarkable voyage and its' attendant perils. After hearing this, Hadrian said that to your merits, ascribed by Aléxandros, must be added remarkable self-possession, unusual in one so young!" Esta lowered her head in humility as she thanked the prefect. "You shall see the Emperor and Empress not in this ancient palace of Rome, but in his new Villa, still being built in Tivoli, a two-hour ride by carpentum. I will tell you more on the way."

The small party left Palatine Hill in Rome for Hadrian's new residence, first carried by lectica until reaching the city gates, and then by carpentum. The road was paved entirely with fitted stones, and the way of over five leagues was landscaped wondrously with Pinus Pinea trees, or "parasol pines" as they are often called, tall cypress trees, olive groves, vineyards, and hazelnut trees. These shaded never ending lawns of trimmed grass, accented by an amazing array of rose gardens. Thus, even the roadway to Hadrian's Villa seemed an enchanted path leading to Mount Olympus.

If villa it could be called, for when they were yet a ways off, they were astounded to see more than a score of magnificent buildings situated spaciously apart on a rising prominence of some one hundred and sixty lugerium.[1] The prefect gestured toward the edifices that could be seen from the carpentum, namely the two story Roccabruna, to the far right with its deep arched porch, the Antinoeion, just ahead, a sanctuary of two temples facing each other, the Pecile, to their left, a large rectangular edifice whose Centum Camerelle alone consisted of 100 chambers and whose upper level was fashioned as a quadriporticus garden with long covered walkways, called the ambulatio, providing space for all-weather exercise.

To the far left of the carpentum they saw the Greek Theatre, with seats for 3,500 spectators, the Temple of Venus, designed with a semi-circular colonnade adorning its entrance, and the Palestra, a monumental complex of many integrated structures, whose center was paved in cipollino marble leading to a great hall surrounded by a double portico with numerous niches whereon were placed many statues. Some sixty rods to the right of the Temple of Venus could be seen the adjacent structures of the Imperial Palace of Hadrian, which

---

1. Approximately 250 acres.

were the Pavilion of Tempe, the Latin and Greek Libraries, the Maritime Theatre, the capacious Heliocaminus Baths, the Stadium Gardens, the Three Exedras, with its many gardens, fountains and statues. These were backed by the incredibly large and spacious palace.

Hadrian's Greek Theatre in his new villa

Their carriage continued up the gradually ascending path of stone, flanked by bourgeoning flora, until reaching the vestibule entry peristyle. Here they were greeted by a guide who, in an hour's time, gave the small company a walking tour of the Canopus, a terraced garden with a canal or long pool of sparkling clear water some fifty rods in length, surrounded by brilliant colonnades and over a hundred fine sculptures, intricately carved. Walking through a tunnel off the Grande Trapezio, they entered the Academy with its stuccoed walls and opus sectile pavements, its entrance guarded by two colored statues of Centaurs, one old and the other young. Beyond the Great Hall were many rooms and on the east of the rotunda stood the Temple of Apollo. To the south of the Academy rose the Odeum, smaller than the others, the theatre could seat 1,000 spectators. East of the Odeum was the Plutonium, or The Temple of Pluto. From here it was a ten minute walk to the Piazza D'oro, a lavish multifaceted structure with floors and walls of finely crafted opus sectile, where different colors of marble and mother of pearl were cut and inlaid to form pictures and ornate patterns. On the north side was fashioned a vaulted vestibule. In the center of the Piazza D'oro was a square atrium surrounded by colonnaded porticoes with a euripus, or canal, running down its length. To the south of this was a cenatio for regal dining, a library, and private latrines.[2]

From the Piazza D'oro, they were escorted through magnificent hanging gardens with twelve terraced waterfalls culminating in a pool of colorful fishes. Hence, their guide introduced the maidens to a matron who conducted the trio to the women's bath, a complex of cold and hot chambers with waters of commensurate temperature, this while the prefect led his male companions to a like edifice. When laved and refreshed, the men were given new togas and

2. For historic detail of Hadrian's Villa, we are indebted to "Digital Hadrian's Villa Project," http://vwhl.soic.indiana.edu/villa/, 2022

tunics. The maidens received new gossamer stolas, long pleated dresses, also worn over a tunic. The stola was much more feminine in design than a toga, for never would a woman of grace be seen in men's attire. Each demoiselle was also given a beautiful golden brooch of great value, gifts from the Empress.

Of this palace, the finest the world had ever seen, Hadrian himself was the principal architect. He had toured the wonders of civilization and with his hosts of mathematicians, engineers, masons, subordinate architects and a myriad of craftsman had wrought his Roman and Greek residence, not upon the ruins of older structures in the city, but on virgin soil in Tivoli where he built everything anew.

Marcius then led Aléxandros, Esta, Eitan, Naomi and Michela into the heart of the Imperial Palace. Emperor Hadrian was seated on a raised platform of marble, on a throne fashioned comfortably so that he might sup while entertaining guests. Next to him his wife, the Empress Vibia Sabina, was seated in like manner. The high semi-circular chamber was lit from behind by many arched windows and flanked by two waterfalls that coursed in cataracts, four rods in height, glistening tightly over the escarpment of rose-colored marble, falling into a pool that flowed flaccidly about the Emperor's spacious stone dais, cooling the great hall wonderfully even in the heat of summer. In truth, this dais was a regal island formed with retractable bridges, setting the monarchs apart from their subjects and servants.

The flow of the falling water could be controlled so as to adjust the sound of it. Hence, when Marcius advanced with his party to the lower dais, the cataract greatly diminished, a roar becoming a pleasant murmur. All in all, it was a dramatic marvel, greater than even Aléxandros had ever witnessed—a spectacle far greater than the greatest theatre could contrive. Though truly a performance, this was no play. This was *real* and must be ascribed to that man who in reality ruled the civilized kingdoms of the world, the commander of the greatest armies from Italia to Africa, Asia, Greece, Germania, Gaul, Britannia and all the Mediterranean nations, and that man was Hadrian, his boyhood friend. Humbly, Aléxandros knelt before his sovereign as did the others in like manner. Of all those present, including the monarchs themselves, Esta was the only person who *remembered* greater splendor, for she, when nearly drowned, had briefly returned to "the center place, the core of all glory, of all creation." There she had seen celestial villas and gardens of indescribable perfection.

The prefect was about to make royal introductions, when the Emperor stood and said kindly, "Marcius, I think we shall dispense with further formalities, for my guest is not a king or general of some distant land, but is the young friend of my friend, the Maiden of Massilia who I have lately heard so much about. Please arise, all of you, sit and sup with us. Surely you are hungry as it is nearly midday. Vibia has commanded this delicious repast and as we eat, let us freely talk with one another without fear of decorum.

Upon hearing this, only Aléxandros and Esta returned the Emperor's smile with ease. The others were speechless—in awe of all they had seen and who it was that stood before them! Nonetheless, after the Emperor took his seat, they sat down before a table laden with succulent meats, cheeses, breads and fruits. Soon, despite their fears, Eitan, Naomi and Michela began to also enjoy the delicious meal.

Emperor Hadrian

The Emperor set aside the leg of baked fowl he had devoured to the bone and said, "The pheasant is indeed good, but what I desired most are sweet fruits set in a delicate tart! Esta, what say you of my appetite and how so is life?"

She looked up happily from her own meal and exclaimed, "I perceive that you are a believer in the philosophies of the Stoic Epictetus, the slave of Epaphroditus of Nero's house, whose own master tortured him and made of him a cripple!

"Oh, great Hadrian, have you not eaten a soldier's fare while in the field and carried a footman's burden upon your back, and this without complaint? Hence, despite the opulence of your palace, if you were found in different circumstance and had but one sparrow to eat, that you would relish and wish for no more! Said the Stoic in Epirus, 'Behave as at a banquet. Is anything brought round to you? Put forth and take a moderate share. Does it pass you or is not yet come? Do not yearn in desire towards it, but wait till it reaches you! Do this and one day you will be worthy to feast with the gods. And if you do not so much as take the things which are set before you and forego, then you will not only be worthy to feast with the gods, but rule with them also.'"

"Ha!" exclaimed Aléxandros, "the games have begun! And you see Publius Aelius Traianus Hadrianus Agustus," using the Emperor's full name, "Esta is not easily defeated!"

Hadrian laughed, "Ah, senator, to *test* is not to *trounce*. And it is a delight to witness personally what you expressed in your missive. Esta, finish this sentiment of my teacher, for indeed Arrian took me to Epirus and there I met the Sire of Stoics. 'Send now, O God, any trial that Thou wilt; lo, I have means . . . .'"

"'. . . and powers given me by Thee to acquit myself with honor through whatever comes to pass,'"[3] said Esta, as she finished his

---

3. Harvard Classics, *The Golden Sayings of Epictetus*, P.F. Collier & Son Corporation,

words.

"Ah," said the Emperor, "that you, sweet demoiselle, *have done* on your voyage from Massilia!"

"But I was not fully proven," she answered modestly, "for I was saved by Maros before I was enslaved!"

Hadrian replied, "None is proven fully until death takes him or her in honor. Complete this maxim, "Thou art thyself a fragment . . ."

". . . torn from God," she answered.

"Mmh," the Emperor mused, "according to Epictetus, what four attributes describe the nature of God?"

"Oh," exclaimed Esta, "that is easily answered. They are *Intelligence, Knowledge, Right and Reason.*"[4]

"And how would the Stoic humble a great sculptor?" asked the Emperor.

She replied, "He said how different is the artistry of man compared to God, saying, 'What human artists work is aught but marble, bronze, gold and ivory . . . But God's works move and breathe. Wilt thou dishonor the workmanship of such an Artist . . . when he not only fashioned thee, but placed thee, like a ward, in the care and guardianship of thyself alone!"

Hadrian was fascinated by Esta's quick and flawless responses. Though he was taught at the very feet of Epictetus, whom he considered sent by the gods to himself, one destined to rule the world, that he might be more fit for his divinely appointed station, yet here was a mere girl who not only had memorized his golden teachings, but seemed their very embodiment! Hadrian considered that the Stoic was much older than he, had suffered much that he might attain so great an understanding. Now, this maiden possessed not a wrinkle

---

New York, 1963, p. 123

4. Harvard Classics, *The Golden Sayings of Epictetus*, P.F. Collier & Son Corporation, New York, 1963, p. 137

in her fair skin! He asked, "Truly, Maiden of Massilia, are you but fourteen years of age?"

"I turn fifteen in two months' time!" she replied pertly.

He laughed, saying, "Only the very young point out how soon they will be older! Now then, what would the Master of Nicopolis say to the man who said or thought he surely must do better with his life—someday—for glad he was that there were years left him *to change!*"

"He would say, 'Friend, lay hold with a desperate grasp on Freedom, on Tranquility, on Greatness of soul, ere it is too late! Lift up thy head, as one escaped from slavery; dare to look up to God, and say: Deal with me henceforth as Thou wilt! Help me be of one mind with Thee. I am Thine.'[5]

"Furthermore, he would say, 'Hercules believed he was God's son, as indeed he was, and went about delivering the earth from injustice and lawlessness.'

"But thou are not Hercules, thou sayest, and canst not deliver others from monsters. Then, purge away thine own, cast forth from thine own mind, not robbers and monsters, but *Fear, Desire, Envy, Malignity, Avarice, Effeminacy, Intemperance.* And these may not be cast out, except by looking to God alone, by fixing thy affections on Him and by consecrating thyself to His commands."[6]

Naomi then spoke timidly, "O great Emperor, may I, Esta's friend since childhood, venture a question?" Her father shot her a warning glance. Had she forgotten her station and his? He had told her that when a powerful lord puts you at ease, remember he may just as easily put you in his dungeon!

---

5. Harvard Classics, *The Golden Sayings of Epictetus*, P.F. Collier & Son Corporation, New York, 1963, p. 142

6. Harvard Classics, *The Golden Sayings of Epictetus*, P.F. Collier & Son Corporation, New York, 1963, p. 143

Hadrian replied, "A friend since childhood, eh? Then, my dear, you've not been friends for long!" Everyone, save Eitan, laughed. "Please say on."

Naomi took courage and said, "As you have been conversing, both Your Highness and Esta have spoken about God, as if there was only One. But then the Stoic referred to 'feasting with the gods,' as though there are many. My friend has tried to answer this question, but still I do not understand, but greatly desire to!"

Eitan hung his head.

The Emperor answered seriously, almost angrily, "Your query has the ring of a Christian's question and strikes at the foundation of the Empire! If there are not gods many, including Trajan, whom I myself deified at his death, then is the Emperor a false sovereign! How could a mere mortal be raised in station to rule the world unless lifted by that which is above the world? Naomi, what say you?"

The maiden trembled and was about to beg mercy on her knees, remembering now her father's admonition. But Esta, touched her arm as she began to kneel and said, "As I have before failed to answer this reservation, may I, great king, try again?"

Hadrian nodded assent. Esta looked steadily at the Emperor and asked, "According to Epictetus, are any 'mere mortals?' That is, any who we call woman or man?" All were silent, waiting for Esta to answer her own question, especially the Man of Power. She continued, "Did he not say, 'I have one whom I must please, to whom I must be subject, whom I must obey: God. He hath entrusted me with myself and said to me: Yet that body of thine is not thine own. I have given thee a portion of Myself!' Then explained Epictetus, 'We are all in an especial manner sprung from God, and that *God is the Father of men, as well as the Gods!* Few rise to the blessed kinship with the Divine . . . Why not a son of God—to have God for our Maker and Father, and Kinsman? . . . Will you not then perceive who you are or unto what end you were born, for what purpose?' Subsequently,"

Esta continued, "Epictetus spoke as if to the great Emperor himself, saying, 'Remember who you are, and whom you rule, that they are by nature your kinsmen, your brothers, the offspring of God.'"[7]

"Esta," said Hadrian, "you have no fear! Forthrightly you use the words of my master to upbraid myself! Few have before done this, and one, an architect, is dead! That is not all, artfully you have chosen select sayings from his discourses and placed them together, as my artisans placed opus sectile to fashion a wonderous representation of a lion in mosaic! Still, you have not directly answered her question: Is there one God or many?"

Aléxandros thought silently to himself, "Answer carefully, wise maiden!"

Esta turned towards Naomi and said, "What two words does Epictetus use again and again to address the Divine? They are 'God' and 'Father.' Naomi, I perceive that Godhood is Fatherhood. May I, most noble Hadrian, refer to the Christian and Hebrew texts to show common association with certain traditions of Greece and Rome?"

"Yes," he answered.

"In what is called the Ancient Testament, for I have studied chronicles of many lands and this one in particular, for in days past the Hebrews were allies of the Republic of Rome, the word for the One God is Elohim, is it not?" Naomi did not answer.

"It is," Esta stated emphatically, "though on some occasions God is called Yhwh, or Jehovah, and there seems to me a reason for this. Now what does Elohim mean in Hebrew? It means *Gods*, plural! Or rather God of Gods! An Abrahamic prophet known as the Psalmist wrote these words, 'God standeth in the congregation of the mighty; he judgeth among the gods." Now these were not strange gods, or what some might call pagan gods or demon gods, for the writer

---

7. Harvard Classics, *The Golden Sayings of Epictetus*, P.F. Collier & Son Corporation, New York, 1963, pp. 118, 120, 121, 122, 128

continues, 'I have said, *Ye are gods; and all of you are children of the most High.*'[8] The Stoic said, 'And who are we that are His children and what work were we born to perform?'[9]

"Do you not see what both Epictetus and the Psalmist are saying? That God is God because he is our Father and that he rules over his children, his heirs, his daughters and his sons, whom he intends to make like unto Himself, if they be worthy—and I think Jehovah must be the Highest Born of Elohim, though I admit I do not yet fully understand."

Esta then turned again towards the Emperor, and said, "Hadrian, as the Stoic said, you were born to a purpose, which you now fulfil. This was true of Trajan who ruled before you. I believe it is true that all who reign do so with the consent of Heaven. But as Agency is given to *choose*, some rule as tyrants, for they regard not their subjects as sisters or brothers. Others rule in likeness of their Father, for such a king knows he reigns as His son, or if a queen, as His daughter. The Greeks call the AllFather Zeus. The Romans call Him Jupiter. The name Elohim, I think, is most descriptive, for He *is* God of Gods. Yet, I also think that in the cosmos there are usurpers, who feign to rule, but in truth are fallen, who say 'I am a son!' but are no longer kin to Deity."

Aléxandros said, "Hadrian, Esta told us something of this concatenation of her thoughts as we journeyed. What do you think of it?"

Hadrian answered, as he looked at Naomi, who at that moment looked years younger than the Maiden of Massilia, and said, "I thank you, *my daughter*, for your question. Ha! Were it not for you I would think Esta a great reciter of the Stoic, when in truth your friend is

---

8. Psalm 82: 1, 6

9. Harvard Classics, *The Golden Sayings of Epictetus*, P.F. Collier & Son Corporation, New York, 1963, p. 141

much more. Like Epictetus, she is a gifted teacher. Like Socrates, she is forthright, but not heated in discourse, nor does she utter injurious words,[10] rather she seeks truth in that which is common to all of us but was not apparent until brought to light by her. In short, Aléxandros, Esta is a philosopher! Who can listen to her, be in her presence, though he is an emperor, and not be made better for it?"

Vibia Sabina then spoke, saying, "My Lady Esta, for to call you a maiden seems an injustice, you are truly beautiful because you are yet a virgin. I pray Artemis that you will continue as you are and though we have reared a Temple to Venus in this, our palace, may you not give that which alone is yours. Tell me, does Epictetus have aught to say on this?" Hearing this, Hadrian scowled, though he said nothing.

"Yes," Esta answered, "both indirectly and directly. Said he, 'To each of us God hath granted inward freedom.' That is to say, the inward voice of our conscience. But he says more, 'These are the principles that in a house create love, in a city concord, among nations peace.'[11] My inward voice speaks clearly to me, as I believe it does to all until silenced by disobedience to the voice of their heart. Perhaps it is Artemis who whispers in harmony with my own thoughts that never will I yield to sensual desire until I am bound lawfully with a man, I pray of my choosing and not one like unto the Jacaian who was slain by the Trierach. Thereafter, for the sake of his true love, and more especially for that of our seed, I hope to be more beautiful as I believe all mothers are."

In saying this, Esta wounded the heart of Vibia Sabina, for the Empress had no children. Nonetheless, she continued, saying,

10. Harvard Classics, *The Golden Sayings of Epictetus*, P.F. Collier & Son Corporation, New York, 1963, p. 139
11. Harvard Classics, *The Golden Sayings of Epictetus*, P.F. Collier & Son Corporation, New York, 1963, p. 171

"Epictetus said, 'Before marriage guard yourself with all your ability from unlawful intercourse; yet be not uncharitable or severe to those who are led into this, nor boast frequently that you yourself do otherwise.'[12]

"Hence, some are taught the ways of Venus in early life and others are blamelessly forced, while others surrender to her desire. The fruit of this is life itself, yet borne untimely, burdensome and often without help of a sire. These children, the blessed hope of creation, are reared by women whose hearts, turned by travail, are righted, for they sacrifice all for the seed of their wombs.

"To me," Esta said, "marriage is sacred, as is motherhood, for it is by this means that we may be goddesses. 'But,' one may ask, 'what of the woman who never marries or whose womb is shut by nature?' I answer, *'Life is timeless!'* We were before! As Socrates said, 'All learning is remembering.' We are now, and we will yet be hereafter. The Stoic whom we revere has said that life is a banquet. Sometimes we must wait for the portion we most desire. You, most honored Empress, are the mother of many nations. Yet, it is my belief that one day, no matter how distant, your womb will bear you loving seed."

Her words had again produced a profound silence. At length Hadrian spoke, saying, "Although Epictetus taught at Epirus, he did not write his own words. However, great is our thanks to our friend Arrian, a senator and philosopher, who wrote the Enchiridion of Epictetus, for he has no peer in taking down, word for word, that which he hears. Younger than me by ten years, his mind is alert and comprehending, as is yours, dear Esta. Even now Arrian is in Rome and it is he who shall be your tutor. Perhaps he will take you to Epirus where the aged Epictetus still lives.

"Finally, I give you that which only a senate or a king may

---

12. Enchiridion 33:7, https://www.gutenberg.org/files/45109/45109-h/45109-h.htm, 2022

bestow. Well did Vibia say it was an injustice to call you a maiden. From henceforth you shall not be a ward of any man, not even of the great Aléxandros! Esta of Massilia, I pronounce you *Esta Hadrianus Agustus, Civis Romanus,*[13] an *Illustrissima Domina Philosophiae,*[14] *cum residentiae in Palatio Imperialis Romae in aeternum.*[15] To insure independence you shall receive from the state treasury a stipendium of a talent of gold per year."

He then addressed the other maidens. "Naomi, it is a valuable thing to *think* for yourself. Yet for Christians this was a forbidden practice under Nero. Trajan, though not radical is his practices still tolerated persecution in defense of the Pantheon. My law is yet more lenient, unless Christians are taken in some illegal act. Yet I declare that you, Naomi of Massilia are *immunes accusationis ad fidem Christianam.*[16]

"Michela, the silent maiden. Glad I am that you were saved by the Empire! That you are Esta's trusted companion is a great thing. Said the Stoic, 'A live coal placed next a dead one will either kindle that or be quenched by it.'[17] Assume then not her looks alone but also her radiance."

Hadrian then spoke to Esta once again, saying, "Although you now *own* a residence in the Imperial Palace of Rome, you shall always be welcome here and may come without invitation. In Rome you shall be close to Lucius Flavius Arrianus, your tutor, one of the wisest of men, Greek or Roman! Certainly, you are aware that Arrian wrote the Anabasis, which chronicles the feats of Alexander the Great, the Cynegeticus on the art of hunting, the Parthica on Trajan's military

---

13. Roman Citizen.
14. Illustrious Lady of Philosophy.
15. With residence in the Imperial Palace of Rome forever.
16. Immune to prosecution for Christian belief.
17. Harvard Classics, *The Golden Sayings of Epictetus*, P.F. Collier & Son Corporation, New York, 1963, p. 153

campaigns, and assuredly you know of his Discourses of Epictetus and the Enchiridion, for these you have so expertly quoted today."

Esta thanked Hadrian most graciously, as did her maiden companions. Before withdrawing, the Emperor embraced Aléxandros manfully and thanked his old friend for bringing such "a diadem" to his knowledge. He commended Eitan for raising Naomi, calling her "so brave a damsel" and also said that the merchant might freely trade throughout the Empire. Hadrian said that *officialis declarationes* would memorialize what was done that day. Sealed parchments would be delivered to the Senate, with copies given to Esta, Naomi and Eitan in the palace at Rome.

Later when Michela expressed her bewilderment at all that was bestowed on Esta, the Maiden of Massilia answered, "Indeed I am astonished! Great also was his gift to Naomi, his warrant that she might believe in her faith, that she might speak and act without fear of prosecution! And, although I am enfranchised as a Roman and given Hadrian's name, it was Naomi he called '*my daughter!*'"

End of Part One

PART TWO

CHAPTER 11
MICHELA'S GIFT

"Come, arise, from sleep awaking,
Come the fiery torches shaking.
Morning Star that Shinest nightly.
Lo, the mead is blazing brightly.
Age forgets its years and sadness,
Aged knees but leap for gladness!"
Aristophanes, from his play "Frogs."

Hadrian's Rome

T he Theatre of Marcellus was far more to Esta's liking than either the Amphitheatre or the Circus Maximus, for the spectacle of drama did not shock her senses as did the brutality of gladiators and charioteers. Yet Arrian said there was much to be learned from the arena and races. His words were to be highly regarded, for in letters, none excelled Arrian in Rome or Athens and few were more knowledgeable in military matters.

Unless attending to his duties in the Senate, Arrian spent two days each week with Esta, either in the palace or attending exciting venues. Although a philosopher, prolific historian and Senator, Arrian had been an able military commander and retained a rugged physic with remarkable features. He was of medium height with thick, close-cut brown hair, dark and curly, his eyes a deep blue. His face and arms were perpetually tanned by the sun and free of scars, attesting to supreme marital skills for he had fought many deadly battles. He was less than twice Esta's age and was Hadrian's junior by a little more than a decade.

Esta looked forward to these meetings, as Aléxandros had returned to Massilia and Esta savored engaging in wit she considered greater than her own. Romans had developed an insatiable desire for *ludi*, their word for sporting competitions, games, pageants and festivals. Originally, they were religious in nature, votive offerings to the gods, fulfilling vows or signifying devotions. Overtime, ludi increased in popularity as they became more secular, splendorous and violent, sponsored not only by colleges of priests, but by consuls and emperors.

For Hadrian's birthday two hundred lions and lionesses were slain in the arenas[1] in the *venationes,* or wild beast hunts. As the demand for *munera gladiatoria,* or gladiator fights, was even greater,

---

1. *Dio,* LXIX.8.2

the public was given six consecutive days of staged combats.[2] Although incredibly bloody, the fights were not always fatal. Flamma, a Syrian Gladiator and a favorite of Hadrian, fought in 34 "games" with a heavy shield and gladius, or short sword. He won 21 fights and was offered freedom four times but chose to remain a gladiator. It was said that Flamma had but one wish, "to die in the arena to the sound of the roar of his beloved crowd."[3] And so he did, at 30 years of age.

Nonetheless, to Esta's delight this day, which was long after Hadrian's birthday, would be spent in an area of Rome devoted to theatrical performances. The Theatre of Marcellus featured a tall, wide stage-front of multiple stories with freestanding columns, extravagantly adorned with heroic statues. Spectators sat in three semi-circular ascending sections. The ima cavea, the nearest to the stage, was reserved for the upper echelons of Rome. The media cavea, immediately behind and above the ima was open to the male public. The summa cavea, the highest section and furthest from the stage, was open to women and children. In the vicinity of the theatre were libraries, shops of every description, museums and many fine restaurants.

Esta, Naomi, and Michela were seated with Arrian, their host, in the ima cavea, beneath awnings. Eponi remained, once again, at home in Esta's chambers, for she enjoyed more their company in the gardens or along the walkways of the River Tiberis.

---

2. *HA Hadr.*7.12

3. https://www.ancient-origins.net/history-famous-people/flamma-0014189, 2022

A celebratory flotilla of Ludi Romani, The Festival of Jupiter

Arrian said to the maidens, "*The Frogs of Aristophanes* is an amusing tale. It is the story of the Greek god Dionysus who so mourns the death of Euripides, his favorite playwright, that he plans to fetch him back from Hades."

The maidens were enthralled as the scene opened with Dionysus walking along side of his donkey, who carried his slave, Xanthias. The act is comical, for it should be the master who rides and the servant who walks!

Xanthias complains, "May I say, I'm so overburdened, that if none ease me, I must ease myself?" The crowd titters with laughter, as also Esta and her friends.

Dionysus replies, "Now is this not pampered insolence! I toil afoot and let this fellow ride and no burden bearing?"

Xanthias retorts, "What, don't I bear?"

Says Dionysus, "How can you when you're riding?"

The slave replies, "Why I bear unwillingly this pouch hung from my shoulder."

The master replies indignantly, "Does not the donkey bear the load you are bearing? How can you bear when you are borne yourself?" The audience laughs uproariously.

Answers Xanthias, "Don't know. But anyhow, my shoulder's aching."

They stop at the door of Hercules, half-brother to Dionysus, and explain his plight, that no poets are left him and despairs for Euripides. Hercules laughs at Dionysus, saying that still he has Sophocles, Agathon and Pythangelus. Dionysus exclaims, "Don't mock me, brother! On my life, I'm in a bad way: such fierce desire consumes me."

Hercules replies, "Aye, little brother. How?"

He answers, "I can't describe it. But I'll tell you in a riddling way. Have you ever felt a sudden lust for soup?"

Hercules declares, "Soup! Zeus-a-mercy, yes, ten thousand times!"

Says Dionysus, "Is the thing clear, or must I speak again?"

The half-brother answers, "Not of soup: I'm clear about the soup."

Dionysus laments, "Well, just that sort of pang devours my heart for lost Euripides."

Hercules: "Mmh, and he a dead man."

Dionysus: "And no one shall persuade me not to go after the man."

Esta whispered to Naomi and Michela, "Imagine Aristophanes wrote this play hundreds of years ago, and we laugh as heartily as did the ancient Greeks!"

Naomi answered quietly, "How is it that in plays the actors can mock the gods of the Romans and Greeks. But if you mention their faults, of which many are told in the chronicles, in but an assembly of commoners—well, you are cast into prison or worse!"

"Not you, Naomi," Esta answered with a giggle, "for you have the Imperatoris edictum and can speak your mind!"

She answered, "Papa tells me that I must still guard my tongue. He says that I would be stoned before the mob heard my defense!"

"Well," said Esta, "I think the Romans and Greeks believe their gods understand 'fun' as well as do men, and even better. So, when things are said on stage they are not taken to heart, unless," she laughed, "it is said of living emperors. Then death swiftly follows, for they cannot laugh at themselves!"

Michela remained quiet. Though they had now been in Rome for a season, living all the while in the luxurious palace and had seen many wonders, still it seemed to her as an impossible dream. Every day she was dressed by servants and given upmost deference. Even stranger and more wonderful was the kindnesses shown her by both Esta and Naomi. More surprising yet, to her young mind, was that she now freely answered when they called her "sister!" Even the great man, Arrian, treated her so kindly as if she were truly a Lady, like Esta. While her friends talked quietly, Michela stole a glance at their host, whose angular features she thought most becoming.

The play continued as Dionysus tells Hercules that he desires to impersonate him, for Hercules had indeed been to hell and back. He says, "'Twas for this I came dressed up to mimic you, that I would be received as Hercules himself by those who helped you before when you went to Hades. Tell me too of the havens, fountains, shops, roads, resting places, stews, towns, hostesses and lodgings, with whom were found the fewest bugs."

Hercules: "Huh. You are really game to go?"

Dionysus: "Drop that and tell me the quickest way to get to Hades."

Hercules: "Hang yourself. No? Then drink Hemlock. No, again? Then go down to the Torch Races and climb to the tower's pinnacle, and when the race has begun and the multitude shouts 'Let them go,' let yourself go."

Dionysus: "Go whither?"

Hercules: "To the ground."

Dionysus: "Oh, that would break the two halves of my brain! No, I will go the way you yourself went."

Hercules: "A perilous voyage! For first you will come to a black lake of fathomless depth, crossed only by Charon, an ancient mariner in a small row boat. A weltering sea of filth and ever rippling dung and plunged therein whoso has wronged the stranger here on earth, or his friend or mother, or profanely smitten his father's cheek."

Dionysus: "You needn't try to scare me. I'm going to go."

Esta again whispered to Naomi, "Do you remember what the cruel children of Massilia called old Maros?"

"Yes," she answered, "Charon, fit only to row the boat of Hades! Yet, ever he was meant to sail the skies of heaven! And now he does!"

Too soon the play was over and the company of four supped at a Greek restaurant known for its roasted quail, cheeses, figs and arugula. Although considerably older than Esta and her two friends, Arrian was much taken with the beauty and intelligence of Esta. As he often did, he turned the conversation towards a topic of merit, saying, "Aristophanes is the unstringing of the bow. It is good to relax and laugh. But even merriment must have restraints and as we dine it shall be Phaedo."

"Oh," said Esta, "I love to talk of Socrates. However, as his death was centuries past and the fun of this night is yet with us, I beg leave to bask in this afterglow a bit more." Turning towards Michela, whom she caught with a bite of bread and cheese in her mouth, Esta asked, "What did you like best, dear sister, the magnificent form of Hercules or the Frogs?"

This caused Michela to choke a little, as she had yet to swallow the morsel, trying in vain to suppress a spontaneous laugh. The result was a sound her friends had not heard before and they all erupted in laughter. Soon she, however, cleared her voice and said, "Why that is easy to answer! For whom did Aristophanes name his play? For Hercules? Nay. He called it 'Frogs.' Oh," she smote her breast with exaggerated feeling, "when the king of the frogs began to croak . . . I mean sing, and in such voice as to melt every maiden's heart, and sang:

> "Through the rushes and marsh-flags springing,
> On we swept, in the joy of singing
> Or when fleeing the storm, we went
> Down to the depths, and our choral song
> Wildly raised to a loud and long
> Bubble-bursting accompaniment!"

Now this short narrative caught her companions completely by surprise, for Michela did not speak the words, but sang them perfectly, as well as did those who performed on the stage of Marcellus, yet far more beautifully and with pure high tones. Never had she sang before in their presence, and truly did not intend to do so then, but so great was the mirth and festive the feeling as they supped in a secluded part of the restaurant, that Michela did that which she often did when cleaning alone in the bakery of Cemenelum.

Naomi exclaimed, "How is it possible, Michela—how did you so quickly learn that stanza!"

Arrian quickly interjected, "Your friends did not tell me, young demoiselle; you sing like a goddess!"

Esta, looked at Michela, smiling widely as she said, "Oh! We did not know, and all this time, our modest friend, you said nothing of your gift!"

Arrian added with growing excitement, "Carmina[4] has been the soul of the Empire since its earliest days, strains of the cosmos, given us by the gods! Hadrian's own musician and rhetorician, Aellus Dionysius is my dear colleague. Michela, I promise: when he hears you, he will demand to be your Vox Tutoris.[5] In a season more, you shall raise your voice not only in the theatre but in the temples to honor our dead and before the games to invoke the attention of Jupiter and Venus!"

Michela, realizing his sincerity and recognizing true admiration in the eyes of Esta and Naomi, could not speak a word in answer. Esta drew the attention away from Michela, for she knew she was close to tears and said, "Master Arrian, such a promise is greater than Michela had ever dreamed! Astonished, she has no words to express the depths of her gratitude. Nonetheless, I know she shall be

---

4. Songs, poems and odes.
5. Voice Tutor

the willing pupil of the much acclaimed Aellus and will strive to master her art and bring you honor. It is a somber opportunity and while Michela thinks on this, let us turn our thoughts to Phaedo and the mortal destiny of the Pater Philosophiae.[6]

"Gladly," said Arrian. "First, however, I do not wish to so swiftly pass over the marvel of Michela! I did not wish to be so bold a patron as to frighten her." He looked at Michela and said, "I believe that a divine attribute of this greatness cannot be taken lightly. Though I heard but a verse, my ear is trained for excellence and I know wherein I speak. Such gifts must be refined by diligent effort and used abundantly for the purpose given, else they are lost to us. This is a law of nature: that which is not exercised becomes a thing of naught. Suppose Flamma ceased to use his daily strength and skill, would not his sinews wither—and if he neglected his physic entirely and became lazy and fat, would we not lose our champion? No longer would he be the Flame but would be weak, common, stirring no man to valor. The young and inexperienced think too little of their youth and the light of heaven they radiate, with its attendant gifts. Hence, Michela, I fear you do not recognize this power latent within you, else by this time you should have already sung for us!"

Naomi asked, "Yes! Well said, our master! And what of that single verse? Michela, how did you know each word of it? Have you heard this ridiculously happy song before?"

This was a question that Michela could answer, and in doing so was able to compose her feelings. She said, "It is but simple rhyme and when words are so fashioned and set to music, they are easy for anyone to recall."

Arrian replied, "There is truth in what you say. Yet you modestly think it quite normal for one to hear this song but once and then sing it in greater perfection than it was heard. It is not. Hence my eager-

---

6. Father of Philosophy

ness to engage Aellus. Esta, is not this a wonder? Michela does not understand this herself. Can you explain it?"

"Yes," Esta answered quietly, "but only to friends who know me and can believe what others will not."

They looked at her intently, as Arrian said, "Say on."

Esta took both of Michela's hands in hers and answered, "It is magic!" Her very touch seemed to confirm the truth of her words. Naomi was surprised that Arrian, the scholar, did not laugh at such a saying.

Instead, he earnestly enquired, "This magic you speak of, can you define it?"

Esta replied, *"There is in life deep magic,* true mysteries wrought and controlled by higher laws than are universally known to men of science and understanding. Yet their operations are common to us. The hawk in flight, his eyes seeing that which no man can see, for afar off the bird-of-prey espies a squirrel waking from its den. Consider in like manner all the myriad creatures of the forest. So also, the morning dawn, unsurpassed in serenity. Then there is the Sun that creates each new day and sheds blessed warmth over the earth and the grasses and flowers that praise its rays. Think also of the Sea and the life of the sea, a world apart from the one on which we live and the tempest, rising from the great waters and inland rushes, raining life upon all that grow in, tread on, or fly above the earth. Consider the little child in the very image of his sire or her dame and its wondrous birth, the beginning of a new body, a body that was not before. Created in the womb, the physical form comes quickly into existence, a fit temple of clay to house an aged spirit that always was.

"And there is fakery, *false magic,* wrought by trickery, cunning conspiracy, not only by wizards, witches and sorcerers but by princes and potentates, those who abide the whisperings of ghosts of the evil dead or spirits of the unborn. These prevail through coercion, or when undiscovered by right thinkers and when their dark secrets are kept from our ken."

Arrian said, "Socrates believed in souls. Are these the spirits you speak of?"

She answered, "More is meant by the soul than this, but often the spirit is spoken of as the soul. Socrates, in part, affirms certain of these truths. He said, 'Our souls must have existed before they were in the form of man—without bodies, and must have had intelligence' in a 'prior existence.'[7]

"Know this, there are two orders of spirits, those virtuous and those wicked. Of evil, there are the spirits of the dead and the never born. Of good, there are spirits yet unborn as well as those who have lived and passed on. Those who are now alive are made sentient by that inward spirit that lives within their bodies, and whether they ultimately be good or evil is yet their own choice.

"Our bodies, no matter how many years upon the earth, are but infants compared to our spirits, for our spirits are eternal and having lived for ages before we were born possess the knowledge of eons with commensurate skills. After mortal birth, the orifice of the mind of the spirit is shut, but not tightly, causing us to forget this prior existence. The Key that may turn this orifice has far greater ken than any mortal woman or man, regardless of their learning. The Key is the Spirit of Truth, possessing infinite understanding. He alone has power to open the hidden recesses of our minds."

Arrian asked, "Is this Spirit *God?*"

She answered, "I do not *remember* that exactly, nor does that seem quite right to me. But I will say He is of the Godhead, as spoken of by Epictetus,[8] who said this Spirit of Truth permeates every facet of mortality. The Stoic quotes Ulysses and Socrates saying, '*I move not*

---

7. *Phaedo*, Harvard Classics, Kindle, location 7725, 7732
8. *The Golden Sayings of Epictetus*, Harvard Classics, XXVIII, location 8658

without Thy knowledge!' Men think great thoughts and invent marvels, such as the aqueduct, and believe themselves clever intellectuals, yet these wonders are but the operations of The Key, the Spirit of Truth, who has opened but a small portion of their spirit mind."

"And how do you know of this Key?" he said.

Esta replied, "I read many manuscripts of many lands, such as Phaedo. When the words speak clearly to me, live within me, then I *remember* them. As Socrates said, *'Knowledge is recollection.'*"[9]

"Did Socrates speak of the Key?"

"No. This was said by another sage, a Jew."

"Do you believe all the words of Socrates?"

"No," said Esta, "only when he remembers correctly. The nature of distant memories are vague. Yet from what is recollected great philosophers, like Socrates and Epictetus, applied Reason. This is important, for we are expected to use the intelligence given us. Yet there is a higher way, a means of acquiring purer knowledge, a surer way to truth."

"What is greater than Reason?"

"Revelation," she answered. "Revelation supersedes Reason. When you are shown something, that is when something is revealed to you, you know it! This is far superior to supposing something. *Remembering is revelation* and to what degree the orifice of the spirit mind is opened by The Key, to the same degree is the certainty of knowing what was revealed."

"Why is not all revealed at once?"

Esta laughed a little and said, "Who but God has the capacity to know everything? The Key turns the orifice slowly, according to our diligence and desire. When we act on truths given, we are given more. It is like ascending a high mountain, step by step. We look to

---

9. *Phaedo*, Harvard Classics, Kindle, location 7653

the heights that must be conquered, yet with each stride our faith is strengthened, helping us believe we may yet attain the summit. When at last we are there, we believe no longer, but *know*. Of course, we may fall and lose ground. Through our own negligence or as a result of iniquity, The Key may begin to close the orifice, which is *forgetting*."

Arrian said, "We began by speaking of Michela's gift. I infer your meaning is that as her spirit is ageless and that in the existence before mortality she acquired skill, perhaps even to the mastery of Carmina, that then, in this life, The Key, even without her awareness of it, opened the orifice of her spirit-self in this regard. Hence, the matchless talent learned *then* is given back to her, that she may sing *now* as one already expert in the art." He was quiet as he thought about what he had just said. Arrian then continued, "This truth more fully explains that which I have always believed, namely the process of Divine Attributes, as I earlier explained! Esta, you act on one's own words and multiply meaning! You are an Invocation—for your goodness has power to invoke The Key and thus the orifice widens for your hearers. Now I understand what an *Oracle* should be!"

"Esta," Naomi said, "Did Socrates, in his reasonings, offer proofs of the existence lived before this one?"

"Yes," Esta answered, "many and some of his reasoned proofs I believe are faulted. Nonetheless, in one area *his remembering, his thinking* is magnificent and I totally believe it is true!"

"What is that?" she asked.

Esta replied, "Arrian, this was also told in Phaedo. Do you know what I am speaking of."

"Most assuredly," the scholar answered. "He spoke of our innate ability to compare almost anything to the perfect ideal. Hence, we can judge physical form with but a glance of our eye—our artisans may sculpt the forms of gods and goddess, of heroes and heroines—

and we judge instantly, though perhaps we cannot ourselves sculpt an ant! We may admire their life-like statues of strength, beauty and grace. Still, we know the sculptures truly are not perfect, that there is no life within the marble and that with time the effigy shall erode.

"Yet even when they are newly carved, *we know* they are not perfect in form! We see exquisite basilicas and temples and likewise make an almost unconscious comparison from what we see to the perfect ideal. Even when we gaze upon a splendid sunrise or sunset, or a beautiful garden or flowing fountain, we may call it perfect— and truly that which is of nature partakes more of perfection than that which is wrought by man's hand—but nonetheless *we somehow know* that there are other vistas far more marvelous, *far more perfect!*"

Arrian continues, "How do we know? How can we make such judgements. One may say, 'I will know it when I see it!' How? Unless each woman and man born into this world has come from another, an existence where perfection is realized fully, completely. Hence, we have all *seen* perfection, perfection of mind, of body, of all nature and this knowledge is within each of us, hidden, as Esta said, in the recesses of our spiritual mind. This is the proof given us by Socrates!"

La Cantante Michela in Rome

CHAPTER 12
WHAT EPONI SEES

"Look carefully at the little stars that fly about and see where they alight upon the blossoms . . . converse not with your maiden friends but with the flora lit by wondrous stella."

Eponi

By a luxurious garden fountain, Esta, Naomi, Eponi and Michela sat reading the work of a poet who was banished by Augustus to a remote region of the Black Sea until his death. Yet Publius Ovidius Naso, known simply as Ovid, was hailed by Arrian as the greatest of the Greek Poets. Upon a marble table was set before the quartet of readers a large codex, entitled Metamorphoses, opened to Book Ten. Each was to read and then explain their reading.

Naomi read:

For as the bride, amid the Naiad train,
Ran joyful, sporting o'er the flow'ry plain,
A venom'd viper bit her as she passed;
Instant she fell, and sudden breathed her last.

Naomi explained, "Here Ovid tells of the bride Eurydice frolicking with water nymphs, I think, running through brooks and flowering meadows, when suddenly she is bit by a deadly snake and dies instantly."

Michela resumed the reading:

Inflamed by love, and urged by deep despair,
Her love leaves realms of light, and upper air;
Daring to tread the dark Tenarian road,
And tempt the shades in their obscure abode;
Through gliding specters of the interred to go,
And phantom people of the world below.

"Well, Orpheus is very angry," Michela said, "and blinded by love, somehow he leaves our world of light and air and descends down the dangerous road to the underworld. His purpose is to tempt or persuade 'shades' and 'gliding specters,' the spirits of the interred, or dead. He calls these 'phantom people' ".

The three maidens and the old dame then read more of Ovid's moving tale of how Orpheus descended into the world of spirits to find Eurydice, his only love. There he met Persephone, the Queen of the Underworld. Esta continued reading, Orpheus speaking to Persephone:

My wife alone I seek; for her lov'd sake
These terrors I support, this journey take.
She, luckless wandering, or by fate misled,

Chanced on a lurking viper's crest to tread;
The vengeful beast, enflamed with fury, starts,
And through her heel his deathful venom darts.
Thus was she snatched untimely to her tomb;
Her growing years cut short, and springing bloom.

Esta said, "Orpheus tells Persephone plainly that he has come for his wife, for he feels she died unfairly, bitten by a serpent in the spring of her life."

WHEN ESTA HAD BEGUN her studies under Arrian she included her friends in the academic endeavor. It surprised her to learn that Eponi could read well. Like Maros, Eponi was from Galatia, the Gallia of the East, long allied to Rome before becoming a Roman Province. Her people were Celts from Gaul who migrated to the highlands of Anatolia in the fourth century before Augustus. They were an erudite clan, possessing many skills needful to the Empire, for the Galatians were mariners and masons, craftsmen and artisans, soldiers and scholars. Eponi's sire had been a teacher in the Phrygian Temple and was a distant relative of the famed King Gordias who tied the Gordian Knot, cut by Alexander the Great. As a child her time was spent weaving and baking with her mother, reading at the side of her father, and playing in the near woodlands, a solitary pleasure for few and distant were her friends. Later, her father became an imperial accountant and was sent by Rome to Massilia to oversee taxes. Yet when she was but a lovely dark-haired maiden, her family was stricken with the plague and all died, save Eponi. Her inheritance was meager and the girl found work in the Market of Massilia. There, she met Maros and grew to love the strong, kindly sailor. When he was gone to sea,

Eponi would walk the quay each evening and look seaward for his return.

~

It was Eponi's turn to read:

> *By the sad silence which eternal reigns*
> *O'er all the waste of these wide-stretching plains;*
> *Let me again Eurydice receive,*
> *Let Fate her quick-spun thread of life re-weave.*
> *All our possessions are but loans from you,*
> *And soon, or late, you must be paid your due . . .*
> *But if the destinies refuse my vow,*
> *And no remission of her doom allow;*
> *Know, I'm determined to return no more;*
> *So both retain, or both to life restore.*

The widow said, "I think Orpheus feels like the 'sad silence' that fills the underworld is like that which he feels in his heart. He begs the queen to give him back his beloved wife. Oh, if Fate could but re-weave life and we could live again cherished moments! Then he says that nothing we have now is really ours, for we cannot keep possessions, for they are but loaned us by Fate and must be repaid. Then Orpheus says ardently that if the destinies will not let his wife go back with him, he will stay in the underworld with her. Restore her life, or keep him, he says. I think he means unlawfully, for he had not yet died." Eponi's voice quivered and her old eyes moistened.

Naomi reached out her hand and placed it upon hers, saying, "Grandmother, how you love Maros and how you must wish to be with him, with a desire as great as was that of Orpheus. Beautiful is the pain of your suffering, for it speaks of undying love."

Esta interjected, "Eponi, how I wish that I could reweave a moment of my life. There is something that you must know and how I shudder to think of it. I am responsible for your greatest sorrow!"

Eponi replied, "My dear Esta, no! You could not have prevented Maros' death!"

"But I could have!" Esta replied sadly but firmly. "You see, when I was about to go down into the darkness of the Necropolis, I felt a warning within my heart that I should not go but return to my room. Because I did not obey this prompting, I was attacked and your dear husband rushed to save me, his life taken in the stead of mine! Oh, if only I would have listened to this unearthly whispering, then would you be yet with him, enjoying these magnificent days together!"

Eponi replied, "That you cannot know, Esta. You were being pursued and the evil man would have tried another day, another way. Maros took joy in giving his life for yours! This he told me!"

All were silent for a time, for there was a quiet, comforting feeling that enveloped this small gathering. Then Eponi spoke again, saying, "Good Naomi, when Maros died you told me that someday I would be with him again. You said that love outlasts life. I have clung to your words, not for his death only, but . . ." She ceased to speak, whether from frailty of emotions or because of some other reason.

Esta said gently, "Oh Eponi, thank you for your kind words to me—thank you for your forgiving soul! Now, I feel there is more you should tell us, for we are your daughters. Please tell us more."

When Eponi could speak again, she said, "We see what lives, but most do not see all."

"What is not seen?" asked Esta.

Eponi answered, "I do not know if you will see them, for no longer are you children and it will be a long while yet before you are aged, as am I."

"Are they magical?"

"Yes. Michela told me of the deep magic you spoke of when you supped with Arrian. I think it is like that."

Esta implored, "Please tell us."

Eponi replied, "Here it would be hard, but soon, if that is your longing."

"Where then?" Esta asked.

"In the forest, in the glow of a dying day," said Eponi. "But now, let us return to the writing of Ovid, for I would know if Orpheus brings back his Eurydice to life!"

Naomi read:

> *From a host of shades that last arrived,*
> *Eurydice was called, and stood revived:*
> *Slow she advanced and halting seemed to feel*
> *The fatal wound, yet painful in her heel.*

Naomi exclaimed, "What joy must have filled Orpheus when he saw a host of spirits, and from these came his only beloved, Eurydice. She came towards him slowly and still seemed to feel the pain of the strike of the snake."

Together they read how Orpheus would be granted his wish with one requisite: that he must *lead* her from the world of spirits into this existence without a backward glance, for if he were to cast his eyes about, even so much as to view the fair beauty who followed him, she would, in that instant, be lost again to him.

Esta read:

> *Now through the noiseless throng they bend,*
> *And with pain the rugged road ascend;*
> *Dark was the path, and difficult, and steep,*
> *And thick with vapors from the smokey deep.*
> *They well-nigh now had passed the bounds of night,*

And just approached the margins of the light,
When he, mistrusting lest her steps might stray,
And gladsome of the glimpse of dawning day,
His longing eyes, impatient, backward cast,
To catch a lover's look, but looked his last!
For instant dying, she again descends,
While he to empty air his arms extends.

There she stopped reading and said, "Orpheus and Eurydice make their way through the silent spirits and walk towards the world of the living, our world. It is a very difficult ascent, but finally they near the surface where the sun shines and are leaving behind the darkness of the underworld. At that point it must have been very perilous and Orpheus fears that his wife might misstep. And so he looks behind him to guide her. Perhaps he thinks that because they are approaching the dawn, he has fulfilled his vow, for who could fault him for helping his wife in the world of the living? But alas, it is not so, for in the instant his gaze fixes upon Eurydice, she dies again! This is a curious thing for Ovid says that after she dies, her spirit descends into the underworld again. What died? Not her spirit. Then it must have been her body. When did she regain it? When she again saw light? This is not explained and perhaps it all was the trickery of Persephone. Ovid finishes his tale with flourishes we need not discuss. But what say you of this story. What truths do you glean from it?"

Eponi replied, "His beloved, though a spirit only, still lived and he was blessed to see her. Yet I mourn that he looked back! If only they could have lived together in happiness again."

Michela said, "I think it speaks to the greatness of love, that it lives through death and that no feat is too great if it will but bring back that which was lost!"

Naomi said, "I agree, but I think that longing alone cannot

change the true nature of life. As Esta has taught us, we lived before now and will continue to live after death. Nonetheless, must we live forever as spirits only, or will we, as Ovid speaks of Eurydice, be brought back into the light of a physical world, the spirit and body reunited?"

Eponi answered, "That is my hope, though it seems impossible. Who has ever lived after they have died?"

Naomi replied, "Such truths may someday be understood. Yet there is so much about life now that is far above my ken. I don't understand such things. How I've dreamed I could fly as the bird. I see a hawk take to the air, but how? I don't know. However, we will live after we die, Eponi! You shall not only see the spirit of your beloved, but one day you will *feel* Maros' arms embrace you. This I know."

Michela asked, "Will someone descend into the underworld, as did Orpheus, and open its prison doors?"

Esta said to Naomi, "I believe you are the one to answer Michela's question."

Naomi answered, "We cannot do that which Orpheus tried to do, that is to fetch back our dead. Hell will affix conditions that can never be met by the upright, for condescension is love that *must* lift. One who guides another cannot lead his loved one detachedly but must watch their footfall and when they stumble must try and catch them. Persephone never had power to redeem, though hell may taunt and grant false hope, but like all of perdition's promises, they are lies. Only One has power to redeem the dead."

Eponi asked, "Can you tell me who He is?"

Esta replied, "Naomi speaks of her risen Lord, *and I am beginning to remember Him.*"

～

A DAY dawned mild and clear. As the maidens and dame partook of the morning repast, Esta said enthusiastically, "Michela, will you be with Aellus today?"

"No," she answered. "In three days more I will again sing with my tutor. You seem exuberant, Esta! What plans have you for us! How I love your adventures!"

"Naomi," Esta said without answering Michela, "Will you be with your sire today? You mentioned he would be coming up from Ostia."

"Nay, not this day. Perhaps in a week," Naomi replied.

"Then," said Esta, "Eponi you must tell your friends, if you will, that today you cannot go to the market with them, though I know you love to do so. Today is the perfect day for you to tell us or show us your secret! We shall take a lectica,[1] then a carriage to Hadrian's Palace. Upon arriving we will send our greetings to the Emperor and Empress, if they are in residence, but we shall not request an audience unless summoned. It is a short walk from Hadrian's Palace to the River Aniene[2] and the riparian[3] forests. Arrian told me that paths have been cleared in the verdure, foot bridges built across the Aniene and that it is a most enchanting walk, shadowed beneath a woodland of wild olive trees, creeping pines, spreading oaks and tall beeches. Small meadows are laced throughout with blooming violets, trailing calendulas, yellow and white cerastiums, purple iris, pink orchids, and regal hicesiaes! Streamlets cascade down rocky falls and wildlife is abundant! There are doves, owls, warblers, robins, kites, redstarts, storks, and we may even see the spectacular hoopoe birds!"

Naomi exclaimed, "However do you remember such detail and of

---

1. Roman litters.
2. Known then as the River Anio.
3. A riparian forest is a woodland adjacent to a stream or river.

a place you've never been to before?" Not waiting for an answer, Naomi continued, "Oh, I would love to walk in such an Eden, but is it safe?"

Esta replied, "Quite! It is part of a large royal reserve. Arrian says that poachers have long since been removed and bandits would not dare enter the sanctuary. He tells me we should certainly see fox and deer, but we should be careful to avoid wild boars, brown bears and grey wolves. But not to worry, Arrian says that seldom do they attack people."

"Surely it is a grand idea, but considering such predators we should request a guard," said Michela.

Eponi replied, "No we cannot, if you would understand what I spoke of. We must go alone if we are to see . . ."

Esta interjected, "The Magic?"

"Yes," Eponi replied. "Nonetheless, Michela and Naomi, have no fears. I have been in forests since I was very young, and as you can see, I've not been eaten yet! Oh, Esta, it is a wonderful plan. Why, we could be in the Emperor's reserve by midday. I can then show you things that perhaps you've never considered and you'll be better *prepared* for that which is best seen in the twilight, if it may be seen at all."

It was a delightful carriage ride from Rome to Tivoli. Esta and her friends were received by the palace servants with great deference and immediately given their customary chambers. Both Hadrian and Vibia were abroad, hence there were no formalities that might have hindered the day.

They were served fruits, bread and cheese and given several light baskets of food and drink to enjoy an evening repast in the woodlands. When Esta refused an armed escort, the centurion gave her a flint striker, an unlit torch and a parchment map, explaining that if they did not return by midnight, guards would be sent to find them. "You will easily see their torchlight and they should see yours," he said. "Do not press through the undergrowth towards the lights, but stay on the trails and you soon will be found. Many a time we have retrieved the Emperor's friends who found it difficult to return to the palace after nightfall—so do not become distraught if you think yourselves lost." Laughing he said, "You cannot go so far in one afternoon that my men cannot find you in one hour!"

As they walked towards the River Aniene, Naomi said smiling, "I think it a good thing the centurion did not even mention bears or wolves!"

Esta replied, "Or great cats, or venomous vipers, or spiders larger than your hands, or dragons breathing fire!"

At this they all laughed, for they felt elated and believed no harm could befall them. The day had only grown more beautiful and before them was a natural garden of splendor, color and fragrance. Stopping upon the bridge that spanned the Aniene, they espied ducks, geese and swans. Nowhere could they see other people, for they were beyond sight of farms and roads. The primitive beauty was only altered slightly by the bark covered pathways, which in truth enhanced the forest and gave ready access to the hillocks, streams, glades and dense canopies of overhanging trees. As they walked on, they called out the names of trees, flowers and forest creatures, deliriously happy and grateful for the shared adventure.

As the foursome descended the gentle slope of a wooded hill, Eponi asked the maidens to say nothing more. Whispering, she led them off the trail and up an easily climbed rocky cleft to an overlook. On this they sat, concealed behind thin leafy boughs that, when parted, proffered a perfect view of a little valley. Two rods distant was a great stand of tall pine trees. Far to their left was a colossal spreading beech, with a girth of at least three rods and a height of ten. Undergrowth was sparse, so that they could easily see to the mossy earth, interspersed with ferns and fallen trunks. Here and there were other beech trees among the pines, but much more slender than their giant overlord. Off to their right was a small marshy pond. Eponi said softly, "Now we must be totally quiet and patient, perhaps for hours. Watch!"

Nonetheless, it did not take hours before they saw squirrels, chipmunks, marmots, dormouse and tiny shrews emerge from holes and nests. Birds began to light upon branches; the sparrow, the white-backed woodpecker, the yellow-billed chough, the red-breasted robin, the scarlet-winged pratincole and, alighting in the pond, a graceful long-billed ibis. As the maidens were obediently quiet, they heard trills, calls, and chirps, an opus[4] of pleasant sounds and watched in wonderment as the animals moved about, searching for bugs or nuts, burrowing in sod or bark, living happily in their own harmonious world, unmindful of man.

"Look carefully, there," said Eponi in hushed tones as she pointed toward the limb of a tall black pine tree. "Do you see a tiny bird. It is beautiful and has an azure-blue crown with dark blue lines passing through its eyes, encircling white cheeks. It has white bars upon its wings, its nape and tail are a lighter blue, its belly is yellow turning grass-green. Its little head is very round, and its beak is black as night."

They nodded and Michela asked what it was. Eponi whispered, "It is a little Blue Parus,[5] whose body is so small you could hold it in your palm. And so I did, for when I was a little girl, I found a chick parus, fallen from its nest and saved it for my own. I found what it liked to eat and nourished it until its wings reached a span in width. I would walk in the woods with the Blue Parus circling above me, then lighting on my shoulder or in my outstretched hands, for it loved me. Not only that, it understood my words and I learned to

---

4. A musical composition.

5. A Blue Parus is known today as an Eurasian Blue Tit, found throughout Italy, a much more colorful bird than its American cousin, the Black-capped Chickadee.

understand the tiny bird's tongue. So doing, I learned that the Blue Parus is the guardian of the forest."

"Whatever do you mean?" Michela asked quietly. "How can such a small fowl be a guardian?"

Eponi answered, "A sentinel need not be a great creature. Rather, what is required are keen eyes and a penetrating voice. Now watch the Blue Parus and listen carefully. It will sing to attract a mate. But if you hear it chirp sharply, in a scolding manner like an angry house dame, then know it is a warning call. Such appeals are made high and low, for each warble has a different meaning. If the parus espies a fox or a wolf stealthy approaching, it will warn its forest friends, from the hare to the dormouse. The gentle beings of this world, those who feed only upon nuts, grass, or insects, *rely* upon the Blue Parus—and when they hear its alarm, they instantly dart into their holes for safety. The parus chirps in a faster cadence when she espies encircling eagles to warn her own race of peril. Still, she cries a different trill, sounding an immediate alarm should she see a raptor swoop earthward to warn hares and other ground creatures of its silent, swift and deadly advance. See how the Blue Parus is now but singing, perhaps with no other intent but to please us, for surely the sharp-eyed guardian knows we are here and that we mean no harm to her or her charges."

This seemed quite remarkable, that a little bird would perch and watch, not only to guard her nest but also concerned for the welfare of many different animals whose only commonality was their innocence.

An hour passed by speedily, for many pleasing sights were enacted before the maidens. All the while, they remained silent, enthralled with a world they had never before considered.

Unexpectedly, Eponi whispered, "Ah, see how the Blue Parus hops about its branch and hear it call its greatest alarm! Now quickly look to the giant beech and see sitting upon a shaded limb, midway to the tree's top, a killer! Do you see it! It is a Goshawk, the most dangerous of the accipiters. Ah! It is taking flight! There! Do not take your eyes off the swooping raptor, for it flies swifter than a racing horse. See it descend within a foot of the earth and weave its flight marvelously through the tangle of the forest. Ah, there, did you see it dart beneath the dead trunk that leans against the cliff, then fly over a copse of fern, gliding powerfully as if driven by a torrent of wind and so low to the earth that surely it seems it must collide with the ground? But no, it flies on evilly enchanted!"

All the while the Blue Parus chirped excitedly. Suddenly, when the goshawk was directly before the maidens, they saw razor talons extend into forest duff, intent on seizing an incautious creature. Then, the raptor was instantly airborne again *with nothing in its claws,* for its intended victim, a ground squirrel, heeding the warning of the parus, had run with all of its might and darted, at the last instant, safely into its den. The speed of the unfolding drama was breathtaking, so vested were the maidens in this world of innocent fur covered beings. The goshawk continued its low-level flight beyond their seeing. Soon thereafter, the little Blue Parus trilled happily.

"What does the bird say now?" asked Michela.

Eponi answered, "Their guardian calls that all is clear and they may safely come out of their dens."

The old dame rose to her feet, saying, "Let us walk deeper into the woods and find a secluded, flowered glen."

Esta asked, "Is there yet more you would show us, for this alone was amazing?"

"Yes," answered Eponi, "now you know of the ken of the forest beings, how they speak to one another and care for each other—now that you understand this, perhaps you will be able to see a magic that is deeper yet."

The three maidens and the kindly woman walked nearly a league more into the forest, and the young ladies were amazed at Eponi's stamina. She led them as if she knew this forest, yet she did not. The old Galatian was very happy, for her countenance was bright and a smile continually lit her face. Nonetheless, she began to behave oddly, muttering incoherently. The maidens could not understand and asked Eponi if she would repeat her words, but she answered them not. Then, plainly enough, the old dame bid them hurry, saying "We must reach the meadow while it is yet day." Nonetheless, she resumed her strange behavior.

Talking among themselves, they decided the widow was listening and speaking to someone unseen. At length Naomi asked Esta, "Do you think Maros has come for Eponi, that her sudden surge of strength is but the quickening that sometimes enlivens the old before their death?"

This saying frightened Michela, who exclaimed, "Oh, that would be terrible, if Eponi should die now! How should we get her body back to the palace?"

Esta replied calmly, "If she should die in this beautiful place, it would be well, for her spirit would leave her body in peace. There *is* a feeling about us I have never felt before. I sense this forest is far more than an emperor's park. We are in a primordial woodland, where, save for this pathway, nothing has changed for centuries, and perhaps has been constant since the dawn of the world.

"Do you remember when Eponi told us it might be difficult for us to *see* something, for we are no longer little children, nor have we attained old age? There must be a truth embedded within her words. I have thought much about this and believe I may know the meaning. Only a little time goes by from birth to early childhood, and there is not much time betwixt old age and death. As the orifice of our spiritual understanding begins to close in the first few seasons of life, so that orifice must begin to open more fully when mortality is nearly spent. Thus, the very young surely know truths, which are forgotten when the aperture shuts and things formally known seem foolish, childish—until they grow old and that knowledge is remembered as the aperture reopens."

Naomi replied, "Well, we are far from birth and death is yet further away from us, or so we hope. How can we then comprehend what Eponi desires to show us?"

Esta answered, "Methinks the Key's presence is felt more easily when we are in the midst of creation, especially when the hills, dells, and streamlets are far from that world crafted by men's hands, and has changed little or not at all from the day it was fashioned by God. Hence, we may supplicate heaven that our minds will be opened, that we may become like little children again. Remember how you used to feel as a child when you ran in the woods, played in a brooklet, chased a butterfly or hummingbird? Was not then the living forest magical to your ken? Think of this day but a few hours back, when we saw the Blue Parus give warning of the Goshawk, saving the lives of its flightless friends! Was not that magical? This is what I think Eponi meant when she said we must prepare our minds."

The sun was sinking low when they came to scattered meadows wherein grew spreading oak trees. Within the shelter of these oaken bullworks were outcroppings of low, flat rocks, like steps. Around and between these crags bloomed countless flowers. Surprisingly, not far from the pathway, there was a solitary monument of stone. Eponi stopped and said, "This is not the only place, but I am told it is the best place in this vast reserve for you to perceive that which I desire for you. I was told we should go to the world wherein stood the Monolith of the Sidhe. Let us sit on a rock at the foot of this stage."

Truly it was like a stage, like that of the Theatre of Marcellus, only far more primitive and private. There was also something quite different that at the first could not be put into words, though each maiden felt it. They sat quietly, as they had earlier when they saw the Blue Parus, yet each demoiselle was not *watching* so much as she was *imagining*.

It was Esta who broke the silence and explained the mystery, saying, "I see it in your eyes, Naomi and Michela, they move about as if some wondrous scene is unfolding before you. Tell me, what do you see upon the stage before us?"

Naomi laughed as she answered, "However did you know? I pictured that we had painted great backdrops of the wild sea and fashioned a likeness of a Trireme in the midst of the waves. Truly what I fashioned in my mind is childish, but as I mentally stand at the helm it is glorious!" She stood upon her feet. "Ah, I command ramming speed!" Naomi leaped from the rock on which they sat to another, her hand flashing left and right as if wielding a sword. "See, I have boarded the enemy's ship!" She plunged her hand into thin air. "The monstrous captain is no more!" They all laughed uproariously.

Esta said, "Michela, what do you imagine?"

She answered, "See the extended limbs of the oak? When I was a child there was nothing more I liked better than to climb great boughs. As I ascended them, they ceased being branches but instead were roadways to far off places." She stepped thoughtfully from the rock and walked towards the tree. She slipped off her gown and sandals, but was yet modestly attired in her undergarments. Soon it became apparent why, for the maiden grabbed a hold of a limb and deftly lifted herself upon it. "Come," she said. "Naomi, you are my Saxon guide and must show me the way to the highest alps of Germania. The limbs are the escarpments in this world. And you, Esta, you shall receive us as the Queen of Agorath, the lost mountain land of wonder. For we shall happen upon your castle in the upper most reaches and you will show us your kingdom!"

Esta and Naomi slipped off their gowns and soon were playing in the tree as if they were children again, playing the parts given them by Michela, inventing in their minds each scene and each danger, heroines all. Eponi watched the drama from the rock, unobtrusively laughing at their antics, as would a mother, shouting praises and cautions. Michela was first to sing, but then was joined in song by Esta and Naomi. When at last they returned to the rock, Michela said, "Ah, this theatre is set with any scene we desire! The trees, the rocks can be anything, anything we . . . what is the word?"

Naomi quipped, "Anything we dream!"

Michela said, swinging her legs back and forth from the low rocky ledge, "This is greater fun than ever I had as a child, for then I was alone, but now I can play with sisters! And oh, Eponi, would I then have had you for my dame! I love you so!"

Eponi said to the maiden, "And I love you, as surely as if you're the daughters I never bore. Now tell me, what did you feel when you were in the arms of the great oak? Did you feel its life, more than ever you did?"

"Why yes!" answered Esta. "Not only that but the tree seemed to be playing with us, listening to us and . . . shapeshifting!"

"Yes," exclaimed Naomi, "I saw battlements rising before us, not branches!"

Michela said, "And when I looked down upon you, Eponi, from truly a great height, I looked down from granite peaks, and you, upon this rock, were not one person but a village of kindly folk and about you were fine houses arrayed with beautiful gardens. When I sang, not only was I joined by my friends, but the flowers about you seemed as little folk who lifted their heads and voices, dancing about with joy. Oh, this is so fun!"

Eponi said, "You have met some of my friends here and now they are yours, for these are truly living beings in this world you have entered. They are just as real as the sparrow or the marmot, or any of the creatures who run and jump, burrow or fly. Look carefully at the flora before you. Look at a solitary flower, like the Angels-Tear there at our feet. It looks like a little person, doesn't it, wearing a white kirtle, with long legs wearing slippers. Its petals are more than its arms, for the Angels-Tear has wings, as if it were a fairy. Do you see it?"

"Yes!" they all answered.

"Each tree, each vine, each flower, each blade of grass is a living breathing being and acts with a certain liberty, or self-agency. Most are good, yet a few are drawn away with dark intent. Though not of our race, they think, feel joy and sorrow, and speak with quiet voices, which the very young and the very old can hear. Look again at the little flower at your feet. Never have I met an Angels-Tear that was not good."

The Flower of the Angels-Tear

Esta asked, "Were these the voices you heard and spoke to today, as we came to this place?"

"Yes," said Eponi. "Even now, you can talk to them as well, for they hear you and love to be loved. Watch a gardener in his garden. See. If he speaks to his flowers, to each one as a friend and compliments their beauty and apologizes for having to prune them back, and so on, see how beautiful they become, more so than if he cared nothing for them. Nature responds to those who love and care for the wonders about them.

"So real are these beings that to some the spirits of the flora take on human form when they gather and celebrate their world. Can this truly be seen? Is this truth hidden in the stories of fairies that are told in every land? Have they great spirits, queens of this magical queendom? This I do not know, for when I speak to a great tree or a tiny petaled flower, they answer me as they are."

The sun set, yet there lingered a celestial glow upon the meadow. Fireflies began to hover about. Eponi said, "Look carefully at the little stars that fly about and see where they alight upon the myriad of blossoms. For an hour or more, converse not with your maiden friends, but with the flora lit by wondrous stella. Walk carefully, never far from the monument. Look again as children look. You will see the magic you saw as a child in the beauties of the night. Do not question the impressions you see, doubting, but let your mind be as free as your spirit. Do not try to explain the sensations you feel, just feel. There will be time later, when you are safe in your beds and think back on this, time then to shape your thoughts into words you can tell each other. Thank you, my own daughters for giving me this day and this night, for allowing an old women to give you something, you who have almost everything because you are young—to give something forgotten and yet so vital to your life."

Angels-Tear Fairies among the living flowers

At length, Esta struck a spark and lit the torch. The four walked slowly back along the path they had come. Quietly they spoke of the day's adventures and shared their affections. Soon it became apparent to the young maidens that Eponi acted quite different than she had earlier when they could hardly keep up with her. Now she walked slowly, and although no complaint fell from her lips, they could tell she felt pain with every step.

Naomi said, "Mother, this eve is so beautiful and this forest so enchanting, why must we hurry back to the Palace of Hadrian? Would we find greater comfort there than here? Nay, see the soft grass is more fit for slumber than a downy bed. We can stake the torch at our sides and simply lie here beneath the starry welkin. The guardsmen will see our torch, for soon they will search for us. We are no worry to them, for it is but a customary thing and gives the men opportunity to leave their spartan quarters and walk about in this moonlit splendor."

They did as Naomi said and soon were talking of the heavens. Eponi said, "The stars are also alive and have voices, voices which now speak clearer to me than ever before."

In two hours more, the old woman was lifted by the strong centurion and cradled silently in his arms, for she could say no more.

CHAPTER 13

SHIPWRECKS

The charioteer was yanked from his disintegrating carriage box and mercilessly dragged behind his galloping quadriga. Esta could see him frantically trying to unsheathe his knife . . .

Ｔt was a short walk from Esta's chambers in the Imperial Palace atop Palatine Hill to a magnificent courtyard overlooking the Circus Maximus in the valley below. A courier sent by Arrian asked Esta to meet him there, explaining that he would bring an "infamous guest." At the appointed hour, Esta and Naomi went to the garden pavilion without Michela, for she spent her days practicing with Aellus at the theatre.

Arrian and the young man with him, rose from their marble seats when the two maidens approached. The young man was of medium height, powerful in physique, angular and handsome in features, possessing dark curly hair, cut close, deep blue eyes and so bronzed by the sun that he almost had the appearance of an Arabian, though the fine structure of his face marked him as a Lusitanian.

"Lady of Massilia," Arrian said, "I introduce you to Gaius Appuleius Diocles, a Spaniard nine years your senior. Known by fanatics,[1] those whose lives revolve around the races, simply as 'Diocles,' arguably the most admired man in the Empire and one of its wealthiest!"

Esta replied, "We are honored to meet you, Diocles." Turning to Arrian, she asked with a smile on her face, "But you said we should meet a man 'infamous,'[2] whereas I hear nothing but praise of Diocles, the *famous* charioteer!"

Diocles said congenially as he bowed to Esta, "Charioteers are a Roman paradox, we are both loved and despised; loved by those so poor they wager little or nothing on our races, and despised by those so rich they throw us bags of gold! Most begin as foreign slaves and triumph as Roman freemen, unless first killed in the circus and made truly free. Considered by the elite to be lower in station than a mercenary, because most have a slave's lineage; yet when first to conquer the seventh circuit are acclaimed victors supreme and are given far more than a gold laden purse but are awarded the palm branch and laurel wreath, the same honor afforded a triumphant general!"

Esta said laughingly, "You have nearly described the 'infamous' Epictetus, has he not Arrian?"

"Indeed, he has," said the scholar, "Epictetus, the freed slave, the mentor of kings! Esta, I wanted you to meet Diocles, for you see he is

---

1. The term "fan" is short for fanatic.
2. "Despite the appeal and stardom of successful charioteers, they were still viewed as disreputable by Roman society. They possessed *infamia* in the same way that gladiators and actors did. The profession of chariot racing was closely associated with slavery, and thus somewhat disdainful to Roman citizens." https://exhibits.library.villanova.edu/index.php/ancient-rome/roman-activities/chariot-racing, 2022

well spoken. He reads the codices of antiquity and though young is a greater sage than many a senator. Also, he has spoken aright, for although Diocles has won hundreds of races and is verily the personification of Mercury, the god of financial gain, commerce and missives, yet his class of charioteers is forbidden to hold public office." Arrian then turned toward Naomi. "And this is Esta's worthy companion, Naomi, whom Hadrian called his daughter."

The Chariot Race, Alexander von Wagner, 1882

Again, Diocles bowed. "Ah, Naomi, I have heard of you as well! Declared by the Emperor *Christianus, qui persecutionem pati non potest,* a Christian who cannot suffer persecution! Hence, I have questions for you that I would fear, for their sake, to ask another."

She answered, "I am no scholar, even of my own faith, but would be pleased to answer you."

"Then let us be comfortably seated. Refreshments will soon be provided," said Arrian. From their seats they could see the entire course of the Circus Maximus. He continued, "Diocles was freeborn in his native land, his sire a sea merchant. Yet he was drawn to racing early in life and when about your age, Naomi and Esta, won chariot races in his homeland of Lusitania. At age eighteen he was invited to Rome to race for the white faction."

Esta interjected, "There are four factions, are there not?"

"Yes," Arrian answered, "the Reds, the Whites, the Blues and Greens. All flags represent prestigious stables who constantly scout for talent in Italia and the provinces."

Naomi said, "It must have been very exciting for you to come from Hispania to Rome and for so dangerous a venture! Did you find immediate success here as in Lusitania?"

Diocles laughed, "No—well, I guess it matters how you define success! I did not win for several years, but I stayed alive—that is success! The charioteers in Rome were far more skillful than ever I had seen. No, I was humbled and shipwrecked in my second race. Fortunately, I cut myself free before hitting the ground!"

"Shipwrecked?" said Naomi, "If you were shipwrecked then however did you race at all?"

Diocles laughed, louder than before, "Although you live in the palace overlooking the great circus, it is certain you have never been to a race! The races are deadly fights and each charioteer commands his own horse-drawn vessel. The corners are perilous straits and often overturns chariots. These crashes we call 'shipwrecks.'"

"How dreadful!" Naomi gasped. "But what do you mean in cutting yourself free? Were you entangled with your downed horses?"

Diocles replied, "Forgive me for laughing! Nothing is known until it is known, and how could you know these things unless taught by someone. Arrian, you teach the world of the conquests of Alexander the Great, and yet have you told your charges anything of the circus?" He chuckled as he added, "Which has greater import?"

Before Arrian could answer, Diocles said, "Was ever a military battle fought beneath the excited eyes of over 200,000 spectators? Many times I have waged circus warfare with 150,000 in their seats and over 50,000 others standing and cheering!"

"Ah, my friend," Arrian smiled as he answered, "I concede my oversight. That is why I invited you here! My dears, a Roman charioteer ties the reigns about his waist, so that in the race they will not drop. One hand carries his whip and with the other he works the tied reins to guide his chariot at breakneck speeds. At his side is his falx knife, to cut the leather reins should he overturn, lest he be dragged behind his horses or ensnared in the wreckage of straps and flaying hooves."

Naomi was even more amazed, and said, "You mean that your chariot flipped and midair, before hitting the ground, you cut yourself free and escaped unscathed? Why that is remarkable!"

Arrian replied, "Not unscathed, as I recall, Diocles, you broke a few bones and were out of the races for weeks!"

Esta asked, "Arrian, how do you know so much about the early career of Diocles?"

He answered, "It was I that saw him race in Hispania and brought him to Rome. I was his patron. Esta, in a better world Rome would have far more scholars, like you, than fanatics. The truth of the matter is simply this: two things matter most to the Roman populace—*bread and circuses*. Two doles are given the masses: free grain and free admission to the Circus Maximus. They are fed and then diverted from riots and unrest through spectacle! I saw in young Diocles a champion charioteer and to my amazement when I learned that he was also erudite, I invested a small fortune in him!"

Esta replied, "You, a writer of antiquity, a patron of the White Flag?"

Arrian answered, "Not the White only. You seem to forget that I was also a military commander. Although many attend the races to see the drama of gory shipwrecks, there are others who see a champion and are stirred to emulate him, for none are more valorous. Charioteers *fight* in the circus, three or four times a week! To win and stay alive, they must possess dauntless courage and must be strong athletes as well as superb horsemen. Yes, it *is* spectacle and many a man lives a life of vicarious bravery through the deeds of the faction he upholds, and such are fanatics indeed. Nonetheless, others, especially young men, see the skill, strength and endurance of a Diocles and are inspired to become like warriors. Though few risk the hazards of the circus, their faction becomes not a white, red, blue or green flag, but ROME itself. Like your father, Esta, they grow to manhood with the desire to fight for their country, upholding it before their own lives."

"Not to mention," said Diocles grinning, "that to back a winner gives a patron wealth and added freedom to write as he desires!"

Arrian replied, "Ha, you have made me a great sum, but a far greater for yourself! Now tell our friends what turned your heart from shipping to racing."

Diocles answered, "It was the charioteer Flavius Scorpus, also a Spaniard. Born a slave, he proved himself in the circuses and bought his own life, becoming a libertus.[3] He triumphed in over two thousand races and died when only 27 years of age. Marcus Valerius Martialis, a Roman citizen and poet of Hispania, wrote in Book X of his Epigrams:

> 'Let Victory in sadness break her Idumaean[4] palms; O
> Favor, strike your bare breast with unsparing hand.
> Let Honor change her garb for that of mourning; and
> make your crowned locks, O disconsolate Glory, an

---

3. A freed slave.
4. An ancient country of Palestine between the Dead Sea and the Gulf of Aqaba.

*offering to the cruel flames. Oh, sad misfortune, that
you, Scorpus should be cut off in the flower of your
youth, and be called to prematurely harness the dusky
steeds of Pluto. The chariot race was always shortened
by your rapid driving; but O why should your own
race have been so speedily run?'*[5]

"I read this when I was very young and also read that 'he lives longest who lives best!' When I saw the chariot races, it seemed to my young mind as if I could see from the eyes of the charioteer and would live each moment of the race with my champion. I could scarce breath when he rounded a turn, and if he fell, I felt his pain. When he was victorious and was applauded by thousands, I felt his triumph as if it were my own."

Esta replied, "Diocles, I marvel that you quote verse so freely. Surely, had I seen you race before this I would have admired your equestrian skill but would have known nothing of the inner man. I think then I should have misjudged you. For although I admire any woman or man in their craft, especially in excellence, yet in athletics it seems that most define keenly their outward form and sharpen wonderfully their prowess, and this is needful in soldiery and is a blessing to those whom they protect, but inwardly they take no care to fashion their intellect and spirit, which must surely outlast the vigor of youth. So, when death comes, as it did to Scorpus, it is saddened yet more, unless he, like you, took with him to the world of spirits a mind rich in truth. There is a price that must be paid to acquire the silver of wisdom found only in codices. I have not read Martialis, his tribute to Scorpus touches me deeply. Please recite another of his sayings."

He answered, "His epigrams are often sardonic, but then I find

---

5. Marcus Valerius Martialis, *Yale Classics*, Page 5617, e-artnow. Kindle Edition.

one that hits the mark. This verse of Martialis states my own lowly ambition and when it is mine, then will I have truly *won*. Says the poet:

> *'The things that make life happy are these:*
> *lands that make no ill return;*
> *a hearth always warm;*
> *freedom from litigation;*
> *a quiet mind;*
> *a vigorous frame;*
> *a healthy constitution;*
> *prudence without cunning;*
> *friends among our equals, and social intercourse;*
> *a table spread without luxury;*
> *nights, not of drunkenness, yet of freedom from care;*
> *a bed, not void of connubial pleasures, yet chaste;*
> *sleep, such as makes the darkness seem short;*
> *contentment with our lot, and no wish for change;*
> *and neither to fear death nor seek it.'*[6]

"Now tell me," said Diocles, "a verse that you cherish."

"Nay," said Esta smiling, "lest our conversion become a competition. Rather I would learn from you and the aspiration you seek. It seems to me that even now you could do as you wish. You have wealth enough to leave the circus and settle with a goodly wife upon country lands. I was raised amid olive groves and know well the value of agrarian life. Why then do you still race?"

He answered with a chuckle, "First I have not found 'a goodly wife.' Have you a recommendation?"

---

6. Marcus Valerius Martialis, *Yale Classics - Roman Classical Literature*, p. 5615, e-artnow. Kindle Edition.

Esta blushed as she answered, "Not I, I am too young! Did you think I . . . "

Arrian, Naomi and Diocles burst into laughter, as Diocles said, "No, I did not think you were recruiting me, as did Arrian before time! However, I must say in sincerity, that someday I hope to find someone *like* The Lady of Massilia!" Esta felt deeply honored but said nothing. Diocles continued, "Anyway, I also feel that I am 'too young' for marriage, and I admit I still love racing too much! You will see however, that despite being a charioteer, I am not temeritous and when a brother dies, I grieve his loss!"

*The centerpiece of a mosaic floor in Trier, Germania depicts Polydus, a charioteer of
the Reds Faction, holding the palm branch and laurel wreath of victor of the race.
Also shown is the name of his lead horse, Compressore.*

Arrian said, "Esta and Naomi, tomorrow Diocles will race his
quadriga of Andalusian horses, that is four abreast. The Hispanic
Andalusian is known as the 'Horse of Kings' and are magnificent
creatures, 15 hands in height, intensely intelligent and beautiful to
behold. Andalusians fiercely gallop down straightaways and with

agility negotiate round the metae posts, the point at which many chariots overturn, killing the riders."[7]

"Hah!" said Diocles, "Arrian always gives more credit to my horses than to me! But what he says is true!"

Arrian continued, "Will you join me in the Imperial Box tomorrow at midday? I will send a lectica to fetch you comfortably to the circus. Perhaps your presence will bring good fortune to Diocles! As Hadrian is yet abroad, I will drop the starting flag as the representative of the emperor."

Back in their apartments, Esta said to Naomi, "What else could I do but accept the invitation?"

Naomi answered, "Of course you could not refuse. But how horrible it will be if we witness the unthinkable, if the chariot of Diocles is overturned and we see his strong body thrown violently to the earth and trampled upon! To think that such a one possessing such ken and wit, could, in an instant and that before our eyes, suffer agony and die—die for what, for gold? Perhaps Scorpus supped also with maidens the day before his death!"

Esta answered her, "Ah, my friend, you are much taken with the charioteer!"

"That is not it. Although his presence is exciting, a result I'm sure of his extraordinary profession! Nonetheless if such a one was killed in pitched battle with enemies, his lost life would be a sacrifice with meaning."

"His lost life?" said Esta. "Have you a portent of his death? You seemed to sense that Maros had come for Eponi, and that very night she died. I think Naomi, you have gifts of your own, perhaps second sight?"

"This is different than with Eponi," Naomi said. "I feel there will

---

7. https://earlychurchhistory.org/entertainment/famous-horses-in-romes-chariot-races/e

be death in the circus tomorrow. Whither it be Diocles or someone else, still it is tragic! One moment a man lives and breathes. His sinews are powerful, and he is goodly in form. The next he is mangled and bleeds out his life and to what end? That the populace might witness spectacle!

"O Esta, you and Arrian speak of the great proof of Epictetus, that we knew purity in our pre-earth estate or lives, for we constantly judge that which surrounds us to a forgotten perfection. All of my life I have heard of the Glory of Rome, and truly that which the Romans have sculpted in marble, in hangings gardens, in temples and basilicas *is* marvelous! But give me the quiet world of Eponi, the forest created by our Lord, where a Blue Parus is a mighty guardian and all innocence 'wins!' Her world approaches far nearer to the celestial than this Roman world, this fallen world of competition where only one may win and all others, no matter how skilled or courageous, must lose, some in agony and death."

Esta replied, "Naomi, what you say is indeed true. But even in the primordial forest there are goshawks and in Eden slithered the serpent. It seems to me there must be opposition in life, for it always has been so, else how can we be proven? Evil is very real and must be fought, even by the small Parus bird. What if the Jacaian had prevailed in our lives? Glad I am for men of war, our deliverers!"

The Jewess answered, "True enough! Offenses fill existence, but why create what is truly a battlefield in the circus or arena to emulate and glorify the death struggle? No enemy is outside of the gate, so let us, as in the theatre, make our own, who shall kill as surely as a foreign army! Ultimately, life will prove it is not an enigma without resolve, the good always to be intermingled with evil. Rather, there must come an end to this Tellus World, this sphere far removed from the center throne of the AllFather. There he cast out Evil and permits it upon this earth only, as you say, to prove us. Oh, that we were already proven for then would the Omnipotent cast

Evil far from us. Yet why can't we do all in our power *now* to rid malignancy from our lives? Why must the populace partake of *spectacle?"*

Esta replied, "Naomi, already you have seen enough of opposition to know your way in life. I will tell Arrian that you will not come, for you feared to see any drama in which the actors might truly die. As he represents the emperor, your refusal might be considered a serious offense, but Hadrian has given you the right to do as you believe—and Arrian will in no wise think less of you. I will tell Diocles that you would love to see his beloved Andalusian horses when he takes them out to practice, but you could not bear to see him risk his life."

MORE THAN ONE hundred and fifty thousand spectators filled the Circus Maximus, for every stone seat was taken and many more stood on the high platform above the tiers. Although the Patron of the race was none other than Hadrian, the Emperor was gone from Italia. The crowds thronged the circus, for at midday there was to be a race of twelve four-horsed chariots, three teams from each of the four factions. Yet what drew the populace was not the number of chariots racing, but the men who held rein. The foremost of these was Pompeius, a gladiator who after earning his Rudis, or sword of freedom, became a charioteer and raced with bloodlust, as if he still wielded a blade and not a whip. Next in ranking was Seuthes, a Thracian slave of exceptional ability, whose callous victories were often hailed by the fanatics of his faction with deadly rioting. It was said that Seuthes had caused more shipwrecks than any other charioteer. The third favored driver was Polynices, known for his cunning in working with other charioteers to literally down their strongest opponents. Conspiring beforehand, his confederates often prevailed in forcing favored champions into the spina, the long wall that divided the two straightaways of the circus, or when racing around the metae, into the conical turning posts at each end of the spina. Only when the track was clear of his adversaries, did Polynices race for victory. Diocles was considered fourth and was known only for his equestrian skill. The other charioteers were also veterans, else they would not have qualified for this race.

"Esta," said Arrian, when they were seated in the Imperial Box of the Circus Maximus, "you are arrayed as if a queen. I knew you would be, for I ordered the palace maidservants to dress you as they would Vibia!" He laughed a little, then continued, "There is a reason for this and be not dismayed or surprised. You see, before Hadrian left Tivoli, I asked of him a boon in exchange for the duties he piled upon me in his absence. He said 'yes' and then added that he wished he could see the effect of this upon the praetors, senators and other elites of the Empire. I was only to do this once, however, *and today is the day!* Before the dignitaries and populace of Rome your station is again raised."

With no further explanation, Arrian rose to his feet and stepped to the fore of the regal balcony. The tumultuous crowd ceased its roaring and became remarkably silent. Arrian extended his hand to Esta, and said kindly to her, "Please stand at my side."

Facing the mammoth stadium, Arrian spoke loudly, and his voice seemed magnified by the surrounding amphitheater, declaring, **"Never has a woman dropped the starting flag in the Circus Maximus, this stadium of antiquity, the largest and most costly structure of Rome, where charioteers from the far quarters of the Empire race, representing not only factions, but kingdoms—never—until today! In the Name of Hadrian, Foremost Sovereign of all the Lands of the World, I present to you Domina[8] Esta**

---

8. Latin for Lady, or Lady Esta of Rome.

Romae, Imperatores solus Pupillus et Repraesentativus Magni Eventus, The Emperor's sole Ward and Representative of this Supreme Event!"

Detail of painting by Jean Leon Gerome, 1883

Arrian handed Esta a white silken cloth, and whispered, "All you need do is drop it." *She did and a deafening roar enveloped the circus and the city as twelve chariots and forty-eight stallions left the starting gates with a ferocity that Esta could have never imagined!*

During the first lap, it was evident to Esta that the three teams of each faction cooperated, maneuvering and blocking opponents—of these Polynices and his color were by far the most aggressive. But when he attempted to drive his quadriga into Pompeius in the second lap, he felt the snap of a deadly lash wrap around his neck and cut into his flesh. Never had he fought a gladiator that could use a whip with such lethality. Polynices tried to strike back with his own twined strand of leather, but as he had finessed his team slightly to the fore, to stem, turn and shipwreck Pompeius, Polynices struck blindly to his rear. Yet, for those few moments, the gladiator whipped him repeatedly until a stroke twice encircled Polynices neck. In that instant, Pompeius jerked so hard that his enemy was pulled off balance. The crowd went berserk as the charioteer fell, not in a shipwreck, but in a fight of his own making and was lost in a melee of dust and pounding hooves. The dead man's team drifted to the outside of the track where it was caught by attendants and removed from the course.

Watching the race was far different than Esta had supposed it would be—the dust almost obliterating from view all but the foremost chariots, scarcely clearing before the next round churned up tawny billows anew. Although they raced with astounding speed, it seemed an eternity between each dip of the dolphins, the markers that counted laps.

The fourth lap found Seuthes to the fore and outside of a rival faction. Behind these thundered Pompeius and two other teams, all nearly neck and neck. Rounding the metae, Seuthes suddenly drove his quadriga hard towards the pylon. Already he was but inches from his foe and the inevitable crash of horses and chariots seemed certain to shipwreck both. Although he was less than half a length ahead of the doomed quadriga, for they indeed struck the flanks of his killing steeds, Seuthes expertly drove his team away from the neighing stallions that careened into the spina and stumbled mightily as Seuthes' chariot shot past unscathed. Not only was his victim's chariot overturned and ripped asunder, its rider hopelessly thrown, but the two chariots that closely flowed, with their eight horses and two charioteers, hit the wreckage dead on. One chariot immediately flipped high into the air, the driver thrown before his own horses that fell, entangled in their harnesses, and struggled with their might to stand, unmindful of the body they trampled. The other coursed over rubble, breaking wheels and box. The inside steed of the quadriga then fell hard upon the track, the stallion's leg broken, pulling the others about it and upon their own charioteer.

Again, the stands erupted with shouts, blasphemes, curses and cheers. Pompeius was on the outside of the disaster and rode undaunted past the three-chariot shipwreck. The other teams also rode through or about it, dangerously swerving to avoid debris, but no more toppled.

Esta was glad Naomi was not there and wished she was also gone from the death field. For when the attendants were able to run to the aid of the broken men and bewildered horses and retrieve what they could before the next career[9] put them again in harm's way, she saw that all three charioteers appeared lifeless. There was no time for kindly attention, and they were roughly handled and put upon litters, as their broken limbs flayed about unnaturally.

On the next lap, one chariot broke apart with no apparent cause but the fierceness of the race itself. Perhaps it struck remnants of wreckage. First a wheel separated, dropping the axle into the earthen track, where it snared the ground like a ship's anchor. The charioteer was yanked from his disintegrating box and mercilessly dragged behind his galloping quadriga. Esta could see him frantically trying to unsheathe his knife, but he was soon knocked senseless between the ground and the draft pole. Attendants on horseback skillfully intercepted the team and Esta later learned the man survived but was badly crippled. After this, several other teams dropped voluntarily from the race, evidently with damaged carriages or wounded horses, reducing the field to half of its starting strength.

Esta searched for Diocles and at length saw him well to the rear of the lead chariots, nearly lost in the dust clouds. She considered this and thought how glad she was that his beautiful Andalusian Stallions, though large and mighty, had not the strength to engage the two lead chariots, for trailing well behind the front runners had kept him out of the hellish fighting. Although surely there would be

---

9. One turn about the racetrack, galloping at full speed.

no purse for one who finished in third or fourth place, she thought it would be a victory just to finish such a battle.

Seuthes and Pompeius alternated in holding the lead. The rearmost advanced and, from behind, whipped his foe, who pulled out to escape the lash, causing him to lose the advantage. Then the savage brutality was repeated, the positions reversed.

Three lengths behind this waring duo, wheeled a hopeful challenger. A length behind this chariot was another, holding close to the inside of the track. Diocles drove his quadriga outside and parallel to this contestant. Trailing to their rear was the last team in the race.

It was in the sixth lap of the race that Esta was able to fully view the magnificent sight of her champion and his colossal Andalusians. The dust was finally disbursed, for the battle raged on with fewer combatants. Diocles rode wide on the track, closer to where she stood, breathless, in the Imperial box next to Arrian. She saw him clearly and he was *not* like the other charioteers who were strained and weary, horses foaming and bloody. Rather, he and his steeds appeared unmarred by the raging contest, exultant—*glorious!*

He stood within the small carriage box of his chariot, perfectly balanced, legs pressed tightly against its sides, his sinews defined and taut, his eyes focused on the galloping quadriga to his four, his whip hand high and cocked, but never falling on his beloved Andalusians. The stallions emulated their master in every aspect, save their muscular might was greatly multiplied. The rhythm of their prodigious strides, each stallion moving wondrously in absolute harmony with its fellows, their rippling sinews, their massive hooves striking the ground in a thunderous, cadence, thrilled Esta! Then suddenly and without any shouted command, crack of the whip or rein, their great heads and necks strained forward, as their bodies lengthened perceptibly, and their hooves fell more rapidly.

Diocles leaned more to the fore as if willing his quadriga to fly down the track. With scarcely a lap to the finish his chariot advanced steadily, easily passing the third team. But how, she thought, could he maneuver through the lead teams that hugged the spina? These charioteers still cruelly whipped their horses and when they could, they lashed each other, determined to win or die.

What happened next caused Esta to shout with as much fear and ecstasy as did the tens of thousands who filled the stands of the Circus Maximus! Diocles' advanced his quadriga directly into the center of the two chariot eight horse mass that was before him, as resolutely as the Trierach had rammed his Trireme into the stern of the Jacaian ship in the Tyrrhenian Sea! Yet they did not collide, as Esta feared they must. For Pompeius' team, who galloped outside of Seuthes', began to give way, his horse's strength fading from all-out exertion over too long a time. His quadriga, sensing the dominance of Diocles' stallions, submissively began to open a gap against the will of their master. This the gladiator was determined not to allow! Turning, Pompeius lashed savagely the right-most stallion of Diocles' quadriga, whipping for its' eyes.

Esta had heard of warhorses fighting *with* their riders, kicking and biting, but had never seen such a thing until that moment! So close was the head of the god-like Andalusian to the hand outstretched in the action of cracking the whip, that it thrust forward, writhing to one side as its jaws snapped tight upon the gladiator's fist! Pompeius was stunned and reactively jerked his team aside while the attacking horse momentarily held its grip. In that instant it seemed that he must fall. But the intelligent stallion, showing its intent was to *win* and not *fight,* let go, so as not to hinder the rapid progress of its quadriga. Pompeius might have nonetheless resumed his warfare, were it not for lost momentum; there was simply not time enough to recover.

For several strides, Seuthes held a slight lead over Diocles, as the two chariots raced toward the finish line. It was all Seuthes could do, to whip and curse his horses, for his chariot was nearest the spina and as Diocles was outside he could do nothing to hinder the noble charioteer who rode beyond the reach of his lash.

The wicked man's quadriga foamed red while the stallions of Hispania lathered normally as if relaxed. Then the Andalusians proved their superior fortitude and desire to win, for they drew ahead, first by a length, and then by two as they finished the race victoriously!

Arrian handed the palm branch and laurel wreath to Esta. The beautiful maiden then awarded these ancient symbols of victory to Diocles, who bowed graciously to the emperor's representative. For a moment, the eyes of each held the gaze of the other with sincere admiration. Following this, Diocles led his splendid stallions again around the track, holding the palm branch in his left hand and the wreath in his right, while the vast crowd cheered uproariously. The circuit was not made trotting, as was customary. Rather, to the astonishment of the spectators, the racehorses performed an equine *dance* as the quadriga drew the nimble chariot along, with elevated and graceful movements, light, swift and agile.

Amazingly, except for a gossamer layer of dust, Diocles, his chariot and his four loyal Andalusians were clean, without the least bloodstain. Many a bag of coin was thrown into the arena and swiftly collected by the attendants of his colors. The far more substantial prize would be given later at a feast held in his honor.

CHAPTER 14
A CHARIOT RIDE

"It would be insane to regard every soldier as Caesar!"

Naomi

Although all three maidens had traveled by carriage, and Arrian had given Esta and Naomi riding lessons, none had ever ridden in a chariot and thought they never should. Hence, when Diocles sent them an invitation to meet him at the Circus Maximus on a day when there would be no races, that he might show them his quadriga and chariot—and give them rides around the course, they were elated!

Michela was spending most of her time with music instruction and voice lessons from Aellus, who, as Arrian had predicted, was much taken with her natural abilities. Yet, as she had no discipline or formal understanding of keys, notes, scales, modes, and Carmina, or

Roman songs, there was a tremendous amount of knowledge for Michela to learn and skills for her to acquire.

Aellus taught the maiden that music was a reflection of natural harmonies found in all of nature, including the Cosmos. To demonstrate this, he would pluck one string of a great Persian Harp that would cause other strings to softly vibrate without being touched, for those notes were naturally harmonic with the first. Music, he said, influenced not only our moods, but our health, happiness and even our behavior. It was unthinkable to the Romans that a sacrifice could be made to the gods without musical accompaniment. So also was music integrated into their lives, from ceremonial pomp to theatrical performances. Aellus explained that just as mathematics plays a vital role in everything, from the measurement of clothes, to houses, lands, nations and even the organizations of the planets and stars, so also, he said, is there a technical structure to Carmina. She learned that Pythagoras discovered that pitches could be described in terms of "string length ratios."[1] Roman music was adapted from ancient Greek melodies and was further revised by Christians who set scriptures to strains, creating unique musical chants that Aellus said were marvelously harmonious. These he warned her against, for although they seemed fascinating and somehow familiar, "they were a contagion that was forbidden to any serious Roman performer."

Unlike Esta and Naomi, who had been schooled for many years, this was a new and thrilling experience for Michela. Hence, time spent with her friends during the day were infrequent, although they supped together in the evening and slept in the same palace apartments.

However, to accommodate the proposed chariot rides, Diocles spoke with Arrian, who in turn arranged with Aellus for a free day for Michela. The day chosen was bright and mild. Arrian escorted the

---

1. http://www.essential-humanities.net/western-art/music/ancient/, 2022

maidens from the palace to the track of the Circus Maximus. Except for a few workmen and a charioteer exercising his team, the circus was vacant.

"Is that charioteer Diocles?" asked Michela excitedly, for she had not yet met the man.

"No," answered Esta. "Yet, it is the appointed hour. Arrian, why do you suppose he is delayed?"

"Ah," Arrian answered, "Diocles is not delayed. He will not come until after he is sure that you have arrived. You see," he laughed, "he loves making an entrance." Only a few minutes passed when they heard the sound of galloping hooves. From the starting gates thundered a quadriga of four Andalusians and Diocles riding his chariot, the stallions and charioteer magnificently groomed, as if they would be seen by 200,000 spectators. Drawing close to his guests, he abruptly reined in his team and stepped from his chariot, bowing deeply. "Diocles," said Arrian with a chuckle, "so splendid are your horses and your own visage, that one might think you had come to perform before Hadrian and Vibia!"

"Why," chortled Diocles, "this is my common manner of attire whenever I am with my Andalusians. You see, they look so grand that I must make intense preparations, lest I look shabby by comparison."

"How true!" replied Arrian. "Well, you know Lady Esta and Naomi. May I introduce you to Michela, whose voice will soon delight the whole of Rome."

He bowed deeply, saying, "Michela, it is with great pleasure I meet the cantrix[2] I have heard so much about! If your voice is as beautiful as you are, I eagerly look forward to a performance!" Then addressing all the maidens, he said, "Who is the first to ride with me?"

---

2. Female singer

Diocles

Naomi asked seriously but happily, "Must we ride as fast as when you came in?"

"Fast?" said the charioteer "That was not fast! My four friends can run much faster—I did not wish to stir up the dust. But no, I promise you all a gentle ride, unless you desire more."

Esta spoke up, "Take Michela first, then myself next. We will give Naomi a little time to gain courage!"

Accordingly, the Spaniard helped Michela onto the carriage box of the chariot. There was room enough for them both, but the closeness of their stance thrilled the young maiden. The ride lasted two laps, the speed gradually increasing until, at the last, the charioteer had his quadriga at a full gallop. That this was an exciting adventure for Michela was easily seen, for shouts of delight, punctuated with amusing screams, were heard continually until she stepped down.

After Esta had taken her place, Michela exclaimed, "Oh Naomi, it is far more thrilling than riding in the Trireme. Tell Diocles to go fast! It is very safe, and you may never have another chance! I can't wait to tell my friends at the Theatre that I rode with the famous Diocles! He is so strong and comely!"

Arrian laughed at this, but Naomi looked more frightened than ever. Smiling, he consoled her saying, "Ask him to proceed slowly and he will be your obedient servant."

Soon the chariot returned and as Diocles helped Esta down from the carriage box, she excitedly thanked him for the extraordinary experience. He then kindly said to Naomi, "You see, your friends are unharmed. What say you?"

Naomi replied with a shaky voice, "I am ready for my turn, only please go slower with me."

Diocles replied, looking steadily into her eyes, "Naomi, I would never want to frighten you!" Then he laughed a little, saying, "How could I, for I've heard of your supreme courage!"

"My courage?" she asked.

"Yes," he said, "You are already proven courageous, for I heard of your conversation with the emperor. And again, you showed fortitude when you refused my invitation to the race. Esta said you did not want to witness the dangers I must face. For that kindness, I do thank you. But was there not more to your refusal? The races *are* violent, something your faith abhors. Perhaps, it was for this reason you did not come and for that I honor you." Then smiling, he continued, "Slower, you say? Well, my Andalusians are fatigued, having run so hard for Michela and Esta. For that reason, I must walk them that they might recover their strength!"

So saying, he lifted the slight maiden, for in stature Naomi was smaller than her two friends, onto the carriage. He put his left hand around her waist, for added support and comfort, while he held the reins in his right.

The others did not hear a command from his lips, nor did they perceive the slightest ripple move along the reins, yet the quadriga moved forward and were soon beyond hearing.

Michela said to Esta, "Oh, did you *see* that? Would that Diocles had put his arm around me!"

After a short time, the charioteer asked Naomi, "What do you think now; are you frightened?"

She answered, "Oh no, not at all! This is not what I expected, and I love it. Walking like this I can keenly observe your wonderful stallions! Their movements are so graceful, so purposeful. They seem to know what you would have them do without a word spoken to them."

Diocles answered, "They are extremely intelligent creatures, and *we* act as with one mind. They are obedient out of love, for they know of my ceaseless affection. They feel changes in my stance by way of pressures through the draft pole; by this and through slight movements of reins, felt foremost by the lead horse, they perfectly understand my desires and respond. When I do talk to them, they comprehend my words. They feel joy, as do I, when they run and I ride. Afterward, they love being groomed by my hand. My quadriga live for me and I for them!"

"Do they like to race?" asked Naomi.

"Ah, that is what they like most! Well, not really. What they like most is to win! They strive together, to cross the finish line first! It is then they show their proud heritage as the finest horses in the world and dance to the astonishment of the crowds!"

"Oh," said Naomi, "Esta told us of the equine dance! Could you show me?"

As they made the turn around the metae posts, coming back into full view, the waiting company saw the quadriga dancing as they had at the race. Michela again spoke, her voice tinged with rising jealousy, "Ah, Diocles did *not* do that with me!"

As the chariot passed, Diocles said to them, "We are having a fine talk, Naomi and I and our four friends. You may wish to rest in the seats, for we shall be a while." With that he resumed walking his horses.

Michela said disconcertedly, "They are just talking and laughing! Whatever about?"

Esta replied, "Well Michela, it seems Naomi enjoys conversing more than the thrill of fast ride. Arrian, do you not remember that Diocles said he had questions for Naomi?"

"Yes," he said, "but I think a chariot is a strange place to get answers."

"Not if you want no others listening," Esta replied.

By this time, Naomi was truly enjoying the chariot ride and the company of the strong equestrian. Esta had told her of Diocles' sagacity and his racing skill, how he won without cruelty and how she was otherwise impressed with him.

"Naomi," he said, "you promised to answer a few questions. Would you do so now?"

"Now?" she asked. "Yes . . . Strangely, here in the Circus Maximus, a place of extremes, there is peace as we talk. Such things as I believe you want to know are best understood when there *is* serenity. Nonetheless, we are in the second lap, and I may not have time to answer so important . . . a thing as . . . well you mentioned my Christianity and I . . ."

Diocles interposed, "You are right, but have no fear for lack of time. We shall not be limited to two laps." He laughed, "My horses can walk for hours, and your friends are in good company with Arrian."

"Well then," said Naomi, "Please speak on."

He replied earnestly, "I often meet Christians, for it is a growing devotion. Yet always they are silent around me. Though I am not an officer of Rome, and should not be feared, still I race before the highest dignitaries of the Empire and I am often seen in their company. This is of their choosing, not mine. I do not need to garner their favor, for I triumph on the track. Anyway, I do not blame Christians for their silence, for though Hadrian encourages tolerance of all religions in his dominions, yet for some reason Christians are truly persecuted in nearly every province, save in the region of Massilia. Under Roman law, an accused criminal is not a convicted criminal, for there must be a trial before one is condemned and punished. Yet the law recognizes inequalities. A citizen of Rome is afforded many protections—these are often sufficient to warrant better treatment and lessor punishments, if found a transgressor. At times a person's position may afford a release without a trial. Non-citizens are treated more harshly, but even slaves are better off than Christians when taken by the law. When Christians are accused of crimes, they are *assumed* guilty, especially if gain may be had from them, for example the confiscation of their property."

Naomi said nothing, for as yet he had not asked a single question. His knowledge of the persecution of her people both pleased and frightened her.

He continued, "Hence Christians are poorly defended and are punished, even tortured to force confessions, eventually suffering unto death by proceedings that are more of mobocracy than Roman law. Hadrian's policy is that Christians *who are found guilty of crimes* should be dealt with harshly, but otherwise let be. However, as an accusation for a Christian will almost certainly lead to condemnation, what chance have they to live peaceably among us? Why, I ask, is there tolerance in the Empire for all cultures, but not for Christians? I have traveled to many lands, and always it is the same, save for Narbonensis and Massilia. Yet those of your faith that I know, like you, are truly good and live kindly. Why, then, this mania? Naomi, this is a difficult question, and you may not have an answer, for you are so young."

Naomi replied, "What you say frightens me, for my father has always warned me to be careful and quiet, for the very reasons you explain. Yet, our Lord commanded us not to be silent, but to teach his truth. Twice I have been blessed in this regard: where I was raised and now the safety given me by our Emperor.

"But I do have an answer for you! This is *not* strange. All other dogmas have as much falsehood in them as are found in Roman myth! What differences are there between the gods of Greece, Rome, the Druids, the Phoenicians, the Egyptians? Each are so similar even names are interchanged, or their Pantheons are equally honored. *However, if what Christianity teaches is true, then everything else is false.*"

"Wow," he exclaimed, "that is put simply and boldly! The question that is put to Christians, which often determines their fate is this: 'Are their many gods or only one?' Now, Naomi, what do you *really* believe?"

"Esta has helped me understand much and has taught me that

there are commonalities in both Roman teachings and in Christianity."

"How so?" he asked, as they once more passed Arrian and the two maidens. Esta waved but did not disturb their quiet conversation.

"Well, she knows how to say things in a manner that I cannot," said Naomi. "This I can say, both Romans and Christians believe that the forces of nature are intelligent—and that the stars and planets, including this earth, *live*. So also the flora, fauna, the sea with its many creatures, and the sky and the fowls of the air and the tempests that rage—all are somehow living things that can *act* for themselves. This, to a great extent, is knowledge newly acquired for me. At least I didn't understand it before, and it has come to my ken through Esta's teachings.

"Why should Christians believe this? *Because all these, including the very elements of creation, are obedient to the commands of Christ, the Creator of all things*, for so the scriptures teach us. He speaks and all of nature obeys him; it *is* so!

"Yet the Roman, the Greek, the Druid, the Egyptian, and so on, they say, in their stories, that each of these forces and each of these living beings are not the servants of God, but they say *they are the gods*—gods who must be appeased if a war is to be won, or their wives or concubines are to bear, or crops are to be harvested, and so on. Recognizing an intelligence and its agency to act, no matter how powerful it is, should not deify the being! A soldier is a thinking man, but it would be insane to regard every soldier as Caesar!"

Diocles replied, "Hah! You think you do not explain things well? Never have I heard it put so simply! Still . . . I could answer you, if I wanted to play the part of a debating senator and say, 'Jupiter is the great god and all lesser gods, or forces, must obey him.' Would this not be the same as your teachings, if I were to equate Jupiter with Christ?"

"Oh," Naomi answered, "I think there are many truths—well, Esta has showed me many similarities of a like kind. This is because, or so I think, that in the beginning of man the truth was known, revealed by the Almighty who wove a grand tapestry of perfect knowledge, strand upon strand, by the hand of Adam, his first prophet and those that God ordained should succeed him. But rising generations, being tempted by carnality and power-lust, often forsook truth and corrupted the doctrines of heaven. Yet in the man-altered tapestries, there yet survived many golden strands of what was, and is, and is to come. You have traveled afar but I only from Massilia to Rome. Yet I have read the codices of many lands and nearly every people yet believe in Heaven's Father and Mother, though the sacred duo are known by different names. The Hebrews calls the Father, Elohim and the Mother, Wisdom. The Greeks venerate Zeus and Hera, their counterparts in Rome being Jupiter and Juno. Certainly, the attributes ascribed to Zeus are far from those of Elohim, for the myth of Zeus is a corruption—still Greeks believe in the true principle of a Father God! So also, each nation has a creation story of how this world came to be, though they vary. What people have you been among that did not believe in the great deluge, the universal flood? These are remnant archetypes and teach many true principles."

"Can you give me another example?" Diocles asked.

"Oh, there are many," said Naomi, "but Hercules will suffice, a man born of the god Jupiter and the mortal woman Alcmene, as taught by Homer, Ovid, Pausanias and Plautus. *This, I believe, is a corruption of the foreknowledge given the ancient seers*, that Christ would be born of the Almighty God of Heaven and Mary, his mortal mother."

"Well," said Diocles, "if a Roman oracle speaks of something that is nearly like unto your truth, then why do you fight it and declare it is surely false?"

"Would it not be false for a man or men to impersonate Caesar?" she asked.

"Surely!" he answered.

"Even if they were rebellious sons?"

Diocles answered, "Then, the transgression would only be greater!"

Naomi continued, "Jupiter is a living planet, and its light can be clearly seen in the heavens when the sun has set. The living Jupiter, the *real* Jupiter, is obedient to the Almighty Creator, who made him as He did every being of the cosmos. That they *are* testify that they were all made by Him. The stars and planets give us their lights as witness to this truth; we *see* them but most of us cannot *hear* their voices. For if all were given us now, we would not learn faith, which is a prime virtue of happiness."

She waited, both to think of what next to say and to allow time for her listener to ponder and perhaps *remember* things which he had once known but had long since forgotten.

Then she explained, "There are those who say they *are* what they *are not!* These are the Fallen Ones! We speak of the Father of All, and truly our spirits were sired by Him. Hence our physical bodies, begotten by our mortal parents, were enlivened at birth by our eternal spirits, divine seed of God! Well, the Fallen Ones were those who rebelled against the Father of All, for they, especially Lucifer, their general, desired to *usurp* His throne and crown and would not wait and strive for their lawful inheritance, but sought, and still seek, to steal a legacy by fraud. These are the unseen *false spirits,* who say they are the creative forces, but they lie! One says, 'I am Jupiter' and another, 'I am Sol Invictus the Unconquered Sun!' They are usurpers, devils who demand reverence, who have their oracles, sorcerers, witches, priestesses and princes. Never do they do that which is good, but always do they seek to deceive and bind. These Fallen Ones fight the true God and how are they unmasked?"

Diocles answered, "Would that I knew? For that is like saying, 'What should I do and how should I believe?' These are questions that have long troubled me!"

She replied, "Ah, The Eternal Good and The Eternal Evil—both have their spokesmen, their counterparts, sent among us. Read and study what these oracles have written! In Metamorphoses, Ovid wrote of Jupiter, whom he says is the King of Heaven, yet he is portrayed as foolish, rash and lustful, the rapist of Europa, Callisto and Semele, and so on. Moses wrote of God, saying that he knew our sorrows and would deliver us from bondage, that he would be our Redeemer. That we might not error unknowingly, He gave Moses commandments, which are given for our happiness and teach us that God is God, with no others before him, that we should rest one day in seven and worship him, that we should honor parents, and not murder, or betray spouse, or steal, or lie, or covet. Ovid's words give men excuse to do evil, to rationalize every debasing action, to follow a depraved father. Moses' words inspire men to do good and emulate the perfect Sire. Now, can you not discern between the fallen and true?

Diocles replied, "I also believe in good and evil, whether seen in the flesh or felt only as spirit, and I think often on these things. Yet we live in this world about us, the world of Rome and Greece! Some of its gods *do* tell us aright! Think of the epigrams of Apollo and Artemis. Think of the oracles Plato and Epictetus!"

Again, the quadriga passed by Arrian, Esta and Michela but began another round, to the consternation of Michela.

Naomi replied, "Oh, that is such a good question! Esta has told me that in the Pantheon there are carnal gods and goddesses and virtuous gods and goddesses, and sometimes the writers of their deeds teach contradictions. She ascribes this to devious scribes! She says we should only follow that which we *remember* to be good, for Esta upholds the doctrine of Socrates, who taught that all learning is recollection—remembering that which we were before taught by the AllFather."

"Well," he answered, "that is helpful, but only in speaking generally. You, Naomi, must believe in an answer that is yet more sure!"

Naomi turned herself about, so that her eyes looked directly into his and said in her young but ardent voice, "Follow Him who has power to save! Which of the gods of Greece or Rome will save you from death?"

He replied, "There is no god who can do such a thing, for when a man is dead, even if his spirit lives on, that is the end of his body, which *is* death, is it not so?"

She exclaimed, "That is *surely* death, but it is not the *end*. Less than one hundred years ago, there truly lived a man, but he was so much more than any other! His name is Jesus, the son of the mortal Mary, the Only Begotten Son of the Immortal Father. From his mother he had power to die and from his Father he had power over death! He was crucified by Rome, because the ruling Jews demanded it of Pilate, governor of Judea. Yet in three days' time, Jesus rose from the dead. His Spirit entered again into its body! This was not seen by a few, but by hundreds! Even the great General of Galilee, Titus Flavius Josephus, the Jew who became a Roman citizen and historiographer wrote of this."

Diocles was astonished and exclaimed, "Ah, this I have never heard before! Say on!"

Naomi replied, "Esta can quote many teachings of philosophers and this dedication of hers has inspired me to also put great sayings into my mind. In his book, *Antiquities of the Jews*, Josephus wrote in book 18:

> 'Now there was about this time Jesus, a wise man, if it
> be lawful to call him a man; for he was a doer of
> wonderful works, a teacher of such men as receive

the truth with pleasure. He drew over to him both many of the Jews and many of the Gentiles. *He was the Christ.*'"

Naomi continued, "Those are the exact words of Josephus, 'He was the Christ!' Now I am Jew, as was Josephus. Christ means Messiah, the One Anointed by Elohim, the Deliverer, and since ancient days our people have looked forward to the coming of the Messiah. Some thought only that such a one would redeem them from the oppression of foreign rule, but that is not the core of our longing. Rather, the Messiah was prophesied to redeem us from the greatest oppressions of all—the oppressions of sin and death!"

"Naomi, please, say on!" he asked of her.

She answered, "Josephus then wrote,

'And when Pilate, at the suggestion of the principal men amongst us, had condemned him to the cross, those that loved him at the first did not forsake him, for *he appeared to them alive again the third day*; as the divine prophets had foretold these and ten thousand other wonderful things concerning him. And the tribe of Christians, so named from him, are not extinct at this day.'[3]

"Now I tell you these things because you have asked them plainly of me. Remember, it is the lawful testimony of the historian raised in station by Titus to become a Roman who declared that *Jesus was restored to life after he was murdered and had been dead three days!* Yet listen carefully. I know these things, not because of the writings of men, though they be as great as Flavius Josephus. I know them

---

3. Flavius Josephus, *Antiquities of the Jews*, Book 18, Chapter 3, 3

because my heart tells me they are true. Christ is not *a* god, He *is* the God of Creation, the Son of the Father Almighty. Any others that claim to rule are false gods."

Diocles said somberly, "It is good you have Hadrian's edict, for without it, Naomi, you would surely die, for who can say such things in this day and not be burned? Yet know this, I am not an emperor, but the power of my arm is strong. I thank you for this—for answering me, though you know so little about me. What power I possess is yours, if ever you are in need and can get word to me."

After this, neither Diocles nor Naomi uttered a word until his charioteer had made yet another round of the track.

Then he broke the silence and said, "Now, we have made nearly five careers. A race in the Circus Maximus is but seven!"

That Diocles would know her friendship did not hinge on any commitment he made regarding *her* convictions, Naomi replied happily, "How can I thank you for this marvelous chariot ride? How I have loved watching your amazing Andalusian stallions! My father trades in most everything, even, at times, in horses. Yet never have I seen any that can be compared to your quadriga!"

He replied eagerly, "What do you say to a final lap of greater speed. A gallop?"

Naomi smiled, "Mmh. How about a trot?"

CHAPTER 15
VITTORIA

A soft light fill'd t' room an there stood a beautiful woman in a'flow'n gown.

Maros

～

In a season since past, Esta hired a genealogista recommended by Arrian. This man, Calvus by name, was a lawyer whose specialty was legalis progenitores, or proving a person's lawful ancestry. This was a most lucrative practice, as proof of bloodline was often a prerequisite for status, station and wealth in the Empire. When she and Naomi met him in the palace courtyard, Esta said to him, "Advocatus Calvus, Arrian speaks highly of you, so highly I may not be able to afford your services!"

Calvus replied, "You are the ward of the Emperor and well known for your literary, linguistic and philosophic attainments, especially for one so young and gracious. Lady Esta, I cannot deny you!"

She replied, "If your charges exceed what I may allot for this venture, I can offer you an exchange."

Esta in Rome

"An exchange, how interesting," he replied. What do you suggest."

"Have you need of a translator in your work?" she asked.

"Always, and it is such a difficult thing to . . . Ah, I see! What a splendid idea! Yes, yes! That is agreed. Now tell me, what can I do for you?"

The maiden handed Calvus a parchment. "Upon this I have written my pedigree, to the best of my knowledge. I confess, in all my studies I should have learned more about my ancestral lines."

"Ah," answered the lawyer, "you would like me to research your family tree, both genus patris and matris?"

Esta answered, "Yes, but that is not all. There is another person, a woman long deceased; I would like you to search out her descent and progeny and have written her name on the bottom of the parchment."

He asked, "Do you think this woman is your relation?"

Esta replied, "I know not, but think it unlikely, as my mama was Celtic and my papa from Italia. While we journeyed from Massilia to Rome, I came across this woman's tomb in Aleria, Corsica. Do you know Celtic?"

"No," was the reply.

"'Fionn màthair mòran,' is more than a name. It is Celtic and means, 'Fionn, mother of many.' There is in the Necropolis of Aleria a statue of a beautiful woman that rises from an ornate sepulcher. That inscription is carved at the base of the sculpture. When I saw it, I wondered, 'A Celt in Corsica? Who was this woman? What did the inscription mean, 'mother of many?' Fionn was certainly a woman of wealth, for her monument was fashioned exquisitely of fine marble. Indeed, if you see it yourself and you look at her effigy long enough, it will seem to you that it is not a likeness only, but is *living* flesh, pure and white! More than this, I cannot say why I seemed drawn to her grave, but there came a feeling into my heart, an aspiration."

"And what was that desire?" Calvus asked in earnest.

"Well," she answered, "that is something quite ethereal and what I ask of you is quite practical."

Calvus replied, "You, Lady Esta, are a most enchanting and beautiful demoiselle. What you ask of me is most interesting. So much so, that I will personally sail to Corsica at my earliest opportunity and see this wonder for myself. Have no fear of my expenses, for this will seem to me as a voyage of leisure and it will cost you not a single drachma. Also, my servants will immediately begin to authoritatively search out your own ancestry."

After her chariot ride with Diocles, Esta received a missive from Calvus, saying he had long since returned from Aleria and desired to see her on the morrow, having learned that which was "remarkable."

Accordingly, Esta and Naomi met with Calvus in the palace garden at the requested hour. After greetings were exchanged, Calvus said, "The statue of Fionn was just as you described it, most beautiful and lifelike, especially when moonlit. I studied it again and again! You may laugh at me if you will, but when I came to an impasse I returned to her tomb in the necropolis. I am certainly no oracle but gazing upon her effigy I seemed mesmerized; then an idea came to mind, which, when tried, produced success."

Esta asked excitedly, "You know who she is then?"

"Most certainly!' he replied. "She was British, the daughter of King Verica, a vassal of Rome."

"A princess?" Esta asked.

"Yes. Her story is extremely interesting. King Verica had been driven from his throne by provinces opposed to Roman rule. Emperor Claudius sent a commander, named Plautius, to Britain to restore the reign of King Verica. On the northern beaches of Gaul, Plautius' troops rebelled, saying they would not fight beyond the limits of the known world. Yet, convinced by an omen they were persuaded and crossed the Oceanus Britannicus.[1] Plautius fought his way north, all the way to the River Tamesis;[2] there he was reinforced by Claudius himself, with a magnificent army equipped with war machines and elephants! Many battles were fought and won. Eleven British kings surrendered at Camulodunum, and a great Roman province was established on the southern extremity of the island. King Verica was reenthroned and Plautius was appointed by the emperor to be its governor.

"Now Verica had a most beautiful daughter, whose countenance was as white as a snowy cloud. Her name was Vittoria, which most certainly was a new name given to her by her sire when his kingdom was restored, for as you know, the name means 'victory.' As a reward, the king gave his daughter to the governor as a most welcome wife, for it is written she was much loved by him. It was Plautius who moved the provincial seat of power to Londonium where he ruled most effectively. Several years later Plautius and Vittoria left Britannia for Rome. Here Plautius was granted an ovation, for the Empire had gained additional territories to the north of his province, in large measure due to his management of the imperial expansion."

Esta interrupted his narrative, "Are you saying that Fionn is the same woman as this Vittoria?"

"Yes! You see, when I was in Aleria and researched the archives and annals, for long has that port city been of importance to the Empire and its records are comprehensive, hence it was an easy matter to find out all about her life on Corsica, for she was a magnanimous lady of substance. Yet, I could find nothing of her origins! She had no birth record in Aleria and there was no mention of her parents. Nothing even of her husband, though I read that she had been married, had children, and so on, but that she was

---

1. The English Channel.
2. Today known as the Thames.

widowed. What to do? I could not guess! Then . . ." he seemed hesitant to continue.

Naomi spoke, saying, "You are a great lawyer, a man of precise order and look for natural solutions, not preternatural. Yet you said that an idea came into your mind as you looked upon the statue. Please continue. You are not in the company of cynics, but two maidens of Massilia. Did not Esta say to you she also had a strange experience when she was in the Necropolis? We cannot then think amiss of you for having a premonition of some sort."

Esta added, "Please tell us all. We shall keep your confidence."

Calvus replied, "Well, it isn't as if I saw anything unusual, except for the uncanny sculpture itself, so living it appeared to be when the moon shone upon it. No, it was the inscription that put me on the right track, ''Fionn màthair mòran,' written in Celtic, as you said. I thought to myself, 'Of course! She was not born in Corsica! Then when did she come to this island and from where?' Of this, there was no record, but I did find records of her that suddenly *began!* Before this, nothing—after this there was much written of her. Fortuitously, I come across a great endowment Fionn had given to a Pelasgian cult of charities, not given to the muses or to dance or fertility rites, as one might expect a cult of the graces to be, but to a most unique domus, a *sanctuary!*"

"What kind of sanctuary?" asked Naomi.

"That I will tell you later. But first," he said, "the nature of the bequest is the thing—it was a great quantity of Atrebate stater, a singular type of coin issued by King Verica of Britannia but still recognized by the Empire. Hence, it was of great worth. In the marketplace of Aleria, it is still in use and these coins are known as Fionns. When I asked a very old woman, a trader, why it was called by that name, she answered, 'Don't you know? All such moneys came to Aleria by the great lady?' 'The Great Lady,' I asked. 'Yes,' said she, 'Hers is the wondrous statue in the Necropolis.'

He gave Esta a little package. "I have brought several of these coins wrapped in this small parchment for you to see."

Coins issued by King Verica 15-42 A.D.

"I thought this was an important clue to Fionn's identity, together with the Celtic inscription and the year Fionn first became known in Aleria."

Esta asked, "What year was that?"

He answered, "817 A.U.C."[3]

She exclaimed, "The year Rome burned!"

"Yes," he said, "set aflame at the command of the insane Nero. Hence, I returned to Rome and with my servants began an intense search of the archives. There is so much from that time, so many claims, so many cases, so much lost property; two-thirds of Rome was destroyed! But my search was constrained by the coins. Was there a connection in these twisted facts? It was then I read in detail

---

3. 817 A.U.C. or Ab urbe condita, 817 years since the founding of Rome in 753 B.C., or 64 A.D.

the history of King Verica, his daughter Vittoria and her marriage to Plautius. Now the former governor of the southern province of Britannia attained the senate when he returned to Rome. His family prospered and Vittoria bore him children, at least six that I could find record of. Then I found the death scroll of Plautius, three years before the fire of Rome. How he died, I cannot yet say. Yet something very strange happened to Vittoria around that time."

"Something strange?" asked Esta.

"It appears," said Calvus, "that she became a Christian! I cannot say this for certain, but there are a number of factors that makes this possible. First, I found court records where Vittoria intervened on behalf of a number of condemned men and women—even a few children—and all were of that accursed sect! These records may be found up to the time of the fire, thereafter, however, they *cease* and no more can be read of the pleadings of this princess of Britannia! At that time, there were also letters written to Vittoria and about her, as also there was official correspondence, for Nero's court had begun an Imperial investigation into her life. One letter describes Vittoria as a lively dame with many children. She was said to be very beautiful, very fair skinned, very *white*, or as you would say in Celtic, *Fionn!*"

"Are you saying . . ." said Esta but was cut off by the lawyer.

"There is more. Of course, we have the evidence that much is written about Vittoria before the fire of Rome and nothing after, and much is written about Fionn after the fire, and nothing before. The coins almost make her identity certain. But then I learned something else. The firstborn of Vittoria was a girl who was given in marriage before her sire died. The man took Vittoria's daughter to his domus *in Massilia!* I have a friend of consequence in that city, who also has the affections of Arrian and the Emperor himself. He is Senator Aléxandros. I immediately sent Aléxandros a missive and asked him if he could identify a daughter of Plautius, a former Governor of

Britannia and a Roman senator until his death. I gave him the approximate date of her leaving Rome for Massilia."

Esta and Naomi were both taken aback with amazement of all that Calvus had said. Esta exclaimed, "And have you heard back from Aléxandros? He is also well known to us, and his words cannot be refuted!"

"Why yes," answered the advocate. "Yesterday I received his epistle and that is why I asked to urgently meet with you. Here is his response." He handed the letter to the maiden.

> "Your request raises questions in my mind, dear Calvus,
>   for that woman still lives in the midst of olive groves
>   and vineyards. She is the old grandmother of Esta, the
>   renowned Lady of Massilia. No doubt, as Esta is
>   honored by the Emperor, you, as a genealogista, have
>   been retained to search out her lineage."

There was more to read, but she could not continue, for tears filled her eyes! Calvus said kindly, "Yes, it is true, dear demoiselle, Vittoria and Fionn are one in the same, and she is *your* great grandmother! Naomi, please read on, for there is more Esta should hear."

Naomi took the parchment from Esta's shaking hands and read:

> "Please use this information carefully, for when I received
>   your letter I found, easily enough, the record of Plau-
>   tius' daughter's arrival in Massilia. Then I came
>   across Imperial correspondence. Evidently, Plautius
>   had died by this time and his wife, Vittoria, was gone
>   from Rome. It was thought then that she might have
>   'fled' to Massilia, for the Court of Nero was searching
>   for her. Nonetheless, Vittoria had not come to our
>   land; that is certain. It would seem that such an

*inquest would defame the daughter, at least in her
own mind, but in our land we thought Nero a tyrant
of the worst order. This is supposition on my part, but
I have known the grandam for many years and until I
searched the records to address your question, I did
not know of her illustrious parents. Hence, I would
assume that Esta is also not aware of her matriarchal
blood line."*

"Thank you, Naomi," said Calvus. "His last comment satisfies my own curiosity as to why you had me search out things that otherwise should have been known to you. Now, Naomi, you asked me what type of sanctuary it was that received the British coins. There are domus journal entries that a great many persons came to the sanctuary, yet there are no records of their arriving at Dianæ Portus. Hence, they were *smuggled* ashore. I found record of more than two hundred and eighty people who were given sanctuary in the Pelasgian domus and two thirds of these were children.

"The commander of the Roman forces at Aleria made a written inquiry into the sudden expansion of residents at this domus, as it could not be hid in so small a community. He was answered by a priestess of the order that they were driven from the mountains by tribal wars, but that they would not be a burden upon Rome, for the Lady Fionn was providing for their care. Now Fionn was known to the commander, for she had built a fine house in Aleria, and although exquisitely beautiful was known as a widow of propriety. Of this, his scribe made particular notice. There were letters between the commander and the priestess. These I have also personally read. He was made aware of the great many children that had come to her sanctuary. As you know, Roman law forbids the housing of orphans, for those deprived of parents must find work or be adopted by relatives. The priestess answered that none of these children were

257

derelict, for all had been adopted. By whom, he inquired. By 'Fionn,' came the response 'màthair mòran, mother of many!'"

Calvus continued, "I found one other official letter of inquiry in the archives of Aleria—from the Court of Nero. It sought to find Roman Christians, whom, it said, had escaped justice after setting fire to the city. Did the commander suspect Fionn and the Pelasgian priestess were harboring these fugitives? We will never know. Nonetheless, formally he stated that no such persons had come to Aleria. Of course, dear maiden, I do not blame the man for being taken by so great a lady, for her beauty yet lives in you!

"Still, I am pleased to bring to your knowledge such an illustrious heritage, for your great grandfather, Plautius, was among the most noble Romans of his era. However, it saddens me to know or, at least, so it seems, that your great grandam was tainted by that odious malignancy called Christianity."

This last statement caused Naomi to involuntarily shudder, and she immediately lowered her eyes, lest Calvus should perceive her reaction. Naomi supposed he must not know of her station and the Emperor's declaration. Yet, she felt his eyes upon her as Calvus added, "Though persecution may not be lawful or rather, I should say that although Vittoria was never prosecuted as a Christian, her association with those people is nonetheless a detestable blemish on her character. It was good she was never found and was not tried in absentia, for among the court records I found damning testimony."

Esta was overwhelmed, rejoicing in her heritage while recoiling at his harsh epithets. With an unsteady voice, she asked, "What disparaging evidence did you find?"

Calvus answered, "In my opinion, it is not conclusive; the confession was made in consequence of threatened torture and hence is not incontrovertible. Also, I find the confessor's profession dubious and believe the man was suffering from delusions. The admission was made by a supposed Christian named Simon who was one among many accused of setting fire to Rome. He was a practitioner of magical arts and was also a Samaritan, a people at odds with the Jews. Nor does it appear that he was allied to the Jewish-Christians of Rome, a considerable populace who lived in poor quarters near the Circus Maximus. This is what I found in Nero's court records."

He handed the document to Naomi to read, for Esta was not yet in control of her emotions. She read:

Interrogator: What was the name of the man who incited his fellow Christians to torch Rome? Say his name and it shall be well with you. Refuse and your own body will be set ablaze!

Simon of Samaria: Nay! Do not kill me! Do not burn me! Please! I will tell you all!

Interrogator: Say on.

Simon of Samaria: It was not a man, but a woman and she is of high station!

Interrogator: You must say her name and how it is you came by this knowledge.

Simon of Samaria: Know you not of the esoteric disciplines of this cultus? I am the foremost magus of these mysteries and possess knowledge that was not heard by hearing and not seen by seeing. How can I then tell you, for you will not believe me? Yet, I beseech you, burn me not!

Interrogator: Say her name and how it is she had the power to effect such an outcome!

Simon of Samaria: She is Princess Vittoria of Britannia, baptized by Paul, the Christian Apostle, who even now is in Rome. Though there be many who are called "saints" in this city, few have such high station as to be Paul's partisan.

Calvus said, "Thank you Naomi. I know this is difficult for both of you. There was one other avowal, given by one of the so called 'saints' that corroborated a major point of Simon's testimony, that of Vittoria's being baptized by Paul. Perhaps you know that baptism is a formal initiation into the discipleship of Christ. However, this witness died while being tortured and, in any case, a baptism evidently entails no legal contract. Terms are not written and hence not signed. It is purely a symbolic gesture designed for the illiterate populace, so no other record could be found to establish the truth of this alleged act.

"Now as a princeps advocatus I must say I think little of Simon's words. For these reasons: he was likely antagonistic, he does not assert that he actually knew Vittoria or the infamous Paul, he was a braggart, a craven, a magician, and admits that he neither heard nor saw the evidence he gives, but admits only to some enigma that he derides as being unbelievable to the Roman mind.

Calvus before the Roman Senate

"Still the accusation was made and, following the precedent of such cases, condemnation would have followed. Nonetheless, Vittoria was never brought to trial and was also not prosecuted in absentia, likely a result of the favorable bias jurists had in regard to Plautius, who was then deceased."

Calvus handed another parchment to Esta, saying, "I have prepared this official document, duly recorded, which validates your heritage as a direct descendant of a Roman Governor and Senator and also a direct descendant of King Verica, a vasal monarch of prominence. Of these failed efforts to connect Vittoria to Christianity and the burning of Rome, I have said nothing—not only because of my regard for Aléxandros and yourself, but because it was never fully proven and could only cause a blemish on your otherwise scrupulous life."

Esta thanked him as best as she could. Seeing her emotional state, Calvus thought he understood and left the two maidens in the garden, satisfied that Esta would forever be in his debt for doing so grand a thing.

They returned to their apartments and Esta lay down upon her bed. She closed her eyes and envisioned Maros as he spoke his final words to her:

"Think not t'at I've lost my senses, for though I'm a dying, yet 'tis sure t'at what I tell ya is true! Last night, Ep soon fell fast asleep, non'less *I saw a spirit*, such as ya spoke of. A soft light fill'd t' room an there stood a beautiful woman in a'flow'n gown. Said she, 'Save my daughter' an she pointed towards t' garden. I jumped 't my feet an no sooner done than t' spirit turned an flew into t' night." Then she remembered he coughed and was quiet for a moment, then said, "I oby'ed, not know'n what I should do, but look'n down I saw a torch fall frum its bearer's hand. So's I grabbed my staff an run t' gate. 'Twas then we fought!"

"Ah," Esta soliloquized, "It was then Maros fought my wicked brother and truly saved my life but lost his own! Yet, Maros saw that which I have longed to see and now that desire is magnified many-fold. He saw Vittoria and heard her voice! By the faithful hand of Maros, *she* saved me. Oh, my own dear la reiremenina![4] Oh, that I too could see her spirit and that she would speak to me!"

So saying these words, her eyes closed and Esta fell into a deep sleep.

---

4. Occitan for great grandmother.

CHAPTER 16

THE JOURNEY

"If you do not find more there than you have here, return quickly."

Esta

∾

Esta began translating for Calvus at once. However, not before he agreed to one proviso: she would not provide a finished translation on any document *she* felt was dishonest or persuasive of wrong doing. Initially Calvus would not agree to this, saying he would not have his works judged by someone so young. However, Esta would not negotiate and proposed a trial. "Try me," she said. "What have you to lose? If you don't like my work, don't use it!"

So pleased was he, not only with her accuracy but the maiden literally transformed foreign documents in the process, clarifying, simplifying, elucidating and adding additional arguments to support evidence. Soon he was using Esta's talents where translations were not required and was immediately praised by his patrons, as if *his* genius was elevated.

Esta enjoyed the work and also felt it very informative. She soon learned that Calvus was active with anti-Christian benefactors. Yet she would work on these cases, if she could in good conscience, hoping to diffuse aggression. For instance, there was one extremely powerful senator, whose patronage advanced Calvus' wealth inordinately, who learned, through Calvus, that not only were his wife's parents of the "hateful cult" but that she also worshiped her Lord in secrecy.

In Esta's presence, the husband demanded that Calvus write up an ultimatum to his wife, threatening divorce if she did not abandon her conviction and provide the names of all others she met with covertly.

Without gaining Calvus' advance consent, Esta engaged the red-faced husband, politely but directly, saying, "You must look at the whole of the matter, and so must I if I am to frame your demands. Will you answer a few questions?" Calvus was greatly dismayed that his aide should take such liberties, but said nothing. The man nodded consent. Esta asked, "Before you learned of this, was your marriage a happy one?"

"Why, yes—better than others, that is why . . ."

Esta cut him off. "Was your wife argumentative, speaking against your own convictions, for you seem to be a man of strong opinion?"

"Why no, that is why I am so surprised at this!"

"Does she manage your domus well?"

"Yes!"

"Is she a good mother to your children?"

"Yes, but surely she is perverting them with this . . ."

Again, Esta interrupted him. "Have any of your children shown any disdainful attitudes towards Rome or the Emperor, or towards the rites and traditions you hold sacred?"

He sighed, "Oh, no. On the contrary. Looking back, I must say she only speaks openly of things of that sort that she must also support, citing certain sensible maxims of the gods and so forth." Esta thought of her own mother. He continued, "However, how do I know what she tells them in private?"

"Are your children open with you and do you care for their regard?"

"Yes, yes."

"Do you feel they are hiding things from you?"

"No," he said exasperatingly.

"A man of your exalted station must speak aright and so must his companion in our fastidious society! Has your wife ever spoken or acted inappropriately among friends or when visiting the senate?"

"No," he admitted.

Esta lightly touched his arm as she said, "It seems to me that you have an exemplary wife, in your own opinion, save for her Christianity. Would not a divorce openly defame her in the eyes of your peers; would it not also negatively affect your children?" Without waiting for an answer, she continued, "Have you considered that perhaps she is such a good wife because of her convictions? She evidently loves her homeland and is indebted to you and our Imperial head for the liberties and bounties she enjoys, true?"

He nodded assent.

"Then you may think about an alternative to such an edict. You may choose to abandon the idea of confrontation. You may choose to do nothing. You may ask yourself questions: 'Do I really want to be quit of her? Though I have great power over her body, do I have absolute power over her mind? If I force her to say things she believes false, will that change her? Perhaps, but would it lift her or degrade her?

Now, you cannot say 'I want her as she was before' and then demand that she change what she *is*. Is it not true, that many of her kind have endured death before denying what you would have her deny? We may proceed to do as you ask, but then *are you willing to see her suffer?*"

"But what if she is found out?" he asked as if bewildered.

Esta answered assuredly, "It would not be our doing, for Calvus holds strict confidences, unless you authorize him to publish the matter. Yet, it is true, she may at some future time be 'found out.' Consider, however, that for this long period, you, her husband, knew nothing of it. Nonetheless, if that time should come, deal with it then. Perhaps you will know much more by that time and will view things differently. Remember, you will always have Calvus as your advocate and his only interest is your welfare. At worst, you will not now endure humiliation, but will face that dilemma at a later time, postponing the pain. At best, you may never experience loss but only gain from this course."

Calvus could hardly believe the outcome of this short conversation! The man put his hands to his face and simply cried. At length he *embraced* Calvus and exclaimed, "Surely, good man, you have trained Esta well! It was wise using her lips to say such things to me, for her manner is gracious and her persuasions excellent. I *do* love my wife and cannot understand myself in this matter, for my wrath was greater than my reason! Never did Esta challenge the rightness of my wrong course, but drew from me that which I know to be true. Now hear me. All that you have found out, all that we have spoken of must be kept in strict confidence. I feel that all will be well. If that is not so, I will not hold you to blame!"

Calvus replied, "Of course, that you can be sure of!" and said nothing more, for he could think of nothing else to say.

His patron replied, now smiling a little, "Hah! What an advocate you are! Had I proceeded it would have surely cost me a fortune. Now

ESTA

then, let me pay you well for such expert counsel and we both shall prosper."

When the patron left, Calvus said only, "He thought it was I who had you say what you did that I would be left free to speak against it, should he have been angered by it? Brilliant! If ever you speak amiss, I will simply upbraid you and disclaim you as an unknowing maiden! Consider yourself redeemed from paying my expenses for searching out your ancestry. I quite enjoyed sailing to Dianæ Portus and learning of the intrigues of Nero and that persecuted band, and must thank you for it. From now on I will pay for your services and no advocate in Rome shall pay you better!"

She noticed that, for the first time, Calvus referred to Christians, not with derision but as "that persecuted band."

As the seasons passed, life was good for Esta and her friends. Michela sang not only in the theatre but in great houses and temples. No one could have supposed that only a few years before the astounding singer of Carmina worked in a bakery. Arrian continued his work in the senate and began writing a series of books entitled *Bithyniaca*, which he and Esta often discussed. Whenever Diocles was in Rome, he and Arrian would take the three maidens riding along the River Tiberis or to a fine restaurant or to some other social event. Although gracious to all, Michela was easily annoyed when his attentions favored Naomi. Yet as Esta was often occupied with Calvus, whose advocacy was no longer genealogista, but foreign trade and affairs of the Senate, Naomi spent many of her days in Ostia working with her father.

Hence, Michela was happy indeed when Diocles came to the city and Naomi was absent. She was delighted when the charioteer suggested they again take the horses out, and this time make it a two-day trip with an overnight stay at a quaint inn. Arrian, Esta and Michela cleared their schedules, readily accepting the invitation.

Michela was the most excited of all on the appointed day. As they

269

mounted, she exclaimed, "What is our destination? I understand the ride to Lake Albano is very pleasant and the inn at Alba Longa is close by and very quaint."

"Nay," said Diocles happily. "'Tis true that way is lovely but too brief for a two-day outing. Rather, we shall ride along the River Tiberis to Ostia. Imagine Naomi's surprise when she sees us!"

Esta laughed and responded, "Oh, Diocles that is a most considerate and wonderful idea! Always she comes to Rome to be with us. How thoughtful that we ride to see her!" As she said this, Esta noticed the disappointed look on Michela's face. Nonetheless, the maiden was ever attentive to the strong athlete during the half-day ride to Ostia.

Naomi was truly delighted with their coming and thought nothing unusual until Michela said quietly to her, "Diocles races in Rome more than ever before, so anxious is he to be with *me*." Nonetheless, Naomi did not alter her behavior towards Diocles or any of her friends.

When they were alone, Esta told Naomi *about* some of her experiences with Calvus, but never revealed details. The "Christian Problem," as some of the senators called it, was a common topic especially at sumptuous dinners. Much to the dismay of certain of his clients and especially one promiscuous politician, a Senator Impius, Calvus made certain that Esta would not be asked to sup with patrons if it was to be a licentious gathering or if Christian humiliation would be displayed. Calvus explained to the elite of Rome that as Esta was a devotee of Artemis, she had vowed not to participate in anything vulgar. Rather than causing difficulties, this only raised their regard for her. Still, Esta gleaned a great deal of information regarding the overall treatment of Christians, arrests, prosecutions and executions. As Naomi saw Esta's effort to help wherever she could and in such a manner as to turn hearts away from the evil of persecution, her love for Esta grew beyond measure.

As for Esta's work with Calvus, it came to an abrupt end when the Emperor returned from his travels abroad.

Trajan was a much different ruler than was Hadrian, his successor. By acts of war, Trajan had sought to continually expand the Roman Empire. This was particularly true of Parthia, a great dominion that Trajan thought was absolutely conquered, for he had seized Babylon and the Parthian capital of Ctesiphon. The Roman senate had even given the emperor the new title of "Parthicus!" Nonetheless, a vast number of Parthian troops had fled from the lowlands of Mesopotamia only to regroup in the mountains of Zagros. From there they began to effectively fight against the Romans, inflicting heavy losses. In the midst of this crisis, Trajan suffered a stroke and died.

Hadrian, the new emperor, wisely sought to end conflict, coalesce power and secure his massive dominions. He declared, "Areas that cannot be defended, should be declared liberated," and hence, the Emperor returned control of local governments to nations he sought to make his allies, not his enemies.[1]

Still there were many uprisings and Hadrian traveled extensively to bring peace and reconciliation to his diverse provinces. He was not adverse to using absolute force, as he did with the rebellion of the Jews in Jerusalem, but he preferred the use of *reason, gifts and diplomacy.*

Returning to Rome, Hadrian met with Arrian, who apprized him of the state of the city. Then the scholar recommended a most unusual solution to assist him in the reconciliation of diverse dominions, from Heracleopolis, to the southeast, to Cappadocia to the east, to Tingitana and Felicitas Iulia to the west, and to Londinium to the

---

1. https://www.zocalopublicsquare.org/2021/09/09/roman-emperor-hadrian-unwinnable-war/ 2022

far northwest. To this Hadrian replied sardonically, "You believe, Arrian, that there is a *single* solution for so many problems?"

Emperor Hadrian riding in Triumph

Arrian replied confidently, "In a way of speaking, yes! I do not mean that one remedy will resolve a thousand dilemmas. Rather, I believe one *person* may do more for you than a thousand others, though they be the finest diplomats in the Empire."

"That," said Hadrian, "*is* a staggering claim. When shall I meet him? For surely, I know of no one individual who could possibly have such skill!"

"Her—I speak of a lady, a maiden and you do know her, but not as I do!"

"What? No more riddles!" asked Hadrian, growing impatient.

"She is *Esta,*" he answered. "In three years' time, since her arrival in Rome, her influence has grown immeasurably, yet few are aware of it."

"How is that possible?" asked the Emperor.

Arrian explained, "Her work is thought to be the genius of Calvus, the advocate. The maiden has become the power behind the numerous and acclaimed works of that arrogant man. Since your leaving he has become the most sought after advocate of the senate! Read these!"

He handed the emperor several conclusive parchments. When Hadrian finished reading, he exclaimed, "My friend, you have spoken aright! Never have I read arguments written so well, so persuasive. Why, the writer tacitly calls out Senator Impius Paetus,[2] known to you and I as a man who can only be moved to action by bribery! Then, expertly recites implicit and explicit needs favoring trade with Bithynia—then demonstrates, with precedents implemented in other dominions, how increased commerce in Bithynia would promote a prosperous peace. Hah! This is excellent! Conclusively, the writer defines the far more expensive military alternative, stating truly that Bithynia is the key to stability in Mysia, Paphlagonia, and

---

2. Paetus: literally, squinty-eyed.

would reinforce our province of Galatia! Why this measure, although intended to enrichen Calvus' trade coffers, is exactly what is needed from Mesopotamia to Armenia. What was the vote?"

Arrian answered, "A conclusive majority! Even Impius approved the measure and without his usual inducement—that I verified. Think not this proves the virtuosity of Calvus, though his name is there affixed. I know for a certainty that this is the work of Esta!"

"Hah!" said Hadrian, "I can almost hear her voice as I read these words. Never shall I forget when first I met the most unusual prodigy. Say on."

Arrian replied, "My king, I believe in the providence of the gods. Esta has been sent to you, *not* that you might raise her station but that she might raise yours!"

Arrian was silent for a moment to allow the Emperor to consider these words thoroughly, then he continued, "Command me that I must tell Calvus that no longer will Esta translate and write for him, for now she is in the service of the Empire. Then, instruct Esta yourself, in every matter of import, in all you desire that she should know. She will quickly assimilate knowledge and understanding of each situation. What is more, Esta will *listen* to your words and will *honor* your desired end. Appoint her as your amanuensis[3] and tell her to write your words as if given of the gods! I tell you, Hadrian, Esta will phrase things in your own style but with added expression. Albeit she is yet a maiden, there is no Roman scribe more eloquent than Esta, no other who can put things in so grand a way nor state things so convincingly. What is more, Esta inherently promotes peace, finding common ground in divergent soil. Olympus has sent Hadrian his own Athena! Esta will spring from your head as surely as did the goddess Athena emerge full-grown from the head of Zeus!"

Hadrian listened attentively to Arrian, his longtime friend and

---

3. Secretary, scribe, ghost writer.

able advisor, who pressed unrelentingly, "Yours is the might to subdue factions, increase the commerce of the Empire and construct dominions of peace and power. No other ploy will so readily assist in so great an effort than combining your strength with the ken of the Maiden of Massilia! Know this also, Esta will take no glory unto herself. Never have I seen such a one! It seems as if nothing in this world can move her off center. Never is she too impressed or too eager. She has become rich, but in no way is she indulgent! There is no scholar, scribe, or philosopher that is Esta's equal, yet she is humble, though not submissive, and seeks ever to learn. It is strange! It is as though she not only comes to us from Mount Olympus but, having walked its golden halls, finds nothing on earth comparable to the perfection she has elsewhere seen."

Hadrian was silent for a time, and then said, "You, Arrian, are a true friend and also one who seeks no honors. Hah! I heard you published a recent history, again of Alexander, but this time you did so anonymously, as if you could hide the style of your writing or the manner of it. It is superb! And now you commend another to me before yourself! Well, I agree with you. Speak with Calvus. Give me a week at Tivoli, then bring Esta to see me. Also, her honest companion, Naomi. To do as you say, Esta will need to travel with my entourage and will need to have her friend with her."

"I will do so," said Arrian, "Oh, there is one other thing you should know about Esta. Calvus came to know her because she desired to learn more of her ancestry. She is a direct descendant of King Verica and may be properly called a Princess of Britannia. This is well attested."

The emperor laughed, "Amazing! Then I think she will be excited to travel with Vibia and myself to the roots of her heritage. In the spring I shall leave Rome, sail to Massilia, thence overland to

Lugdunum,[4] Augusta Vindelicorum,[5] to Cetium,[6] to Colonia Agrippina and thence to the north shore of Gaul, then sail to Londinium, Britannia."[7]

Esta and Naomi spent the winter season at the Imperial Palace in Tivoli where Esta sat frequently with the emperor and his advisors, with Naomi helping afterwards scribing copies. Little time was left the maidens to visit with their friends. Occasionally, Arrian and Diocles called at the new palace, but never did Michela accompany them. So it was that as spring approached, Esta took a carriage to Rome to see her, in the company of four guardsmen, as Vibia recommended. She found Michela at the Theatre of Marcellus, rehearsing for a play where she was featured as the lead singer.

"Michela," said Esta, "very soon Naomi and I are leaving with the Emperor to sail to Massilia, as we have said. From there we shall begin a long overland journey through Gaul and Germania and will ultimately sail to Britannia. I have asked Hadrian if he would allow me take you as far as Massilia where arrangements could be made to take you to your family in Narbonensis. He not only approves of this, but he told me I may say to you that when you desire to return to Rome, you may do so as you please as his charge." She gave a parchment to Michela. "Present this to any imperial captain at any port and you will be given passage to Ostia, with an attendant, for it is not advisable that you travel alone. I know this has long been your desire!"

Michela looked at the parchment, signed by Hadrian's signet and was taken aback. "Thank you, my dear friend for this," she said. "But

---

4. Present day Lyon, France.
5. Present day Augsburg, Germany.
6. Present day Sankt Pölten, Austria.
7. Travels of Hadrian, https://i0.wp.com/followinghadrian.com/wp-content/uploads/2022/08/0.The-travels-of-Hadrian-and-the-Roman-empire-c.-125-FH.png?ssl=1, 2022

I cannot leave Rome. My presence is needed, for I am to sing at many festivals and plays. Also . . ."

"Also," Esta finished her saying, "there is Diocles? Ah, I fear, my friend that your devotions for him are greater than his are for you. You've heard what he says about marriage, that he still must race in many lands, but that someday—and there is an end to his talk of a family. Listen to me, Michela, I long to see my brothers and sisters again and especially my old grandmother, if yet she lives. Blood ties are more important to me than ever I knew, ever since Aleria."

"Hah!" Michela laughed, "Ever since your brother almost stole you away to Jaca—that made you love your family?"

Esta knew she had blundered, for never had she told Michela that which Naomi had long known. She answered, "No, that was also when Eponi truly became our adopted grandmother; it was at that time I began to long to know more about my own lineage. Michela, you don't know how or why you were separated from those who should be closest to you. This is an opportunity that may never come again! Take it! Go and find your kindred. Return to them a lady of importance, a singer of Rome. Stay for a season and if you do not find more there than you have here, return as quickly as you desire! Soon thereafter you will hear of Diocles when he races again in the Circus Maximus. Pick up with him where you leave off now; there is little that will change in his life for years to come!"

Michela answered, "What you say may not be true. When you and Naomi are gone, then Diocles will see me differently. Then I will not be just one of 'the three maidens,' but he will see me for myself! When you return to Rome you shall find me a married woman, whose husband is the heroic charioteer and I will yet be more renowned as the greatest singer of Rome. What I say *is* possible. Together we shall rise above our class and our happiness shall be boundless!"

Esta offered no more advice to Michela but wished her every happiness.

In three weeks' time, a company of over two hundred left the Imperial Palace at Tivoli, led and followed by a host of legionary. Among the imperial entourage were engineers, scribes, architects, artisans, skilled carpenters, masons, bakers, maids and, of course, two maidens, Esta and Naomi. They were especially honored, for Hadrian invited them to ride with Vibia and himself in his regal carpentum.[8] Hadrian was ecstatic to once again commence a great journey, for he loved to travel far more than to stay at residence in his palace, though it was the most luxurious in the world. He said to Esta, "My dear, you cannot truly be well learned until you are well traveled. You will see wonders and perhaps experience a few privations, but shall be better off because of them. Already your influence has been keenly felt in the Empire, though few beyond my counselors know of it. My thoughts and orders, put in words by you, have largely settled affairs to the east and south of Italia. Yet there is much to be done in Germania and Britannia. What say you?"

Esta laughed, "We are ready, are we not Naomi, and will be pleased to ride astride at your side when the road is too rough for a carriage!"

Naomi added smiling, "for that matter, to walk if the path becomes too steep to ride!"

At this, Vibia protested.

---

8. An elegant four wheeled carriage with leather strap suspension, spacious and richly decorated.

CHAPTER 17
BELDAM

"After the most straitest sect of our religion I lived a Pharisee . . .
Why should it be thought a thing incredible with you, Agrippa, that God
should raise the dead?
. . . I verily thought with myself, that I ought to do many things contrary to
the name of Jesus of Nazareth.
Which thing I also did in Jerusalem: and many of the saints did I shut up
in prison, having received authority from the chief priests; and when they
were put to death, I gave my voice against them.
And I punished them oft in every synagogue, and compelled them to
blaspheme; and being exceedingly mad against them, I persecuted them
even unto strange cities.
Whereupon as I went to Damascus with authority and commission from
the chief priests,
At midday, O king, I saw in the way a light from heaven, above the
brightness of the sun . . ."[1]
Paul

---

1. Acts 26

The Emperor's ship was a floating palace, complete with private quarters, heated baths, a massive covered deck roofed with terracotta tiles, supported by ornate columns and floored with mosaics. Although designed for deep waters, it sailed mostly within sight of the shoreline and was accompanied by a fleet of triremes, quadriremes and the massive quinqueremes. The weather was propitious and the voyage from Ostia to Massilia required but six days. Vibia loved to play board games, including Latrones, Scripta, and Tabula and found Naomi an excellent companion in this pastime. Esta was occupied with writing dispatches, decrees and epistles for the Emperor bound for far and diverse destinations, including Aleria, Caralis, Caesarea, Olisipo, Brigantium, Legio, Aquitania, Tarraco, Colonia Agrippina, Mogontiacum, Cetium, Londinium, Camulodunum, Eboracum, and Lugdunum. Some of this correspondence were orders of preparation concerning the present journey. Most of this work, however, was the business of operating the western provinces of the Roman Empire.

One stop was made in Genua. The Empress went ashore to see the local sights, accompanied by Naomi and the Imperial Guard. This was Naomi's second visit to the city and a grander adventure than the first, for Vibia treated her as a daughter. They chatted constantly and laughed a great deal. They did what might be called shopping, though never did Naomi see an exchange of coins for clothing or other items they acquired, and she was left to wonder whether a steward afterwards made payment or if it was simply expected of local merchants to provide wares to the Empress. As the day went by, she concluded it must be the former, for the acquisitions were enormous and every store keeper was overjoyed with their visit. Hence, Naomi thought, payment of some type must be made.

Esta stayed aboard ship with the Emperor who sumptuously entertained dignitaries of Genua. To her surprise, Hadrian introduced her not as his amanuensis, or his officialis scriba, but rather as "Princess Esta Verica of Britannia, Consiliarius Imperialis Romae."[2] Such an honor was totally unexpected. Indeed, Esta did not know that Hadrian was aware of her lineage, for Arrian did not tell her what he had told the Emperor. This introduction became customary whenever the maiden was introduced thereafter. Nonetheless, her duties were unchanged, although she noticed much more deference was given her by the luminaries who constantly vied for Hadrian's attention than she formerly received.

In Massilia, Esta and Naomi were finally given time of their own. The Emperor and Empress were engaged in approving the final plans for their overland journey and a week was given the maidens to visit with their friends and family. They called first on Aléxandros, to whom they were so indebted for the help and kindnesses he had given them. When he saw them, the senator was amazed at how time had enhanced their beauty. They were fourteen when he had last seen them and now they were seventeen years of age and were both exquisite in form and dress. Formerly, Naomi looked much younger than her age and was as thin as a reed. Still slender, the Jewess had become remarkably feminine. So it was that as Aléxandros escorted the two maidens around Massilia, both to see familiar faces and to meet new friends, the eyes of all men, young and old, followed the two demoiselles with animated admiration.

When Esta asked Aléxandros to arrange a carriage to take them to her old villa, for it was growing late, he replied, "Would that I could take you, but unfortunately my presence is required elsewhere this evening, for I did not know of your coming. Nonetheless, I will

---

2. Imperial Counselor to Rome.

have Ophelos, the Procurator Archivi[3] of Massilia, take you. He will be most obliging."

Esta asked, "How do you know? He also may be engaged. Let us trouble no one without notice, but let me hire a carriage."

"I assure you," Aléxandros replied laughing, "Ophelos or a hundred other young men would do battle to be your escort! Hah, there he is now." A tall man of fair complexion and lightly colored hair, not yet thirty, was then leaving the senate house walking towards them. Aléxandros motioned for him to join them. As he drew near, he said, "Senator, I have been looking for you! Everyone is talking about the Maiden of Massilia and her lady companion, that they have returned to our city, and if I were to find them I must first find you!"

"True!" chortled Aléxandros. "Nor can anyone so much as speak to them without my express consent, for they are my sole charges!"

Ophelos replied smiling, "Your sole charges? Then I must inform the Emperor and Empress immediately."

"Oh!" Esta exclaimed, suddenly concerned, "Have they sent for us?"

"No, no," said Ophelos, "I was but jesting—but that I wanted to meet you is no jest."

"Stop that," said Aléxandros, smiling.

"Stop what?" said Ophelos.

"Speaking to the maidens, for you have not been introduced," said Aléxandros. Then he said formally, "Princess Esta Verica of Britannia, Consiliarius Imperialis Romae and Domina Naomi Romae, formerly of Massilia, may I introduce you to my over confident friend, Ophelos, your carriage driver who will take you to your ancestral villa."

"Oh, that would be my pleasure! Excuse me," he said, "I will

---

3. Manager of the archives.

return shortly with the senatorial carpentum!" So saying, he left them without further comment and without waiting for the maidens to greet him.

"Impetuous fellow," said Aléxandros, "but an excellent man. I think you will enjoy his company, for he is a scholar. Although from Massilia, he spent nine years in Greece before returning last year. Hence, Ophelos knows little about you, but I would trust him with my life."

It felt strange for Esta and Naomi to revisit old sights, having been gone for over three years. Ophelos was much calmer when he returned with the carriage and almost concealed his excitement, for never had he such beautiful passengers. Naomi asked him about his experiences in Greece. He answered affably and told of several adventures, none overstated. Then he asked the maidens about their friendship, their childhood years and of Rome. Esta was impressed that he did not ask a single question about the Emperor or the Empress. When they reached the villa, Esta noted sadly that without Maros' care the olive groves and the vineyards were not as lush as in former days. Still her old home was very lovely to look upon.

Esta had not sent notice of their coming. Her second eldest brother stood in the doorway to the courtyard, having heard the carpentum approach. Esta said to their escort, "Ophelos, we have not told you of a tragedy that befell our home before our leaving, which truly was the cause of it. Know only the offender is dead, as are my parents. As I know not how my family will receive us, please wait. We shall find the matter out, for I long to see my brothers, sisters and especially my grandmother. If all is well, we shall send for you to join us. Perhaps we shall stay. If not, we would ask that you take us to an inn. Would this uncertain plan cause you any difficulty?"

Ophelos was taken aback by this sad summary but replied submissively, saying, "Have no thought of me, for it is a pleasant evening. I will walk along the palisade and look out to sea. When I am needed, call out and I shall come." He helped the maidens step down, bowed and silently left their company.

The brother starred at them, saying nothing, for he did not know who would be calling in the senate carpentum. Not until they had nearly reached the portico did he exclaim unbelievingly, "Esta? Naomi? Can it really be you?"

"Yes," his sister replied.

He embraced both maidens with more tenderness than either expected. "La menina told us you would come back before she died and here you are! She can walk only with our aid but her mind and tongue are as sharp as ever. We are about to enjoy the evening repast. Your attendant is no commoner. Please invite him to join us as well."

Esta replied, "Oh, it is wonderful that grandam still lives! May we also abide for an evening or two? We would be glad to sleep, as in former days, on the balcony."

"Of course!" he replied.

Soon all were gathered to sup. So congenial were they, one to another, and especially towards the two maidens that in light of Esta's words, Ophelos could not perceive what difficulty they had endured. Nor had he heard anything from Aléxandros or the other senators of the family's misfortune.

At last, her brother asked Esta if she would be comfortable in telling that which had befallen herself and Naomi since their hurried departure from Massilia. Notwithstanding Ophelos presence, Esta told all, with the exception of the Vision of Fionn given Maros and her discovery of their grandmother's regal lineage. From the youngest to that most elderly woman, they listened in rapt suspense to her every word.

When Esta described the ramming of the Jacaian ship by the Roman Trireme and the horrible death of their eldest brother, they listened silently. Of course, they knew of this from the missive sent by Aléxandros regarding the passing of the legacy of the domus, but the awful event did not come alive in their minds until they heard Esta describe the sinking of the vessel in vivid detail. Nonetheless, it was evident that Esta felt sorrow for his death and more especially that he died without hope of redemption, for contrary to the maxims, he thought more of riches than honor. Of his murdering their parents, she said nothing.

Naomi tenderly added her thoughts to the narrative, explaining how she felt when Maros and Eponi died and how she was more amazed by the Emperor than she was of the splendor of Rome, for Hadrian had called her "daughter."

At times the family cried and at other times they laughed with delight, so animated were the two maidens in the telling of their incredible story. When they finished, Esta said to their host, "Papa and mama left me a small heritage."

"Yes, of course," her brother answered, "I have it for you."

She replied, "If it is needed to help sustain the groves and vineyards, please use it for that purpose."

He responded happily, "The first year was difficult, but we all worked hard and rejected the offers of the money lenders. This last year was prosperous indeed and we have remained debt free. All the while, I kept your inheritance apart from our trade and have the whole of it for you, including mother's necklace redeemed by Eitan, which he sent to me by courier after you were safely in Rome."

Esta answered sincerely, "My heart is full of gratitude for your diligence and kindness. May I ask what has become of the widow who once was our sister?"

"Strange it is," said her living brother, "that after the magistrates of Massilia conferred our sire's legacy upon me, causing her absolute disinheritance and this to her utter horror, for the care of her children was hers alone—it was then that a representative of Senator

Aléxandros, in effect, dried her tears, for he gave the unfortunate mother a lawful legacy of a considerable sum. This, he said, did not come from our sire, nor even from our eldest brother, who had done such wicked things as to cause her ruin, were it not for this unexpected bequest. He also explained that a covert enquiry exonerated her of any involvement in her husband's schemes and evil designs. Hence, with the legacy she might reside in Massilia in honor. This she has done and lives with her young family not far from here. Have you, dear sister, any knowledge of this mysterious legacy? I have since asked Aléxandros of it, but he would tell me nothing."

A feeling of intense joy filled Esta's heart, for her desires had been fulfilled by that good man—to the blessing of an otherwise poor widowed mother. She answered, "Oh, I am so happy to hear such tidings, but I am afraid I cannot explain the legacy, save that it must come of heaven, as do all good gifts! Now, dear brother, regarding my inheritance, I have no need of it and ask you to do with it as you will. Surely you know the circumstance of each member of our family and will be just in its distribution."

"What of the necklace? Surely as you are now in Hadrian's court, you could wear it with pride as befitting one shadowed by regal station!"

Ophelos, who had to this point been silent, exclaimed, "Do you not know that Esta has been proclaimed by the Emperor to be herself of royal blood right, that she is 'Princess Esta Verica of . . .'"

Esta placed her hand on his arm, interrupting this disclosure, saying, "Ah, my new friend, Ophelos, please say nothing more of that at present. As for the necklace, I know it is of great worth and speaks of our father's love for our mother. Yet I believe they would both have us use it for good. Please sell the necklace. Eitan's agents in Massilia will secure a fitting price; use the moneys for the benefit of our family; if there is no pressing need I ask you to seek out the unfortunate in Massilia, or elsewhere, and give until it is gone. I must soon leave to do the Emperor's bidding and will not be here to see to this."

Overwhelmed by learning of her imperial rise in station, and more importantly, feeling of her supernal wisdom and unselfishness, her brother replied, "Dear sister, never did I know when you were a child that there lived a goddess in our domus. I even admit that sometimes we . . . I do not mean to confess that others in our family felt as did I . . . sometimes, I was jealous of you and our sire's attentions on you. Sadly, I did not rebuke our brother when he was intent on sacrificing you to Jaca! Forgive me, please! And thank you for entrusting me with your inheritance. I shall not fail to do as you have said! Perhaps by doing well in this thing I may in some measure make recompense for past negligence!"

Esta and Naomi stood and embraced each member of the family. Even Ophelos gladly received their offered affection before he left. As he drove the carriage back to Massilia he considered both maidens. Esta, as a princess, was well above him and though astounded by her, he could not let his mind dwell too long on her extraordinary gifts. He concluded that Naomi was altogether different, yet beautiful still. The Jewess was empathetic, loyal—perhaps the loveliest, the finest maiden of *his* station he had ever met!

"La menina," Esta said to her grandam, I would like to speak with you in the morning, when you are well rested."

"No," said the old woman, "tomorrow may be too late. Come sit by me and let the others rest this night. You have many questions for me. This I know. And there are things I would tell you which have long been hid in my heart."

Soon they were alone and Esta asked, "La menina, how did you know I had questions for you? For such a long time you have not seen me nor did I say such a thing as we supped."

The grandam answered, "Mmh, will you think me foolish—I who told you that your own experience was foolishness and was only a consequence of delirium? I who did nothing to relieve your awful burden when the hellion of Jaca came for you and did nothing more than chant a malediccion on that evil seed of mine!"

Esta kindly replied, "Was not the petition answered, to my blessing and their destruction? Who can say but that your malediccion was but an answered prayer."

Hearing this, the old woman laughed and said, "Then it was not uttered as faithlessly as I had supposed. Well, I will tell you. You may not believe me, but this you will know for surety, I am about to die and who would be so foolish as to lie as they look over the great abyss?"

Esta said simply, "I will believe you."

Her grandmother replied, "Not since I left Rome as a young bride had I seen my own mother, until—well I knew of her changing beliefs, as did my sire, before he died. Yet he did not mock her, as did I, for I thought myself wiser than she who bore me. Yet few others knew of her . . . what I called her 'madness.' I told myself that I should have inherited a rich dominion in Britannia and a legacy in Rome! But I knew the Emperor hated Christians. Christians were good for nothing, but sport! Nero gave Christian children to lions in the arena! Smeared with pitch, he used them for torches in his gardens! What would happen to me if it became known that I was the daughter of such a one? Hence, before it was known, I married and fled here, to Massilia."

Esta put her hands upon her grandmother's shaking hands. You raised my mother to be a good and loving dame, one who believed in the maximus of Apollos, which are ever worthy devotions."

"Yes," she answered, "that I did! There was no shame in the gods of the philosophers. It was also a safe path for us. Your mother, my own daughter, became a votary of Apollos and Artemis, for they upheld her manner of thinking, for strangely she was so much like the grandmother she had never met, though I taught her nothing of Vittoria's beliefs. Not long after I left Rome, the tribunal of the Emperor found out my mother, discovered what she had become! My father was then long dead and enquires were made in Massilia of Vittoria's whereabouts, for it seemed that she had also fled Rome. I knew not where she had gone. Then was I afraid, afraid for myself and for my children. Never did I speak of the only legacy I believed that she left us—shame."

"La menina," Esta said, "you spoke of not seeing your mother after you left Rome, until when?"

"You are always perceptive, my granddaughter, and in this you rightly surmise. I had not seen her until recent days. Twice she has come to me. The first time I dismissed seeing her, for I said to myself I was sleeping and it was but a wishful dream. I awoke from that dream feeling wonderful. It was so peaceful. She was as I remembered her, beautiful and kind, not at all like the woman I had made her into, the foolish, despised Christian, persecuted for believing what the elite scoff at—the type of person who is spit upon, stoned, beheaded or burned. She came to me in that dream and told me I should soon die. When I came to my senses, I disbelieved that I had actually *seen* her, except that I did believe that Nyx would soon come for me."

Esta asked, "You said 'twice.'"

"My maire came again but seven days past. This time she came through the arch of the portico, where I sat alone thinking of my life and of you! Yes, my daughter, how I longed to see you before I died. I considered that all my children are around me, all except my evil grandson, who is dead already, and his mother, who he killed, and you, my fair one. *She* walked into our little courtyard while yet it was

291

light, but the lightness, the brightness of her person was greater! When I saw her, I thought of how you told me of the 'Burning One.' I knew, somehow, that she was not that person, but I also knew that she was somehow like Him. I could say nothing, for I knew I was awake, truly awake as I had never been before and was astounded, speechless! I saw her as surely as I see you now before me. I cried at the sight of her, for seeing her as she was, *I knew she had not died in shame!* Then I found my voice and pled with her to forgive me."

Esta asked, "What did she say to you?"

"She told me she loved me. I asked why she had not come to me before, to show me the way? Mother said she had done so many times. She had warned me in dreams and in omens. It was then I remembered how I felt at certain times, though I did not know why! Sometimes I gave heed to these premonitions, without under-standing them. Oh, it came to me then that I had forgotten her visits of the night and all she had done for me after she was dead, for I saw her works clearly—I do not understand but they were shown to me. Senseless creature that I am, I also had forgotten all that she had done for me when she was alive! Many thoughts, many wonderful memories flooded over me of her loving attentions and great deeds —but these are not what you should hear but this: she said, 'Our daughter Esta is well. You will see her, if that is your desire, before your death. Tell her what you know, what you had always known but had forgotten.'"

Esta said, her eyes wet with tears, "Oh La menina, that is the most wondrous thing you ever told me! Do you know that your mother saved *my* life—that in spirit she came to Maros as I was being carried away in the Necropolis of Aleria? Old as Maros was he fought and prevailed!"

"Nay," said the women, feeble in body but not in mind. "My mother never was given to speaking of her marvelous deeds, not in life nor in death. When she came, she did not remind me of her goodness, of her relentless search for truth and her passion of giving! How is it I was so blind, so fearful of the might of Nero and yet did not fear the omnipotence of the Almighty God?"

To this Esta had no answer, but inquired, "Did you know how your mother became a Christian?"

"Oh yes!" La Menina replied, "There was in Rome a considerable number of Christians and not all were of the lower cast. This infuriated Nero and his factions. Of all those who had come from Jerusalem there was a bold fellow who possessed an incredible and fearless ability to testify of these things—that Jesus defeated Death Itself and rose from the grave after being crucified by a Roman governor. This man himself had been a persecutor of Christians and was not only a High Jew, but a Roman Citizen! When I heard him speak, he told a little of his own history and never did I learn more."

Esta exclaimed in astonishment, "You heard him speak? Who was he?"

She answered, "He was an orator and went about using his skills to destroy the disciples of Jesus, and this after His death and rising. But he himself was changed, for the risen Lord appeared bodily to him and challenged him, for how could this persecutor not believe when he saw Him alive? After this he was known as Paul and was ordained an Apostle and became one of the twelve men who governed Christians. After some time, Paul was arrested in Jerusalem and because he was a Roman citizen and appealed to Caesar, was sent to Rome. There he lived for several years and, though under arrest, had a house. Though he could not leave it, others could freely come to him. First Jews came to his dwelling, but they rejected his words. Then came many others, called Gentiles by the Jews, for so did they call all who were not descended from their fathers. Among these were many Romans, Britons, Greeks and so on. Many of these were aristocrats, like my mother who took me with her to see and hear this man. Though his speaking was great, I thought I understood why the elders of the Jews rejected him. Already I had reached my majority and thought for myself—too much so, for I had become arrogant. This man, though Roman, was horribly maligned! He was derided and cursed by most everyone I knew and these were men and women of power! Hence, I never returned with my mother to see this Paul. Later, when he was beheaded by Nero, I feared even more. I had *listened* to him speak and in the eyes of the tribunal that made me guilty of a crime worthy of death!"

Esta said quietly, "Please chasten yourself no longer! Grandmother, this was a difficult thing and many felt as you did."

"Yes," she said firmly, "many did fear and for good cause, if they loved this world and its pleasures. But that was no excuse for me, for *I remember* that when the apostle spoke, before I allowed doubts to supplant his words, I felt an incredible something in my heart, something that cannot come from any man, a joy, a hope that what he said was true. This did not last long, for I allowed its destruction."

"Did Vittoria join the Christians?" Esta asked, "A man told me she was baptized by Paul."

"Yea and nay. Mother would tell us of his teachings and that she knew he spoke the truth. She said that knowing was not enough but that it was required to enter into a covenant, which covenant was sealed by the act of baptism. I remember clearly how she described this sacred rite. As the devotee was immersed in water, they were to immerse themselves wholly in the teachings of their Lord, leaving forever the outer world with its pantheon of deceitfulness, killing the old person with its falsehoods, being laid in a watery grave, then rising out of the water in likeness of His rising from the tomb, cleansed, reborn anew. It was a covenant of the heart, without written contract, witnessed by witnesses, a solemn ritual performed only by ordained emissaries. Mama was secretly baptized, that is, the ceremony was done covertly that it might not be known by Rome. Paul could not leave the confines of his house, but another man, ordained by him, went out into the country, to the shallows of the River Tiberius, to a secluded bend and stood in the water with her, spoke the rite and laid her wholly under the flowing stream. Mama said that never was she so happy as she was at the moment of her cleansing, for she had entered the Gate of the Kingdom of Heaven. And to think, I thought her deluded when I was the one mistaken! But there is more you should hear, and I grow weak."

"Rest then, grandmama," said Esta, "and we shall talk again when you are stronger."

She answered, "Nay, still you do not understand and that is why I had to see you before . . . I do not think that I shall be as my mother, who had power, after her death, to appear to Maros and to me! What I have yet to tell you must be said while yet I can speak from these old lips. How I supplicated heaven then, after she came to me, that I might see you! How I prayed to convince the AllFather of my desire to tell you things. 'What things?' I thought. What had I known but had forgotten? Each day from then till now, I have given my strength to find out that which I should speak to you."

"*I will listen!*" Esta replied sincerely.

She tried to speak, but her voice faltered. Then with great effort and with renewed control, the dying woman said, "You told me yourself, 'Life is timeless.' I scoffed at your words, thinking you were delusional because of your drowning. Soon I will go, yet will I live and so did I live before I was born a babe! Now, I did not live as some beast of some rudimentary race. Nor will I live after as some other type of being. Do you recollect when, as a young maid, you read to me from Phaedo?" Esta nodded. She continued, "The re-embodiment spoken of by Socrates is false, though other of his teachings are true, that we learn anew what we had for ages known before our birth. Most of all I remembered what Vittoria, my own mother, told me as I was about to embark on the ship and leave Rome. She said, 'Oh my learned and self-wise daughter. The day will come when you will know that what I have tried to teach you is true. You *are* a spirit daughter of God the AllFather! Of all the Father's children, his First-born Spirit was his Only Begotten Son in the flesh! He is our One and only Lord! Think,' mama said, 'remember who you are. Remember who He is, your Redeemer!'"

Esta was overwhelmed by this and could only ask, "Are you a Christian then?"

"Yes," she answered, "as much as I *now* can be, for how can I observe the sacred rite, for we have killed Paul and those who held keys."

"Keys?" Esta asked, and she thought of her conversation with Arrian and her telling him of the Spirit of Truth. Was there more to this that she might learn from her grandmother? "What do you mean by keys?"

She replied with a trembling voice, "Though I believe surely, yet is my understanding weak. Are your questions sufficiently answered?"

"It is strange that I do not remember all that I wanted to learn from you," said Esta, "and yet you have taught me so very much! I love you and I am filled with gratitude for all you have said."

"Then hear my last words to you, Esta. You are to be like your great grandmother, like Vittoria, who in life was a beautiful mother, a glorious Beldam, and who in death serves still her children."

La menina closed her eyes and slept. When morning came, she still breathed but did not open her eyes. All the while, Esta did not leave her grandmother's side. Sometime after night had again fallen, the maiden was roused by a gentle breeze. Faintly, so very faintly, she saw the spirit from the garden of Aleria take the hand of another young woman and lead her quietly away.

CHAPTER 18

THE EPISTLE

*"Every foreign land is to them a fatherland,
and every fatherland a foreign land."*

Anonymous

E arly on the morning of dies Solis,[1] Esta and Naomi walked
among the gardens and monuments of the Agora of
Massilia. For a long time they strolled in silence, enjoying
the quietude before others were out and about. At length Esta said to
her companion, "Naomi, often you went with me to the Temple of
Apollo or Artemis. Yet never did you take me to worship with you. As

---

1. Romans called the days of the week after seven celestial bodies that could be seen
with the naked eye, namely the Sun, Moon, Mars, Mercury, Venus, Jupiter and Saturn.
Dies Solis literally means the day of the Sun.

I think on this, never have I seen a shrine or temple to your Lord in Massilia!"

Naomi replied, "In times past, our ancestors worshipped in Synagogues or in the Temple at Jerusalem. Jewish Christians were cast out of both." She let out a little laugh as she said, "As you know, those who cast us out are now themselves castaways and with the diaspora those synagogues and temples are in ruin. Still Christians gather often in private houses or in the wilderness. It is our hope that one day we shall build sacred buildings in which to meet. One reason why we have not been persecuted in Massilia as in other lands is that, for the most part, Christians here are like my father—they are silent."[2]

"When do they meet?"

"The first day of the week," Naomi replied.

"Ah, this very day! We have only a few days left that we may call our own, for soon we shall leave Massilia. Naomi, please take me with you to worship as you do!"

She answered, "I don't know where they will meet for I have been so long away and always the place was changed. We will have to make inquires."

"Then lead on," Esta exclaimed.

Her friend answered somberly, "It may be difficult. You are known to everyone now as an Imperial Counselor to Rome. Legionary are everywhere about, for Hadrian has many soldiers in the city and we can hardly venture unnoticed. Not only shall suspicions arise in fear of us by Christians, but I believe others are watching us—my sire said there are always watchers."

"What do you mean, watchers?"

"There are those like Calvus, that is before you *turned* him. Some

---

2. "Early Christians were silent in the face of Roman power, choosing to pursue the way of peace." https://christianscholars.com/silence-a-christian-history/ 2022

are of high station and others of low. Inwardly, they are the same. They hate Christians and blame every difficulty on us, saying we have offended their gods. If gain can be made, they will traffic our lives. Vibia told me . . ." She stopped abruptly.

Esta asked, "Please continue. Tell me what Vibia said."

"Oh, Esta, it is so hard to say it!"

"Please, I must know!"

Naomi answered, "The Empress said that you have enemies—you are envied for the influence you have over her husband, that every favor granted a person or faction leaves others jealous if they are not given the same or more. Not everything done is done by tribunals. There *are* covert murders. She told me to warn you but you were so impatient to see la menina and with her passing, I decided to wait. Anyway, after we left Genua, the Empress said the danger would likely come as we traveled overland in the forests of Gaul or beyond."

Esta answered resolutely, "You are always my friend and confidant. Yes, I know that if I openly avowed Christianity, all we've gained, in wealth and honors, may be forfeit and more. There are lolls in storms but always the tempests of injustice return. Nonetheless, Vittoria did not weigh the consequences of the True Way but embraced it with all of her heart. As I think on this, I don't believe her spirit warned Maros to save me only that I might enjoy a privileged life! Also, Vittoria appeared to her daughter not only for la menina's benefit but that I might understand as well. I think I must speak to your priest and . . ."

Naomi interrupted, saying, "Nonetheless, what you are *now doing* is of great import! Your work with the Emperor is helping to establish peace throughout the Empire! What could be more vital? Because of you, Christian persecutions have diminished and tolerance is growing! These are weighty matters."

Thoughtfully, Naomi continued, "Long have I thought that this is why you were led to Rome—a learned friend of Christianity in a high place, who is not herself a Christian! Yet, if you should worship with us and it was found out and in some way made to appear perverse by your enemies, who can say what would happen? Vibia told me there are still executions—she has told me that Hadrian's safe warrant given me may work in direct opposition to the intent of the edict, for it openly declares me to be a Christian. Hence, she said, there are those of the elite who say I must die! She said this is why she took me with her when we landed in Genua. You were safe aboard ship and my safety was assured by the Empress and the Royal Guard while walking in the city."

Esta was shocked and said in dismay, "Naomi, I had no idea of the threats made against you, although I suspected I had made enemies after leaving Calvus. When I went into Rome to see Michela before we left, the Empress arranged to have guardsmen accompany me—something I thought strange, for often we had ventured alone in the country and in Rome."

"Well," said Naomi, "I have told you! Now what are we to do?"

Esta replied, "Your father's house, here in Massilia, is it still kept by his servants?"

"Yes."

"Are they to be trusted?"

"I think so but do not know! It has been so long since we left."

"Is there one at least who is a true Christian?"

"Yes, a steward and his wife."

"Then we must hasten to your house where you can quietly speak with him and beg his confidence. We must alter our appearance, disguise ourselves as best we can and have him take us to their place of meeting. Can this be done?"

"Oh yes," replied Naomi enthusiastically. "Yes, and always my sire keeps carts to bear merchandise. We could hide in a cart, covered by a blanket and other things on hand and the steward could drive us there and back. Oh, I hope he is there! When we leave again, as ourselves, it would be thought, should we be observed, that we simply rested in my old home for a few hours!"

Fortuitously, Naomi and Esta were met at her sire's house by this man of middle years. He and his wife were about to leave for the very purpose that would satisfy the maiden's desire. Changing their vestments, Naomi and Esta, with shawls covering their heads, climbed into a donkey cart, boarding hopefully unseen within the stall. His wife placed a blanket over them and sat atop the headboard of the cart while the man walked at the side of the cart, leading the ass. In this manner they traversed the streets of Massilia without difficulty. When they were beyond the city a half a league's distance, they stopped at a farm house. Behind this, in a copse of trees, the maidens slipped from beneath the blanket and carefully made their way into the house where they joined the gathering of Christians.

Naomi introduced Esta to their leader, a man who would not be called an elder or a priest, but said he was lo fraire, or simply a brother. Later Esta learned why he used this appellation. The meeting was very much to Esta's liking and was without pomp, consisting of prayers, singing and well-mannered discourse. When it drew to a close, Esta asked lo fraire if she could pose a few questions.

He answered, "We are pleased that you joined us today. We know who you are, Maiden of Massilia and Rome. Long have you been a true friend to Naomi, who is like a daughter to all of us. How may I help you?"

Esta replied, "Over the years Naomi has told me much about your faith and I have read the old annals of the Jews and the codices of John and Paul and other texts about Christianity, some antagonistic, for at the time I worked with an advocate of the Senate. I have learned that my great grandmother, Vittoria, was baptized during the reign of Nero, that she fled from Rome to escape death and lived a charitable life in Aleria. I feel peace when Naomi speaks to me of your Lord, when I read His words, and today when we met. My grandmother, who you may know for she lived with us before her recent passing, came to believe as did her mother. On the eve of her death, when I asked if she was a Christian, she said to me, 'Yes, as much as I *now* can be, for how can I observe the sacred rite, for we have killed Paul and those who held keys.' She did not tell me what this meant and I do not understand."

He answered, "I knew of your grandmother but didn't know her. I am so glad she told you this, but she must have learned of the Lord before she came to Massilia, or she learned by reading, for never did she join with us. Yet what she said was true of the rite of baptism. Had you read the codex of Matthew you would better understand her words to you, for in that sacred writ it tells how Jesus gave the 'keys of the kingdom of heaven' to the apostle Peter. Later, in the same book, it is told that the other apostles were given this same authority, that 'whatsoever they would bind on earth should be bound in heaven.' The power of God can only be given by ordination by one who holds these keys, or by one who is authorized by a key holder, or in other words, by a priest who is authorized by an apostle. So also must saving rites be performed by a man who possesses these keys, again an apostle, or by a priest authorized by an apostle. A man so ordained cannot give others this power without the authorization of a key holder. Do you understand?"

"Not entirely. Why cannot those who hold this power of God convey it to others without authorization from an apostle? If such received it aright, why cannot they then give it aright?"

"Mmh," he said. "Let me put it like this. You know a great deal of the government of Rome, do you not?" She nodded assent. "Does the Emperor appoint men to rule when he is absent from Rome?"

"Yes," she answered.

"Suppose one such appointed person desired to leave Rome and travel at leisure among the Greek Islands. Could that man arbitrarily give the Emperor's authority to another man of his choosing?"

"Certainly not," said Esta, "not without Hadrian's express direction."

"Suppose when Hadrian left Rome he gave those in power that edict, that they might appoint local rulers. Would such appointments be lawful?"

"Yes!" she answered.

He continued, "But then suppose that those whom Hadrian appointed to govern were all killed. Could the local rulers appoint men to replace the official representatives of the Emperor? Or could they even appoint other local rulers?"

"No," said Esta, "no man of himself can assume the Emperor's authority! If Hadrian's authorized representatives were killed, then must an appeal be made to the Emperor to replace them, *wherever* he may be! Until then, there would be a power void in Rome."

She thought for a moment, then offered her own explanation, saying, "There is the question of the senate, when we speak of this worldly empire, but I understand what you are saying. I think it is this: Jesus ordained his apostles to be his official representatives and gave them power to choose local priests to govern in their own lands. These powers held by the Twelve must be the 'keys of the kingdom' of which you speak. So long as the apostles lived, for if one died, another could be appointed, the Christian Church would be rightly governed and local priests could be ordained to minister sacred rites, such as baptism."

He replied, "You are very astute and are correct. When your grandmother told you 'We have killed Paul and those who held the keys,' I believe she meant 'we,' meaning that in the past she regarded herself as a non-believing Gentile, and they in truth did kill the apostles. An apostle is more than a disciple, that is to say a follower. Remember, an apostle is a key holder, for even after Christ's ascension to heaven, by the Power of the Holy Spirit, the Spirit of Truth, the Lord personally revealed his will to the Twelve and thus the church was directed by the Lord himself. After the deaths of the apostles, there was no one left on earth who had the authority to appoint other key holders. Holy men, like Polycarp, were truly ordained as priests by the apostles, but such men were not given the authority to perpetuate this power. Polycarp was not an apostle. Hence, with his death, and others like him, we are left without the authority of the Emperor of Heaven. Only God can appoint others when, according to His pleasure, we are worthy to receive new key holders, new apostles. I believe this will not be until we learn as a people to honor his servants whom he sends among us, and will not stone them, burn them, crucify them, or take off their heads."

He let the truth of his words sink into Esta's heart, then he continued, "I knew a true priest in Massilia who was ordained by the apostle Phillip. Before he died, this old priest sent for me. He told me that he could not ordain me to the priesthood without the authorization of at least one surviving apostle. He sadly exclaimed with a trembling voice that he had not heard from any of the Twelve since the last of their number, John, was exiled by Domitian to the Greek Island of Patmos, some years before. He said to me, 'You must lead our people as a brother only and assume nothing more—*assume no authority where it is not granted aright.* Remember, God's house is one of order and we must enter His sheepfold by the door and not try to steal over its walls. Wait patiently, but believe and teach others to believe. Our natures are eternal. We are eternal. One day the Risen Lord will also raise us and somehow, before that day, we will receive every necessary rite of Heaven. This is truth, for Paul spoke even of baptisms for the dead.'[3]

"Esta," he continued, "I believe I know your desire. I am not a

---

3. 1 Corinthians 15:29.

true priest and know not where I can send you to find one, if any yet live. It is a hard and a very sad thing, but I believe there are none alive. I cannot baptize you, but still you can be a devout follower of the Lord. You must wait for the blessing of the immersion covenant."

Esta thought of the words of Epictetus, where he said that life is like a banquet and in due course, we will ultimately receive that which is presently denied us. She answered him, "We must do our best, to be lights in a darkening night, knowing that dawn will come with the Daystar. You have helped me more than you know, for I knew not what I should do and now I know what I must do."

"What is that?" he asked.

"I will do as my grandmother said, I will strive to be like Vittoria and do good wherever I am led, among whatever people, and so long as I have high station, I must use it wisely to protect and defend truth. You spoke of the Spirit of Truth, the revelatory power by which the Apostles exercised their keys. Now I understand thoughts that were before given to me. Though for a time apostolic authority has been lost to the earth, I can receive guidance from our Lord by following the impressions placed in my heart and mind by this same Spirit. *I can learn His will for me and then I must do it!*"

Lo fraire replied, "You are an elect lady, young Esta, sent to earth with divine purpose. How quickly you perceive! I may never see you again, for Naomi tells me you will soon leave with the Emperor. I have a gift for you. It is an epistle written by an unnamed Christian to a man called Diognetus. It is not scripture. It was not written by an apostle, but by a man who I think was a true priest for he was a disciple of the apostles. This was given to me by the old priest of Massilia when he asked me to carry on his work, as you say, as best I could. I have made copies on parchment and would like you to have this one. You will find it an excellent way to tell others of Christianity, though it may incite their anger for it denounces the pantheon."

He gave her a small scroll entitled, "The Epistle to Diognetus."[4] Later when Esta was alone in her room at the inn appointed by the Emperor, she read the missive and was absolutely amazed. She then asked Naomi to join her and the friends read those passages Esta thought most important.

"Please Naomi, begin at the first and tell me what thoughts are brought to your mind." The Jewess read:

> "Epistle to Diognetus
>
> "Since I see, most excellent Diognetus, that thou hast shown an eager desire to understand the religion of the Christians, and art making precise and diligent inquiry about them, what there is in the God whom they trust, and in their worship of Him, that leads them to look beyond the world and despise death, and neither recognize as gods those who are counted such by the Greeks, nor keep the religious observances of the Jews; and what is the nature of the affection which they exhibit towards one another; and why this new

---

4. This epistle is published in its entirety in:
    Early Church Classics THE EPISTLE TO DIOGNETUS
    BY THE REV. L. B. RADFORD, M.A. RECTOR OF HOLT SOMETIME FELLOW OF S. JOHN'S COLLEGE, CAMBRIDGE LONDON SOCIETY FOR PROMOTING CHRISTIAN KNOWLEDGE Nouthumre Land Avenue;
    43 Queen Victoria Street, Brighton: 129, North Street;
    New York: E. S. GORHAM 1908
    Ecclesiastical historian Carl Joseph von Hefele dated this Epistle *before* the BarChochba (Bar Kokhba War) in the reign of Emperor Hadrian. p.18
    "Nothing is known of Diognetus. He may have been the Stoic Diognetus who was the instructor of Marcus Aurelius, the future emperor. Doulcet endeavored to prove that Diognetus was a pupil of Dionysius the Areopagite, and a witness of his martyrdom. Kestner, regarding Justin as the author of the Epistle, supposed that Diognetus was induced by the young Aurelius to consult Justin on points of inquiry." p.44

race of men or profession of life has come into the
world now and not earlier . . ."

Naomi paused in her reading and exclaimed, "How interesting!
Whoever this Diognetus was, he must have been an exceptional man
to have devised such questions! I had never thought about this last
one—why Christianity is perceived as a new religion."

Esta replied, "As you are a Jewish Christian, your people have
long looked forward to the coming of the Christus, the Messiah. To
you and those who are converted to truth, Jesus fulfills the Messianic
promise. But to others it seems as if this faith suddenly appears with
Jesus's earthly ministry. Please continue." Naomi read:

> "—I welcome thy zeal, and I pray God, who bestows
> upon us the power both to speak and to hear, that
> it may be given to me to speak in such a way that
> thou mayest be most helped by what thou hearest
> . . .
>
> "Come now, purify thyself of all the ideas that preoc-
> cupy thy mind, put aside the familiarity that
> misleads thee, become as it were a new man from
> the beginning, since thou art about to listen to a
> doctrine which is itself a new thing, as thou
> thyself didst acknowledge; and observe not only
> with thine eyes but with thine understanding
> also, what is the real nature and form of those
> whom you Greeks describe and regard as gods. Is
> not one of them stone, like the stone that is
> trodden under foot; another bronze, no better
> than the utensils molded for our daily use;
> another wood, already decayed; another silver,
> requiring a man to guard it against theft; another

iron, corroded by rust; another earthenware, no
more comely than that which has been prepared
for the meanest service? Are not all these made of
corruptible material? Are they not wrought by
iron and fire? Was not one of them fashioned by a
stonemason, another by a brazier, another by a
silversmith, another by a potter?

"Are they not all deaf, blind, destitute of life, of sense,
of motion? Are they not all subject to decay and
corruption? These are the things that ye call gods,
ye serve them, ye worship them, and ye become
completely like unto them.

"For this reason ye hate Christians, because they do
not regard these things as gods."

Esta interjected, "Naomi, what does the writer mean when he
says that those who revere idols become like them?"

She answered, "The worst case is the easiest to unmask. Think of
the suffering of pagan victims, slain on sacrificial altars, sculpted of
marble. The chiseled rock cares nothing for the anguished innocent
and their screams of pain. It cannot act aright, for the stone is a
dumb god, without feeling, as also are they who ply the sacrificial
knife without natural sentiments. I have often thought that no
person could do such things and still be a person. They must first
give up their humanity in order to consort with devils, or the carnal
gods masked as idols crafted by men's hands."

Esta replied, "Ah, your words are as powerful as his!" She was
quiet for a time as she considered what Naomi had said. What would
she do if ever called upon to witness such unthinkable brutality? If
she had not the power of the Emperor to back her, not so much as a
solitary guardsman for assurance, would she have the courage to
raise her voice in defense of the defenseless at the risk of her own life

—especially if threatened with torturous death? Silently Esta thought a prayer, pleading that never would she be tried in such a manner. Then she considered the sufferings of the Lord and felt ashamed, realizing that His example must entirely govern her actions, regardless of consequences.

"Naomi," she said as she contemplated these things, "next, the friend of Diognetus describes the Christian lot, a most peculiar circumstance! Before we read this, what would you say, Naomi, is the true homeland of Christians?"

"Our homeland?" she answered. "Do we come from any place—a *common* land of nativity? What a strange thought. I can't think of any! Jerusalem was once the home of my Jewish people, but no more! Now Christians may be from Asia to Hispania. What does he say about it?"

"He undoubtedly sees things as you do. Start and read from here," Esta said as she pointed to a certain place in the manuscript. Naomi began reading, but did not at first grasp how the writer could agree with her, for she did not fathom how there could be a homeland for the diverse followers of Christ. She read:

> "I think therefore that thou hast now learned suffi-
> ciently that Christians are right in holding aloof
> from the vanity and delusion of the pagan world,
> and from the pride of the Jews . . .
> "For Christians are not distinguished from the rest of
> mankind by country, or by speech, or by customs.
> For they do not dwell in cities of their own, or use
> a different language, or practice a peculiar life.
> This knowledge of theirs has not been discovered
> by the thought and effort of inquisitive men; they
> are not champions of a human doctrine, as some
> men are. But while they dwell in Greek or

barbarian cities according as each man's lot was cast, and follow the customs of the land in clothing and food, and other matters of daily life, yet the condition of citizenship which they exhibit is wonderful, and admittedly beyond all expectation. They live in countries of their own, but simply as sojourners; they share the life of citizens, they endure the lot of foreigners; every foreign land is to them a fatherland, and every fatherland a foreign land.

"They marry like the rest of the world, they beget children, but they do not cast their offspring adrift. They have a common table, but not a common bed. They exist in the flesh, but they live not after the flesh. They spend their existence upon earth, but their citizenship is in heaven."

"Of course," Naomi exclaimed, "I do understand! Our homeland is not of this earth, but of heaven! As Paul wrote, we are but 'strangers and pilgrims on the earth.' As you say, we have forgotten the far country of our heavenly homeland, yet we hope to return there."[5]

"Exactly!" said Esta. "Now here he speaks of the paradox of persecution. He does not give reasons for irrational behavior. He only states what is! Read on."

"They obey the established laws, but in their own lives they surpass the laws. They love all men, and are persecuted by all. They are unknown, and yet they are condemned; they are put to death, and

---

5. Hebrews 11: 13-16

yet they give proof of new life. They are poor, and yet make many rich; they lack everything, and yet in everything they abound. They are dishonored, and their dishonor becomes their glory; they are reviled, and yet are vindicated. They are abused, and they bless; they are insulted, and repay insult with honor. They do good, and are punished as evil-doers; and in their punishment they rejoice as finding new life therein. The Jews war against them as aliens; the Greeks persecute them; and yet they that hate them can state no ground for their enmity."[6]

Naomi ceased to read and exclaimed, "How well he tells of our plight and how we strive to follow the Master's words, 'If any man smite thee on thy right cheek, turn to his the other also.'[7] This he expounds and more!"

"Now let me read this," said Esta. "Listen to the beauty of his words as he tells how the Creator of the Cosmos was himself the Heavenly Emissary sent to us."

"It is no stewardship of merely human mysteries with which they have been entrusted. But God Himself in very truth, the almighty and all-creating and invisible God, Himself from heaven planted among men and established in their hearts the Truth and the Word . . . sending to men not a servant, as one might imagine, or an angel or

---

6. L. B. RADFORD, *Early Church Classics THE EPISTLE TO DIOGNETUS,* New York: E. S. GORHAM, 1908. pp. 52-56
7. Matthew 5:39

ruler, or one of those who administer earthly things, or of those who have been entrusted with the ordering of things in heaven, but the very Artificer and Creator of the universe Himself, by whom He made the heavens, by whom He enclosed the sea within bounds of its own, whose mysteries all the elements faithfully observe, from whom the sun has received the measure of his daily courses to keep, whom the moon obeys as He bids her shine at night, whom the stars obey as they follow the course of the moon, by whom all things have been ordered and defined and placed in subjection, the heavens and things in the heavens, the earth and things in the earth, the sea and things in the sea, fire, air, abyss, things in the heights above, things in the depths beneath, things in the space between—He it was whom God sent to men."

"Now," Esta asked, "How was He sent? Like a Roman general with a great host of men-of-war?"

Naomi replied, "I know better than that! He sent Him as his humble Son, submissive, though all powerful! Yet I am very interested to know how the author of this amazing epistle describes His first coming." She began reading once more where Esta pointed on the scroll.

"Did He send Him, as a man might think, on a mission of domination and fear and terror? Indeed He did not, but in gentleness and meekness He sent Him, as a king sending his own son who is himself a king; He sent Him as God, He

> sent Him as man to men, He sent Him with the
> idea of saving, of persuading, not of forcing; for
> force is no part of the nature of God. He sent Him
> as inviting, not as pursuing man; He sent Him in
> love, not in judgment. For He will [yet] send Him
> in judgment; and who shall stand before His
> presence?"[8]

Naomi's eyes became wet and she could read no more for a time. Seeing this Esta suggested they walk the path that led from the inn to a wooden bridge spanning a streamlet in a quiet glen but a furlong distant. There were Roman guards about the inn and near forest. Although the day was fast closing, more than an hour of daylight yet remained. Hence, the two maidens walked the way believing they were safe, although unknown to them they were watched furtively by enemies.

A tall legionary saw the maidens leave the inn and make their way down the verdant path. Although young, he was a veteran of a least one battle, for a scar extended from his left cheek and disappeared beneath his tunic. He smiled as he greeted the two demoiselles, saying, "I see you are without escort. Allow me to accompany you."

Esta answered, "We only desire to gaze upon the brook from the old footbridge as dusk falls. We shall call if the need arises."

He replied politely, "Ah, most noble lady of Rome, I would be untrue to my station if I allowed you to venture beyond my sight this eve. I will follow a short ways behind and will not otherwise intrude."

By this simple act, Esta and Naomi's lives were spared without

---

8. L. B. RADFORD, *Early Church Classics THE EPISTLE TO DIOGNETUS,* New York: E. S. GORHAM, 1908. pp. 68-71

their knowing of an unseen deadly peril. Hence, they walked to the bridge and back to the safe haven of the inn, talking of the beauty of the closing day. Back in their chamber, Naomi picked up the Diognetus parchment, asking, "What else would you have me read?"

Esta said, "Of the nature of Deity as understood by pagan priests compared to that taught by true prophets, the eye-witnesses of His glory. Begin here." Naomi read:

> "... Dost thou not see that the more [Christians] are
> punished the more their numbers increase?[9]
> "... Who among men understood at all what God is,
> before He came? Or dost thou accept the vain and
> foolish theories of those famous philosophers, of
> whom some said that God was fire, and others
> that He was water, and others again some other
> of the elements created by God? But these notions
> are but the trickery and imposture of magicians.
> No man ever saw God or made Him known [save]
> God revealed Himself. And He revealed Himself
> through faith, to which alone it has been granted
> to see God."[10]

Esta remarked, "Now sadly it is true that men, even those considered chosen, such as your forebearers, proved themselves rebellious and disobedient. Yet here he tells of a clemency exceeding that of the most gracious worldly prince who strives to reign in

9. L. B. RADFORD, *Early Church Classics THE EPISTLE TO DIOGNETUS*, New York: E. S. GORHAM, 1908. P. 71

10. L. B. RADFORD, *Early Church Classics THE EPISTLE TO DIOGNETUS*, New York: E. S. GORHAM, 1908. pp. 72-73

semblance of the Son. For as one strives to emulate heaven then are they no more deluded on earth. Listen to this."

> "When the time came which God had ordained to manifest His own goodness and power He did not hate us or reject us or take vengeance upon us, but showed His longsuffering and forbearance; in His mercy—*He Himself took up the burden of our sins, He Himself gave His own Son as a ransom on our behalf, the holy for the lawless, the innocent for the guilty, the just for the unjust, the incorruptible for the corruptible, the immortal for the mortal.* What else could cover our sins but His righteousness? In whom could we lawless and ungodly men be justified but in the Son of God alone? O sweet exchange! O inscrutable operation! O unexpected blessings, that the lawlessness of many should be hidden in one righteous person . . . having now revealed a Savior powerful to save even the powerless . . ."[11]

Naomi exclaimed, "Ah, his words thrill me! How different are the ways of God compared to worldly kings! Here emperors feel justified in destroying the rebellious. In all of history, when was there a monarch who not only forgave rebels but actually bore their afflictions, suffering in their stead? Not only that, no other besides the Eternal Creator could purge his creation from every fault and transgression, recreating us, refining us, purifying every woman and man

---

11. L. B. RADFORD, *Early Church Classics THE EPISTLE TO DIOGNETUS,* New York: E. S. GORHAM, 1908. p. 76

who believes in Him and submits to His counsel and commandments."

"Yes," replied Esta, "and He did so in perfect love." She read on:

> "For God loved men . . . whom He formed after His own image, to whom He sent His only-begotten Son . . . how wilt thou love Him who so first loved thee? Loving Him, thou wilt be an imitator of His goodness. Wonder not that man can be an imitator of God; by the will of God he can.

> "For happiness consists not in exercising lordship over a neighbor, nor in wishing to have advantage of weaker men, nor in possessing wealth and using force against inferiors. Not in ways like these can a man imitate God; such ways are far removed from His majesty. But whosoever takes up his neighbor's burden, whosoever is willing to use his superiority as a means of benefiting another man who is in this respect his inferior, whosoever bestows upon the needy what he himself holds as a recipient of God's bounty and so becomes a god to the recipients of his bounty, he is an imitator of God. Then though thou art yet upon earth thou shalt behold that God ruleth in heaven, then shalt thou begin to speak the mysteries of God . . . then shalt thou pass judg-ment upon the deception and delusion of the world, when thou hast learned to know the true

life that is in heaven, to despise the seeming
death here, and to fear the real death there!"[12]

"Now consider how this missive is brought to an end. Although
the writer does not give us his name, he tells us who he is, a follower
of the Christian prophets. He speaks of two symbolic trees of antiquity, two companions in eternal erudition.[13] Naomi, please read
again."

> "It is no strange message that I preach, no unreason-
> able argument that I pursue; but having been a
> disciple of the apostles ... I now minister rightly
> in my turn to those who become disciples of the
> truth ... who become thereby a very paradise of
> delight, producing in your midst a fruitful tree of
> abundant growth adorned with fruits of rich vari-
> ety. For in this ground hath been planted a tree of
> knowledge and a tree of life; but it is not the tree
> of knowledge that destroys, it is disobedience
> that destroys ...
> "Not without significance is that which is written,
> how God planted from the beginning a tree of
> knowledge and a tree of life in the midst of the
> garden, indicating thereby life through knowl-
> edge ... There is no life without knowledge, nor is
> there sound knowledge without true life; where-
> fore the two trees are planted the one beside the

---

12. L. B. RADFORD, *Early Church Classics THE EPISTLE TO DIOGNETUS,* New York: E.
S. GORHAM, 1908. pp. 77-78
13. Extensive and profound knowledge.

other . . . Let thy heart be knowledge, and let thy
life be the true word understood in thy heart.
"Bearing the tree thereof and taking its fruit, thou
shalt ever reap the harvest that is desired in the
sight of God, which the serpent toucheth not, and
deception cometh not near to defile; and Eve is
not corrupted, but is trusted in her maiden purity.
And salvation is set forth plainly, and the apostles
are interpreted, and the Lord's Passover advances
on its way, and the seasons are kept and are
arranged in order, and the Word rejoices to teach
the saints, the Word (which is Christ) through
whom the Father is glorified, to whom be the
glory forever. Amen."[14]

Naomi had never heard of this epistle before and was much
taken by it. However, what she was most grateful for was that her
esteemed friend was finally and entirely allied to that cause and to
that life she deemed essential. With tears the two maidens embraced
each other, filled with happiness and joy. Naomi, cried, "My sister,
long have I prayed and dreamed of this day when you would understand truth as do I and I should comprehend truth even as do you!
This Letter to Diognetus has been the katalysis[15] which has
dissolved our divergent views, merging them into wonderful unity."

To this Esta could add nothing, for her friend, in so few words,
had said all that was in her own heart.

No sooner had they dried their eyes than a servant called at their
door, saying that a man named Ophelos asked if they would sup

---

14. L. B. RADFORD, *Early Church Classics THE EPISTLE TO DIOGNETUS*, New York: E.
S. GORHAM, 1908. pp. 80-89
15. Greek progenitor of catalyst.

with him, that he awaited their pleasure at the garden portico of the inn.

"I am so pleased that I found you had returned, for I called on you twice already this day," said Ophelos, smiling. "Esta, given your grandmother's death, I have not wanted to intrude and as Naomi is always with you, well I have . . ."

Seeing his hesitation, Esta replied, "We are delighted to see you, are we not Naomi?"

"Oh yes!" said her friend, "and we haven't much time before our leaving!" No sooner did she speak these words than she regretted saying them, knowing it sounded over anxious.

Nonetheless, Ophelos brightened considerably and said, "Well, that is partly why I have come! Let us eat and I will tell you all."

After they were seated, Esta asked, "And what shall you tell us that we do not already know concerning our leaving of Massilia?"

"I hope you will not be disconcerted at me for this," he said cautiously, "but I spoke with Aléxandros and he spoke with the Emperor about my request."

"Your request?" Naomi asked.

"Ah, you must think I cannot command my tongue to say clearly an entire thought. I assure you when I am about my business, I talk well enough. Anyway, I suggested . . . I asked if I might join the Emperor's company to map his journeys, for I am also a traveled cartographer. Hadrian gave his consent! I pray you will allow me, when you deem it appropriate, to be your escort."

"We have guardsmen," said Esta smiling.

Naomi quickly interjected, "But Esta, they hardly ever speak with us, decorum and all. I think it is wonderful, Ophelos, and we shall be glad of your company whenever we are not needed by the Emperor or Empress!"

CHAPTER 19

SICARII

"Then it was that the Sicarii, as they were called, who were robbers, grew numerous. They made use of small swords, not much different in length from the Persian acinacae, but somewhat crooked, and like the Roman sicae; and from these weapons these robbers got their denomination; and with these weapons they slew a great many; for they mingled themselves among the multitude at their festivals, when they were come up in crowds from all parts to the city to worship God, and easily slew those that they had a mind to slay."[1]

Flavius Josephus

---

1.   Flavius Josephus, *The Antiquities of the Jews, Kindle Edition, p. 397.*

The Captain of the Sicarii

From a distance, two Sicarii, hired assassins from Cosa, watched the maidens on dies Solis, one a young man who had killed but one person and the other an older Sicarius,[2] the leader of their band. They saw them walk across the Agora, then hasten to Eitan's house. When they saw a cart emerge from a stable behind the lodging, the commander stealthily followed it while the other watched the house. The Cosan who trailed the cart knew he had guessed aright when he saw the cart pull into a grove of trees near a rustic cottage. For immediately thereafter, he saw the man who had led the donkey cart, the woman who rode on its headboard *and* two maidens with shawls over their heads, leave the stand of trees and enter the cottage. As he saw no other persons about, the Cosan made his way quietly to a window and saw a large gathering of people within.

"Christians, no doubt," he said to himself retreating to a furtive vantage point. Sometime later he saw most of the people leave the cottage. After this, he saw the two maidens clearly as they also walked from the stone house, less cautiously than when they had entered, for their shawls were about their shoulders. The two demoiselles were indeed Esta and Naomi. He soliloquized in a whisper, "Ah, it is a pity, they are so beautiful. Perhaps, if I choose well the place, there will be time enough for ludo."[3] He followed the cart back to its stable and finding his confederate, said, "They hid in the cart."

"Where did they go?" asked the younger Cosan.

"They are Christians—not just Naomi but Esta as well. They went to a secret meeting. We must strike when they are again so foolish as to be without their guards but now there are too many people about." He laughed, "Esta is too self-assured for her own

---

2. Sicarii, plural; Sicarius, singular. The Sicarii were Jewish terrorists, zealots who hated Rome. Yet, the Sicarii thought nothing of killing Jews as well as Romans.

3. Sport or game.

good." He grinned mordantly. "Perhaps before we cut their throats, we can indulge a little, even persuade cooperation by threatening to tell of their Christianus cultus."

The other loutishly chortled, "When?"

The first answered, "We shall watch always, sleeping in turn during the night. If we do not do it here, we will find the chance there," and he pointed to the east. "We can take our time. For a thousand denarii, we can afford to be patient, but it would be best to have it done before Avignon."

"Why is that?"

"From Avignon, I am told, the Emperor's entourage will be pulled up the Rhône in water coaches, until reaching Lugdunum."[4]

"Ah, yes," the second man said, "a slow and difficult journey is that, roped to horses that pull from the shore! How long do you suppose it will take?"

"Never have I made it. Maybe three weeks. If by Avignon we have not done the deed, we will leave our mounts and follow afoot; a hard task, but they must put ashore afore each nightfall. Though there shall be many in that company, surely the maidens will take respite, to bathe and such, and that alone."

The younger Cosan asked, "When we split the blood money, how much is half a thousand?"

"Ah," said the first, "half—your share—will be a hundred denarii!"

The foolish one replied, "A hundred! That is a lot to kill a traitorous Jewess!"

The chief Sicarius smiled as he said, "It is the other maiden, Esta, who carries such a price on her head. She is a great Roman, a knowing sorceress!"

The young Sicarius asked, "When will our brothers join us?"

---

4. Present day Lyon.

The captained answered, "If Esta yet breathes when the Emperor's company reaches Lugdunum, six others will give you aid, for notwithstanding this venture I have other work for them." He laughed, "But then you'll be able to count your wages upon one hand!"

"Ah," replied the other, "that would be a shame but I suppose it is only fair. Why are they not now with us?"

"Oft times, one man or two is better for such work," replied the veteran assassin, "and in the end it takes but one dagger to open the great vein." This he said, for the captain was haunted by those he had killed and wanted no more ghosts about him.

Some time passed before the young Cosan said, "Say, I've been thinking. Could an untrue Jewess be taught aright, be compelled to uphold the cause of *herut?*"[5]

"Certainly," said his captain, "Why do you ask? Would you take the beautiful Naomi to wife? I think she is too smart for you, Lamech. Still, if you decide to bed her always instead of a quick ludo, that will not alter our contract with the Sicilians, for only the Roman maiden *must* be slain. However, I will only allow your taking of the Jewess as full payment for your cutting of Esta's throat. You shall not receive one denarii for the death act but I shall keep your share, and Esta's corpse will be your *damim.*[6] Remember, you will be required to subject the living one harshly, lest her cries endanger us!"

The hellish command excited Lamech and he answered, "I will surely do it! No more than my hand and my knife is needed!"

"Good," said his captain and he laughed inwardly, doubting not that the stupid young man would do the dreadful deed and receive no silver for it—but a fighting wench instead who must always hate

5. Freedom as expressed passionately.
6. Blood money, bloodguiltiness. The implication is that Lamech will be a bridegroom of blood.

her abductor. The commander preferred to violently ravish a conquered and helpless victim rather than subject himself to a nagging woman. Hence, he reminded Lamech, "Remember, if the place and time be right, I will embrace the Roman before you kill her. It will only take a few minutes and you can use the time in getting to know your new wife."

Thus, the foul Sicarii talked with each other as they went about their business of watching Naomi and Esta, waiting to draw daggers with little risk to themselves. Their band of Jewish robbers were fanatics, hating Rome and loathing Christians with equal fervor. They often spoke of the rise of their exiled nation to world power, led by a prophesied Messiah commander who should vanquish their enemies. Before the destruction of Jerusalem, their murderous sect numbered many thousands. Many of the atrocities committed in the Holy City were of their doing, thinly veiled pretenses to incite uprisings against Rome. Now they were scattered abroad with their countrymen. If murders were the means to advance the obsession of their aberrant vision of herut, so much the better, for they delighted in bloodshed.

In the Roman Senate, there were those who secretly condemned Hadrian's consolidation of the Empire. Rather, they looked back upon Trajan's expansionist wars with nostalgic relish and desired to again "spoil" their subjects, not solicit compromise. These conspirators, led by Impius Paetus, furtively hired a small faction of the Sicarii to kill Esta, for they recognized that much of Hadrian's genius in the uncanny empire-wide reconciliation was due to the maiden.

When Senator Impius first saw Esta on the dais of the colosseum, he was smitten by her beauty. Subsequently, he connived to steal her virtue but could not so much as approach the maiden alone. In public, Impius was routed by Arrian, who readily perceived his foul intent. Nonetheless, the shrewd politician soon recognized that she was becoming a formidable adversary. His *occulta cohortis*[7] used Sicilian agents to negotiate with a rogue troop of the Sicarii so that the assassins knew not the identity of those who hired them. Then, if for any reason the murderous plot became known, the blame would fall on Roman hating Zealots. These were the greatest Jewish antagonists of the Empire and were called by Josephus "The Fourth Philosophy," the first three being the Pharisees, the Sadducees and the Essenes.

HADRIAN'S RETINUE was impressive indeed as it left Massilia and included the royal guard, his wife, Vibia, imperial secretaries and advisors, craftsmen, engineers, architects and men and women of letters.[8] Esta and Naomi rode in a carriage with the Empress, while Ophelos rode his own horse with two guardsmen, sometimes to the fore and sometimes to the rear of the company. As the official cartographer, he was given leave of the Emperor to move about freely, surveying their route.

On the third day, Ophelos fell back a half league, intent on ascending the highest hill along the trail to obtain a birds-eye vantage point. He left his mount with his two guardsmen while he climbed the hillock afoot, for the crags were too steep for horses and his guards were too encumbered with their armor to scale the rocks. He reached the summit in an hour's time and sat down upon a ledge. He saw the emperor's company distantly and the trail before and to their rear. He wrote his observations upon a parchment and was about to begin his descent when he espied two horsemen emerge from the forest. They rode the trail following Hadrian toward

---

7. Secret band
8. https://member.worldhistory.org/article/1892/hadrians-travels/ 2022

Avignon. The strange thing was that he did not pass the two men by the time he and his guards caught up with the main body. There were divergent paths that crossed the road and so, he concluded, they likely rode down one of these.

That evening, Ophelos supped with Vibia and her attendants, including Naomi, while Esta met with Hadrian and his staff. Trying not to concern Naomi, he said to Vibia, "While I was mapping today upon a hilltop, I saw two riders trailing your company, yet later we passed them not. Likely they turned off the main road for some other destination."

"Or," Vibia said, "they gained the forest when they heard you approaching behind them. Hence, they took cover and when you passed by are still trailing us. Thank you for being observant, Ophelos. I will send out searchers before dawn." Then the empress resumed her meal.

Ophelos wished he had not spoken in Naomi's presence, for he saw her concerned expression. Afterwards, he asked if he might go for a walk with her and so they casually traversed the encampment, talking. Their conversation was most enjoyable and he felt he had diverted her thoughts when she proved he had not by saying, "For the past week I have felt unseen eyes upon Esta and myself. I feel that we are surely being followed."

He replied, "Oh, I'm sure it is nothing. What I said to the empress . . ."

Naomi interrupted, "Ophelos, if we are to increase in the regard we have for each other, then you must not disregard that which I tell you! We, Esta and I, have been through many dangers and neither of us are given to hysterics. There are reasons why our lives *are* in peril, though we travel with the Emperor and Empress and with their strong legionary!"

He answered decidedly, "Then I shall never be far from you!"

The guards who searched for the two horsemen returned the

next morning without success. Two days more passed unhindered. The afternoon grew hot when the company halted. They stopped at a long bend of a streamlet, a tributary of the Rhône that flowed but a few furlongs distant. It was sheltered along one side by a steep bluff that faced the stream and on the other side by the rapids of the Rhône. The Imperial Guard set up their camp near the trail at the head of this wooded bench, ascertaining that it was unlikely that intruders would approach from the river or over the vertical face of the bluff. The far end of the escarpment fell off abruptly into the Rhône River.

Vibia commanded the company to refresh and clean themselves. Servants brought basins of water to a secluded glen. Fires were kindled and the basins heated for the comfort of the Empress. The elite men of the entourage, together with Hadrian, walked down to the shallows of the Rhône to wash, while the privileged women and maidens bathed along the clear running rill protected by a few Eunuchs.

Esta was euphoric with the idea of washing off the grime of the journey, as was Naomi. It seemed to them an impossible thing for malefactors to penetrate the security of this natural defense walled by cliffs and swift current. Hence, feeling assured they carried sandals and clean clothes in baskets and waded knee deep upstream a short distance to enjoy greater privacy. Soon they came to a grassy bank where they could still hear the laughter of the other ladies, although they were beyond sight of all, including the armed eunuch.

Esta and Naomi disrobed and placed their soiled garments aside, then plunged euphorically into a deep pool of crystalline waters. Their athleticism and youth triumphed over the coolness of the stream and soon their lissome bodies were accustomed to the temperature of the water. The sun was still well above the horizon and the maidens could leisurely enjoy their swim. The pool, which was formed in the lee of the far bank, stretched some ten or twelve rods' distance opposite the shallows where they waded. This was an ideal length to race from end to end, a sport they had enjoyed years before in Lacydon Bay of Massilia.

Naomi challenged, "See the outcrop of rock there at the end of the mere? On the count of four, I'll race you to it! ONE, TWO, THREE, FOUR!"

The two demoiselles, unhindered by undergarments, moved swiftly, like graceful naiads, down the length of the pool, with Esta winning by a single stroke. "Back to the start, cried Naomi enthusiastically. ONE, TWO, THREE, FOUR." This time the Jewess prevailed, also by a single stroke.

The two maidens stood waist deep, laughing. Esta, panting heavily for she had exerted herself with all her strength, said, "This race will prove the champion!" She shouted, "ONE, TWO, THREE, FOUR!"

The two swimmers were nearly equal in skill and were equally tired, reaching a point abeam the rocky ledge at the same time. They climbed out of the water and sat upon the stony shelf, drinking in the last warm rays of the sun, for it was near to setting. Naomi exclaimed, "Look at our skin, so lathed and cleansed. Ah, it is so beautiful here!"

"Yes," said Esta, "and so quiet!"

Naomi replied, "I think it is because we are on the far side of the stream and a little ways beyond our baskets. Otherwise, we could surely hear the others."

Aside from the murmur of the stream, all was hushed. They lay down on their backs on the warm ledge and looked up into the muted blue sky, accented by white clouds tinged with gold. Naomi said, "I think our laughter must have frightened away the small creatures of the forest." Hence, they conversed softly, hoping to see wonders such as Eponi had showed them in the woodlands of Tivoli.

For some time the two maidens talked, enjoying immensely each other's company and the tranquility of the place.

"Did you hear that faint rustling?" asked Esta. Let us be still and say nothing; perhaps we shall see a hart or a hare." They rolled over on their stomachs and looked intently toward the trees at the base of the cliff, from whence they heard the slight sound.

THE TWO SICARII had heard the approach of Ophelos and his guardsmen, as Vibia had divined. The captain was taken aback to think he had let Romans get to their rear where they could have espied them. Therefore, the Sicarii did not pursue Hadrian's company after Ophelos and his guards passed, but waited a day, thinking soldiers might be sent in search of them. This proved true and again they waited until the searchers turned back. Then they followed again with greater care.

When the Romans made camp in the long bench that ran between the high bluff and the Rhône River, the Sicarii tied their horses well off the road and made their way on foot, keeping in the shade of trees to scout out the encampment. At first the captain was very discouraged, for it seemed the only way of approach to the interior of the dell, where Esta would be found, was through the tent city of the Imperial Guard and the numerous sentries that were posted at its head!

As they had no means or desire to try the copious flow of the Rhône, they backtracked to the land from whence rose the high flanking bluff. Moving cautiously down this length they discovered two things. First, they had a commanding view of all that transpired far below. The two Cosans saw the Emperor and his male court washing in the Rhône. They also saw the Empress, dames and demoiselles bathing in the streamlet. They were mindful not to make silhouettes of themselves, but found they could speak in low tones without discovery. Hence, they continually made ribald discourse. Secondly, they discovered the face of the bluff was nearly vertical and was impossible to scale. Perhaps, the captain said, they would find clefts somewhere that would permit their descent to the base of the cliff. Still, they had not seen the two maidens who were the purpose of their quest. So it was they continued unseen down the bluff in the direction of the Rhône.

Ophelos was walking with the men toward the river as he scanned the bluff beyond the streamlet with his mapping mind. He knew the women would be bathing in this long tract of woods and meadows and began to second guess the wisdom of the captain of the Imperial Guard. Truly, the bluff was unassailable near the road and then down most of its length. But he saw with keen eyes that there was one "V" notch in the vertical face, a furlong from the river that ran twisting from the base of the cliff to the summit of the escarpment. Without voicing his concern, Ophelos quit the company of his elite companions. Armed only with a walking stick of hardwood, he made his way through the woods towards the "V" in the bluff, easily fording the streamlet.

"Ah," said the captain of the Sicarii to the lout following him, "what did I say? See those crags up ahead. There may be a sharp bend of the escarpment—a way down!" But the young Cosan hardly heard his commander, for he was peering over the bluff with absolute astonishment. "What?" said the captain. "Ah, I see them. Quick, back away! *We have them if we are not found out.* They are resting, perhaps sleeping, as dull as two eggs laying in a nest!"

Obediently the other retreated and the two killers hastily made their way to the crags. The commander continued his assessment, saying, "What fortune is ours! They sleep alone, apart from all others and their guards, thinking this quarter is safe from attack. Now then, do as I do, move like a spider from hold to hold down the face.

Remember your new wife is almost yours if you fail not in this one thing."

The Sicarii and Ophelos had correctly surmised that the "V" in the cliff was indeed a vertical path that allowed both ascent and descent. The two Cosans were half way down the bluff when Ophelos was crossing the streamlet near its convergence with the Rhône. They would reach the ledge before the cartographer and they carried daggers sheathed at their waists.

The captain now whispered commands to his solitary soldier. "The best plan can be faulted and always an escape must be thought through. For us, it is the Rhône. Its rapids may kill us or quickly carry us away. This only if we fail and alarum is screamed." Nearing the base of the cliff, he continued. "Now we must move with stealth. This will not be difficult as fresh grass grows near the streamlet and it will muffle our footfalls. In one leap, you must fall bodily upon Naomi, your hand gripping her mouth so that no sound can escape her. I will do the same with Esta and shall indeed take a moment for myself, for no better place could be found than this! You must also hurry and bind your bride with the cord you carry—tightly! I will have Esta firm in my grasp so you can easily cut the great vein. Then you must carry the Jewess back here and I will help you get her to the top. I think they shall not come looking for the maidens until night-fall and will not find our trail until daybreak. By then, we shall be leagues away!"

As the Sicarii carefully began to cross the meadow grass, the young Cosan tripped on a dry branch, rustling its leaves. This is what the maidens heard, thinking it was a small animal. A moment later Esta again heard a hint of movement, but saw nothing. She placed a finger on Naomi's lips and then began to slowly back off the ledge as her companion did the same. The two maidens lowered themselves into the pool below the outcropping, slipping without sound into the water. Naomi was about to swim away, when she felt the pressure of

Esta's hand on her arm, stopping her. Beneath the ledge, they could stand upon their feet with their heads above the waterline. Esta moved carefully, as far as she could, back up under the outcropping and lowered her head so that only her nose was above water. Again, Naomi did the same.

They waited but a moment before they heard an older man say, "What? Where could they have gone? I saw them here, not a minute ago!"

Fortuitously, as the maidens had slipped into the pool, the view of them was then momentarily blocked by brushwood.

The younger man replied as he quickly looked upstream and downstream, "I see naught! The water is clear—I can see to its bottom! They are gone! Captain, you said that *Esta* was a clever sorceress! Perhaps she . . ."

"Shut up, you fool!" he angrily retorted. "I didn't mean that and no one can disappear! Even when we kept our cover to surprise them, we were within easy range of hearing. Yet I heard not a sound, not a splash! There must be a hiding place. Quick, find them! ***Kill them!***""

It was then the maidens, only a few feet beneath the rock, heard a sudden commotion as Ophelos fiercely struck the younger Sicarius's head with his staff. So distracted were the two men and so intent did they look upon the stream that they did not hear his approach. The stricken Cosan fell from the ledge into the pool, turning the waters near the maidens red with blood.

The captain drew his dagger and faced Ophelos laughing sardonically, "Hah, you have a stick and I've a blade!"

He was, in truth, the superior fighter. With his first thrust the assassin's hand shot behind Ophelos' descending staff and cut to the ribs of the cartographer. Yet, Ophelos did not cry out in pain, but quickly seizing the hand gripping the dagger, pulled the assassin toward himself, dropping his staff and clenching his arms about his enemy, holding him fast in a standing embrace—this as he worked backwards, one foot, then another, until they toppled from the ledge into the pool.

Ophelos was far younger than the older Cosan and his lungs much more capable. The two fought on, but Ophelos prevented his foe from surfacing until he felt him weaken and drop his dagger. Yet, the captain wickedly kicked Ophelos in the face and made the surface. He no sooner took his first gasp of air than he caught a glimpse of a maiden's hand, clutching a large stone, descending forcefully! The blow was well directed and struck his temple, cutting his eye. The fighter pushed Esta back and made the bank, wheezing —then ran with his remaining strength down a trace near the stream—running for the Rhône.

During this frightful moment, Naomi had reached their dazed friend and helped him gain his feet on the rocky bottom of the pool. She saw that the killer had inflicted other wounds in his body, for it seemed that blood was everywhere. Yet Ophelos quickly found his voice as he ascertained they were no longer in danger, for the young Cosan floated face down and was carried with the gentle flow of the streamlet towards the river—this while his commander was nearly gone from sight, running like a wounded fox.

Ophelos said, almost in a cheerful voice, "Have no fear. I have suffered no major hurt and will keep my eyes lowered while you find your vestments. Hah, they cannot be far!"

Obediently the maidens swam upstream to their baskets as Ophelos slowly made his way across the pool to the shallow bank. Indeed, he did not look up, for he no sooner made the meadow grass than he closed his eyes, faint with blood loss. Naomi stayed with him, pressing moss into his cuts, until Esta returned with men. He was carried quickly back to camp, given wine while his wounds were cleaned and seared. Before an hour past, Ophelos rested beside a warm fire, Naomi at his side.

A village on a tributary of the Rhone River

CHAPTER 20
SATURNALIA

"Remember that you must behave in life as at a dinner party. Is anything brought around to you? ... Does it pass by you? Don't stop it. Is it not yet come? Don't stretch your desire towards it, but wait till it reaches you. Do this and you will eventually be a worthy partner of the feasts of the gods."

Epictetus

Hadrian was aghast at the averted tragedy, consequently dismissing the captain of the Imperial guard. How was it, he questioned, that a young cartographer detected the fatal flaw in the security of the encampment? Guards should have been posted along the bluff and more especially at the "V"— also down the length of the Rhône, which, though tumultuous at this section of the river, was still passable. The body of the younger Cosan was found wedged with flotsam near the confluence of the streamlet and the Rhône. He was found to be a Sicarius by markings on his body. The captain escaped, but several men saw him dash into the rapids, below the confluence and believed his fate was sealed.

The Emperor issued an edict that any Jew found along their intended route should be arrested and if found to be of the Sicarii sect, executed. Mounted couriers were sent with this order to Avignon, Lugdunum, and to Mogontiacum, the capital of Germania Superior.

Ophelos was thanked and rewarded heartily by Hadrian who gave him a perfectly balanced pilum, or javelin. This, he said, should replace his staff, which though proven effective against the Sicarius, was much more lethal and could be thrown effectively from a distance of six rods. Hadrian also gave a Ophelos a jeweled gladius, or short sword, which in craftsmanship and value was equal to his own.

As for the young man's injuries, they were numerous, though none were deep and he was congratulated for having fought off a skilled cutthroat. Because of the wounds Ophelos suffered in his legs, he could not walk any distance. Vibia insisted that he ride in her carpentum, much to Naomi's delight. Though recuperating, the Empress found his conversation much to her liking and was captivated by his knowledge of Greece.

Hadrian astounded the Imperial Guard when, after discharging their captain, he declared that he would be their commander for a time and would *walk* at their head. After the mounted vanguard departed to scout the road, Esta approached the Emperor with a request, saying, "Sire, riding in a carriage is tiresome! Might I stride at your side?"

He laughed, "Well that you may *try*, I grant you! However, I shall not hold back on your account. My purpose is to aggressively lead my men! Nonetheless, I would be glad of your company for as long as you can keep up, for there are many matters to discuss." So saying, he gave the order to advance. There were some legionary in the company who had before marched with their Emperor and had seen him outstrip his retinue.[1] These were therefore not surprised at the assertive pace Hadrian set, but they were entirely amazed at the strength and endurance of Esta, for that day the company made 8 leagues, arriving in Avignon before nightfall, and never did the maiden falter.

The following morning, the Emperor mounted his magnificent stallion and led his entourage through the city in regal splendor. For five days more they remained, as Imperial engineers, architects and craftsmen made plans for generous improvements. Hadrian lifted the status of Avignon to a Roman colony, designating it "Colonia Julia Hadriana Avenniensis!" A small number of his staff were appointed to oversee the construction of buildings, roads and a bridge to span the Rhône. The majority of his company then departed in a flotilla of river coaches bound for Lugdunum, save for the principle body of the Legionary, who marched northward along a rough road paralleling the Rhône, led by a newly appointed captain. At pre-determined points of landing, the company reunited once again for the evening respite. Then each morning they resumed their separate modes of travel.

Esta and Naomi were thrilled with the new adventure, so very different than traveling by ship on the open sea. At certain sections of the river, the waters were deep and slow moving. At such times, sails were raised and they moved stalwartly *with* the wind *against* the current. Often the river narrowed and the waters were beset with rapids. Then long ropes were drawn between the vessels and powerful draught horses that pulled the water coaches steadily upstream. Esta was often engaged with the Emperor, leaving Naomi to enjoy the mutual company of Vibia and Ophelos.

---

1. https://member.worldhistory.org/article/1892/hadrians-travels/ 2022

The countryside through which they sojourned was incredibly beautiful. At times rolling hills could be seen from the Rhône, magically arrayed in flowers of the same hue. Birds flocked along the river in abundance; plovers and terns, black-necked grebes, green-yellow finches, the fast and low flying merlins, the distinguished looking herons, sandgrouse, tiny pipits, Egyptian vultures, a host of varieties of eagles, owls and graceful pink flamingos. Picturesque chateaux and hamlets dotted the primal landscapes. The weather was mostly moderate, making travel aboard the water coaches effortless and exquisitely pleasant.

One morning, when they were two weeks into the river journey, Vibia approached Ophelos, who was laboring diligently with his mapping. The empress said, "You know, Ophelos, you seem highly intelligent for one so heedlessly unobservant!"

The cartographer, who was much recovered from his injuries, was taken aback by her words and replied, "Your Highness, is of course, right!" He looked down at his sketches of the course of the Rhône and then studied the shoreline. This endeavor had occupied much of his time aboard the river coach. "Mmh, it is true, I indeed missed a considerable landmark in my drawing. I think I must have been distracted!"

"No, no," Vibia laughed, "your folly is that you are *not* distracted enough!"

Ophelos put down his codex of open parchment. Returning her smile, he stood and bowed, saying, "Empress, I am ever your servant. What would you have me do?"

She answered as if the matter should be readily foreknown, "Not for me!" Vibia gestured toward Naomi who stood at the prow looking shoreward. "What man could always be near such a beautiful maiden, one who likely saved his life when he was kicked senseless by an assassin, and seem to prefer putting down lines and ciphers on parchment instead of wooing her favor? Know you not that she is loved by Diocles, the richest, the most daring, the greatest charioteer in the Empire? It is certain that when we arrive in Lugdunum, Naomi will find missives awaiting her! With the gentle touch of her hand, she will break the seals, open and learn anew of his undying love! Better it would be for you, Ophelos, to have her troth *before* Diocles wins her heart with persuasive letters, for though he is an equestrian he is erudite and a most skillful poet!"

The young man asked leave of the Empress and walked straightway to the bow of the water coach. For the first time he put his arm gently around Naomi's waist. She had not heard his coming, for the sound of the river had mesmerized her, and the maiden startled at his touch. Nonetheless, it felt wonderful and she immediately turned about, so that his hand glided around her form and came to rest upon the small of her back. She looked up excitedly into his face, and smiling said, "Ophelos, you look so much better!"

He replied, "I have recovered more than my health but my senses also! Do you know that I love you?"

Naomi giggled, "How should I, for you have never said so! Even now you ask me what I know and do not say outright what you feel for me! That is the way with you, you . . . "

Ophelos put a finger upon her lips as he said, "Naomi, I do love you! I believe I loved you from that first night when Aléxandros asked me to escort you and Esta to her old villa. Why do you think I asked the Emperor if I might be his cartographer on this long journey?"

"Oh that!" she answered, "Why you saw an opportunity to raise your station, of course!"

"Yes," he said, "that I did! For I knew if could but win your love then never could I rise higher!"

Nothing he could have said would have touched her heart more. Yet she answered, thinking well into the future. "Before I requite the affection I have longed for, I must ask your thoughts . . . "Naomi hesitated, not knowing exactly how to phrase her words. Often she had thought through what she might say to Ophelos and had never settled on a way to say that which she knew must be said. She continued carefully, saying, "You say you love me. What makes me, me? There are many pretty girls in Massilia and thousands in Greece where you lived for years. If you have not loved before . . ."

He interrupted her, saying, "Never like this."

Naomi continued, "Then if you have never loved another as you love me, there must be some distinguishing feature I have—something more than the way I talk, or look, or move, for I know myself and in none of these do I excel and many are the demoiselles who exceed my grace. You, Ophelos, are an accomplished man, strong, intelligent and very kind. You are established and your way in life is certain. Hence, your wealth is assured. What you do not now have that you rightly desire, you *shall* obtain. Hence, you turn many a lady's head and can have your pick of the lot!" She laughed, "Even Vibia is taken with you; good thing for me she is already taken!"

"You speak," he said sincerely, "of your *Christianity*, your belief in one God, one Redeemer, one Lord."

"Yes," she replied.

He said earnestly, "I do not understand your faith and have heard much against it, especially in the Senate. Nonetheless, this is what I think: I believe it is true that your convictions, the kindness of your faith and its goodness has molded a lovely maiden into the finest person I have ever known! Only truth can so fashion the miracle that is you, Naomi. As Hadrian has declared that none may hinder you in this regard, so I promise that never will I be an obstacle to your worship and always will I defend you."

Her answered shocked him. She said, "That is good, but it is not enough. I do love you, but suppose you asked me to be your wife, and I . . . "

"Ah," he interjected quickly, "That is what I do ask! I know you would accept nothing less from me but a faithful promise to be your loyal husband, for I know you are not a coquette to dally with love or to bind yourself to a man who is inconstant!"

"Still," she answered thoughtfully, "there is more and we have *time* to see if our love ripens as it should." Hearing the words "our love" thrilled the young man. Naomi continued, "First, my father must know, or learn rightly of our intent and then he must give his consent. I will not marry without it. Here is the hard part, for when he is informed by such a one as Aléxandros, for example, of your character and devotion, I believe he will love you as well! Nonetheless, I know my father and he will *not* give his consent unless you become one of *us!*"

Naomi was quiet for a time, letting the import of her words take effect. Then she said, "Know also that I believe that in a true marriage the husband and wife should become one and not just when joined in the connubial sense. This merger of passions cannot happen, *at least for me,* unless *before* the vows are taken my beloved believes in the truths I hold most dear."

He drew her closer to him as he said, "Naomi, I do want to understand your faith, and I will try. Yet I cannot promise to believe. It seems so strange to me that a man *crucified* could somehow rise from the dead. I must be honest with you."

To his surprise, she replied, "Oh, I am so happy that is how you feel!"

"What?" he rejoined quizzically. "I don't understand!"

Naomi smiled as she replied, "This, Ophelos, will not be the last time you don't understand me if I am truly the daughter of she who bore me. My father often said that never could he love anyone but my mama! Also, he told me that just when he thought he understood her, he found he did not! Yet, when it came to their core beliefs, they did indeed understand each other and that perfectly."

The maiden laid her head against his chest as she said intensely,

"I am happy you answered me as you did, for I cannot, I will not even try to convince you of any of the truths I hold sacred. I know that if I did, I should miserably fail! Only the Spirit of Truth can implant *within* you the faith and knowledge of Christianity. I can only be a teacher, not a persuader, for that power is not given me or any other mortal instructor. Christ was no man, but is God, all powerful! So powerful that His Testator, the Spirit of Truth, can speak to you without speaking words to your ears. Ophelos, you only need to be a hearer, a contemplator, one who is willing to ask the AllFather the questions of your heart, especially as you read the sacred codices and have courage enough to receive unspoken answers. I believe you will most assuredly feel these answers even as you now feel the sun's warm rays upon us."

He replied, "Oh, that would be wonderful. Even now I feel peace as you speak to me! Nonetheless, as it is up to me to obtain these answers, I must honestly say that it may be I cannot know of these things, as do you. I know of Athens and you do not, because I have been there. When it comes to these things, I think you have been where I have not and perhaps never can go!"

Lifting her head she looked into his eyes, saying, "How grateful I am for your honesty! If after your sincere investigation you still think these things strange or impossible, yet will you ever have my regard, for you, Ophelos, are a man worthy of the greatest esteem. I know you would never lie to me to steal my affections."

Germanic Woodland

"Then what?" he asked.

"Then we could never be wed, for I must also be honest with you! Yet I have no fears. How can I fear the truth? It is like the love you feel for me. Did I ever try to persuade you to *feel* this for me?" She laughed, "Did I say, 'Ophelos, these are the most excellent qualities I possess,' then boastfully multiply my virtues before your eyes. Such a narrative might conclude with, 'So then! We have established that you *must* love me! Have I not convinced you to do so?" and she softly laughed, but he did not.

"No," Ophelos replied quietly, "never did you persuade me to love you, but you drew near to me, so near that I could feel a radiance never before felt."

With eyes moist, Naomi humbly said, "I thank you, Ophelos, for such a compliment and will strive to always be worthy of your words. Then this is what I suggest: Write an epistle to Eitan, my sire. Your letter may be attached to the Emperor's correspondence to Rome so that it may be surely received by my sire in Ostia. Also, send a copy of it to Aléxandros in Massilia and ask him to stand as a witness of your good nature. He will quickly send his own words to my father and they will forcefully attest to your fine character, for I know you have his admiration. Write whatever words you desire and do not ask me to assist in the writing, but say his answer may be returned by the same means, though it will take many months. During the interval I will give you what codices I have, testaments of the Lord. Read these. Ask whatever questions you have, first ask them of Esta, for I would rather that she be your teacher than myself."

"Is Esta also a Christian?" he asked incredulously.

Naomi replied, "I think it best that you not ask that question, of me or of her. Nonetheless, there is no one so versed in philosophy and the religions of men than Esta. She well understands the dogmas of the those who uphold the pantheon and has even spoken of these things to the Emperor and Empress and, I think, to their entire satisfaction. What is more important in this instance, is that Esta thoroughly understands the texts of Christianity, the doctrines of my faith and the means to be used to discover their truths. You may say in your missive to my sire that *I have said I will not marry you unless and until you believe for yourself that which you are learning.*"

Ophelos answered, "Naomi, I will do this! Even if my actions seem slow to Vibia, for happily the Empress chides me, implies that I must be thought a fool if I do not quickly obtain your troth, I shall patiently abide—and wait for two things: the gift of truth that I must feel within and your sire's consent."

The following day, Ophelos presented a sealed letter to Hadrian and asked that it be sent with his government correspondence to the Port of Ostia. When the Emperor saw Eitan's name upon the folded missive, he surmised its content, saying, "Ah, it is about time! Vibia has told me of your love for Naomi, hah, not that she needed to tell me! Yes, your pleading will be sent and I warrant that Eitan will surely receive it!"

He then placed his hand firmly on the young man's shoulder and said, "I have called Naomi my daughter. Vibia feels likewise, though the maiden is both a Jew and a Christian. As for myself, this affection for her came suddenly upon me and was entirely unexpected. All I can say is that, as we met, she showed courage in a most simple, yet direct manner. Almost the maiden invoked my wrath, but then Esta spoke and explained the way of things. I felt peace and my eyes were opened to Naomi, and how I wished then that she was born of my blood! Hence, I am her defender and in this sense her father too. As you have watched her on this journey, I have watched you. You have my regard as a fitting companion. Yet know this, I will watch you yet and command that always Naomi be treated as an Imperial Daughter of an Emperor!"

SPRING PASSED into summer and summer into fall. The Roman government, embodied in Hadrian and his court, passed through Lugdunum, where many were added to his entourage,[2] and Mogontiacum, the capitol of Germania, where he inspected military installations between the Rhine and the Danube Rivers. From Mogontiacum he also commanded the building of the Germanic-Rhaetian Limes, a great wooden wall marking the northern limit of the Empire in that region of the world. Traveling hundreds of leagues, Hadrian continued to march with his troops, never setting foot in a chariot or horse drawn conveyance, abiding and supping in his legions' camps, reinvigorating their discipline.[3]

During this campaign, which took him as far east as Cetium, Hadrian met frequently with tribal leaders, vassal kings and their courts. At such times Esta and Vibia would accompany him. Not only did Esta write for him, but often, in difference of her eloquence, the Emperor would have *Princess Esta, Consiliarius Imperialis Romae,* speak for him. Always, she amazed her hearers and was extremely effective in advancing Hadrian's principals of self-government under the Roman Protectorate.

The Imperial entourage wintered in Mogontiacum. Nonetheless, advance troops were sent west to Colonia Agrippina and Forum Hadriani, a new city established at the estuary of the Rhine and the North Sea, to prepare the way for the coming journey. When the weather broke at the start of the new year[4] they planned to traverse

---

2. "Hadrian's travelling entourage may have included as many as 5,000 individuals, including his wife and her staff, imperial secretaries, personal friends and advisors, officials, servants, guards, architects, and craftsmen, but also men and **women** of letters." https://member.worldhistory.org/article/1892/hadrians-travels/ 2022
3. https://member.worldhistory.org/article/1892/hadrians-travels/ 2022
4. March was the first month in the Roman year.

the Rhine by boat to Forum Hadriani and would thence sail to Londinium, Britannia. With great anticipation, the Emperor intended on introducing Princess Esta Verica to the isles of her ancestral legacy.

THE WINTER UNFOLDED with incredible beauty; great snows blanketed giant fir trees, rolling meadows, majestic mountain peaks and deep valleys. Esta and Naomi had never seen such dynamic contrasts of towering heights and dizzying depths, veiled mystically in morning mists and heralded brilliantly by kingly sunsets of crimson and gold. The month of Mensis December[5] had come and they eagerly looked forward to Saturnalia, the Roman festival honoring Saturn, their god of husbandry, abundance and peace. Saturnalia was the celebration of the year, a time of feasting and giving of gifts, of beautiful decorations of ornaments, wreathes and lighted candles.[6]

---

5. Mensis December was the tenth month in the Roman calendar, now known simply as December.
6. Much later this festival would ultimately become the Christmas of Christians.

Festival of Saturnalia

The Emperor Hadrian and his Imperial Company were sheltered in comfort in the regal apartments of the magnificent Fortress of Mogontiacum[7] on the bank of the Rhine River. In the Great Hall of the palace the Roman and Germanic Courts attended the Emperor and Empress in the high feast of the wondrous season. As they partook of the banquet of smoked meats, boiled roots, leeks, cabbages, baked fowl, dark bread, rich cheeses, wines and ales, they conversed happily and gave their closest friends small gifts and missives of affection—and this to the delightful accompaniment of skilled musicians.

On a sudden the Emperor arose. Seeing this, all were immediately silent. He said, "Although the year is not yet ended, still the harvest is long past and the days of travel are hindered by such snows as we shall never see in Rome! Glad I am for that!" Everyone laughed as Hadrian continued, "You, my vassals of Germania, are not only my subjects, but my mighty brothers and your provinces are the strong northern bastions of the Empire! How we of Rome are bound to you and your people! The endowments given to rebuild your fortifications and walls of defense, to rebuild your cities, and not only with basilicas to house your senates, but to construct arenas for your chariots, and theatres to lift your spirits, and aqueducts to bring you clean water from the mountains and hot bathes to cleanse and comfort your bodies—these endowments are the gifts of my Empire to this loyal and stalwart people!"

---

7. Mainz, Germany.

High Feast of Saturnalia

All stood upon their feet and hailed the Emperor with raised steins and shouts of praise. When the din subsided, Hadrian continued, saying, "Traditionally we give gifts during the Feast of Saturnalia and I have seen you this night share such tokens of love with those about you. Hah, I have given Vibia a beautiful necklace made of gems from the mines of Germania and she has given me a beautiful toga, yet," and he laughed, "I cannot wear it here in Mogontiacum, but must wrap myself in furs, lest I die of frost. It will wait until I return to Rome!" All laughed and were well pleased with their Emperor, for never had such a ruler come among them. "Now you may know that Vibia and I have no children. Yet we have come to love two maidens dearly. The first you all know as my Consiliarius Imperialis Romae, for often you have heard her speak," he chuckled a bit, then went on, "and I would say that if you were truthful, you must confess that you prefer Esta's animated wit, ken, and elegant voice to that of your Emperor's." Again, the host laughed, but not too much.

"The other maiden, you may not know," said Hadrian. "She is Naomi, the one I first called 'my daughter.' Naomi, rise and please come to me, for I have a gift for you, and bring with you Ophelos, my *Officialis Iter Socium, and Primus Cartographer Romae,*[8] and most importantly *Heros et Salvatorem Filiarum Mearum,*[9]—that is right, bring him too as the gift is also for him."

---

8. My official traveling companion and the foremost cartographer of Rome.
9. The hero and savior of my daughters.

Naomi, "my daughter."

Hand in hand the young man and maiden approached the head table of the Emperor and Empress. Still standing he gave Naomi a tied scroll, saying, "Here are six parchments tied together. The first was written by Ophelos and humbly seeks your sire's consent that he may take you to wife. It is addressed to Eitan, the Merchant of Ostia, Italia. The second is the epistle of Senator Aléxandros, who vouches for Ophelos in an illustrious way, also sent to Eitan. The third was written much later, by Esta, and is also written to your sire. As nothing should be hid from your Emperor, I have read all of these. In Esta's epistle she tells Eitan of a discovery made by Ophelos, which finding must be held confidential and so cannot be shared in this gathering, but was necessary to Esta's recommending the union and that without this development the marriage could never be. The fourth and fifth letters were written by my own hand and that of Vibia's, telling your father of our many adventures on this vital journey and also advising him that we heartily support the request made by Ophelos, for we know that his daughter loves and honors this worthy man. The sixth and final epistle is your sire's answer to you. It is rather lengthy, but well written, for I find that he is quite erudite. He speaks most graciously and gratefully to myself, the Empress, the Senator and especially to Esta, whom he says is the greatest of all maidens, save for his own Naomi. Incidentally, he also gives consent for you to be wed, according to your own desires."

By the time the Emperor finished speaking, Naomi could not control her emotions and was crying, nay, sobbing with tears of joy, as were Vibia and Esta. During the many months, Ophelos and Esta had often met to read and talk, fulfilling the charge given him by Naomi. Yet neither had spoken to her of the change wrought in his heart. Naomi wanted to ask, but dared not, for she had promised to remain aloof from his investigation. Always was he kind and loving when she was near, but always did he include others with them as wardens to assure his virtuous conduct. Of course, Hadrian and Vibia *had learned* of this silent change in Ophelos; first from Esta's letter and then when they questioned her directly. Yet even the Emperor and Empress told no one, not even Naomi.

All who were gathered were impressively moved by the affections of Ophelos and Naomi, for it is a truth that all good souls take vicarious joy in a love story. They knew very little of that which was unfolding before them, save that a strong young man had sent a letter to the father of a beautiful and noble maiden, asking for her hand, that there was some extremity to be satisfied before they could be rightly bound and finally, that the highest powers on earth, with Esta's assistance, had provided the needed aid.

Vibia stood, her eyes dried, and said with prodigious excitement to the gathering, "You, our friends, are invited to attend another festival on the morrow, the wedding feast of Ophelos and Naomi!" She then looked directly at Naomi. "Now I also have a gift for you, my daughter. The Emperor gave you six parchments tied in a scroll. Naomi, turn yourself around and see who enters the Great Hall! He is the *courier* of Rome who has journeyed long and braved many dangers and storms that he might arrive in Mogontiacum before this, the eve of Saturnalia! He comes at my behest, for without your speaking I knew your heart's desire. His presence is my gift to you!"

The maidens could not believe their eyes as the Captain of the Imperial Guard escorted Eitan to the dais that he might embrace his daughter.

Zur Matte in Roman Germania

PART THREE

CHAPTER 21

RUITH

"My body weeps . . ."

Naomi

❧

S
he heard his voice again. How she loved the sound of his words, spoken so gently and yet so manfully. She knew that all he said was true, or rather would be true, for he spoke of the future. He called her by name and yet he did not call her "Esta." It was her name, an appellation as familiar to her as were *the ages.* Later she pondered that thought. When was she first given that name? She had forgotten it and had not been called _____ since she came to this country.

She loved not only his speaking but the touch of his hands upon her head as he said, "Daughter, the time and place appointed you[1] to

---

1. Acts 17:26 And hath made of one blood all nations of men for to dwell on all the

sojourn on the earth are at the beginning of the abandonment, for man did not receive the Dayspring[2] to lighten their way and hated those whom He chose, for all are slain, save one and he is removed from their midst. Yet before the second day[3] of darkness is spent, He will reveal the Light again and this before the glory of His coming. Sadly, many generations will pass in shadow, for long is this time in the reckonings of that country. Still, all are precious in His sight and *He will send valiant ones there who shall not be deceived but shall accomplish that which is needful, that Truth be not wholly forgotten,* that the Enemy may not triumph but be checked in his doings, that his emissary spirits be exposed in their deceits. You, _____, are given the power to discern spirits while you dwell in that country and shall be a bearer of light. The intelligence you have attained in this ageless land shall not be diminished in that telestial sphere, so far removed, and shall be a persuasive blessing to those who desire peace. You will be born a fair daughter in the lineage of _____ whom you love from your days together in this land. Even now she lives in the spirit realm of that far country for her mortal estate is fulfilled. There you will also become a beautiful mother and will be given choice sons and daughters for many generations, even until the end times. *Power will be given you in life and in death,* that they may be led aright, even all your seed who desire truth. The Enemy knows the valiant and labors to destroy them. As the Dragon seeks to devour *the child,* so will his sycophants crave thy seed, but because of thee they shall *not* prevail."

The sounds of Colonia Agrippina woke Esta from the vision of the memory she dreamed. She had not seen the blessing, had not

---

face of the earth, and hath determined the times before appointed and the bounds of their habitation.

2. Luke 1:78-79

3. 2 Peter 3:8. The abandonment will not last more than two days, or two thousand years before.

again traveled down the Incredible Passage to the Core of Creation, but while she slept the maiden had heard—had remembered words spoken to her by . . . by whom? Had she forgotten so soon? Quickly she sat up, retrieved parchment and began to write. Oh, it was so hard, so fast was it fading! She wrote these words, "Men have abandoned Him, have slain the chosen. There will be a period of fearful renunciation, a time . . . how long a time? Generations? Then will He return. I am born of an illustrious mother. By what name was Vittoria called before? Ah, I do not remember! I *will* yet be a mother and will be given power to help my children in times of danger. What was said? Yes, he promised, 'Power will be given you in life and in death!' The Enemy knows . . . knows what? Ah, he and his spirits know *us*, the mission given to us before we came—ah, we are to be light bearers during the darkness."

She sat back and looked at what she had written, knowing it was incomplete. She contemplated and prayed and at length wrote her thoughts, "Some are chosen to be born in the light of the day and others in the night. My world is steeped in pagan shadow and my calling is to lift my lamp. No, I am to be a lamp. I must indeed be a slight luminary compared to the Daystar! Yet I will truly bear whatever portion of His brightness He chooses to give me. Oh, that I might live when He returns, when his chosen again walk the earth. Still, I am grateful for whatever good I may be good for. There was something said in my blessing about peace. Perhaps that is why I was sent to Rome to further peace. It seems wars never cease and common ground must be found!—that is unless we war with unseen beings—devils who to seek to destroy us—there can be no compromise with the never-men."

Esta was most lonely in the evening hours. For many years Naomi had been her cherished companion. She was the perfect confidant and friend. She was, of course, very happy for Naomi and Ophelos. Seldom were the two apart. Naomi, she knew, was one of the valiant souls spoken of in her blessing. Already she had conceived and would soon be herself a beautiful mother, a Beldam. Esta considered her own station and read over the words she had just written once again. "I *will* yet be a mother and will be given power to help my children in times of danger." She looked over the blessing again and again. Nothing was said that she could remember about her being the voice of a powerful Emperor. She knew unabashedly that she had helped to establish peace, but that peace was a type of amiable commerce and had little to do with the eternal truths that now governed her life. True, such stability reduced the suffering caused by conflict and in that measure she felt gratified. Yet, becoming a mother was indeed a vital part of her blessing and it seemed was the most significant measure of her life's purpose.

Esta laid back down upon her bed, for it was hours until morning. She was so somnolent yet fought back sleep, for there were so many important things to consider. She was to be a mother, yet presently knew no man that she desired to marry! Whom did she esteem? Arrian, Diocles, Aléxandros? Lately Esta desired romance in her life. Perhaps the love and affection that Ophelos gave Naomi and that she so willingly returned made Esta desire a love of her own. She thought of Eros and knew the awakenings she felt in her body were real and purposeful, yet as she considered the men she knew, well they just didn't seem to fit. Fit what? She was too tired to sort through such things and so she turned her mind to that promise of future motherhood. Esta knew her own mother well, a kind and forthright dame. She had always loved her grandmother, but now she understood her so much better.

Then she thought of Vittoria, her valiant and beautiful great grandmother and it seemed she knew much more about her than was *reasonable*. Had Vittoria come to her in forgotten dreams? Had they conversed, laughed and planned together? It seemed that she could almost remember . . . Then Esta thought of her children. Did she know them? She had been told who her great grandmother was to be even before she was born. She knew the dogma of predestination was not a true precept, save for two things, the time and place of our coming to this earth—these two things are fixed for everyone.[4] This thought thrilled Esta, that perhaps she already knew her daughters and sons for many generations from her ageless past. As Vittoria had waited for her birth, so she would wait for theirs. Her eyes closed and she seemed to see faces, beautiful maidens and stalwart young men, one was called a Condesa—and she dreamed the most wondrous dream.

THE JOURNEY to the coast of Forum Hadriani was fraught with spring storms, causing the Imperial Company to hold up in Colonia Agrippina for nine days. This afforded the expectant mother relief while Ophelos lovingly attended to her every need. Esta, however, was nearly always engaged with the Emperor, hardly less than if he were in Rome. At length they reached the sea between the continent and the Islands of Britannia.

It took more time to make ready for the crossing of so great a company than did the actual voyage itself. It would have been a pleasant sea journey, save for Naomi's distress, for she suffered violently on the crossing from motion sickness. Ophelos, Esta and the Imperial physician did all they could to ease her malady that was aggravated by her pregnancy.

Londinium was much more rustic than Esta had envisioned but it pleased her very much. Although it was nothing like Massilia,

---

4. Acts 17:26 And hath made of one blood all nations of men for to dwell on all the face of the earth, and hath determined the times before appointed, and the bounds of their habitation.

where she was reared, yet it felt as if she were returning home. Many vassals came to the Fortress of Londinium, their entourages in trail, to meet with Hadrian and his court.

Making ready for Britannia

Almost nightly the Emperor hosted feasts for his regal subjects at which time proclamations were given, gifts were bestowed and announcements made regarding the building of new roads and defenses in all but the most northly territories of the isle. At each of these banquets, Esta was introduced as *Princess Esta Verica of Britannia, Consiliarius Imperialis Romae.* The effect of this was quite astonishing to the maiden. Though she was well received throughout Gaul and Germania, here in Londinium it was considered quite extraordinary that a Roman aristocrat of so lofty a station was one of their own, a princess of the noble lineage of Verica.

Many a nobleman, especially those who were yet to marry, approached the Emperor motivated not to win his favor but hers and to see her more closely. Nonetheless, what amazed Esta were the number of "cousins" she had. It seemed that almost all were as expert in genealogista as was Calvus of Rome, for they could easily site their bloodline back to her great great grandsire, albeit through incredible machinations of uncles and aunts, nieces and nephews, marriages and adoptions! As amusing as this was, still she found that she very much liked the Britons, their intellect, cheerful natures, good humor and especially their active imaginations!

Each evening, before Esta retired to bed, she would visit Naomi. Since the sea voyage she had become quite ill in the last days of her expectancy, seldom eating without forfeiting that which she ate and often she was feverish. This was a grave concern, for Naomi had become wane and, despite her swollen belly, was otherwise incredibly thin. Hadrian had his best physician attend her. Nonetheless his treatments seemed only to make her dire situation worse. Ophelos confided to Esta that the medicines his wife took only aggravated her condition and that each bloodletting brought her closer to death.

He told her, "The Imperial doctor himself has no faith in his doings. He told me, out of Naomi's hearing, that if she does not soon begin to mend, she will die, if not now, then surely in child birth! Oh, my friend, what am I to do? I heard of a woman, a Druidess, some say a sorceress—but she is said to be a healer with a knowledge of things unknown to the bloodletters of Rome. I know this sounds terrible, but I am desperate; hence, six days past I sent for the Druidess. When she comes, how am I to judge such a one? To give my dear wife over to a stranger, one who may invoke powers of gods I have forsaken, surely that would offend our Lord, would it not?" Before Esta could answer, he added, "Julius Caesar wrote that the Druids were among the most important classes in Britannia and were to be honored and never taxed. Could it be he esteemed them aright?"

"What is her name?" asked Esta.

"Ruith,[5]" he answered. "She lives in the woodlands between Colchester and Linnuis."

"However did you learn of her?"

"A British Baroness came to see Naomi, having heard of 'her dying!' She said that only Ruith could save her, for she herself was helped by the Druidess when she delivered. Even stranger, the Baroness brought a small bird to me, said it was a 'colm' and told me to affix a tiny parchment on its leg—my summons to Ruith! This I did and let loose the bird, which flew northward. Ah, I feel so foolish!"

Esta replied tenderly, "Ophelos, you have done well. We don't know if Ruith is an enchantress who invokes dark powers or if she is a woodland physician who understands the remedies of nature. Many medicines are made of plants and animals, from the bark of an oak to sage and from pig to serpent! Every land in the Empire has its practitioners, for illness is everywhere found. Only in the great cities do men study to become authoritative physicians, and some, I believe, know less of natural cures than do these rustics. That Ruith helped a woman of station is a good recommendation. Let us meet

---

5. Ruith, Celtic word meaning to run or chase after.

this Druidess that I may question her. Fear not that your small missive will reach Ruith. A colm is a wood pigeon, akin to the messenger birds used by Roman generals."

Ophelos was greatly relieved and embraced Esta as her brother. Nonetheless, when Esta went to Naomi's bedside, she saw how inordinate her appearance was altered in a single day! Naomi's skin was so pale it seemed translucent, her eyes were sunken and glazed, her hair disheveled and wet with fever. Immediately, Esta sent a servant to Hadrian, begging her leave that she might constantly attend her dear friend.

When the Imperial physician examined Naomi the following morning he told Esta and Ophelos, "There is only one way to save her life. I must incise her womb and deliver her child by caesareo,[6] the procedure by which the first emperor of that name was born." This he said in Naomi's hearing.

Weakly, she implored, "If that will save the life of my babe, then you must do so."

The doctor answered, "Nay. It is too early, but it will save your life."

The Jewess replied with tightly closed eyes, "Then forebear and I will live a while longer that my child shall be born alive."

As he was leaving, the physician asked to speak with Esta alone. In the anteroom he said to her, "The life of this young dame is important to the Empress and the Emperor. If I do nothing and they learn I could have saved her life, my own might well be taken."

Esta asked, "If nothing is done, how long does she have?"

He replied, "That is hard to say. Life is both fragile and tenacious. However, after four days, the outcome will be less assured."

"Then leave her in my care for those four days," said Esta forthrightly, "and *do not* attend her. I will nourish my friend using what

---

6. Caesarean.

knowledge I possess or may be given me of Providence. If by the fifth day she is not improving, we will talk again of the caesareo. Should she die, I will tell Hadrian and Vibia of these, *my* instructions to you." Smiling, the man nodded assent, for inwardly he did not believe Naomi's life could be saved regardless of what he did for her. He thought it probable that she must die immediately of the shock of the caesareo surgery. Now, no blame should fall on him.

Esta was at Naomi's side as Ophelos slept in an adjoining room, when Naomi opened her eyes and said feebly, "Esta, did I tell you that my own mama died giving birth to me?"

"Yes, both you and your sire have told me of that night, both sad and wondrous."

"Maybe," Naomi said haltingly, "that is the way of things in my family. Who knows but what my grandmother died giving birth to my mama? I only know my father, who has always been so good to me. Perhaps, it is only right that my life should be taken when my baby is born."

Esta said carefully, "I don't think that is the plan of Heaven for you. Try to get well, lest both you and your babe perish! You have not fulfilled your appointed time to deliver!"

"Ah," answered Naomi, "I had forgotten about that. Oh, it is so hard."

"So hard?" questioned Esta.

"So hard to keep trying. I just want to fall asleep and never waken."

"That you must not do, nor even consider. I think your body is indeed spent and your pain must be severe. Yet, think of what you have already endured! We have been through so much together. Think! You saved me when I should have died in the sea! Then you were about to marry a man you didn't love and I was promised by my brother to a foreign devil! How we conspired to win the right to live our own lives! You were so brave and daring! Oh, the journey that followed. You prayed us through to a safe landing at Aleria when our Trireme should have sunk in the tempestuous sea. Remember the night I was abducted, then saved by Maros and the sea battle that followed? Oh, the memory of it still thrills my heart! Think of all we experienced in Rome and how close you came to infuriating the Emperor when you challenged the validity of the pantheon! Hah, you have no fear! Then not an hour passed before he called you his daughter! Think of the last day of Eponi's life, of the marvels she showed us! Oh, then there was your ride with Diocles— remember how envious you made Michela?"

Finally, at this, a hint of a smile passed over Naomi's face. Esta continued, "I could go on and on. Think of the Sicarii and how Ophelos saved us and then how you saved him!" She squeezed the hand that was already cold to the touch. "Naomi, your life has been preserved time and time again. Are you called of heaven to bring a new life into the world? Yes! Yet, is your life's mission only to bear this babe? Or rather, is it God's will that you raise your child, love Ophelos, her sire and live for them, as well as for me? Surely, that is what you must do!"

Naomi asked quietly, "You said 'love her.' Shall I bear a maiden?"

Esta laughed a little, as she answered, "I thought, mayhap, I'd put you to sleep, for you closed your eyes again. Hah, I see you *are* listening. Mmh, I don't know why I said 'her.' But it does feel right to me! Hence, what shall you call your infant maiden?"

"Oh, I will call her Eponi!" Naomi said with greater strength.

"Now you are talking sense! *You will* call her Eponi! Then as she grows and she hears her mama call her name, she will delight in your loving summons. Even now Eponi loves the sound of your voice as she rests in your womb. As the years pass, she will always cherish the sight and sound of you and your loving touch, for you will be an excellent mother, sent of God for this all-vital purpose, to do for your daughter what no one else can do! You will instill in her heart the truths of the Lord that she may walk in His way."

Naomi smiled as she replied, "Oh, my dear friend, you infuse little Eponi with joy for I feel her move inside of me, affirming all you say! I promise she will not hear me speak such doubtful things again."

Naomi was soon fast asleep. An hour after midnight, a servant entered the bedchamber and said quietly to Esta, "A woman has come from afar, in response, she says, to an invitation from Ophelos. I told her I would show her an apartment where she might rest for the evening, that the matter could wait until the morrow. To this she replied, 'Nay, that will be too late.' As she is insistent, should I awaken Ophelos?" Esta replied that she would speak with her.

The woman who waited in the anteroom was older than Esta by a score of years. Her attire was plain, yet she was well groomed, slender, stood erect and possessed symmetrical features and an intelligent bearing; hence Esta was not surprised when she spoke with a learned tongue. The woman bowed slightly to Esta, saying, "I am Ruith and have come from the woodlands south of Linnuis. Ophelos sent for me, saying I must come at once lest his wife die."

Esta replied, "Please sit down for there are things I would ask you." She directed the servant to bring their guest food and drink, then continued, "I am Esta. Though not of her domus, yet the wife of Ophelos is my beloved sister. Naomi is with child and is indeed suffering nigh unto death. Ophelos told me you helped a Baroness who was in a similar circumstance. He also said you are a Druidess, a healer. Can you tell me more of your art?"

Ruith answered coldly, "You wish to know my fee, do you, for a Druid sorceress invokes no powers without first palming gold."

"No," said Esta, "I will gladly pay what you ask. Yet, before I entrust you with the life of one so precious to me, I would know beforehand what gods you implore and what medicines you will use, for I have some knowledge of your craft."

The woman answered curtly, "I will speak only with Ophelos. If you have knowledge of my 'craft,' then why have you not already healed the poor dame?"

Esta looked more carefully at the woman. She was not dressed as an enchantress. It was obvious Ruith was not impressed with Esta's high station, if she even knew of it. That she had come far, had traveled nights as well as days, to help an unknown woman, spoke well of her. Esta doubted that a Druidess would forsake all comforts to make such a swift journey. It was also clear she did not respond to interrogation.

Knowing she had offended the woman and perceiving that this traveler possessed merit, Esta answered, "Her husband lies exhausted in yonder room. Please come with me and see Naomi. I only ask that you tell me beforehand what course you will take if you decide to help her. Know that the Imperial physician does not see how Naomi can recover, yet he recommends caesareo. Oh, I shudder to think of her trying to endure such a thing in her weak condition. I believe the surgery would kill her."

For the first time the woman looked emphatically at Esta. She arose, not having touched the food set before her, and said, "Let us see Naomi."

Esta closely observed Ruith as she looked intently upon the sufferer. She said, "Please hold the lamp high and let the light be guided by my gaze." Her eyes were wet as she gently touched the fevered brow, which roused the girl from sleep. Ruith said with great sincerity, "Oh Naomi, I am so happy that Ophelos asked me to come and do what I can for you. How I prayed that you yet lived, for I *knew* that you and the life you carry were both in peril. My dear, can you answer a few questions?"

Now the Imperial Surgeon had asked nothing of Naomi, for he

said he knew all that was requisite. Naomi was relieved to tell of her pains. She replied shakily, "It is difficult to breath without my breath causing great pains in my back. I feel regular tightenings below my stomach and between my legs. These were infrequent a few days ago. Now they wax stronger and my body weeps bloody water from where I will deliver, yet I have some weeks to go before my time is fulfilled. Finally, I burn with heat, then shake with cold. Then it seems I become oblivious to my surroundings and at last I rest without pain for an hour or two, only to awake and feel again the pain. All food is repellant and all drink abhorrent to me."

Ruith responded, "Ah, how well you explain yourself! Your mind is yet lucid. That is a very good thing! Now, I would like to see your form, for much can be ascertained by looking. Is that allowed?"

"Yes, please yes," said Naomi.

The healer turned to Esta, saying, "Please have the servants bring me boiled water immediately, in four vessels and a rod length of clean linen." Esta instructed the servants as she held the lamp for Ruith. The healer removed Naomi's bedclothes as soon as the first basin of hot water was given her. Tearing off a portion of the linen, she bathed Naomi gently while carefully studying her body, especially her abdomen. Then she prepared a poultice from leaves, bark and sage that she took from a satchel she'd brought and placed this poultice between Naomi's thighs. She covered her with clean linen, over which she spread warm blankets. "Now Naomi, I am going to place many pillows beneath your back and head to lift your upper body without disturbing your lower. This will help you breathe easier."

Having done this, she said, "Naomi, your body is not listening to your spirit and is so grieved by the innocent babe it carries that it wants to expel your child before its time. We cannot let this happen, can we?"

"No!" Naomi answered in a pitifully fierce manner. "She must live!"

Ruith replied, "Then I want you to fight for life, your own as well as the precious being in your womb! Speak often to your unborn. Already it is a knowing person who can think and act with a will of its own! You say it is a girl, then tell her how much you love her and want her to live. Say that she too must strive, must endure! I would like to prepare a broth for you to drink, made of bone marrow, oak, sage, garlic, nettle and other leaves, sunflower seeds and the pulp of black yams. You will find my preparation strangely pleasant to the taste, calming and nourishing. May I do this for you?"

"Oh, please do," said Naomi.

Ruith left for a time with the servants and returned with the special broth. Esta was surprised that the aroma was indeed agreeable. At first, Ruith could but wet Naomi's lips and tongue. After a few minutes of gentle persuasion, she slowly spooned the broth into her mouth until, to Esta's amazed joy, the bowl was empty. Then Ruith whispered, "My daughter, I know not who you supplicate in times of exigency, but may I offer a petition to heaven?"

Naomi opened wide her eyes and said, "Please do!"

Ruith knelt by her bed and said with closed eyes, "Father, I have come as bidden and have done all that I could do this night. My powers, though needed, are slight. Thou art Omnipotent. I beseech thee to give Naomi the strength to overcome this great illness and be healed every whit. In the name of our Lord, Thy Son. Amen."

Soon Naomi fell into a deep sleep, for having been nourished for the first time in days, she could truly rest. Ruith arose and addressing Esta and the servants, said, "Naomi will not awaken until midday. I too need rest and will now gladly receive a couch."

It was so. Naomi awoke when the sun was at its Zenith. Color had returned to her face and her eyes were bright. Still weak, she no longer felt faint and the weeping fluids had dried completely. With the help of the servants, Ruith had already prepared fresh fruits and dark rich bread, spread with honey. These were given in small servings to Naomi, whose appetite grew with each passing hour. When Ophelos saw his beloved and learned all that had been done for her, he wept with joy and thanked Ruith profusely.

On the fifth day, the Imperial Physician returned, as promised, astonished to see Naomi so recovered. He said self-assuredly, "Ah, my treatments proved effective in the end. All that was needed was a little time for my medicines to produce this predictable result."

Esta, smiling, said nothing of Ruith, but replied, "True, you are most skilled in the healing arts. Now, you should attend to your other patients and give Naomi no more of your expert care for she is well! I will most assuredly tell Vibia the excellent news."

The weeks passed and Ruith stayed on as Naomi's midwife. She carefully guarded the expectant mother's diet, providing drinks made of grains and new wine, while serving fresh boiled roots and soft cheeses. Soon Naomi quit her bed, save for evening repose and was able to walk with Ophelos along the Tamesis.

Esta returned to her imperial work but still visited with her friends each evening. One night she found herself alone with Ruith and said to her, "You, our dear helper, are an enigma, for you are no Druidess. As no one becomes a true healer without receiving instruction from someone expert in this skill, can you tell me where and by whom you learned the healing arts? You are already proven! I ask only for my own benefit."

Ruith replied, "You sit at the side of Hadrian."

Esta said reassuringly, "What you tell me shall *not* be told others."

Ruith answered, "The Druids of Linnuis and Colchester are cruel and barbarous. In the name of the sun god and the moon goddess, Baal and Ashtoreth, they torture their victims before stealing their lives. The sufferings of the Britons under these priests and priestesses are immeasurable, even my own family died at their hands. When a maiden, I fled to kin who lived in Glastonbury and was there taught truth and learned of cures that invoked the aid of no gods, but One. Only then did I return to the woodlands south of Linnuis near my old home. I learned to use the fears that are embedded in the minds of idolaters to keep the Druids out of my forest. Over time, with heaven's help, I built a fine cottage and have made it a sanctuary for those preyed upon by pagans. My work is small, for I can only help a few, both in my woodland and to whatever land I am called; yet it is sufficient to give purpose to my life."

Not long after this, Esta was again at Naomi's bedside as Ruith delivered Eponi. As the healer lifted the newborn and placed the beautiful infant upon her mother's breast, carefully severing the cord and gently bathing the two with warm water, Esta esteemed Ruith greater than any physician of Rome. Without her, this truly wondrous delivery would not have been and these precious lives would surely have been lost!

When all was quiet, Esta said to Ruith, "Mother, when you return to your cottage in the woodlands of Linnuis, may I come with you? Hadrian is riding north to build a great wall that will mark the extremity of his Empire in Britannia and I need not accompany him. It is my desire to live with you for a season, in your cottage, and there serve and learn."

Ruith answered, "Why yes! That will be glorious."

CHAPTER 22
WOODS

"Let them see their fears!"

Ruith

Hadrian provided mounted guardsmen to escort Esta and Ruith to the healer's forest home, telling Esta that he would meet her back in Londinium the following spring, for he desired that she then accompany him across Oceanus Britannicus to Belgica, Aquitania, Narbonensis and Tarraconensis.

The Emperor had recommended they travel with him aboard his Imperial ship on his voyage north, where they could put ashore at Abus Estuary.[1] From there it was scarcely a two-day ride to Linnuis. This did not please Ruith, who desired to travel overland from

---

1. Known now as the Humber.

Londinium to her home, which journey on horseback was a good nine-day ride. Esta explained to Hadrian that she must acquiesce to Ruith, for the woman must have some fear of the sea, but added that she also desired to see country that they would otherwise sail past.

Nonetheless, Esta wondered how it was that Ruith had come to Linnuis so swiftly, for she must have come on foot, as she had no horse. Ophelos had said that he had let loose the pigeon approximately seven days before she arrived. How fast can such a bird fly? Could it fly to Linnuis in a day? Esta did not know, yet Ruith arrived in time to save Naomi's life. How was it, that allowing a single day for the pigeon, Ruith traveled so a great distance as to outpace mounted riders by two days?

Nonetheless, the allotted nine days for the northward journey proved accurate and was accomplished without difficulty. Yet, the Roman guards were dismayed when they came to a crossroads atop a hillock near Linnuis, for Ruith thanked them as *she gave them leave to return to Londinium.* Their captain objected and addressing Esta said, "The Emperor charged us to see you safely to this woman's abode. There is naught but a Druid shrine and flowing spring upon this summit. We cannot, in good faith, leave you, Lady Esta, in this wilderness!"

Esta had learned from their frequent association that Ruith often did not explain herself and that her actions were habitually perplexing, though in every case she discovered later the reasoning behind her curious behavior. She turned in the saddle to Ruith and asked, "As these good soldiers have traveled far with us, protecting us from all hazards, should we not have them camp at your cottage where they can sup and rest for a day? It cannot be far distant."

Ruith replied, "You may stay with your guards but they cannot come into my woodland." So saying, she began to walk her mount down the crossroad.

Esta apologized to the captain, who protested, saying his

concern was for her and not for himself or his men. She replied, "Please, I must do her bidding, as I am her guest. Have no fear for my safety, for I feel no foreboding and must thank you for our safe journey. I wish you a speedy ride back to Londinium." Obediently, the guardsmen turned about while she quickly rode to catch up with Ruith.

When Esta rode again at the side of Ruith, she asked, "There must be good reason for you to refuse the giving of hospitality. Please tell me that I may understand."

Ruith replied, "I said only the truth. Men-or women-of-war[2] cannot come into my woodland, lest their eyes betray them and they later tell others that which is not. The more such are allied to violence, the more this is so."

"What of valiant warriors sent of the Lord?" Esta asked.

Ruith answered, "Such are not allied to violence, but peace, though of necessity they have shed blood and will be received by us if it is succor they need." She turned from the crossroad and made her way into the forest, with Esta riding close behind her, though at first there was no apparent trail. Soon however the path was plain enough and the beauty of the woodlands grew marvelous. So unexpected was this that Esta was reverently silent for never had she seen a forest so magnificent. The Alps of Germania were more grand than the hills about them. The River Rhône far more tumultuous and abundant than the small streamlets that coursed here and there, yet there was something indescribable about this woodland with its variety of stately trees and its flowered meadows. As Esta thought on this it seemed to her that the *life* of this forest was more . . . more *alive*. Oh, she wished that the aged Eponi could see this with her!

In an hour more she espied a wondrous thatched stone cottage. Nothing about it was ornate, indeed it was the very antithesis of the

---

2. Such as the Greek Amazons of Pontus.

grand houses of Rome. Its walls were made of white limestone and the mortar that joined the quarried stones appeared to be made from cemented sands of the same substance, for it could hardly be seen winding about the rocks. The effect of the whiteness of it, contrasting with the verdure which closely sheltered the house and the rustic color of the thatch, tinged with moss, was remarkable and extremely inviting. The door and windows were well set, though somewhat irregular, which only added to the quaintness of the dwelling. Nothing spoke of defense for so isolated a house—no open plains about it to espy the approach of an enemy more easily. Rather, towering evergreens rose immediately to the rear of the cottage, while flowering plum, redbud, cherry, blackhawk, hawthorn, dogwood, cornel and wide-leafed maple trees grew in even closer proximity, framing the dwelling with natural grace. To the fore of the cottage door bloomed an enchanting profusion of red and white roses, lupins, iris, trilliums and herbs such as ginger, rosemary, cloudberry, sage and poppy.

Further removed were vegetable plots and grassy meadows wherein grazed together goats, horses and forest deer. Amazingly there were no fences about, not for defense nor to retain domestic animals. An amiable hound, sleeping lazily in the shade of a great oak, looked up at them without barking. An emerald green woodpecker, perched on the near trunk of a sweetgum tree, sounded a muffled cadence to the melodious trills of blackcaps, nightingales, robins and other songbirds. A young woman came to the cottage door, looked out at them and waved her greeting.

Ruith's Enchanted Cottage

Esta exclaimed, "Ah, Ruith! How is this possible?"

Her friend smiled happily, saying, "Come inside, there is more to see. Our horses will be attended, our equipage removed. I see smoke arising from the chimney. You will soon taste the most delicious porridge that ever warmed your mouth. As we sup, I will tell you how this came to be."

The young woman embraced Ruith, welcomed her home and then did the same to Esta, though not calling her by name. Ruith introduced her, saying, "Esta, this is one of my helpers, whom I love as a daughter. Her name is very much like your own, Efa."

Esta replied, "Efa! What a beautiful name, old Celtic for Eve, our first mother! How appropriate as you verily live in Eden!"

"That I do!" said Efa. Then addressing Ruith continued, "Two are wholly well and gone from us since you left for Londinium. Two Ceosans[3] have come to us and abide in the loft. The mother and her children are yet here and I think will be for another season."

Ruith answered, "You have done well, Efa. Come Esta, meet our friends before we eat, for they will lift your disposition more than food."

Half of the cottage consisted of six bedchambers, furnished each with a comfortable featherbed, a well-made table and two chairs. Two of these were occupied; the first by a dame of middle years and a young maid, the second by three boys, all convalescing. A stout staircase led to a spacious loft wherein other youths were recovering from grievous burns. None were able to rise from their beds, but two of the boys. These ran to Ruith's extended arms, a happy greeting. The matron said kind words to each of her patients and all expressed

---

3. Ceosan were persons sacrificed in mock trials by fire, typically they were forced to jump through a raging Bonfire. Only if they survived three such tests were they allowed to live. Even then no assistance was given the Ceosan. Hence, death would normally overtake them in a short time.

gratitude, except one who remained silent as he was burned so badly he could not speak.

The other side of the cottage consisted of a great room, wherein were fashioned cupboards, a great hearth, several large tables with chairs, and against one wall was placed four more beds, about which curtains could be drawn. Another young maiden was at the kettle, spooning porridge in two bowls, which she set upon the table. She smiled as she said, "Ah, Mistress Ruith, you and your friend must be weary from your long ride. Come sup. The porridge is hot! I have also set out fresh spring water to quench your thirst, cold and clear!" Greetings were shared and then the maid lifted a tray of the same fare to feed others in the cottage, saying, "Won't it be grand when all can come and dine together!"

Esta and Ruith were alone at the table, enjoying the repast. At length, Ruith answered Esta's question, saying, "We lived in a village, not far to the north of this woodland and three leagues east of Linnuis. My sire in his travels had passed through Glastonbury where he learned somewhat of Christianity and became a believer in the Almighty Father and his Only Begotten Son, our Lord. These things he taught us when he returned. I was the youngest of his children but still I remember how I felt inside when we prayed and worshiped together."

"What did you feel then?" asked Esta.

"Absolute peace. Yet as our family were the only Christians in our village, if we could be called such, for even my sire had not been baptized, we thought it necessary that our beliefs should be kept secret. As a Druidic overpriest lived near us and as all those we knew were druids, this was a difficult task indeed."

Esta asked, "Why was your father not baptized when he was in Glastonbury?"

She answered, "The brothers and sisters of the abbey founded by

Joseph of Arimathea were teachers only and said they had not the authority to perform sacred rites."

"What happened to your family?"

"I was so excited about what my father told us that I shared what little I knew with a maid my age. She told her sire and we were found out. Now we had wronged no one yet we were bound and taken to the summit where you and I quit the company of your guardsmen. What happened there is hard to tell, so heinous were the acts of those devils, for men and women they were not. My sire and brothers were ritually 'tried by fire.' I saw their agonies and heard their screams until they were nothing but charred stubble. My dame, sisters and I were violently humiliated. They were burned but I was not, for after they finished their brutality, they thought I was dead. In truth I could see nothing more, so swollen were my eyes, nor could I move, so shocked was my body. Yet, I heard the overpriest say, 'Leave her for the beasts of the forest to devour.' He laughed as he said, 'the maiden is silent and only living sacrifices can be given the flames of Baal.' A woman spoke and I knew her voice, my friend's own dame, a Druidess, a sorceress, a fiend—she added sadistically, 'Aye! The Ceosan's cries must be heard afar till reaching Mount Zaphon. Silence is mockery to Baal, yet her flower taken is sufficient for his consort.'"

Ruith continued, "Now the Druids believe that Baal lives on Mount Zaphon[4] with Ashtoreth, or Astarte his consort. That the demon gods live there can be no doubt and are known in other lands by different names, such as Zeus and Hera. They hate anything that has to do with the true Lord. Still, the devils live not far away as they often possess the very bodies of their mortal disciples—for no

---

4. https://www.metmuseum.org/toah/hd/cana/hd_cana.htm#:~:text=In%20a%20-land%20dependent%20upon,30%20miles%20north%20of%20Ugarit, 2022

human could be so merciless and cruel, save they had abandoned their own will to the unborn spirits of hell."

Esta exclaimed, "Left in such a desperate strait, how did you live?"

"Hours after the Druids quit the summit, I recovered enough to drag myself to the spring, where I sipped a little water. I tried, but could not even stand upon my feet. The next day I was found by a kind merchant and his wife who, with their company, were bound for far off Exeter, for they heard my moans. Carried in their wagon, I did little more than live, but I could speak. Knowing of Glastonbury from my sire, I asked to be left there. I was kindly received and after a long while both body and soul recovered. For seven years more I lived and served among Christians, becoming a healer. I did not marry, for after what was done to me, never could I bear. Yet I longed to be a mother, to nourish and to heal.

"Then one night I dreamed a dream. The thought that was foremost in my mind when I awoke was that my art was most needed in the very place where I was wronged! I considered how many others were or must be sacrificed upon that summit. How many still breathed after being maimed or burned in their sadistic rituals, being left, as was I, in the agony of silence. I knew that Druids feed copiously on the living, that always there must be new offerings. Hence, I returned."

"However did you find such courage?"

"I reasoned that nothing could be done to me more than had been done. I had no delusions of greatness but felt that if I could save even one silent victim upon the summit, as the merchant and his lady had saved me, well, that one would be worth my life."

Esta listened intently to Ruith's story but questioned, "That you returned boldly is certain, a test and manifestation of faith and fearlessness! Nonetheless, how is it that your woodland is so altered, so lifted above natural enmities, so protected as to be a haven for your sufferers?"

Ruith replied, "I left Glastonbury alone and afoot, for by then I knew well how to live and thrive in the forests and God has given me robust legs that can best a mounted rider in a days' time. Alone, I could easily bypass the hamlets of Druids, for they have their signs, some secret, but I knew them. When I came to a village of descent folk, I would yet be wary and would study the ways of those who lived there from the cover of shrubs or trees, for I was stealthy as a fox. Hah, I had become so strong and agile that I could glide up a tree like a cat and often would ascend a great oak in the middle of their dwellings before dawn and not only look down upon their doings but hear them converse!"

"Why did you do this, if you needed not their food for your journey? Why not hasten back to your awful summit?"

"It was summer. I loved the journey. I needed time to consider how I could do that which seemed impossible. More importantly, I wanted to do good. Everywhere there is suffering, bones that are broken in accidents, fevers from sicknesses, women who have need in bearing—and too frequently are the bonefires of the Druids and those piteous Ceosans they leave crying afar to Mount Zaphon!"

"Ruith, never have I known such a one as you!"

"Oh, do not praise me, for I could do nothing save power were given me. And I found along the Fosse Way an abundance of need, for there is much suffering in the common experiences of our people and frightful need because of pagan ritual. Most always the skills given to me proved effective. I did much that summer, but the greatest joys came to me when helping a stricken dame, like Naomi, deliver safely.

"So I continued until I was but a league from the summit crossroads, still unknowing as to what I should do. Yet I had made plans. I thought of building a cottage of stone in the near woodlands where never man came, save to hunt. I prayed that I would not be found out before I had saved at least one from the summit. I determined that perhaps I could move about, disguised as a pagan sorceress and make my habitation feared, for I had learned that courage is of heaven and cowardice is of hell. Though I know well the secrets of the dark arts and could feign the part I had decided to play, yet I vowed that all that *I did* would be in harmony with truth and would never use my healing skills for ought but the giving and preserving of life.

"Of course, I knew of the enchantments of sorceries, and that not all were fakery, but conjured by those allied to unseen demons—and I knew these were but the black charms that work in opposition to the inexplicable blessings given of heaven, that which is termed the miraculous, for to God nothing is impossible, not even the raising of the dead. Of the former, I had seen much. Of the latter, *none*, save for the miracles of nature and life that surround us always. Still, through healing, I saw the effects of good herbs and how a broken limb could be set so as to slowly mend. But as for a parting of the Red Sea, or restoring the sight of one who is blind, these were things for me to read in sacred codices and I sought not for such things.

"This was the condition of my mind as I walked the Fosse Way. Then I saw a man in the distance and was about to retreat into the shadows of the forest, when a sudden impression came to me that I should not but rather hail him. 'Ah,' I said to myself, 'he must be in need and there is some good I can do.' Hence, I ran to him and when I drew near and before he spoke to me, said, "My friend, I see you are an aged man and have journeyed far. You have no satchel and hence no food to strengthen you. My craft is to glean from the woodlands as if cones were pomes. If you will allow it, I can soon make a delicious repast and would hear of your travels."

"What did he say to this?" asked Esta.

"Nothing, yet he smiled and followed me a short ways to where a stream flowed down from the summit spring. He sat upon a downed limb and watched while I kindled a fire by striking my stone and boiled water using an open urn I carried. Into this I placed roots, dug in his presence, and garnish I had in my bag and soon we supped.

"Only then did I take the time to notice him closely. His hair was streaked with white and there were lines about his kind eyes. His garments were rustic and his staff of uncarved wood. Nonetheless, despite these marks of age and poverty, his bearing was regal, erect, his actions, even to lifting his food were quick and knowing. More than these was the feeling I felt in his presence and the burning of my heart.

Then of a sudden he said, "Ruith, what is it you now desire?"

"Ah!" exclaimed Esta, "how did he know your name? Was he truly not a stranger to you?"

"I thought I had never seen him, but when he spoke my name, he was no stranger to me. Who he was, I did not know and to this day am yet uncertain. But I felt, somehow, he was a holy man; that I was not sent to him, but that he was sent to me."

"How did you answer his question?"

I answered, "Let them see their fears, that they hinder not my works."

"He replied, 'Ruith, you are proven. We have seen your doings. *It will be as you ask* and this woodland will be the sanctuary you desire *if* you bring none here, save those who have need and those who are sent. *To these you shall be a Beldam of Heaven.*'"

"Then he smiled as he said, 'Daughter, never wear disguise; be who you are. Your foes will indeed see their terrors. Your countenance to them will appear more dreadful than the fiends they worship, your home more forbidding than the great abyss. *To them you shall be a Beldam of Hell*, a horrid mistress of Bel.'"[5]

---

5. Beldam has two meanings, the one the antithesis of the other:

"Was it our Lord that had come to you?" Esta asked.

"No. I knew he was not." She answered. "After that he arose and left me, walking away swiftly until he was gone from my sight. I turned and crossed the road, where the forest was more dense. I waded through a marsh and coming to higher ground walked into the heart of the woods. In a beautiful sunlit meadow, I knelt in prayer, thanking God for what had been given me, for I doubted nothing. At this spot I began to build. No sooner had I laid but one course of stone than a man and his daughter came into the meadow from the far side of that copse of trees," and she pointed out a window. "He said that it was a hard thing for a lone woman to build a house of rock and asked if they might help me. 'Where is your home?' I said to him. He answered that he had none, for they were Christians and had fled from a far land, that only he and his maiden were left alive. To this, I said, "Then yes, please help me build my home and yours. It must be large, for soon others will also come.'

"We soon discovered our forest was indeed enchanted, for there is such a thing as a blessed enchantment. The creatures of the forest did not fear us, for we ate not their flesh. The waters of the stream-lets never fail, even in heat and always are clear and sweet. We have winds, but never gales. The ground is fertile."

Ruith continued, "In several days more, a woman found us, whose story was much the same as ours. Soon she became wife to

---

The first is Bel or belle, meaning beautiful (or in the Akkadian, Bêlit, meaning lady) coupled with dam or dame, meaning mother—making Beldam, the compound word meaning **Beautiful Mother**.

The second is Bel, meaning Baal, the pagan god, coupled with dam, meaning mistress—making Beldam, the compound word meaning **Baal's Mistress**.

"The worship of Baal was popular in Egypt . . . Through the influence of the Aramaeans, who borrowed the Babylonian pronunciation **Bel**, the god ultimately became known as the Greek Belos, identified with Zeus." https://www.britannica.com/topic/Baal-ancient-deity, 2022 the widower. The four of us built this cottage and so quickly was it done that we were amazed!

"Every now and then some hunters would come upon our abode. But when my eyes met theirs, the killer's eyes filled with terror and they fled when none pursued. Once, my helper's wife ventured into the hamlet of the overpriest on the far side of the summit, as she desired to purchase cloth. It was there she heard talk of the great sorceress who lived in these woods and of her dark dwelling. Those who said such things said also they were lucky to escape with their lives. A shopkeeper told how the overpriest boasted that his rituals on the summit must have empowered a Druidess with its blood sacrifices. As she had not come to him, the overpriest would not go to her, nor should anyone, he said, venture into her wood that desired to keep their life.

"Thus was the promise given me brought to pass by preternatural means. Often, we go to the summit, especially after ceremonious feasts, such as the Festival of Midsummer's Eve or The Dæg of Blodniht, where homage is paid to Baal in the Ritual of the Bonefire. Although we cannot prevent the carnage, we do lend succor to the few who survive by bringing them here. Also, there are those who pray their own way to my woods and still do I travel to find those in need, leaving my homing birds here and there as faithful messengers. It was in this manner that Ophelos sent for me."

As a young maiden in Massilia, Esta had dreamed of learning from the masters of Rome and Athens. Never could she have thought that one day she would become an apprentice to a legendary healer in a woodland forest. Ruith became fabled in all the towns and villages near Linnuis, known to those who feared her as a terrible witch and known to those whom she healed as a gracious mother. For a year,

Esta was Ruith's companion. She learned how to rapidly traverse a forest, making ten leagues in a single day—more than she had ever ridden on horseback and more than when she strode along the Rhône path at Hadrian's side where no obstacles barred her way. She learned the healing arts, ministering to many injured souls, for the dark pagan cults were deeply embedded in that province of Britannia.

Of her dangerous adventures only one will be told. The man she saved was not a Christian, for there were few in the realm, nor an enemy of the clan who sought his life. His wife and three of his four children had recently died of an illness that left pock marks on the skin of its victims. A High Druidess kept the tribe in superstitious obeisance and was held in more fearful regard than their old over-priest. This was because she did not shrink from wielding the bloody sacrificial knife herself. This sorceress struck fear into the hearts of her people, saying that the dread disease was the handiwork of the goddess *Cailleach*, or the veiled one. The Druidess commanded the men in the hamlet to bind the hands of the poor man and his surviving child, a maid of eleven years, and take them to the summit shrine. In the dark of night, they kindled a Bonefire. In the phan-tasms of its ghastly light, the Druidess caused a deep sleep to over-power the man, it was said by enchantment but was truly nothing more than her pricking his skin with a drugged barb. The bindings of his hands were cut and he was laid oblivious upon a stone altar. The ritual was designed by this enchantress to play upon the minds of the villagers with dreadful anticipation, striking their breasts with terror.

Druid Sacrifice

The night sky was overcast but was slowly clearing. She decreed that when the moon was unveiled, or rather when the clouds parted so that the lunar orb was unhindered by mists, she would stab him in the stomach, so that writhing with pain he would be roused from his slumber. In this helpless state he should then be cast into the Bonefire, together with his Ceosan daughter.

Nonetheless, when the maid saw her sire fall by means of the drugged barb and the men lift him upon the table of rock, in desperation she broke free from the woman who held the rope that bound her hands and ran swiftly into the blackness of the woods. The sorceress laughed at her escape, saying the beasts of the forest would yet make of her a sacrifice, that none should pursue her but all tarry, as the moon might be seen at any time. Hence, the people did linger in the flame's light, drinking aged ale, while the old druids spoke omens and the Druidess stood at the side of the altar with knife unsheathed.

Though the young maiden's hands were tied, her feet were not and she swiftly ran—where to she did not know. Although the dark woods frightened her terribly, the horrid scene she left behind terrified her more. At first she ran down the road but fearing pursuit on the open way, she turned into the woods. Strangely, as she continued her flight, the maiden felt herself growing more calm with each footfall. Then she espied the light of Ruith's stone cottage and was soon at its door, crying for help. Immediately, the girl was admitted, her hands loosed and she was warmly embraced. Ruith was gone, some twenty leagues distant, where she was needed as mid-wife. Nonetheless, Esta had stayed behind, feeling that her help might be required in the woodland. Hearing the maiden's story, she left the girl in the charge of her companions and went alone to the greensward summit, not knowing beforehand what she should do.

In less than an hour she stood in the cover of the night looking into the midst of Druidic ritual. The clouds had not yet disbursed, but soon would do so. Already the Sorceress held her knife unsheathed, ready to slay the maiden's sire who lay upon the stone altar, the moment the direct rays of the moon should illuminate the victim. Esta had thought the drama would already have been played and she would find nothing on the greensward, save a smoldering Bonefire and the man's remains. Yet, there he was, still very much alive and the foul deed not yet done. What was she to do? Esta could not bear the thought of watching his killing!

She of course had no guardsmen, was but a young woman and was weaponless. Before her were not only old druids, dressed in long white robes, but a host of men bearing swords and shields, no doubt the guards of the High Druidess who stood ready to strike the stuporous man on the altar. Behind these were scores of villagers, apparently drunk with ale and savagery.

Esta knew she had not a moment to decide her course of action. If only Ruith were with her, for she bore the guardian promise. Or was that only effective in her woodland? In Londinium she seemed no different than any other. She determined to act forthrightly, to command obedience in the name of the Emperor, for was she not his consiliarius, his official advisor? Yet if she invoked his power without being flanked by Imperial guards, would they but laugh and make of her a Ceosan? That was, she decided, most likely. It made no difference to Esta that the maiden's sire was not a Christian, for all life is life.

What she did next was all that she could do and Esta expected that it would surely mean her death. How do you reason with savagery and how do you command without power to enforce your commands?

Nonetheless, Esta stepped forthrightly into the Bonefire's light just as the clouds unveiled the moon's rays and the Druidess raised her dagger high. **"STOP!"** Esta shouted in their own tongue and dialect. All turned to see who it was that gave the command, but especially the High Druidess, who straightway and with the ferocity of manner that only a devil can enact, glared intently at Esta. Her eyes wildly hideous! Esta continued her edict, **"IN THE NAME OF THE EMPEROR, CEASE THIS BUTCHERY!"**

The sorceress reacted instantly and with the hand that held the knife, wheeled round, pointing the blade at Esta as if it were a scepter, as she rejoined angrily, **"SEIZE HER!"**

Esta had but one defense: her strong athletic legs. The maiden spun about and fled. Yet already a guard of the witch was nearly upon Esta and the man caught hold of her outer gown and would have captured his prize had not the dress cloth been but a light weave, which ripped in his grasp. This only freed the maiden to run unencumbered. The long months of swiftly traversing the country-side with Ruith was then put to life-saving use, for the prey possessed far greater agility and speed than did her pursuers. Yet nearly the whole company of Druids and villagers gave pursuit, torches held high, yelling fiendishly, filled with lust, for most had in the instant of her command set their eyes upon her. She was exquisite, the most beautiful maiden they had ever seen! The men craved her but the Druidess even more, for *Cailleach* had whispered to her mind that a Christian stood before them, a Ceosan of exceptional worth! Like a mad pack of wolves, insensate with hatred, the drunken mob ran after her, spreading out at the further command of the Druidess, who yelled insanely, "ALLOW NOT HER ESCAPE, BUT KILL HER NOT! GOLD TO THE MAN AND MATCHLESS PLEASURE WHO TAKES HER!"

The night was dark and clouds once again enveloped the sky, shutting out heaven's light so that many stumbled and violently fell headlong. Nonetheless, Esta *saw* as if the moon were full and bright. Like a doe, she leapt over downed branches, hedgerows of black-thorns and deadly ravines. Gradually, without weariness, she circled about the mob, marked by torchlight and made her way with an uncanny pace towards the mystic woods of Ruith.

Not all the villagers had dulled their senses with liquor, nor had all followed chase. There was one woman, not yet in middle years, a widow who grieved with the man when his wife died, who then stood at the side of the stone altar, frantically beating his chest, trying desperately to rouse him from the induced lethargy. Failing in this, the woman seized a fire brand and struck his side. His eyes opened in pain and he started so fiercely that he fell off the altar. She grabbed his arm and exclaimed, "Haste! Rise! We must flee lest we die!"

Slowly the two left the greensward and disappeared into the forest—fortuitously in the direction of the stone cottage. So engaged were the Druids and their followers in chasing Esta, that none saw their escape. Yet the man could not venture far, for he was impaired by the lingering effects of the Druidess's potion. Hence, they were laying upon grass in the dark recesses beneath a beech tree when Esta found them. She and the woman were able to again get him to his feet and support his arms and slowly walk to the Beldam's cottage. His little daughter could hardly believe it when she saw her father alive and all were overjoyed in their delivery. Esta explained that God had saved them all for an important purpose. In this cottage and wood they were safe so long as they forsook the false gods of their village and were willing to learn of the true Lord of heaven, He who had saved them from destruction. Trauma is a significant teacher and the hearts of all three were prepared to learn.

The man soon recovered and when Ruith returned she found him diligently building an addition to the cottage, for he was a skilled craftsman. This new structure joined the lodge at a right angle and consisted of six bedchambers, three on each side of a central hallway. The woman and the little girl were also busily engaged in helping and in the process were learning to love each other. In a month's time, they considered themselves Christians and desired to return to the outside world as a new family. Ruith gave them a horse and enough provisions to make the journey to Glastonbury, for that is where they desired to make their new home. Esta felt supreme happiness in their happiness.

From such experiences, Esta learned that our Father in Heaven loves all of his children. The would-be Ceosan, though formerly pagan, had become a devout disciple of the Son of the Father. Esta knew not what his past had been, but believed he was intent on doing good for the rest of his life. It was hard to do so, living in that era of growing darkness, but she believed he would persevere. She was glad for men like him, women like his new wife and children like his daughter.

Esta had also learned more about the calling of a Beldam, the calling of a being a beautiful mother. Ruith had been given a superb gift, that of reigning in a Provisional Sanctuary, a woodland of a similar order as was the Paradise of Eden, where Evil fled in fear of itself and where enmity between the races of living things seemed somehow suspended. In this woodland, death was still possible but was manifest mostly in the cessation of avarice, carnality, mistrust and faithlessness. For those who already desired goodness, this forest somehow added immeasurably to that desire. If they responded to the greater light they were given, other virtues were bestowed, including courage, faith, devotion, selflessness and heal-ing, both of body and spirit.

Ruith's asylum was only a small tract of a few hills, streamlets and her remarkable cottage. When she ventured from it, as when she left to save Naomi and her babe, Ruith left knowing that she was stepping beyond the perimeter of her preternatural forest fortress, that she was again vulnerable to the common misfortunes of life and thence had need to exercise greater faith and judgment, courage and care—that she would again be risking life as she strived to serve and save. Nonetheless, as Ruith was fearless and did not fear death, she was always willing to answer the calls or impressions that came to her.

Esta also learned that Ruith's powers were not hers, that even when she was within the misty woodland she was but Esta. The maiden enjoyed the protection of Ruith's forest, but not to the extent of its' Mistress. "One day," Esta soliloquized, "one day perhaps I may be given such a gift . . . one day when I have proved myself to be a Beldam such as Ruith!"

When it was time for Esta to return to Londinium and fulfill the pledge she had made to the Emperor, she embraced Ruith, wept and promised to one day return. "You have been a mother to me and how I hate to leave this place of true enchantment. The labor here is endless but so is the peace it brings."

Ruith answered, "I will see you again, Esta, as you say, here, before I die."

The Orchard of the Beldam

CHAPTER 23

A SIMPLE TASK

"On the bleak shore now lies the abandoned king,
A headless carcass, and a nameless thing."

Virgil

For the first time, Vibia noticed that Esta was taken aback as her husband introduced a nobleman of Gallia Narbonensis, saying, "Domina Esta de Roma,[1] this is Lucius dux Carcaso[2] de Foix, who not only is an architect expert in the working of stone but is governor of Provincia Nostra. [3] You would have met him earlier had you sailed with us last year to Northern Britannia. His work on my wall is finished and he will travel back with us as far as Carcaso."

---

1. Lady Esta of Rome.
2. Known after Roman times as Carcassonne.
3. Our Province, or the first Roman province north of the Alps.

Esta replied, "You are from Foix? I don't believe I have heard of the place."

Although her response might have been taken as an afront, implying that his home was so insignificant that it was unknown, he was not offended. Firstly, she smiled warmly and he was immediately impressed by her unusual grace. Secondly, indeed not many people knew of Foix. He answered, "Have you been to Carcaso?"[4]

"No, but it is a well-known oppidum on the banks of the Atax River,[5] a vital trading center linking the Mediterranean Sea with the Ocean of Atlas,[6] the continent of Gaul and the Aragonese Mountains. I admit, it is strange that I have not been to Carcaso, as I was raised in Massilia, scarcely seventy leagues distant."

He replied, "You are quite right. Carcaso was found to be important strategically to Rome six hundred years before Augustus. It is an impressive fortress and commands a hilltop view of the Atax Plain. Never has it been taken by our foes! Hence, all know of the primary citadel of Provincia Nostra. Yet there is another oppidum, if it can be called such, that lies two days journey to the southwest of Carcaso, built strongly upon the thumb of a great rock, a knee, as it were, at the base of the Aragonese, known as Castrum Foix. For beauty, none can compare with Chateau Foix, my ancestral home."

Hadrian laughed, "Lucius thinks that by using the title 'de Foix,' he will publicize its fame! However, I do admit that the Castrum Foix is indeed the guardian fortress of the Aragonese Pyrenees, and stands as a sentry over the essential overland route between Gaul and Hispania."

Vibia interjected, "Sadly, as Ophelos was recalled to Massilia in

---

4. Fortification or fortified town.
5. Known now as the Aude River.
6. The Atlantic Ocean was known as the Ocean of Atlas.

our absence, taking, of course, Naomi and Eponi with him, we shall be glad of his company. Don't you agree, Esta?"

Lucius dux Carcaso

The maiden's cheeks were still colored. Lucius was Celtic, as was Esta, his hair dark, like hers. He was of medium height, strongly built with intelligent features and although he had attained thirty-two years in age, yet he was unmarried. And he was a proven prince, having commanded and prevailed in battle. Even more to Hadrian's liking, he wisely administered peace in his realm. As a younger man he had learned to quarry and set rock so accurately that a knife blade could not be forced between the adjacent stones of his structures. His fame in this regard had come to the emperor's attention and hence his work on Hadrian's Wall.

Esta replied, looking searchingly at Lucius, "As of yet, I know so little about you. But as Vibia has an uncanny ability to discern character, I am quite certain I will find you to be a man of goodness and wit. Hence, yes! I am glad you will be traveling with us."

Esta had enjoyed the journey from the woods near Linnuis to Londinium. As Ruith had walked the distance in answer to Ophelos' entreaty, so also did Esta, a challenge to herself. Although she followed the Roman roads, she took to the forest whenever she espied others about. As Ruith had sought for opportunities to help when traveling from Glastonbury to Linnuis, so Esta did likewise, exercising great caution each time she made herself known to villagers. Nonetheless, she did not traverse that great distance unarmed but carried a lightly concealed Pugio beneath her mantle. The Pugio was a dagger, the length of the blade being two spans of the maiden's hand, with a small bone handle that fit her palm perfectly. It was an earlier gift from a Roman courier whose leg she had set. The Legionary had broken his leg near the Ratae Baths as he attempted to save a cart from overturning. As the baths were close to Ruith's woodland, Esta learned of the good man's plight and offered help. So grateful was he, that he gave her his Pugio, keeping his Gladius. From his bed, he instructed Esta in how to properly grasp and use the blade.

She had made the journey in fifteen pleasant days of walking and running, staying only four nights in the cottages of those she served. Otherwise, only her mantle and the boughs of evergreens covered the maiden at night or in rains. Only once was it necessary to draw the Pugio from its sheath when a man threatened to accost her, but quickly changed his mind when he saw the knife glistening in the moonlight and quickly observed how easily she managed it.

When Esta arrived in Londinium, she went first to the domus of Ophelos where she sadly learned of his family's departure, for the maiden had longed to see her dearest friend and new babe again. Still dressed in her soiled mantle, she found Hadrian and Vibia in their regal apartments, having arrived but two days before. The Emperor could hardly believe it when he learned that Esta had made the long journey safely, without escort and afoot. When he praised the feat to his wife, Vibia chastened the maiden and commanded that she should never risk her life so foolishly again. Esta said nothing to the Emperor and Empress of her newly acquired healing skills or of her many adventures, the least of which was the recent passage south. Vibia ordered her attendants to bathe and dress Esta in finery, after which she was introduced to Prince Lucius. She had become quite used to the feel of the hidden Pugio against her form and no one would have guessed that the dagger was concealed on the slender maiden.

Preparations were made immediately for the voyage and journey south to Durocortorum[7] and soon the Emperor's court were aboard the Imperial fleet, sailing south across the Oceanus Britannicus. Vibia and Esta were walking the deck when they saw Lucius standing alone near the prow. Vibia said to Esta, "I'd like to sit for a while and gaze upon our fleet. It is quite a sight to see such massive vessels move upon the waters. I love it and think I could live my life

---

7. Now the city of Reims, France.

quite well as a seafarer! Why don't you join the prince for a while and get to know him better?"

Empress Vibia

"It is a beautiful day to be aboard such a splendid ship, is it not?" said Esta as she approached the young governor of Carcaso. "You and the Empress are of the same mind, for Vibia also contemplates the majesty of the imperial ships."

Smiling, Lucius turned about and said, "Esta, I was hoping I might see you this morning! Hah, the fresh sea breeze plays wonderfully with your glorious hair!"

"You like my disheveled look?" Esta laughingly asked.

"Why yes! And I think I prefer your plain traveling dress to your exquisite gowns, for until now I never saw you but in silks." Since their first meeting, Lucius had often dined with Hadrian, Vibia and Esta and they had enjoyed many pleasant conversations. He continued, "Now you look more like a maiden and less like a princess or consiliarius!"

"Ah," she replied, "it is strange indeed that the Prince de Foix prefers the common to the illustrious!"

"At least," he answered, "you refer to my humble home of Foix, rather than the great Carcaso or my Province of Narbonensis. For in Foix, I am truly myself and there I am nothing more than the prince of my family."

"Does your sire not live then?" she asked.

"Nay, but my loving dame is yet alive, and I have three younger sisters, with children, and one little brother, all reside in Chateau Foix, a heaven to me."

Esta replied, "Yet, you were not thinking of such pleasantries just now, for when I drew near your brow was furrowed. Lucius, what troubles you?"

Normally, the prince would have never answered such a personal question, especially from someone he hardly knew. Yet, even then, he felt he could never set aside a question from Esta as a thing of naught. Also, that she was so attentive as to perceive his disposition was something he thought extraordinary. He answered, "Ah, you must forgive me. You are quite right; I was regarding this Roman armada that carries not only Legionary but the Court of Rome! Within sight upon these waters, in distance less than a league, there is more wealth and power than in the whole of Narbonensis! I speak to you, Esta, as if I had long known you and can share confidences. The Emperor and Empress are good people, perhaps the best rulers the Empire has ever known. Well, perhaps, this makes no sense to you."

Esta answered, "Truly, what you say to me shall not be said to another. I do not believe, Lucius, that you envy their station nor lust for their power, for there is melancholy in your voice."

He replied, "Yes, indeed, for when I look out at this incredible display, I think of the obsequious imperial court with all of its intrigues. It is the same in my province, just the same, except in Foix. There only the nobility of families are regarded, for there every sire and dame are held in high regard and children truly honor and obey their parents. In Foix I am not called Prince but sire, though as yet I have no sons or daughters. It is such a simple way to live, one of thoughtful labor and caring, not for silver but for one another.

He continued, "Ah, it is hard for me to explain. When I was a young commander of Carcaso and had won a battle against the barbaric Aquitani, bringing them in subjection to Rome, the Emperor Trajan exalted my station, appointing me *princeps* of the province, which Hadrian yet sustains. How my inclinations have changed since I first gloried in the glories of man! I hunger, Esta, for something greater than all that sails before us. Esta, have you seen suffering?"

She answered simply, "Yes." Esta felt herself fortunate that Lucius was in a reverie, for she desired to know foremost how he *thought*. Esta believed that seldom did the man reveal to others what he had already said to her. "Though I have not been a warrior, I have seen carnage. You will not offend me. Please say on."

He replied, "Perhaps you have read the writings of Publius Vergilius Maro?" She nodded that she had. "Think on these lines he wrote in his second book:

> *"'Thus Priam fell, and shared one common fate*
> *With Troy in ashes, and his ruined state*
> *He, who the scepter of all Asia swayed,*
> *Whom monarchs like domestic slaves obeyed.*
> *On the bleak shore now lies the abandoned king,*
> *A headless carcass, and a nameless thing.'"*[8]

Esta said, "How well the poet speaks of the vanity of high station and the miserable end of those who live for this life only. Had Priam lived well, his death would not have left him a 'nameless thing,' regardless of his mutilated corpse. Lucius, do you find solace from these cares in your worship of the gods?"

He looked into Esta eyes, then suddenly smiled as he answered, "Ha, what I tell you now might well cost me not only my 'high station' but also my life—*if* it were told he who is foremost aboard this ship! *I do not sacrifice to the gods, not to the least of the pantheon or the greatest. I do not believe in them!* Though I find inspiration and truth in the annals of the poets and believe in the virtuous maxims inscribed on the monuments of temples, I do not hold to the notions of gods that destroy in a fit of jealousy or exalt devotees on a whim. No Esta, all nature is in perfect order, all things abide by eternal laws. Who decreed these and who created the perfections and beauties of life, from the birth of a babe to the seasons that govern the harvest, I cannot say—I do not know. Yet there must be a supreme Creator and there is *right* purpose in all that he does. There are almighty decrees I

---

8. Virgil, *The Harvard Classics*, Volume 13, P. F. Collier & Son Corporation, New York, 1937, p. 119

do not yet understand; there has to be more to life than is presently seen and always I search for the *meaning of things*. One day I hope to comprehend what now is incomprehensible to me. such as the laws of brevity, suffering and death! How are things to be made aright when so much *seems* unjust or at least unfair?

"Ah, Esta, how I muse with you! You must think me a strange man indeed. You said you would not tell others my ramblings and I knew instantly you were sincere! I suppose that is why . . . no, there is something else." Erratically, his thoughts leaped from one point to another. "You are unlike anyone I have ever met. It is not only in your outer self, for in beauty no other woman is your equal—rather it is your *internus spiritus* that radiates virtues most excellent. Well did Hadrian tell me . . ." He stopped speaking, feeling he had said too much.

Esta rejoined, "Please continue. What did Hadrian tell you?"

He answered gently, "He said, 'Esta is Domina Romae, Domina Imperii."[9]

Esta was accustomed to adulations but as she had *seen* the truly divine and knowing she was yet far beneath celestial perfection, she was honestly humble. She accepted praise that was appreciation but would not dwell on it. Servile praise or flattery she abhorred. Still, the effect of Lucius' compliment upon the maiden was very different than anything she had before experienced. "Thank you for trusting me," Esta replied. "I think I would very much like to see Foix."

THAT EVENING, as Esta rested, she thought of all those who were beloved to her. Memories of her mama and papa, grandmama, her faithful family and especially Naomi, who was more dear than her

---

9. Esta is the Lady of Rome, the Lady of the Empire.

own sisters, old Maros and Eponi, her friends in Massilia, including Aléxandros, and those friends she had gained in Rome, Michela, Arrian, Diocles and even the Emperor and Empress, for Esta knew they loved her as she loved them, and oh, Ruith, the Beldam of the Woods, what wonderful adventures they had shared—and when she thought of Ruith, Vittoria also came to mind and then, with closed eyes, came other faces whose names she could not remember—these memories like the powerful surge of the sea rolled over her and about her, filling her soul with gratitude for immeasurable blessings.

Esta was resigned to the loss she felt for those gone: her parents, la menina, Maros and Eponi, though she believed she would again be with them after she had lived this life. She was grateful for Vibia and Hadrian, who were yet with her. She greatly missed her association with Arrian and Diocles, but oh, how she longed to be with Naomi, to talk as they did when they were girls walking along the shore of Lacydon Bay—and how she wanted to play with little Eponi and watch her grow into the image of her saintly mother!

Nonetheless, Esta realized that something had changed deep within her, for she was beginning to love in a way she had never loved before. Always she had *felt* passionately. But of a sudden a great desire seemed to eclipse all other loves and longings. She questioned, "How could it happen so soon?" Then another question came into her mind. "Was Lucius a stranger when you met him?"

She answered in soliloquy, "No, he is no stranger to me. Perhaps in meeting Lucius I have met a wonderful memory. Yet, I must be careful, for this is land and sea I have never crossed. How his image now dominates my sky! Nonetheless, there are many whom I love *who are fixed* in my firmament, for each has been a light unto me and will be so yet, and the greatest of these is my Daystar!"

Esta thought on her Lord, then lit a candle and read from her most cherished codex. She read for hours, pondered and prayed until He was again foremost in her heart. Yet it was strange, for even as

Esta set her thoughts in order, Lucius became even more to her. "Of course," she thought. "Love is a gift of God. The more I love the Giver, the more he gives me."

THERE WAS much imperial business to conduct in Durocortorum and Lutetia.[10] Hence, Esta was ever with the Emperor and fulfilled her duties with continued distinction. The southerly journey to Carcaso was less demanding and most of the time Esta rode at the side of the prince in preference to riding within Vibia's carpentum, even when it rained. This was, of course, noticed by the Empress and was pleasing to her and the Emperor. Soon the prince and princess's names were heard in accord, such as, "Will Lucius and Esta be supping with us tonight?" Nonetheless, when the company retired for sleep each evening, Esta always slept alone with her servants.

Carcaso was far more massive than Esta had imagined it to be, possessing double curtain walls, moats, bastions and high towers overlooking the Atax River with Colonia Julia Carcaso just beyond the gates, a flourishing town of shops and well-built houses. Yet within the fortress there were not only the essential components of defense, a keep, quarters for legionary, stables, an armory and an administrative basilica, but there were additional shops, an inn, several restaurants and even an amphitheater. The order and management of Carcaso were extremely impressive and spoke well of its' Prince.

A host of couriers awaited the Emperor in his coming to Carcaso and he was occupied from the sun's rising to its setting with Esta writing answers, dictates and military dispatches. So also was Lucius reengaged in the affairs of his province so that for two weeks he

---

10. Now Paris, France.

hardly saw Esta, save to infrequently sup with her, and that was possible only by Vibia's insistence.

Then, during the third week, Lucius and Esta were summoned by Hadrian and Vibia. The Emperor said to them, "Within a month we shall leave for Hispania and I will need Esta's skill, especially at Tarraco and Legio. At present, however, I do not require her services. You, Prince Lucius, govern the Narbonensis as I do the Empire. You have chosen your officers well and they manage your affairs perfectly in your absence. Hence, you may leave Carcaso, if that is your desire, and you may take the princess with you and enjoy the early summer in some other place. I hear that Foix is quite beautiful in this season."

Lucius replied, "Foix is lovely in every season, but thank you, Sire. How I have desired to show Esta my home!"

"Yes," said Esta, "He has told me so much about it that I can scarce wait to see it!" She looked at Vibia, as she continued, "Your kindnesses to me shall always be remembered and treasured, and perhaps this most of all. Though you rule a vast empire, yet you both understand the singular purpose for which each person lives. Most often alliances are made in our world without consideration of the heart. How well I know this fact as I think about the averted tragedy of my youth! Thank you. I thank you both! Might I ask a question?"

"Certainly," said Hadrian.

"After you visit Legio, will I yet be needed? Surely, you will continue your adventures, for not only do you thrive as your traverse your dominions but also do they thrive by receiving your personal attentions!"

The Emperor smiled as he said, "Esta, always are you needed. Nonetheless, after Legio I believe you will have accomplished quite enough for the Empire, should you desire to fulfill another office. Now, I think I shall disclose something that you must consider." Vibia gave him a disgruntled look. "The Empress disagrees with me on this matter. Lucius, after you return Esta to Carcaso to join us, you will remain here, or at least in the Narbonensis. You may, of course, talk of future plans with our beautiful Domina Romae, but *you may not take her troth*. As Esta's sire is deceased and as Aléxandros is no longer her guardian, I must act the part, even though I gave her independence long ago. You know already that Esta is no ordinary maiden, that she has rare gifts and is second only in my eyes to the Empress Vibia. Still, she is a demoiselle whose feelings may overrule her thinking. Show her Foix and all you hold dear. Then release her back to us for a time. I know that you could not ever think or feel otherwise than you do now, for who else would have the power to win your affections after you have known Esta? None! Hence, I do this thing for Esta's sake, to give her time to confirm her desires. After traveling with us to Legio and assisting with matters in that city, she may do as she pleases. Esta will surely go to Massilia to see her family and Naomi—or she may return to the great city where she is loved, to Rome, for surely Esta will want to see Arrian again, her tutor, Diocles, who adores her, and Michela who worships her. Of course, she may also return to Carcaso or Foix, as she wills, be it soon or late. I caution you, Lucius, it may not be for many seasons."

During this time, Esta listened with bowed head. When Hadrian was finished speaking, she lifted her eyes to meet his and advanced, kissing him on the cheek. Then she embraced Vibia and speaking to both, said, "Hadrian, thank you for always you have directed me aright. I will do as you say. Vibia you are so understanding! How good you have been to Naomi and to me."

Lucius also answered, saying, "I have thirty glorious days to be with Esta, that she might see my home and family. I will protect her from all men and especially from myself, for I will not place her under any obligation and especially from bearing my seed until such time as she herself chooses to become my wife. We shall not speak of her troth until she returns from Legio—*if* she returns to me. Sire, I would not want it otherwise. How unfortunate are alliances which are coerced, entered with misgivings or misinformed. Time alone begets wisdom."

Hadrian smiled warmly and said, "Lucius, you are indeed a prince!"

IT HAD BEEN SO VERY LONG since Esta's brother had conspired with the Jacaian to take her captive. Nonetheless, this villainy instigated the purposeful and wonderful adventures that followed their treachery. It seemed to Esta, as she left Carcaso with her attendant maidens, riding at the side of Prince Lucius, that all things had coalesced for her good and she was filled with joy.

The countryside through which they passed was verdant, the little hamlets quaint and peaceful. In his own province and on a journey of less than two days, the prince agreed that they should have no need of guardsmen. Esta was grateful when protected by Legionary, but also felt such an escort marked those they guarded as persons of import, tempting thieves and those who would extort ransom. Also, at her request, the prince put off his costly raiment for sensible traveling clothes. Her own attire was nearly the same as her three servants, so that the appearance of the five travelers was comely but common. The effect of this left Esta feeling nearly as free as when she left Ruith's Woodlands traveling alone. They also agreed not to publish their departure or speak of their station, so as not to rouse interest or deference. Lucius thought it excellent that he should arrive in Foix unannounced so that Esta might see the natural manner of his people.

Verdant countryside

Late in the day, the little company of four maidens and one man stopped at a dominant mountain knee, called Mons Securus, or safe hill.

"If you desire to rest in a cottage," said Lucius, "we may ascend afoot a rather steep pass to the summit. Atop there is a small fortress and several dwellings. We shall be welcome for already they have seen our coming. Or we may sleep beneath the stars, for the night is warm and clement."

One of the attendant maidens said cheerfully, "Oh, please, Lady Esta, may we spread our blankets on the soft grass? It is so beautiful here and surely there is no danger!"

Another of the maids said, "No danger? Are there not bears in the Pyrenees?"

"We shall be safe enough," said Lucius. "My steed will wake me if anyone or anything comes near us. Horses make excellent sentries if your ears are trained to hear their signal neighs and whinnies."

The four maidens lay close together, while Lucius put his bedroll near their mounts, though still within easy speaking distance. After supping, they laid down, but none were as yet somnolent. For the sake of propriety, Esta's blanket was furthermost from Lucius. She asked, "The towering mountains to the south of Mons Securus have such a poetic name. Lucius, why are they called the Pyrenees?"

He replied, "The ancient Greek King Bébryx ruled the mountainous kingdom of Aragon. Of all the virgins of all the dominions of Greece, his daughter, Princess Pyrène, was considered most fair. So beautiful was she that the demigod Hercules sought her for his own, but Bébryx refused the warrior and sought to punish Pyrène for being so exquisite as to attract his love. Angrily, the king threatened to disfigure her face.

"Hence, she fled from Aragon and sought to hide from her sire in the great underground labyrinths that are found here. These caves are immense and make hollow such mountains as Mons Securus, Lombrives and Niaux, but two leagues from Foix.

"Alas, the princess happened upon the den of a she bear! The claws of the great beast did unto Pyrène that which her father had failed to do. Screaming, she bled out her life in agony. Hercules heard the torments of his dying love, but found her too late. Tenderly, he buried Pyrène deep in the heart of these mountains, whose name became that of her own."

"What a sad and beautiful story!" said Esta.

"How frightful!" said another damsel. "Are the bears hereabouts truly killers?"

"A she bear will always defend her cubs," said Lucius. "Otherwise, no, unless driven by fierce hunger or crazed. Have no fear, but rest. We shall leave at first light." They talked more of the unhappy fate of Pyrène. Then to ease their innate fears of vicious beasts, Lucius spoke of the night sky and its wonders. Hence the maidens fell asleep in peace, as did he.

Nonetheless, the eyes of a brute were truly upon the maidens and their solitary guard. More than a year and a half had passed since the two Cosans had failed to capture Naomi and murder Esta. Still, their Roman conspirators had not recalled the promised blood money for the deed. It will be remembered that the chief Sicarius had been injured by the descending blow of the rock in Esta's hand. Nonetheless, he had made it to the Rhône and despite its torrents had survived the river. Their attack, hindered by Ophelos, led to a score of Sicarii deaths, a result of the Emperor's decree against the Zealots. For this reason, the captain was rejected and spurned by his own men. Yet, the veteran assassin believed that Hadrian, with Esta, must return to the south of Gaul and had been biding his time, recovering and plotting. The former chief of the Sicarius had clandestinely met with his Sicilian handlers, touting the fact that no one had come closer to killing Esta than had he. His proposition was "simple." He would trust no confederates, not the Sicarius or even a sole companion. As no other person would know his plans, he could not be compromised. The assassin stated the obvious, as his victim was protected by the might of the Emperor, to actually take her life would be extremely perilous for her "executioner." Hence, his fee would not be a thousand denarii, but ten thousand and his retainer a "mere two hundred denarii." It took months for the Sicilians to work their way through the dark intrigues of their trade. Nonetheless, at length, Senator Impius was informed of the plan and immediately approved it. Soon thereafter, the Sicilians swore a *sanguis foedus*[11] with the Zealot.

Ten thousand denarii is a great sum, especially for one man. The Cosan put off the garb of his clan and when he heard tell of Hadrian's arrival in Carcaso, he hastily made his way to the fortress on the Atax and entered the citadel in disguise, more that he should not be seen by Sicarii than by Romans. He could scarce believe his good fortune when he espied Esta, recognizing her instantly despite her common dress, leaving Carcaso *without* an imperial guard!

Trailing the small company of five without being noticed was a simple matter for the killer. He had not seen the prince before and, as he was dressed in common guise, thought him less than a Legionary. His task was simple. He did not need to capture Esta. He considered what an easy thing it was to murder in dark woodlands when there is but one man to give chase. Slowly and quietly, the Sicarius advanced, his right hand grasping the hilt of his dagger.

Lucius heard the scarcely audible neighing only an instant before he heard a slight rustling of a maiden's blanket and gown. He carefully arose and withdrew his sword from its scabbard, thinking at first his mount had been troubled by an owl or some such creature

---

11. Blood pact.

and did not want to disturb the sleeping maidens. All was quiet and Lucius was not yet totally alert, for he sensed no danger.

Then every sinew in his body tensed and more especially the grip on his blade, for he suddenly saw a horrifying sight! Three maidens were yet asleep, while Esta was on her feet and astoundingly in a fighting stance! She held a Pugio and faced a barely discernable figure, a crouched man whose glistening steal reflected dim rays of moonlight. No doubt he had intended on silently slaying the princess, but her ears had been more acute than even the trained hearing of the prince. In a trice, Esta reacted, drawing the Roman dagger from its hiding place while quickly gaining her feet. So focused was the maiden on the fiend that she had not so much as cried out for help.

As he looked upon Esta, the Cosan was surprised but not overly concerned. He was angry with himself that she had heard his approach, or rather that she was alerted by a horse and knew the meaning of the alarum. At first, he doubted that she actually saw him in the black shade of night. Then, somehow, their eyes met—at least her unflinching gaze looked steadily toward him. In the next moment he saw the man also arise, somewhat sleepily. Well, he must act while the man was yet three strides distant and not fully roused from his lethargy. Then the Cosan remembered Esta's swift action in the streamlet and how it nearly cost him his life. Now she was armed with a Pugio and seemed to know its proper use. Yet his very life proved that no foe had ever beaten him with a blade and surely this maiden would be less of a challenge than soldiers he had killed.

The Sicarius lunged swiftly like a striking snake! With startling speed, down came the Pugio, deflecting the thrust but not entirely, for the point tore through the shoulder of the hand that held her dagger, which fell useless to the ground. In the next instant, the assassin would have driven his steal into Esta's heart. That he could not do, for his own was pierced by the prince's sword.

CHAPTER 24
FOIX

"Love Foix, 'Tis a pretty little town.
Love Foix, 'Tis a pretty little town.
These are the words to the melody of the Calandra Lark."

Blanche de Foix

L ucius examined the gash in Esta's shoulder by torch light, aided by a maiden attendant. In the wars, as he desired to not only be a fit commander but also to help his injured men, the prince had learned fundamental surgical skills. The princess lay very still upon her blanket, for the pain was severe. He tore her stola free from her shoulder to expose the lacerated skin. In his equipage Lucius carried a small satchel, which he handed to the maiden. "Give me a swath of linen as long as your arm." Bundled, he pressed this firmly into the wound and held it for several minutes, staunching the copious flow of blood. To his astonishment, Esta did not cry out, though he knew the pressure increased the pain. Lifting the linen momentarily, he looked closely at the injury, "Mmh," he said thoughtfully, "the thrust was a strong one and would surely have taken your life had you not parried the stroke! Still, it is deep and has cut through vital sinews that control movement. I will cleanse your poor shoulder with wine. Using sutura,[1] I will first try to mend the sinews before they retract and are lost to us. Then I will close the wound. Until this is done, the hurt will be much worse. Please, I beg of you, drink freely of the wine." This he said, for she had not yet drunk of the cup offered by another attendant.

Dawn came before Lucius finished his task, for he needed the sun's light to see clearly. After applying several layers of linen, wrapping the shoulder and affected arm tightly, he smiled and said to his patient, "You, my dear Esta, are more stoic than any maimed soldier I have served. But now, the pain will ease a bit and I believe you will begin to heal."

She returned his smile and said clearly, "Thank you! Twice this night you have saved my life. First you killed my killer. Then, I would have surely bled to death had it not been for your skill."

"Hah," he retorted, hoping to cheer the sufferer, "My skill? What about your own! Where did the Pugio come from and how did you react so deftly as to deflect the death stroke?"

Despite the pain it caused, Esta laughed a little as she answered, "Why on my person, hidden. I have carried it with me since I left the woodland near Linnuis."

He bent over and kissed her forehead, saying, "Ah, I knew not that I loved an Amazon! What a fighter you are! Never when I embraced you did I detect the weapon! Now rest. We shall not leave this camp for a day or so, not until you feel able to ride, for the trail is

---

1. Roman word for suture.

quite rough between Mons Securus and Foix. I think a litter would be more difficult for you than to ride horseback."

She replied weakly, "Give me but an hour or two and I promise to stay on my mount. I am so anxious to see Foix!"

He answered, "If you can stand it, that would be best! Mon la maire[2] is renowned as a healer. The sooner you lay upon her soft bed the better you will be."

As Lucius attended the horses, a maiden asked him, "What of the Cosan? Would you have us bury him?"

"Nay," he replied quickly, "leave him. He is fit food for the beasts of the forest. If he bears a purse, divide the silver among the three of you."

In a short while, Esta rose to her feet and to everyone's delight there was some color to her cheeks. Her servants carefully removed her blood stained and torn sleeping stola and dressed her in comfortable traveling clothes adjusted for the use of one arm and hand. Lucius lifted her upon her mount but gave her not the reins. These he held and trailed Esta's horse at the side of his, while with her good hand she steadied herself by holding onto one of the pummels.[3]

All the while they journeyed, despite her weariness and distress, the princess made brief comments on the beauty of the countryside. Indeed it was glorious and verdant! Hills rising into majestic mountains, meadows watered by clear streamlets, brown hares darting about, deer, mountain goats, and fox aplenty, fowls, small and large graced the air. Once they waited while a bear and her cubs crossed the path well to their fore.

Though in consideration of Esta's condition, Lucius set a slow pace, they nonetheless arrived in Foix while yet there was light.

---

2. My mother.
3. It is thought the Roman saddle had four pommels.

Several boys and their papa were working a field as the small company rode past. The father looked up and immediately recognized Lucius. Smiling widely, he ran to the trail and gesturing with both hands raised, exclaimed, "Mon Paire,[4] long have you been gone! How we have missed you and see how my sons have grown." This he said as he pointed towards them.

A young dame attending her goats saw them next and also ran to his horse, reaching for his hand in greeting. "Oh, mon Paire, we are so glad you've come home! Who are these demoiselles you escort?" Before he could answer, her eyes fell upon Esta and seeing blood seeping slowly through her clothes, exclaimed, "Oh, you are injured and yet you ride! Please rest here, I will quickly fetch mon lo marit[5] and he shall take you in a cart to Chateau Foix!" So saying, she swiftly ran to the village while Lucius helped Esta from off her horse and laid her gently in the shade of a spreading tree. Soon the dame returned, and kneeling beside Esta said to her, "He will be here very soon. He is hitching our donkey to the cart and placing clean straw inside that you may be more comfortable. The ride up to Chateau Foix is steep! Here is goats' milk. It will help you mend." She handed her a chilled urn. "We have an ice cave, just outside our town, where we keep our milk and cheese."

Esta took a sip of the milk and said sincerely, "Ah, it is the best I have ever had, so cold and delicious!"

The cart arrived and again Lucius gently lifted his love. She was glad it was large enough for her to lay inside. As its sides were but posts she could see the village quite well, though she lay upon her back. One of the maidens sat beside her in the cart as concerned townspeople approached them and kindly expressed concerns. Her servant said to her, "Lady Esta, some of the words these people

---

4. My Sire in Occitan.
5. My husband in Occitan.

speak I understand and some I do not. Yet it is a lovely, flowing way they talk!"

She replied, "Here, they speak a more pure langue d'Oc,[6] than is spoken in Massilia, where because of trade many tongues are spoken and affect what is commonly said."

"They speak so differently here than in Lutetia," the attendant observed.

Esta was glad to talk a little, to distract her from the pangs that shot through her with every jolt of the cart. She answered, "In northern Gaul, langue d'Oïl[7] is spoken, yet many of their words are blended with ours."

Esta lifted herself, resting her weight on her good elbow. "Look about! See how every cottage is flowered, from window sills to colorful edgings of stone fences and pathways. The grass is so green in hue and every abode is built sturdily, every stone in its place, every timber set aright, so artfully, so picturesque! Homely cottages along the streams and aside meadows; others set well in the hills with cobbled paths leading to their doors. And there, atop the knee, the Chateau! Have you ever seen such a beautiful place as Foix?"

The Roman maiden replied, "Ah, it is true! I should rather live in Foix than in Rome!"

The ass, led by its kind owner, began pulling the cart up the steep ascent to the little summit whereon was built the Chateau that gave its name to the village. Her guard let down, Esta winced and her friend squeezed her hand in sympathy. The wound began to ooze more liberally from jostling about, her countenance paler. Then her eyes closed as mercifully Esta slipped into a deep sleep. She did not

---

6. Language of Oc, or Occitan.
7. The ancestral "oïl" evolved into "oui," or the language of "yes," known now as the French tongue.

open them again until the following morn, well after the sun had risen.

Chateau Foix on the Ariège River

She awoke in a quaint and clean room, resting on a soft feather bed. Lucius slept in a nearby chair. At her side sat a gracious dame of some three score years.

"Ah, Esta! I am so glad to see your eyes are clear! Your body could endure no more and so it took rest without taking your leave! I am Blanche de Foix, hah, the dame of that slumbering man. Last night, he would not sleep but watched over you while I removed the linens from your wound and carefully examined his handiwork. I will say this only because he will not hear my praise, but his surtura was excellent! I cleansed it again and placed a healing poultice upon the wound. Now tell me how you feel."

Esta smiled, feeling a great peace in this woman's home. She said, trying to rouse her strength, *"You are a Beldam, a beautiful mother!"*

She replied, "That is such a nice thing to hear. Again I will say something because I know my son cannot hear me. Dear la filha,[8] I would be your Belamaire[9] if that is your choice! Lucius told me of his love for you and the Emperor's wise edict. So, you see, I must hope with him! But you did not tell me how you feel. Nonetheless, I can see! Though your eyes are clear, you are very pale and have lost a great deal of blood getting here. Yet I promise, you shall get well if I am allowed to care for you."

"How long?" she asked.

"Hah!" the dame exclaimed. "In the outside world, a month, maybe two. But here, if you do as I say, a week!"

"Yes! Yes!" said Esta, "I will do as you say, exactly, for I must recover soon. I want to see Foix and the Pyrenees and all that Lucius has told me of. I want to be *with* his family, not cared for by them— by you, that is!"

---

8. Daughter in Occitan.
9. Mother-in-law in Occitan.

"Hah," the Beldam laughed again, "You are as impetuous as he said. That is good! And you are believing. Now you must do two things if you are to heal aright and use your arm again, as if never stabbed by that evil man."

"Just two?" asked Esta.

"Well, maybe three," said the dame. "First, you must drink *my* Ambrosia. Second, you must sleep without care. And the third thing, perhaps the most difficult, you must believe! Believe that when you awaken you will be whole."

"Of what is it made and how does this Ambrosia work? I have some knowledge of healing herbs," said Esta, "and also I know of the legends of the ambrosia of Mount Olympus."

The dame answered, "Somehow, I feel it is you who will tell me, for Lucius says you understand both the temporal and spiritual nature of life. This I can say, my Ambrosia is not of darkness but light; not of the gods of Greece or Rome, nor is it their food or drink that is said to confer immortality, spoken of by the poets.

"Esta, because of who you are, for all have heard of the Lady of Massilia, the Domina Romae, I will tell you that which I have told no other, not Lucius or my own daughters—and this that your mind may be at ease. Later when you are well, we shall go there."

"Go where?" asked Esta.

"To a mountain grotto that was shown me by my grandmama. Deep in a wondrous cave there is a narrow ribbon of amber, hidden in the stone. La menina told me that long ago it was resin from a tree of magic, that is the sap of it possessed healing powers. Not only this, but the essence of this tree lives yet in the flora in the valley of the grotto. La menina taught me how to sparingly harvest a little of the amber, reduce it to powder and combine it with the nectar of the bee, the blossom of yellow lutea, coneflower, valerian root and the juice of the Aragon tangerine, but only that which can be gathered in the valley of the grotto. This with a little cinnamomum must be cured, then gently boiled to become the elixir of my ambrosia. Do you understand?"

Esta replied, "Grandmama Blanche. I believe that all healing comes from our Lord, whether by means which he gives us naturally, from the earth, or through faith in Him, our Creator. Of this I will tell you more, later, when I have strength. You have my trust, *because of who you are,* I believe your Ambrosia makes use of these two means. Please, I will partake of your healing elixir as I ask in my heart for His blessing."

In the chamber was a hearth and upon the fire a small iron pot, boiling with an aromatic draught. Esta watched as the dame dipped a wooden ladle into the bubbling amber and poured the brilliant elixir into an earthen cup. The instant the ambrosia touched her lips, Esta felt a magnificent burning that seared not her flesh and was pleasant beyond description. Slowly she sipped the delicious nectar and felt its radiating warmth spread throughout her body, but especially in her wounded shoulder. When she had savored the last drop, Esta closed her eyes and dreamt of the Beldam she wanted to become.

It seemed to the princess that she slept only an hour. Yet, when Esta sat up, she noticed that Blanche wore different garments and Lucius was gone from the room. She heard the trill of a songbird through an open window. Blanche saw her awaken and said, "Do you know what the Calandra Lark is singing?"

"No," said Esta smiling. "Do you understand her voice?"

"Why yes," said Blanche, laughingly, for though gifted, she did not possess the same understanding as old Eponi. "I think she sings, *'Love Foix, 'Tis a pretty little town. Love Foix, 'Tis a pretty little town.'* Those are the words that fit well her melody! Don't you agree?"

"Oh, yes!" exclaimed the princess. "Foix is the prettiest of towns and the Lark the loveliest songbird to sing its fame!"

Suddenly Esta was astonished as she realized she felt no pain!

With her left hand she cautiously felt her right shoulder—it was no longer bound by linen, nor was it covered by the poultice. She touched the skin beneath her gown, feeling for the wound. There was none, only the small rib of a scar! She pulled back the robe and looked at her shoulder—it was healed! She lifted her right arm and moved the fingers of her hand with ease! "Oh, Blanche, how could this be in but an hours' time?"

"Not an hour, my dear! You have not opened your eyes for six days." The dame said this as if that were quite enough time to accomplish so great a feat. Blanche continued, "Although daily I roused you just enough to sip a little broth and drink a little more of my Ambrosia! Now you must be very hungry! Rise and I will help you dress. My family is most anxious to meet you, as are the villagers of Foix. First, however you shall sup. Oh, Lucius will be so happy to see you up and well!"

Blanche's children and grandchildren and Esta's attendant maidens were enjoying the morning repast when the princess descended nimbly down the long staircase that led from her bedchamber to the Great Hall, followed by the grandam, at a much slower pace. Her foremost maiden rushed quickly to embrace her, exclaiming, "Lady Esta, we've been so worried as we were told that none but Lady Blanche could serve you! Ah, just look at you, moving as if never you were injured! Truly, there is magic in this enchanted chateau!"

Esta returned the embrace, saying happily, "I *am* well! Entirely so!"

Immediately, she was surrounded by Lucius's family who were as delighted as her maidens, although it was the first time they had met the princess. All were enthusiastically polite, even the little children and all welcomed her to their home. Blanche, who by then had joined the spontaneous celebration, introduced her daughters and youngest son and then her grandchildren, whom she liberally praised.

Lucius was outside, chopping wood for the fire, when he heard the commotion and put down his axe. "What is this?" he exclaimed as he entered the Great Hall. In two strides his hands were about Esta's waist and he lifted her easily as if to better see that she was indeed well. "My Lady," he said joyfully, "you are a wonder!"

As he put her gently upon her feet, she replied, "How expertly you knit my shoulder and what extraordinary care I received from your mama! By your care and hers, my Lord has blessed me! I am healed, Lucius, and," she laughed, "so hungry!"

After they supped, Lucius was able for the first time to walk about the village with Esta, her hand in his. Though by no means a city, yet there was much to see and so many wonderful people to meet. The summit upon which the chateau was built was but the prominence of smaller hills that immediately surrounded it. In the dells between these prominences wound two rivers, whose confluence was in the heart of Foix, and many streams. Artfully, wooden and rock bridges spanned the rivers and larger tributaries. The streets at the center of the town were paved with stones, as were most of the lanes and pathways that led up and down, twisting and turning, to the many cottages and shops. Flowers and gardens were abundant, as were shade and fruit trees, including apple, pear, peach, cherry, fig, apricot and plum. The laughter of young children seemed everywhere about them, as plenteous as the trills and chirps of songbirds and squirrels. They climbed the limbs of spreading oak trees and somersaulted down grassy banks or raced nimbly along low rock walls, imagining some great adventure.

To the north were hills of greater height, but to the south and southwest rose the incredible pinnacles of the Pyrenees Mountains, still capped in snow. Throughout the many little valleys were open fields, wherein fathers and sons happily labored. Dames and daughters sang as they washed clothes in brooklets, or baked in common earthenware ovens, interspersed here and there throughout Foix for convenience. Doors were mostly open and others were seen within their homes spinning wool. Upon distant meadowed hills were shepherds with their flocks.

The prince and princess walked slowly, greeting everyone they met, young and old. Esta was amazed, for Lucius knew most every name, and when he did not, he made inquiry in a most genuine manner. One young man said to him, "Sire, it makes us all so happy that your beloved has recovered so soon!"

"Ah," he laughed, "word travels throughout the village like a swift wind, for Esta but left her bed this morning!" He grasped the youth's hand and continued, "Your father is David, our skilled forger of iron, is he not?"

"Why yes!" he replied.

"Is your name not the same as his?" asked the prince.

"Yes, Sire, I am indeed David, son of David de Foix."

"From the looks of the heft of your sinews, you also must tend the forge."

"Sire, that I do and am learning the blending of ores. Already I craft swords tempered in the cold waters of the Ariège!"

Lucius replied with a smile, though he knew well the path, "David, show us the way to your great hearth, for I would like Esta to see the skills of our smith." The young man led them down cobbled steps and through a maze-like walled passageway, then to a stout but narrow wooden bridge that crossed the Ariège. In the lee of a cliff was a natural cave that had been enlarged by its owner. Down a hewn channel of rock on one side of the cavern floor ran a steady streamlet of alpine water, diverted upstream from the river. Near this was fashioned a large furnace whose inward draft was drawn from tapered leaden pipes that ran below the surface to the face of the cliff and whose upward draft ran vertically a rod in distance chiseled through solid stone to the slope above. In the center of the furnace was the bricked fire pot and charcoal bed. Although furnished with a bellows, the cunning drafts and design of the forge caused the furnace to produce astonishing heat without further blowing the fire. The elder David embraced his prince, but called him "Sire" as did all whom they met. Then he bowed graciously to Esta and told her how happy he was that she was well.

Esta spoke both to the father and son, saying, "I have not seen such a forge as yours, not in Massilia nor in Rome!"

"Aye," said the son, "Foix is known for its strong but flexible steal, the finest in Gaul and Germania—and perhaps in the Empire. How our blades are fashioned is a secret known only in Foix. All of our friends can easily find this forge, but no outsider knows of it!" He walked over to a shelf and from it took a glistening sword, which he handed to Lucius. "Sire, this is steel that I have wrought and fashioned." His father looked on proudly. "At first," said the young David, "my blades could not withstand fierce combat, for my father tested each, and all failed—or they would not hold an edge. But now . . ."

The elder smith interrupted his son as he grasped the hilt in his massive right hand, "But now, withdraw your own sword, the work of *my* own hands and cross blades with me as I brandish my *son's* blade!"

Swiftly the son stepped back, as did Esta. Although it was mock combat and no bodily thrusts were made, still it was a wonderous thing to see the Roman general and the powerful forger smite blades with a terrific din. At length, Lucius laughed a great laugh as he sheathed his own and asked to examine the other. Looking down the length of the sword first and then carefully inspecting the edges, then lastly the hilt, he exclaimed, "'Tis true! There is none finer than this—from Persia to Britannia!" The apprentice smith smiled widely at the prodigious compliment.

Lucius and Esta visited many homes, enjoying immensely the

kind and sincere hospitality of each. Wherever they went in the village there was no pretense, only mutual admiration. Amazingly, there was no want in any household nor was there manifest any idleness. Yet they found some who were sick and one who was dying. In the latter cottage, Blanche already attended the sufferer, but confided there was little that could be done.

Later, as daylight was turning to dusk, the two were walking down a forest trail a league from Foix, as Lucius desired to show Esta a high waterfall that cascaded like a veil over natural terraces of mossy rock. Only forest sounds could be heard. Suddenly Esta stopped and slipped her hands around his neck, saying, "How strong you looked when you came in from chopping wood! How easily you lifted me with your hands about my waist!" She laughed a little. "Yet, it has been a long day. We have walked leagues and still there is more to show me. But you, my prince, must be very tired and no doubt have not the strength to lift me again!"

Promptly Esta was not only lifted, but thrown straight up into the air, then caught by strong arms, not at the waist, but cradled as if she were a slight child. This the maiden had not expected and was stunned, frightened and delighted in successive instants. He laughed, "*You* shall never tire me! Nonetheless, I am amazed at your own strength, for this is the first day of your wellness. Yet, 'no doubt,' you are at last near fainting and must needs be carried!"

She did not ask to be set upon her feet, but looking steadily into his eyes, said, "Only once, my prince, have you kissed me and that was upon my forehead when I lay wounded." Softly their lips met, then, and many times thereafter as they walked in moonlight back to the Chateau de Foix.

For the next twenty days, Esta grew to love everyone in Foix, but especially Lucius' family. Her own papa and mama had been so very good and their domus a caring one. Yet there was something very different in Blanche's home and Foix was very different than

Massilia. That city had been only tolerant of clandestine Christians, but in Foix there quickly grew overt interest in Christianity. Not only Blanche's family, but nearly everyone in the village were eager to learn of truths that countered the inconsistencies of predominate thinking. Not that Esta was critical of those who upheld the gods. There was one old woman who was a devotee of Hypnos, the god of sleep, who claimed that her dreams were messages of warning and not to herself alone but to anyone who would listen to her. Others believed in Pan, especially shepherds. While certain farmers built shrines to Priapus in their fields. Others talked of Zephyrus when the wind blew, and so on. To these Esta answered, but only if she were asked, that there is intelligence in *all* life. Nonetheless, she said, we should implore the Creator of life and not worship His creations.

Each evening, after the last repast of the day, Blanche and her family gathered in the Great Hall, as did many villagers, for all were welcome. Lucius often told different aspects of Esta's story and then she would tell stories from the Lord's Testament. The people of Foix were very intelligent and many were literate. Always they had questions for Esta, which she kindly answered. She had brought several Christian codices with her, including several copies of *The Epistle to Diognetus*. These she gave to Blanche to keep in her librarium for anyone in Foix to read, as they desired. Still, Esta explained, that she was *not* a priestess, nor did she know of anyone living who was a true priest of the Lord. Hence, she taught it befitted those who accepted the teachings of the Risen Lord to *live* by the light they were given and patiently wait on Him—that *ultimately all would be given of heaven, in this life or the next*. The effect of these evenings of spiritual discourse were as amazing as the healing of Esta's shoulder and arm. In twenty days, most of the people of Foix, including all of Blanche's family, called themselves Christians and had some understanding of what that meant.

The attendant who had ridden in the cart with the princess

when she was wounded begged Esta that she might stay, for the demoiselle was in love with a young potter who asked for her troth. Romans considered servants, slaves, but not Esta. She freely gave consent and wished her every happiness. Nonetheless, in one regard it grieved the princess, for she also did not want to leave Foix but was yet under the command of the Emperor.

The day before Esta left the village, Blanche led the maiden to the valley of the grotto where they took from the cave a small amount of the precious amber and gleaned from the dell the nectar of the bee and the herbs requisite to make Blanche's Ambrosia. These were carefully sealed in wax and placed in a stout but small urn for Esta to take with her.

The morning following the whole of Foix bid adieu to Lady Esta, shedding many tears. She told Blanche how much she loved her family and again wished her former servant happiness. Then Esta told all who had gathered how grateful she was that such a town of goodness was on the earth, that nowhere had she seen a more upright people. Then she spoke as an oracle, saying that their village would be a place of retreat forever—a sanctuary for the persecuted followers of truth.[10] Again Esta told of her love for each of them and said she hoped one day to return.

Then, astride their mounts, the Princess and her two maiden attendants left Foix, led by the Prince. The next day Lucius delivered his beloved to Hadrian and Vibia in Carcaso. Soon thereafter the Emperor's company left for Hispania. As Lucius watched Esta depart, he felt such pangs that he thought he must die. How long would she be gone from him? A year, maybe two? Perhaps that was the wrong question. Would she ever return? So much can be changed by time. He thought back to their conversion on the Emperor's ship

---

10. Foix and especially the nearby summit of Montségur was a retreat for persecuted Christian Cathars in later centuries.

when he said, "One day I hope to comprehend what now is incomprehensible to me, such as the laws of brevity, suffering and death!" She had taught him so much; then why did he feel this parting so deeply?

CHAPTER 25
THE LAST DAYS OF ESTA

"It is with the greatest of sorrow that we announce the sudden demise of Princess Esta Verica of Britannia, Consiliarius Imperialis Romae, lost at sea."

Emperor Hadrian

Esta's Ship in a Stormy Sea

Tarraco[1] was the chief city of the Roman province of Tarraconensis and the richest on the Mediterranean coast of Hispania. Possessing a fine port, a fertile plain and sundrenched shores, Tarraco had long been a favored retreat of emperors and the senatorial class of Rome even before the days of Augustus. Its vineyards produced some of the finest wine in the world. Its farms were renown for flax, a most versatile seed from which oil is extracted, also its fiber is twined into exceptional linen, damasks and lace. Culturally, Tarraco was truly *Roman* with an amphitheater, temples, forum and walled walkways interspersed with magnificent porticos with sweeping views of the city and sea.

Hadrian had summoned legates and rulers from Tarraconensis, Baetica and Lusitania, the three principal provinces of Hispania, to Tarraco for a great conventus, or assembly. Many Roman senators would also be present for their fortunes were vested in Hispania.

In the basilica of the forum of that great city, the emperor said to the princess, "Esta, in political matters, you've come to think as do I. Always do you amiably *strive* to resolve contentions peaceably and seek for common ground between disparaging factions. Quickly do you learn that which is most important to the chieftains of every land, from myself or through your own investigations and then you put into words, written or spoken, convincing arguments that further mutual good, which is always my intent. This said, still the greatest reason for your popularity in my travels is your linguistical skills. Somehow, everywhere, you speak the native tongue as if you were one of their own. Indeed, they soon consider you as such. Hispania is second only to Italia among all my dominions!"

"It is such a wealthy country," said Esta, "and yet it is distraught with strife, especially in Baetica, where olive oil and grain latifundia[2]

---

1. Modern city of Tarragona, Spain.
2. Huge landed estates.

produce massive exports destined for Rome and Athens—this while the smaller landowners are continually displaced, as they have not the slaves or capacity to contend in the marketplace. Many of these farmers are former Legionary who, like my own sire, were granted lands when they left the service of the Empire, then forced off their groves and fields by the senatorial class who dominate the latifundia. While everyone extols the virtues of agrarian life as the soul of the Empire, many thousands have been forced to forsake the soil of Baetica to the cities, especially Rome herself, and there live off the dole."

Hadrian replied, "Again, Esta, that is an accurate summary. Ever since the days of Tiberius Gracchus, emperors have fought the greed of senators who covertly own the great estates. Profit is preferred to life and slaves, many from conquered lands, are but livestock to their owners. Still, it is one thing to quell an uprising of slaves and quite another when the protestors are dislodged Legionary! As you speak to the assembly, speak to self-interest first and to the heart, second."

The Emperor spoke first in the assembly and promised that which was pleasing to his hearers: new aqueducts, temples, roads, amphitheaters and basilicas throughout the principal cities of Hispania, the cost to be borne by Rome. He spoke of increased trade and profit, the taxes of which should in the end offset the investment made by the Empire for these gifts. As senators were in many instances exempt from paying taxes, they heartily cheered Hadrian's oration.

Then others were called on to address the conventus. Legates spoke of provincial needs and civil unrest. One prominent freeman, a former Legionary and landowner, a man who had gained the support of many of his fellows, spoke at the Emperor's request—a most unusual occurrence. The man, who had been a great military commander in former days, denounced the latifundia and its human degradation, a crime, he said, committed against the veterans who had fought the wars protecting Rome and had won the very slaves owned by senators. His address incited the assembly almost to mob violence and sentries were required to restore order.

After this, Esta rose to speak. Although she had often represented Hadrian in many lands, yet she seldom spoke before Roman men, for not even an empress was held by many of the senators and legates to be an appropriate counsellor for "men's business." There were those present who had witnessed Arrian's introduction of Esta in the Circus Maximus. This, however, was vastly different, for not wagers but vested fortunes were at risk whenever the Emperor called for a conventus in imperial provinces. There were also faces among the crowd whose secret intent was known only to their companion conspirators; these were the senators who had hired the Sicarii and their master was yet the treacherous Impius. These were men with dark countenances and smiling faces, who delighted in the illicit gain of manipulated warfare and desired only superficial accord in dominions where they were the predominant landowners, a coerced compliance with lethal consequences of disobedience.

For a moment, in elegant beauty, she stood in silence before the conventus. Then smiling Esta said, "Rulers of Rome, vassals and legates of the Emperor, Senators, Proconsuls, Romans, commanders of men, though Consiliarius I do not intend to tell you your business, but rather I desire *to think with you* for an hour. That is far safer than to dictate what should or should not be done to achieve a certain end. For if done and the end is not realized, I should be proven a falsus advocatus,[3] like half of those learned men who appear before the magistratus." Light laughter coursed through the assembly.

Esta continued, "I was told there was one soothsayer of Cordoba who attended the sick young son of an illustrious praetor in Lusita-

_____

3. False attorney.

nia. The haruspex[4] commanded that a calf be slain, the savory meat prepared for his dinner and the entrails brought to him for examination. After supping to his fill, he then looked briefly at the praetor's son and that from a distance, for the child was indeed very ill and thought contagious. The soothsayer then said to the praetor, 'Have no fear, the viscera divine a full recovery and a long life for your boy. Such a prophecy is worth a hundred denarii. Make payment at once for I must leave for Baetica!'

"The praetor replied, 'That is a great sum and must be raised. Stay another day. I will pay you tomorrow.'

"To which the haruspex hastily asked, 'But what if the boy dies during the night? Do I lose my fee?'" The conventus erupted in laughter.

Esta then greeted each province in their native tongue, speaking briefly of local virtues, before continuing her address in Latin. The effect of her beauty, intelligence, wit and provincial familiarity was mesmerizing.

"Hispania is a great land," Esta continued, "abounding in riches, drinking freely from the cup of prosperity. Still, conflicts arise, as has been told, symptoms of national malaise, though soothsayers say otherwise. What are the causes? Is there a cure or is unrest a necessary evil of any people, no matter how well ruled? In times of privation, want must be endured, for what wine can be shared when vineyards are dry and desolate? Yet, seeing we are now in abundant times each must be careful not to fill their own chalice avariciously, lest they find they hold the Cup of Pythagoras! Remember how the Philosopher of Samos designed a cup as a jest to teach the consequences of greed among his friends; when it was filled too full, a

---

4. A soothsayer who interpreted omens by inspecting entrails of sacrificed men or animals.

siphon caused the cup to drain all its contents through its base, spilling all upon the ground.

"Is not Hadrian a liberal Emperor? Does not Rome freely give, knowing it sows gifts as a worthy husbandman to be returned with profitable increase when the harvest is come? My own sire was a soldier of the Empire, who having accomplished his days bought groves and vineyards in Massilia. Would he have served so faithfully had he thought there would be naught for him when his time had come but a Roman dole? If, through avarice, a man gains more than he can protect, how will he keep that which he thinks to be his own when his foes make war on him? Well has Hadrian established the furthermost boundaries of the Empire and withdrawn from dominions beyond those limits. Well has our Emperor returned many governments to the governed and what is the result? Peace, trade, prosperity in far off Germania, Britannia and Persia! Your task is to do in Hispania what Hadrian has done abroad!" Certain men applauded, while others seemed to stir in variance.

Esta spoke in a slightly elevated manner, saying, "What of slaves? Does bondage make one less than a man? Does wealth and power make one more than a man? When Nero ruled, did not the legions of Hispania unite in opposition to that wicked prince? Did not Epictetus, a Greek slave, become one of the greatest philosophers of all time, the educator of Emperors? Man is man and though he may worship immortals, he is but mortal clay and will soon live out his breath. What then is he? A slave may become a great teacher, like Epictetus. A man of elevated station may fall and be declared a public enemy by the Senate and cravenly take his own life, as did Nero. What legacy will you leave after you have breathed your last and what shall be my own?" The assembly fell mostly silent, for Esta had remarkably pricked every man's conscience.

She pressed the point, "Should subjects fear their rulers? Perhaps, but they should possess a greater passion, a love so great they are willing to die in defense of the Empire. What is requisite to engender such love? Each freeman should be able to merit undeniable possessions, that which is his own and cannot be unjustly taken. Never should a ruler of Hispania overrule the edicts of Emperor Augustus, the first emperor who began paying pensions to Legionary of twenty or more years of service, by forcing these veterans, through trade or by order of the law, to relinquish their lands to expand latifundia."

As Esta continued, most of her hearers again made applause and succinct comments of approbation. Nonetheless, there were those, particularly certain senators of Rome, who glared intimidatingly.

Nonetheless, the princess spoke confidently, exclaiming, "Now I speak to your self-interest. Is it better to store or to sow? Suppose a husbandman hoarded seed in urns and sowed not his fields, but used his grain only for bread for many years. How long would he have increase? Though his stores were great, his seeds would ultimately die and though planted, not a kernel would grow! Therefore, in your bounty, be liberal with the seed of your plenty, as is Hadrian! He is an Emperor who lives not for his own aggrandizement, but to better every province in his Empire. He desires the happiness of every Roman and the wellbeing of every servant of Rome, though he be a lowly slave, as was his teacher, Epictetus. He seeks that every province should govern well itself—*though if it does not do so, the Emperor will command his Legions to set things aright!*

"As this conventus cannot alter the Emperor's decrees, it would be wise to examine the unsettled affairs of the three provinces of Hispania, find common purpose and be united in resolution. Hence, before the assembly is dismissed there should be less need for Imperial edicts. Remember, provoke not one another or those in your charge; wisely conciliate and regard both high and low as men of purpose."

When Esta took her seat next to Hadrian, the Emperor said

quietly, "Well done! Nonetheless, you must never be without guards so long as you are my Consiliarius Imperialis. You spoke as an oracle and I saw many eyes that adored you and others that wish you dead."

Later, at the great feast of the conventus, Hadrian introduced Lady Esta to Mateo the legate from Cordoba of Baetica, a man he had known for a decade and one who had served him well. He was a man of great wealth and station who owned the largest estate in his province, whose lands were partnered privately by notable senators. "Esta," said the Emperor, "you have been formally announced to the entire assembly but it is likely that you know few, if any, of my companions or legates. This is Mateo de Cordoba, who insists on meeting you personally. You will find him singular in character and fiercely devoted to his pursuits."

In consequence of Hadrian's introduction, Esta extended her hand, which Mateo kissed with bowed head. As they were in the company of many others, Mateo drew Esta apart that he might speak more freely with her. He was a man of striking and powerful presence, articulate and well spoken.

After pleasantries were exchanged, Mateo said frankly, "Domina Romae, in but a few hours you have entirely captured my heart! I could not take my eyes off of you as you spoke, nor as you have been socializing! Perhaps you noticed me as well?"

Esta shook her head. "No?" he asked as if that were impossible. Esta smiled bemusedly and looked for signs that he was baiting her but saw nothing to indicate a lack of genuine intent.

He returned her gaze with adoration, saying, "Well then, now you see me and no other! I must truly unburden my soul, for I mustn't allow this special moment to pass without telling you that which you most desire to hear."

As she said nothing, he continued, "Dear Esta, it is as if I had known you all my life, or rather it is as if I have longed for one as perfect as you since the day I first became a man! You are exquisite, a goddess, more beautiful than Venus and as wise as Juno! For years I have heard of The Maiden of Massilia, for your fame is spoken everywhere! Of course, you have enemies, so does everyone who is great! I heard you spoken of in derision among some rabble of Rome when I was there two years past. If I knew then what I feel now, I should have slain those vipers! Now hear me and do not think I speak rashly! *You must come with me to Cordoba and become my wife!* My waiting to marry is at an end! I alone can protect you, not only now, as does the Emperor, but always, even until you die!"

Esta raised her eyebrows in disbelief and looked searchingly at the man. Was he speaking in jest? No, she decided; it was either a ploy or else amazingly he spoke sincerely! She had heard of the passions of men from Cordoba and knew well the passion of the nobleman from Jaca! Smiling she answered in a direct manner, "I suppose anyone can look after anyone else until they die, especially if death comes quickly!"

"Oh," he answered, "I am such a fool! Of course, of course, but that is not what I meant. I . . ."

Esta interrupted him, saying, "You tell me it is as *if* you longed for someone like me. That is different, is it not, from *actually* wanting someone like me. It rather seems a confession that you have settled for women quite different than I. Señor Mateo, you are indeed a good-looking man of considerable charm and wealth. Have you had many loves?"

Clear thinking was not a strength of the legate from Cordoba. He replied quickly, not understanding her implication, "Why yes, of course, many! That is why I can speak with such authority when I say that you are the most beautiful of all!"

Esta decided not to attempt further exploitation of the man's foolishness, although his complete overconfidence was amusing. Surely, his amours were seldom, if ever, refused. As Mateo was evidently unmarried, he must have impetuously considered that "waiting" for his perfect mate must now be rewarded, though surely he had never waited for anything in his life; hence this astounding attempt to woo her deepest affections by trivial sentiments! What of his mention of her enemies? A true conspirator, she mused, would not make such a slip. Or was he so expert and powerful in his own eyes that he thought himself exempt from caution? Did he think her beauty should not be wasted in murder? Better, perhaps, to frighten her a bit to more easily win her over? No, she thought to herself. No true confederate of killers would so entirely violate the protocols of intrigue.

All this passed through her mind in only a moment of time. Esta replied, smiling kindly as she spoke softly in his native tongue, for a Roman senator was talking to friends nearby, "Señor, no puedo enamorarme de usted a primera vista."[5] Then she spoke normally, saying "A great man, such as yourself, cannot have taken the time to think things through when he offers so much so soon! Nonetheless, I can from this moment be your true friend if you will be mine."

He answered enthusiastically, "Ah Esta, you are truly perfect! How did you learn the dialect of Cordoba? You speak as if you were born in my city! It is my loss, of course, for I would be more than a friend to you. Yet, it is also much gain, for never have I had such an amiga as the Domina Romae! Now this I will do. Never have I lived the virtues you advocated in your speech to us. But from this moment, I am a changed man—an ally to insignificant landowners! I am not great and they are not small. We are all men! This is how it must always be: you speak and I will do!"

Esta answered earnestly, "Are all in Cordoba so forthright as you? If so, I must someday visit your city, for I hear it is most beautiful."

He answered, "Mmh, sadly not. I am the best. Still, you must

---

5. Sir, I cannot fall in love with you at first sight.

come to Cordoba and forget the faults of my countrymen. With you upon its streets it shall be the most beautiful of all cities. If ever I may do a kindness for you or yours, please ask and it shall be done."

Villa in Tarraco, Hispania

She replied, "Mateo is a name that means 'gift of Yahweh or god' in Hebrew. Your friendship is truly a great gift! Mateo is also the name of the Christian writer of one of the books of the Lord's Testament—or as it is commonly written, Matthew. Is it not so?"

He answered, "I know so very much, yet about this I know but little. My great grandmama told me something of this before she died."

Esta said, "Mateo, you must learn all you can of his book, for I believe you are already a kindred soul of this writer of truth."

"This I will do!" He promised. "Truth? I confess I have not lived before for truth; it was not a consideration. Yet, I do not lie. Now I am a changed man and will live by the truth of this book! May I write to you after I have read it? You may have other things to tell me to do. I think it would please my great grandmama, if she looks down upon me, which of course she must do."

"Certainly," Esta answered. "Read Matthew and the other books of the Testament, if you like. Then write to me, not at Rome, but to Foix, a small village west of Carcaso." Thus, it was that Esta made a true friend of Mateo, a companion to the Emperor. Later such an office was signified by the title of count, or conde.[6]

As legate of Cordoba, the principal city of Hispania Baetica, Mateo proved true to his promises and indeed proved instrumental in the fair distribution of lands in that province. He also read The Book of Matthew and subsequently read every Christian codex he could purchase. Thereafter Mateo de Cordoba was thought to be the strangest prince of Hispania, so *giving* was he. Yet he did not write an Epistle to Esta, for when he heard the news of her he only wept.

Strange are the meetings of life! No matter how brief they may be, directions can be changed. So fleeting was Esta's invitation to

---

6. The word is derived from the Latin, comitem, meaning companion, or in the context of nobility means companion or attendant to the emperor.

read a small codex that it could not be supposed to have altered a good life and made it better, but such was the case. Yet, this was not the end of that which came from their knowing one another and more especially that Mateo *knew* of Foix.

In mid-autumn the Emperor's company arrived in Legio,[7] called after Legio VII Gemina, or The Twins Seventh Legion, named after the legendary twin founders of Rome, Romulus and Remus. The work that Hadrian did in Legio was principal to elevating the martial skills of that historic legion. He soon proved to the Twins Seventh that he not only relished the soldier's life, but was a master of the arts of warfare and possessed endurance greater than their strongest warriors. Vibia said to Esta, "Only my Emperor prefers sleeping on the earth and eating dry bread to the repose and delicacies I offer." She laughed as she said this, but Esta knew that it was a painful truth. Yet for this, Hadrian was beloved of his army. Still, there was not much for Esta to do in Legio and she wondered at her being there.

Then, one day, Hadrian supped with Vibia and Esta. He said, almost casually, "Well, we shall both miss you." He handed Esta an official parchment. "This will requisition an Imperial ship in any port of the Empire. I would that you should first sail from Tarraco to Massilia and visit our daughter and her child."

Vibia unwrapped several elegant stolas and regal dresses, several fit for a little maiden. "These," she said, "are for Naomi and Eponi. Tell them of our love and say it will not be long before we shall come to Massilia ourselves to see them."

Hadrian resumed his instructions, saying, "From Massilia you may go wherever you will. If to Italia, you have apartments in either Rome or Tivoli, in either palace. If to Foix," he laughed, "I think you must take residence in only one place, the Chateau! Incidentally,

---

7. Modern day León.

Foix is the only town where I shall not require guardsmen about you night and day, for Lucius has proven himself your able protector!"

Smiling, Esta answered, "It will be to Foix. My head and my heart agree. My love and longing for Lucius grows only stronger each day we are apart."

Hadrian then looked at Vibia seriously and leaning forward spoke quietly, saying, "Good. Then there is one thing more that must be done. Did you know, Esta, that as we traveled from Tarraco to Legio, six would-be assassins were discovered by my elite Legionary and executed?" Shocked, she shook her head. He continued, "There are still those in the senate who believe the warring polices of Trajan should supplant my own and they are convinced, especially after your oration in Tarraco, that you are a great threat to their aspirations. Two others, the last we know of, were found near your quarters and killed but yesterday. Sadly, I foresaw this eventuality in Germania and Britannia, so effective were your persuasions in opposition to those who oppose me—which is why I wanted you to yet accompany us to Legio. So loyal are they here to me that I hoped to ferret out those who would take your life."

Esta replied, "Oh, my dearest friends, I . . ."

Hadrian interrupted, "There is more to explain—one thing more that must be done. As I said, you shall be guarded as Domina Esta de Roma until you leave for Foix. However, tell no one of your intended destination. *At that time there shall be a sad proclamation given, for we shall announce your sudden and unexpected death.* Before this is made, a secret dispatch will be sent to Carcaso or Foix, to be read by Prince Lucius alone. Thereafter, in expert disguise you will be taken by ship or carpentum with but one of your trusted maidens, escorted by my elite guard, to Foix. Never can your face be seen by others until you are safely there. I will leave it to Lucius and his dame, Blanche, to warrant that Foix will forever be your secure sanctuary. My dear Esta, this is the best hope you have of life."

WHEN NAOMI LOOKED up from her spinning and saw Esta at her
doorway, she leaped to her feet and ran to receive a tender embrace.
Eponi toddled about and loved the attentions her mother's dear
friend heaped upon her. Ophelos too was overjoyed at Esta's coming
and begged her to stay until the vernal equinox. Yet Esta could not be
persuaded, for she said she desired to winter in Rome and see
Michela, Arrian and Diocles and resume her work for the Emperor.
As Naomi and Ophelos had not met Lucius this seemed quite
natural. It was hard for Esta not to tell Naomi of the man she loved,
but Hadrian had impressed upon her the absolute need of secrecy
regarding her future in Foix if, she was to have a future at all.

The two friends called upon Aléxandros who was so excited to
see Esta that he wanted to host a celebration for all of the city to
honor the renowned Maiden of Massilia. However, after reading a
missive from the Emperor disclosing the dangers facing her, given
him by the captain of the Imperial escort, the senator decided to host
a private feast. Besides Sebastian and others of their old friends,
Esta's family jubilantly attended the banquet.

Soon the winter storms came and yet Esta left Massilia on a
tempestuous sea, ostensibly bound for Rome. The Emperor had
arranged for three vessels to make the journey and only the captain
of one of these was privy to the Emperor's plan. This captain
commanded the small fleet under an alias, obedient to Imperial
orders. Aboard his ship was Esta, an attendant maiden, the Emper-
or's own seamen and a faction of Hadrian's elite guard. In blustery
weather the small fleet left the Port of Massilia late in the day, a most
unusual occurrence, for it was said that the commander delayed his
departure in the hope of more clement seas. Hence, upon the vast
Mediterranean, under cover of night, he separated his ship from the
other two triremes and reversed course. Before daylight his single

vessel drew near the Port of Narbo, well west of Massilia. From it was lowered a rowboat, wherein were ferried two maidens and two guardsmen. A prearranged carriage met the four at the pier of Narbo, its driver also under strict orders of the Emperor and rode immediately from the quay northbound into the Pyrenees. Without notice, the ship left the Port of Narbo to report to Hadrian the following day at Tarraco. There the ship was given a new insignia and sailed with a new assignment for Caralis, the commander under his true name.

Several days later, Hadrian received a dispatch from Massilia stating that the ship bearing Esta was lost at sea. The blame was placed on its captain who, it claimed, had foolishly left port in a winter storm. By this means, Esta's death was convincingly contrived. Thereafter, the Empire mourned the loss of its Domina. Nonetheless, before the celebration of Saturnalia, the illustrious maiden, in altered guise, arrived safely at the Chateau de Foix. Having delivered Esta safely to her new home, the Imperial escort left Foix for Tarraco, reporting the following month to Hadrian of the success of their mission.

Vittoria was greeted elatedly by Blanche and her family. Soon the whole of the town pressed into the Great Hall to welcome the familiar face, now known by a new name. As Lucius was gone to Carcaso, a furtive courier was sent with word of her coming. The moment he received the glad news, Lucius immediately left the fortress and on his fastest horse raced for Foix. In her long absence, time had passed slowly for the man who loved the illustrious Maiden of Massilia. Yet as he galloped homeward, it seemed to the anxious prince that furlongs were longer than leagues. Still, he quickly outdistanced his escort and midway exchanged his spent mount at the garrison of Mirepoix. The same day Lucius departed Carcaso he arrived at Foix, not weary in the least, although the same could not be said of his exhausted steed. Sentinels, having espied him afar, apprised Vittoria, who ran from the Chateau de Foix down the cobbled path to meet him as he rode into the village. Leaping from the saddle, he lifted her slender form into his arms, cradling her as he had in seasons past beneath the moonlit waterfall, kissing her again and again. At last he spoke, exclaiming, "Ah, my one and only love, you have come home to me! I can scarce believe I truly hold the princess of my dreams! Is it really you?"

She answered, filled with joy, "It is I!" she laughed. "Thanks be to our Lord, I am here! I am yours, no more to serve the Empire but you and the family that will be ours."

In but three days the lovers were wed. The rite was held in the *Christian* chapel in Foix, where the guests were trusted villagers, one and all.

CHAPTER 26
VICISSITUDES

Vicissitudes [1]

"The Theatrum Romanum Cordoba presents Michela de Roma, maxime musica Artifex imperii, [2] *esposa* [3] *of Diocles, renowned Charioteer from Hispania who has run an unequalled 4,257 races. This will be Michela's last performance, for Diocles has at last quit the arena and with Michela will live serenely in Praeneste."*

Announcement posted in Cordoba, Baetica, Hispania

---

1. Changes regarded as natural in human affairs; changes in circumstances, uncertainties or variations of fortunes or outcomes. Oxford English Dictionary.
2. The most splendid musical artist of the Empire.
3. Wife.

C aesar Titus Aelius Hadrianus Antoninus Pius became the Emperor of Rome, succeeding Hadrian in 138 A.D., or 891 ab urbe condita.[4] The prosperity of the Empire continued under the reign of Antonius Pius and the spectacle of the arts flourished as never before. Great soloists were paid enormous sums to perform throughout the provinces. The famous charioteer from Lusitania, Diocles, who had competed in 4,257 races over the course of a career lasting more than two decades, winning first place in 1,462 races and placing in another 1,438, wanted to show his homeland to his beautiful new wife, Michela of Rome and Narbo. They had known each other for over twenty years, yet had not married, preferring the adventures of racing and the adulation of the theatre to a settled life. Nonetheless, Michela had long loved the charioteer and no one else. On the other hand, Diocles had silently languished for the Christian Jewess, Naomi, a dear friend of Michela's. Naomi, however, had married Ophelos, a senator of Massilia, years before he attained that exalted rank. Yet it was not only the thrill of the highly dangerous races that diverted Diocles from his cherished thoughts of Naomi but also his secret conversion to Christianity.

In Rome and everywhere the charioteer raced in the Empire, he covertly sought to assist persecuted Christians and help them in their poverty. This he handled with as much skill and cunning as he did his horses at Circus Maximus. His winnings were so great as to make him as wealthy as a senior senator of Rome, yet he lived modestly! It was a wonder to everyone, save those whom he served, what Diocles did with his money!

---

4. 891 years since the founding of Rome.

Diocles

Although Michela was taught many truths by Naomi, Esta and old Eponi, she nonetheless slowly adapted to the popular beliefs of her close associates in the arts. She sang to the gods at Roman rituals, she sang of the gods at the theatre, and she walked before their effigies ceremoniously on feast days. None were her equal and she was everywhere praised.

Then, many years after his return from Hispania, Michela sang before Hadrian and Vibia in Rome. Following the performance, she was summoned to appear before the Emperor. Hadrian said to her, "Although tonight I enjoyed greatly the excellence of your voice, yet think of another time, long past, when I called you 'the silent maiden' and advised you to kindle the radiance of Lady Esta, who was then your companion. Still, Michela, I would that you might be so lustrous!"

Michela answered, "O great Sire, Esta was indeed the living coal who warmed the charcoal of my soul. Sadly, her brilliance was quenched when she was lost while I was yet a young maiden. Nonetheless, I thank you for this remembrance and promise I will strive again to merit a semblance of her radiance."

Hadrian and Vibia both smiled as he replied, "You humbly answered aright. Yet you will never find such happy luminosity so long as you seek the idolization of those you do not even know or care for."

Michela was shocked, for never had she been so upbraided directly by one whom she so revered. Hadrian continued, "Who is it, Michela, you desire most to please; whom do you love most of all? To whom you would be most true?"

The great artist bowed her head but did not answer. Hadrian continued, "If *self*, such is not entirely wrong! For Michela to be true to Michela—for you to truly love yourself, which is to say, to regard unabashedly your own worth, for one cannot keep secrets from oneself, is to be *one* with your innermost conscience, a rare thing. On the highest level, if you desire to please self so that you learn to live without degrading remorse—that is a noble pursuit. Yet is there another, someone greater than self, whose love you desire to merit? To love one's country and to have that requited is a great virtue. To love the AllFather, whom Rome calls Jupiter and who Esta called God, and to have Him regard you as an elect daughter is greater still."

The Emperor reached out and took hold of the hand of the Empress, which action both surprised and pleased Vibia. He said, "I grow old and will soon be Emperor no longer. Glad I am that there is one who will yet cherish my company. Michela, I would rather have this woman's affection than the love of all the Legionary of Rome. Is there someone who has such power over your own heart? Do not fear to leave the theater for his sake."

A SEASON PASSED and Diocles returned to Rome. He called on Michela, as was his custom, after he raced. She said to him, "For this long time you have known that I was yours for the taking, I whom the crowds of Rome adore. I am still beautiful, am I not? You prefer my company above all other *demoiselles*, do you not? Still, you bind me not to yourself."

Diocles was taken aback, for never had Michela spoken so with him. It was true but he did not know how to answer her. She continued, "I have come to an understanding of myself. The populace and the pantheon are both deceivers, promising what they cannot give. No longer will I serve either. I remember and I am trying to remember more—that which was taught by the best friends I ever had, so long ago. I am trying to recall the truths of sweet Naomi and Esta and Eponi. I don't believe it is possible to forget, really forget, things so important. Somehow, I believe there is part of you, Diocles, that has become more allied to these things than what is known by me or by the many others who know you."

Hearing this, Diocles looked at Michela more intently than ever before. She returned his gaze as she said, "Help me remember truth —if you are my true friend, help me. Though I may never be bound to you, yet I desire to be worthy of your regard. It is time I lived more for heaven than for earth."

He replied quietly, "What of your art?"

She answered, "I will no longer live and sacrifice for my art but only in praise of truth. Soon I will leave the theater. I still have life before me and believe I can change; I hope to become again what I once was—or what I was once becoming."

After this, Diocles and Michela began to see each other often— and talk. Slowly, and over several years his affection for her grew into love and gladly did this warmth replace his memories of Naomi.

One day, Diocles said to her, "Michela, no more will I race! I have bought a beautiful domus in Praeneste and desire to there raise more than colts. It is a small village, without the politics of a metropolis, where a man and his wife can quietly abide and serve truth. Michela, I have grown to love you. Have me for your own and I will take you back to my homeland, to Hispania, to Lusitania to meet my papa and mama and my family. Then we will forget the crowds, yours and mine, and we will return to Italia and settle quietly in Praeneste and raise sons and daughters."

SOON AFTER THEY WERE WED, Michela's manager, old Aellus Dionysius, arranged for her to sing a farewell performance in Baetica.

Michela sings in Baetica, Hispania

In the audience was the most eminent prince of the Province, Conde Mateo de Cordoba. She sang so beautifully that it brought tears to his eyes. Michela did not sing of the gods, but sang of the love of a woman for her beloved and also of her love of heaven. After the performance, he invited the illustrious couple to lodge at his estate where they might rest from their journey, before commencing another to Lusitania, which they gratefully accepted.

The following day, as they enjoyed the morning repast together, Mateo found to his delight that Michela and Diocles knew the Lady Esta of Rome before she was reported to have died at sea near Massilia. "I met her but once," he said. "There was a conventus at Tarraco. I heard Esta speak. After, I asked that which I had to ask!"

"What was that?" said Michela.

"Why, I asked her to marry me! Of course, what else could I do?"

Diocles was incredulous, "After you heard her oration and without knowing anything more, you wanted Esta for your wife?"

Michela interjected, laughingly, "Hmm, Men of Baetica are more decisive than those from Lusitania, though both are of Hispania!"

Mateo inquired, smiling, "Señor Diocles, did you not take this fair cantante the moment you set eyes on her?" Diocles shook his head. Mateo continued, "No? Hah, you became too much of a Roman then, before you met her! But no, I did not ask Esta to be my wife until Hadrian introduced her to me and our eyes met. Then I loved her!"

Michela was highly intrigued. "How did she answer you?"

"She said that she could not decide so quickly. That was reasonable as she was a Celt, though she spoke as if she were of Cordoba! Then told me she was my true friend and said I should read a book written by a Hebrew whose name is my own."

"What did you do?" inquired Diocles.

He answered, "Who could but hear Esta's voice and not do as she asked? I obeyed."

"You read the codex of Matthew?" said Michela.

"Yes!" he said enthusiastically, then added, "Oh, that Esta had lived! How I wanted to write her and tell her I had proven my promise."

Michaela asked, "What was that?"

"That I was a changed man!" he said. "Well, she was gone and I labored with my soul that she might not look down, with my grand-mama and be disappointed in me. Two years passed and I met my wife. She bore me a daughter, whom I named Esta."

"What does your wife think of that—naming your child after a woman you loved?" asked Michela.

Mateo answered candidly, "I don't know. She died giving birth. So I have raised Esta, my own daughter, and her love is sufficient. She is always my companion and no one shall marry her who is not worthy—and he must be a man willing to be joined to my domus!"

"What does Esta say about that," Michela retorted.

"Of course, nothing," he answered frankly.

Diocles asked, "Is Esta of age to be married."

"She will be of age when I find her husband. Alas, there are none in Cordoba who are not faulted." His eyes fell upon the sword sheathed at the side of the charioteer. "Diocles, may I examine your blade? It looks most excellent!"

He handed his sword to Mateo, who stood and cut the air before him with several strokes. "This, my new friend, is the finest I have seen, though I have thought the steel of Hispania to be supreme! May I ask where you secured such a sword?"

Before he could answer, Michela asked Mateo, "Does Esta carry steel for her own safety, I mean should it be for a last defense?"

"Why no!" he replied.

"Please forgive me, but I think this might also interest you and we are alone." Michela withdrew, from an artful hidden fold at her

473

side, a slender Pugio, a much smaller companion blade to that of her husband's.

"Asombroso!"[5] he exclaimed. "The workmanship of both is supreme! Magnifico! I must have their like, the sword for me and the Pugio for Esta! Now where may I buy?"

Diocles answered, "We would give them to you, dear friend, except that they were wedding gifts to us. I confess that our fame and the announcement of our marriage brought many gifts to us from far parts of the Empire. Yet, we received a box that was quite unusual. It was from Princess Vittoria de Foix, near Carcaso, a most excellent lady that we have never met! With the gift was a missive that read, 'Let these blades protect you, whom I love, always. As the sword is emblematic of His word, wield your weapons only in defense of truth.'"

Mateo seemed stunned. He said, "I have heard of Foix! The first time was long ago."

"Who told you of this town of Gaul? Have you also heard of its princess?" asked Diocles.

"Mmh," said Mateo. "Forgive me, there are things that must not be spoken."

"Esta," said the Conde de Cordoba to his daughter, "I would very much like to go on a journey of adventure, and this before I am too old to do such things. I also feel that I have neglected in teaching you certain skills, such that must not be used except for a last defense."

"Papa," said the beautiful maiden, "whatever do you mean?"

"It is a secret," he answered. "I want to have a Pugio made for you, that will fit your hand perfectly and be balanced for your

---

5. Astounding.

strength. There is only one place that forges the finest steel. There, I am sure, we shall find a master of the sword who may teach you its use."

Esta was immediately excited and exclaimed, "Oh, papa, when shall we go?"

"Soon, when the snows melt in the lower mountains of the Pyrenees. We shall not take a carriage, but ride mounted to the sea. Then we shall sail to Narbo, with our horses aboard. From Narbo we shall ride to a city, the name of which you must not tell another. It is there we shall have swords forged, one for myself and another, a Pugio, for you."

"What is the name of this secret city?" she asked.

"Do you promise not to tell?"

"Why, yes, papa!" said his daughter.

"Foix! Foix, a small village not far from Narbo."

The sire and his damsel enjoyed each other's company perfectly as they rode, sailed and rode again. They passed through beautiful villages, open country, enjoyed propitious seas and finally traversed the peaceful lands of Narbonensis.

As they stopped at an inn on the main road to Carcaso, Esta inquired, "Papa, everyone speaks so much of the great fortress of Carcaso and Prince Lucius, the commander of the castle and governor of the province, should we not rather venture there? Surely, such a place would have the finest steel and master swordsmen aplenty to teach me the art! You could ask the prince what he should do, if he had a daughter like me."

"Ah," said the sire. "You think there should be more gallants in such a fortress? Perhaps you desire romance before swordplay?" he laughed.

The Peaceful Lands of Narbonensis

"Well, every governor knows of Prince Lucius, as do I," he said. "A most excellent commander and I would gladly meet him. I believe he does have a daughter like you—several—and sons too. I am told he is a sire of ten children! But no, that is not our purpose. We ride for Foix!"

The terrain quickly became more mountainous as they traveled west from Narbo and scarce were the hamlets. Nonetheless, they came across isolated cottages where rest and sustenance could be purchased. All whom they met were kindly and hospitable. However, at one small domus, Mateo asked the owner if he knew of the forge of Foix, for he was interested in buying fine swords. The man answered, "There is no forge in Foix, though there be unknown smiths that live beneath the ground in caves high in the Pyrenees, known for their craft. Surely, there be tradesmen in Carcaso. You must buy there, for neither I, nor any man, can tell you of the furnaces hidden in the dangerous labyrinths of the mountains." Mateo thanked him and left as if bound indeed for Carcaso, much to the joy of his daughter. Nonetheless, when next they came to a crossroad, Mateo turned again for Foix, much to her disappointment.

Yet, when they rode into the village of Foix, Esta exclaimed, "Oh, father, it is a such a beautiful town and the chateau upon the summit is so lovely! Never have I seen its equal."

Mateo and his daughter, Esta's namesake

Mateo agreed, and knew then why the Esta of long ago had wanted to live in this enchanted place in preference to Rome, believing that she must have preferred tranquility to the energetic commerce and culture of the capitol of the world. Soon they ascended the steep pathway leading to Chateau de Foix. A strong young boy, younger than Mateo's Esta, met them near the stable and offered to care for their mounts, directing them towards the main gate of the chateau. "Strange," said the sire, "there are no guards about!"

"Why, there is no need," answered Esta. "There is such peace in this place; you can feel it!"

Mateo knocked at the door and a happy young girl opened it, smiling widely. "Welcome to Chateau de Foix! I am Esclarmonde. We hope you have come to stay with us for a while! How can I help you?"

"Is this chateau an inn?" asked Mateo.

"Oh no," said the maiden Esclarmonde. "But kind strangers may stay here for we always have rooms and love to hear of far-off places. Now," she said politely, "what is it you would like?"

The conde replied, "May I speak to someone older than yourself, I mean no disrespect to one so gracious, but I have business to do."

Esclarmonde bowed and seated them in the Great Hall to take their rest, saying she would fetch her grandmama. Soon a lady of more than four score years entered, saying, "Welcome to Chateau Foix. I am Blanche, the matriarch of this house and village. You have traveled far—from Hispania?"

"Why yes," answered Mateo's daughter enthusiastically, as she daintily curtsied, "we have come from the south of our land. It is with pleasure I meet such a great lady as are you, Gran Dama de Foix. My name is Esta de Cordoba."

"Esta?" Blanche asked in disbelief. "I have known only one other by that name." She looked at the sire and said, "Señor, how is it that you gave your hija this name?"

Mateo answered, "A long time ago, I met Domina Esta de Roma when she traveled with Emperor Hadrian at Tarraco. So impressed was I with her, that my hija is her namesake. But let me tell you why I have come."

"Please continue," said Blanche, seemingly unmoved by what he had said.

"Last season I met the great Roman charioteer, Diocles and his beautiful wife, the famous Michela, who sang for us in Cordoba. He wore a magnificent sword and she carried, hidden, a superb Pugio, though smaller than most. When I asked where such steel could be purchased, Diocles said he knew not, but that they were gifts from Princess Vittoria de Foix. This lady they had never met! Hence, we have come alone for we understand there must be some secrecy about these items and where they are forged. I desire a sword for my own use and a Pugio for Esta. Also, a tutor for her that she may learn its use. The cost is of no consequence."

"That is all?" asked Blanche. "You wish to buy swords? They can be had easily in Carcaso."

"Hmm," said Mateo. "There is more. Diocles and Michela are my new friends, but they are old friends of she who was lost at sea, the grand lady for whom my daughter is named. I ask myself, is there something else revealed in that the Princess of Foix should send such gifts? Know that Conde Mateo de Cordoba is a man of trust, never to betray!"

"I will see," said Blanche. "Esclarmonde, please show our guests to the fine chambers overlooking the Ariège. We shall sup midday, that is, the entire family, for we are many. Please join us then."

An hour before that time, Vittoria and her daughter, Esclarmonde went to the portico off the apartment overlooking the River Ariège. Leaving her mother seated on the balcony, the young maiden knocked on Mateo's door and invited the Conde and Esta to join them. Vittoria arose when she saw Mateo, smiling warmly. Astonished, he looked at her in disbelief.

Vittoria was extremely beautiful, slender and dressed modestly in the fashion of her village. Nothing in her vestments conveyed high station, yet her carriage was regal. She exclaimed as she took his outreached hands in hers, "Ah, Mateo, I see you are indeed a changed man! And this is Esta, who is, I perceive, a maiden of greater goodness than her namesake." She embraced the demoiselle and said to her, "Esta, already I love you. How all of my children will enjoy meeting you, for they will cherish you as a sister!"

Mateo looked steadily at Vittoria, overwhelmed and interrupted, saying, "Is it really you? How I hoped it was you, that you lived—that you were not lost in the shipwreck! I thought to myself that it could be true, that this was done by Hadrian, that you might survive! I knew rumors of senators that spoke evil of Domina Esta de Roma. Terrible men! Men to despise!"

"Yes, Mateo," she replied, "The assassination attempts multiplied. The Emperor saved my life with an elaborate ruse. It was hard to leave, to be thought dead."

Esclarmonde looked very puzzled, "Mama, I do not understand."

She replied, "I am Vittoria, but many years ago . . . well, I will tell you later—but what I always wanted to be is what I am: a wife to my husband, your father, and a mother to you and all my wonderful children!"

Mateo exclaimed, "No es possible! Princess, you cannot be the mother of so many—it is said of ten?"

"Yes, it is true, I am a mother of many. My husband and these are the greatest joys of my life." She stood with one arm around Esclarmonde and the other cradling the shoulder of Esta. Vittoria continued, "I think Esta will be most interested in meeting my eldest son, who is but a few years older. He is named Lucius, after his sire and will be at the midday meal. But now, let us sit and talk, for I would learn of your life and will tell you mine, for I know my story is safe with my true friend."

Esta, known as Vittoria

"Yes! Yes!" said Mateo, "then tell me next what I must do. It has been so long since I heard your command!"

The view of the Ariège River and the village below was idyllic. Señor Mateo first told his history as he had related it to Michela and Diocles. He added details of how the reading of the codices had changed him. He exclaimed, "Paul I like best! How I wish I could have met him! He was decisive, like the steel of Foix! I am that way! Before he knew the truth he thought he was always right, even when he was wrong! Like me!"

This made Vittoria laugh, then she said, "My great grandmama *did* meet that resolute apostle! She heard Paul teach in Rome before he was executed. Her name was Vittoria, the name I took for myself when I could no longer be known as Esta, my given name, lest I be slain by the enemies of the Emperor."

The maiden Esta exclaimed, finally understanding the enigma, "*Ah, then I was named after you!* Always has my father told me of your goodness. How I have wanted to live worthily, to be fit to bear so great a name as she who was renowned in all the Empire, who made peace between provinces and taught my own father how to be fair to his own people! Because of your influence he is beloved in Baetica. It is wonderful! Wonderful that you are yet alive—that you have continued—and now are a beautiful mother. Oh, how I want to be just like you! Tell us of your family!"

Esclarmonde added, "Oh yes, mother, never did I know you lived such an adventurous life! Please tell us all!"

Vittoria answered, "For a long while I served Rome as I traveled many lands, teaching conciliation among the nations. I loved most of all my time in Britannia, where your grandsire, Esclarmonde, in generations past was a great king. There also I served a powerful and noble Beldam and together we saved the lives of many who would have otherwise died by Druidic hands. At last, I journeyed with the Emperor and Empress to Tarraco where I met Esta's sire. Now all this time, there were assassins, men hired by foes of the Emperor whose intent it was to kill me—to silence my voice."

The two maidens were kept spellbound by Vittoria's story, as also was Mateo. She continued, "So it was I sailed from Massilia aboard the Emperor's ship in a fleet of three vessels. The captain who commanded this ship, under Hadrian's orders, left the escort when night fell upon us. Oh, I was very frightened, for I knew well the dangers of a tempestuous sea and the storm that tossed us about was terrible! Yet before daybreak the captain had skillfully sailed to Narbo as the tempest was abating. I was rowed ashore with my faithful attendant. She is with us yet and is now also a dame in Foix! From Narbo we rode concealed in a carriage and I was delivered safely to Prince Lucius, whom I had long loved. It was said that I died in that storm, lost at sea! Hence my enemies were appeased. Hah! That did not happen, as you can see, for here I am! Still, it was required that I live secretly among my friends of Foix, each faithful, each silent! I had to take a new name and live a new life—a most glorious life it has been!

"Prince Lucius and I were soon married. Oh, how wonderful were those days! To be snatched from the jaws of death and received safely into such a paradise as this! The Prince, for always he is *my* prince, seldom left Foix but gave command of Carcaso and the province to able men and spent his days and nights with me! Never had I thought such a love could be!"

Esclarmonde smiled, for the maiden loved to hear her mother speak lovingly of her sire. "Blanche's family were ever so kind to me, as were the villagers, and oh so protective! Yet the years passed and never was there an attempt again upon my life. Hadrian's plan was a gift of happiness to me, though I greatly missed my friends." She said this as she looked at Mateo.

Vittoria continued, "At first, Lucius would take me hiking in the mountains. As I was very fit, these little journeys were so fun and were very romantic. I loved to see him lead the way and he said I was like a mountain goat, for we ascended many an escarpment that was so steep it was frightening to look down! Then we would reach some outcropping or summit and Lucius would take me in his arms and press his lips upon mine. Oh, my daughters! To have such a man be your husband is to have the greatest blessing heaven can give, save for that which follows.

"In the early part of the second year of our marriage, our little prince was born to us and I insisted that his name be that of his father's. Lucius was so energetic that it was all that I, Blanche and others of the family could do, just to keep up with him! He loves everything that has to do with life, from the smallest bird to the largest bear! Also, our boy loved soldiering and aspired to become like his father. Now truly, there is no other swordsman his equal!" All the while Vittoria spoke of her son, Esta was captivated!

"In pleasant succession we were blessed with our other children," Vittoria continued, "Cécilia, Jourdain, Roger, Esclarmonde, Felicia, Ramon, Phillipa, András and our little Leon. It was Roger who met you at the stable and who cares even now for your horses. Though quite young, he is a true equestrian and is more skillful than many a stablemaster twice or three times his age! If he does not sup with us, it will be because he is off galloping astride his favorite mare. Who can hear his mother's call when he is leagues away from the Chateau? Yet always is Roger home when it is time to stable his mount." Then she laughed contagiously, "Though if I am yet to find him, he will likely be asleep in the hay, for he prefers a barn to a bed! Well, it is time to sup and meet the family. All in all, with my sisters and brothers by marriage and their many children, we shall sup with more than fifty in the Great Hall of Foix! We shall not see the Prince for a day or two more, for he is in Carcaso."

Mateo and Esta were greeted with tremendous cordiality and made to feel instantly at home. As they supped, many questions were asked about Cordoba. When Mateo answered, everyone laughed, for he had such an amusing way of saying things. When Esta replied, all were fascinated, for she had a gift of telling that was truly enchanting. Young Lucius, especially, was thoroughly captivated by her.

When the Prince returned to Foix he was likewise delighted with their guests. Over the years, Vittoria had told her husband all she could remember of her impulsive friend from Hispania, of his wit, sincerity, and considering their brief association, his remarkable devotion to her. Nonetheless, he was surprised that his wife had understated Mateo's fidelity and impetuosity! Soon, they too, were fast friends, delighting in each other's company. With his eldest son, Lucius took Mateo and Esta to the forge and introduced them to young David, now the master smith. Without delay, the requested sword and Pugio were fashioned expertly.

However, it was not David who taught the condesa the skill of using her blade, but young Prince Lucius. Like his sire, he was strong and confident, possessing a manly form and extraordinary features. Yet, he was mild and gracious in his manners, qualities inherited from his mother. He delighted in showing Mateo and Esta the majestic Pyrenees above Foix, riding sure footed steeds until paths became too precipitous. Then they would dismount and ascend on foot, leaving their horses to graze. The father observed how quickly his daughter would slip her hand into the firm grasp of their escort and how eager he received it, for the views from the sheer heights of the mountains were indeed breathtaking. Often in high meadows, Esta's skill in swordplay was improved by crossing blades with both Lucius and her sire. Always such adventures were filled with lively discourse and much laughter. So pleasant were these days that soon a season passed and still the conde and condesa remained in Foix.

Then one day Mateo said to young Lucius, "I have a grand estate in Cordoba. This you know, for I have told you of it."

Lucius laughed, "Yes, Señor Mateo, you have, many times!"

"Well," said the Conde, "I have no son, and my only heiress has no husband! There is only one thing that can be! You must take Esta as your wife and be my son! All that I have is yours!"

Lucius was incredulous, "You want to give me your vast estate?"

"No," Mateo answered forthrightly, "I want to give you Esta—*she* is all I have! Of course, you must take the other as well, but that is of little consequence."

The Prince and Princess of Foix gladly gave their consent and a most glorious wedding was held in the chateau, where the guests were Blanche's family and their dear friends, the villagers. So it was that Vittoria, the same who was once Esta, first had grandchildren born to her not in Foix but in Cordoba.

Seasons swiftly passed. Vittoria's nine children who were with her yet at Foix grew happily, filling her life with unmeasured joy. Lucius told her that her beauty alone was unchanging, which made Vittoria smile. Still, she saw wrinkles in her reflection where before her skin was smooth. How she loved her husband even more as he aged. Often they read the codices of the Lord's Testament together and to their children. Daily they knelt as a family and supplicated God in the name of His Son.

There were challenging times when Vittoria constantly fell to her knees when sicknesses came, as when Blanche died, or harder yet, when Phillipa was taken. The former sorrow was soon replaced with happiness, for they knew Blanche had lived a full life and had embraced and received every light given her of heaven. The later sorrow was never far removed from Vittoria. Although she believed the spirit of her daughter yet lived and was in the paradise spoken of by the Lord, still she yearned to rear her child, to see her grow into womanhood and fulfil her divine calling as a wife and mother. Often she thought of Lucius' "Law of Brevity"—how quickly the years were passing, how swiftly life was irrevocably altered and supplicated God for greater understanding.

Nonetheless, the Chateau de Foix was repeatedly blessed with joyous times. Jourdain was next to wed, followed by Cécilia and Felicia. Esclarmonde, who was most particular in choosing a companion, was not married until her 28th year. These marriages brought the gladness of many births and although only Jourdain's family lived in the Chateau de Foix, the others were not far removed, save for Lucius, the eldest.

Antonius Pius, although highly regarded by many, was not as respected as Hadrian had been, for he never left Italia and the close alliances of the provinces began to wane. Northeast of Carcaso, wars broke out and the Empire called upon the elder Prince Lucius to lead his Legionary into battle to aid in subduing these rebellions. Roger, who had long been knighted,[6] rode with his sire as far as the Danube, where the last battle was fought. As when a young commander, Prince Lucius valiantly led his army from the fore, never sending men where he would not fight himself. The conflict was sore and many lives were lost.

On the last day of combat, a singular stronghold on the enemy line was not only holding firm but making headway into the Roman ranks. If this could be taken, victory would surely follow. If not the defeat of the Legionary was likely, for it was known that their foes would soon be mightily reinforced. Prince Lucius and his Carcassonian cataphractarii, swiftly rode to meet this terror, while other formations hesitated, their commanders leery of the odds.

Lucius, astride his great warhorse, led the attack. He was the point of the spear, hurling into the mêlée, followed closely by his mounted men. Yet so rapid was his advance that they could not flank

---

6. A Roman knight was an Eques, a noble skilled in horsemanship and the use of arms; he was of an equestrian rank, a class directly below the senatorial class.

their general. Even Sir Roger's steed could not keep pace with his sire's stallion and the warrior who, though now aged, fought as ferociously as Flamma, the Syrian gladiator who triumphed twenty-one times before he was slain. So it was with the Prince of Carcaso, who at the onset reaped death, his sword a fatal scythe, until a heavy blow from a battle-axe unseated Lucius and he fell headlong from his steed, grievously wounded. Nonetheless, his calvary broke through the stronghold and soon all of the forces of Rome steadily advanced. Roger, aided by his fellows, bore his father, in a state of delirium, safely to the tent of a cautious commander—a captain that had stayed well behind the line of combat.

The campaign proved successful but when peace again prevailed, only the son returned to the Narbonensis, for the heroic Prince never regained his senses and at last succumbed to death. Not only the Chateau de Foix, but great houses throughout the land mourned his loss. Four unmarried sons remained at Foix with Vittoria: Roger, Ramon, András and Leon. Without her sons' close attentions and deepest affections, Vittoria would have died with grief.

SUMMER HAD AGAIN COME to the Pyrenees when seven visitors were announced at Chateau de Foix, arriving with an escort of twenty Imperial guards. These were admitted into the chateau while the Legionary remained watchful, taking strategic positions without.

Vittoria could scarcely believe her eyes as she entered the Great Hall and saw Michela before her, with her husband, Diocles, and three of their children! Two other old friends also greeted Vittoria, Arrian and Calvus! The children were soon occupied by Leon, as he led them outdoors to explore the village.

After exclamations of loving surprise were exchanged, Arrian, still agile and hearty, explained their unexpected coming. The soldier turned scholar was very distinguished in his bearing and, as he constantly exercised his mind in prolific writing, his intelligence advanced with his years. "It became my custom," he said, "to visit Praeneste whenever I desired absolutely serenity. There Diocles has built what I think is the finest villa in Italia with stables and a magnificent farm near streams where the catching of fish is both an appetizing and pleasing pastime. Michela wondrously rules his domus and their children are exemplary. The three youngest you have met." At this compliment, the beautiful mother smiled proudly, for it was nothing to Michela if someone applauded her melodious voice but meant everything when her children were praised. Arrian continued, "Often I admired a particular wedding gift they received from a mysterious lady of Foix, a sword and Pugio of excellence! When last I was shown these, Diocles mentioned a strange comment made by Mateo, the forthright governor of Baetica, in their regard. Fortunately, I never forgot this peculiarity. Then, recently, I returned to Hispania to do the Emperor's bidding, for still I am of some use in the Empire, and called upon the Conde de Cordoba. To my surprise, Mateo, though yet alive but suffering in his heart, had recently quit his station and his son-in-law provisionally acted in his place, awaiting confirmation from Rome. This I had not known! The young conde, husband to the beautiful Condesa Esta, a lovely mother of two daughters and one son, is an outstanding Roman and leader of his Hispanic province. But who he was I did not know. Hence, I spoke privily with Señor Mateo who explained his 'noble son' was from Foix. Then I remembered what Diocles had told me and said as much to Mateo.

"Trembling he asked, 'How well did you know Domina Esta de Roma?' I answered that for a long time I was her tutor, until such time as only she could teach me. Unsteadily he replied, 'I feel you loved her, as did I. Is this so?' Taking his old hand in mine, I answered that it was. Mateo continued, "This you must keep secret and knowing who you are, for you were also a companion of the great Hadrian, I must tell you,' and he whispered in his own tongue, 'Mi hijo es Conde Lucio de Cordoba y Foix, hijo de Esta que ahora se llama Vittoria de Foix, esposa del principe Lucio, su padre, muerto en la Guerra.'[7] Then Mateo told me of his wondrous journey with his daughter to Foix and all that happened in consequence."

Arrian turned to Vittoria and grasped her hands in his as he said, "Esta, the greatest, the finest, the most beautiful lady I have ever known, I cannot tell you the joy I felt when I learned that you lived— that you had not perished in the sea! Oh, how I wept for joy and Mateo with me! Empowered as I was, I immediately approved the appointment of your son as Governor of Baetica, quickly finished my business in Hispania and returned to Italia and Praeneste."

Michela interrupted, "My dear friend, when we learned that you were yet alive and of your happiness here in Foix, we too were overjoyed."

Nothing more was said for a time, for Vittoria held her hand against her heart, with bowed head and closed eyes, as tears coursed down her cheeks, all the while keeping hold of Arrian's hands.

At length she regained her composure and said, "Oh, my friends, thank you for making such a long journey to see me. How I have longed for the day when I could again see your cherished faces and feel the warmth of your presence! Always have I loved you! Michela, Diocles, how glad I am that you are wed and are living after the manner of true happiness, for you have left the accolades of fame for things far greater! Arrian, though I may wound your heart, yet I must ask, did you every marry?"

He replied sadly, "No Lady Esta. I thought when I was young that I must chase my careers, first in the Empire and then in scholarly

7. My son is Count Lucius of Cordoba and Foix, son of Esta who now is called Vittoria de Foix, wife of Prince Lucius, his sire, killed in war.

pursuits until I was 'accomplished.' Then, I told myself, I would find a fine woman and together we would have a family. But you must know the reality of my affection is this: only one woman captured my heart and she was so very young and so much above me. When I thought she was lost to life, I grieved without measure. Hadrian knew of my suffering, yet told me nothing, though I know the Emperor trusted me entirely. I can only think that he felt, perhaps, if I knew you had given your heart to the Prince of Foix my grief might become too much to bear."

Esta leaned forward and kissed the cheek of her friend, saying, "Ah, Arrian, always are you my equal. I am so sorry for your pain."

He replied, "There is always purpose to life, in all that we endure. I found satisfaction in my labors and have done much good, I think. Now my joy is full, for you are truly alive!"

Vittoria looked at Calvus, who had been silent. She said to him, "Were it not for you and the work you did for the young maiden of Massilia, my name would not now be Vittoria! It was you who gave me the knowledge of my wonderful great grandmama and changed the direction of my life! Oh, I was so pleased when your heart began to soften, for I perceived that you were becoming a man of *feeling*."

Calvus answered, "What you say is mostly true. You speak of my old hatred of Christians. Because of you and Naomi I was forced, despite my innate faults, to begin to see truth where before I only saw fanaticism. Yet I must confess, never have I fully muffled the allure of power and wealth. Nay, were it not for Arrian and Hadrian, for Arrian had greater influence on my soul than did the Emperor, my associates in the Senate would have still won me over and I would be forever lost! Yet now, I see, that perhaps it was Heaven's purpose that I was still *thought* to be allied to the shadow government of the Empire."

"Whatever do you mean?" asked Vittoria.

Calvus replied, "That is why I have come. Never have I lied to you, though often I tried to persuade you of what I thought were deceits—only because I was then blinded. Hadrian's brilliant subterfuge has indeed preserved your life. It is humorous to me that the captain of your vessel took payment of two senators to have you killed! Hah! What a man! He obeyed the Emperor's orders while he was made rich by Hadrian's foes! Nonetheless, this pretense of death has kept you alive—until now! Although heretofore a bulwark that defense is now shattered."

Vittoria exclaimed, "It has been so long! Why would anyone *now* seek my life?"

"After your death was faked," said Calvus plainly, "your legacy became a greater tool for Hadrian and those senators allied to his non-expansionist policy or cause. *You rose to the station of a martyr!* Hah! That is hard for a living person to do! Often would the Emperor and others in league with him—often would he speak your words and powerfully invoke the memory of The Lady of Rome! So great did this incite the passions of many in the City, that a movement arose to deify you and build a Templum deae Estae dicatum et consecratum![8] Of course Hadrian knew your death was but deception and also knew that you, above all people, would be woefully offended at such an act. Therefore, he enlisted my aid, as one who understood your Christian beliefs—and how, even in death, you should hate such a thing! Hence, I forthrightly opposed your 'temple' and those who petitioned the erection of the edifice. Hah!" He laughed again, "by so doing I greatly pleased those who thought me even more allied to their anti-Esta schemes!"

Then Calvus grew very somber, saying, "Now, Princess Esta, listen carefully. He who now rules this Empire is not the man that Hadrian was! The strife we are beginning to see is desired by that same faction that hates your memory—or rather, they did hate your

---

8. A temple dedicated and consecrated to the goddess Esta.

memory. Now, they, once again, hate *you* and again conspire to *kill you!*"

Vittoria exclaimed, "But how did they learn I was yet alive?"

He replied, "When Prince Lucius was dying, his last words were heard by another commander, a confederate of those who desire that Rome should again be at war to enlarge the Empire." Calvus took a small parchment from his pocket, saying, "Your husband, though delirious, said a type of prayer to you, which was written down by this commander. Though feverish, it was said he spoke clearly. This is a copy of his pleading." Calvus read, "'Esta—Vittoria, my beloved, oh that I might return home before I die! Praise God that you perished not in the deep and lived to raise our children. If only I could see you again!' Thereafter, he called your name repeatedly."

Calvus gave her the strip of parchment, as he said, "Now, Arrian came to me, as I am still an advocatus, for he is one of the few who knows of the power you had in my life—how because of you I began to forsake our gods. Arrian wanted to know what had become of your estate, for he desired that it be covertly returned to you. He was shocked as he told me the news of your life—shocked because I was not surprised, for already I had learned of the words your Prince whispered as he died. I told Arrian that your riches were of no account, for though your death was a pretense in the first instance, *in the next it should sadly be assured.* I explained to Arrian that previously I told Antoninus of these things and he said there was nothing he could do. Our new Emperor was almost fitful, exclaiming that to officially recognize you lived was to implicate Hadrian in falsifying your death—that there was a delicate balance of power in the Senate that might easily be upset! Of course, Arrian would not hear of this, but using his office he arranged transport, by sea and by land, sending immediately for Michela and Diocles, and we have come to give you warning."

Vittoria was astonished and grateful, expressing both sentiments to her friends. Arrian and Diocles swore on their lives that they would defend her! Nonetheless, she asked, "How long before the army of assassins descend upon Foix?"

Calvus answered, "Truly, I was surprised to find you here and living yet peaceably. Nonetheless, honestly, if you have more than hours, you have not more than days before you are attacked."

Esta replied with confidence, "Foix, my family and friends must be spared! This is what must be done. We must assume that your coming to Foix with guardsmen is known to those who desire my death and your very presence signifies the truth of my husband's words. Is it not so? Yet without your forewarning I must surely have perished and many whom I love with me. How I thank you! None-theless, despite your greatest efforts they will kill me unless I disappear to a place where no one can follow. I know of such a place; it is real and is in a wilderness known only to myself."

Esta continued persuasively, "We must leave this very hour! You, my dearest friends, and your Imperial escort should indeed leave with me. I will only take a few belongings and my four strong sons who, as yet, have made no marriage vows. Together we shall leave Foix in plain sight that the spies of the conspirators shall see us. We shall take our journey without rest to Carcaso, which we can make by tomorrow eve. There, my husband's warriors are still loyal to me. From Carcaso, I and my four sons will disappear that very night. No one will know where we shall go, not even you, my rescuers. That I have quit Foix in the light of day will save the village and what can those murders do to the great citadel of Carcaso? You then must straightway return the way you have come. Let it be known in such a manner that it will be believed that you know naught of my leaving! Truly, my disappearance will be as much a mystery to you as to anyone else! Thus, your lives shall also be preserved from those who hate me, though I know you would be faithful, even unto death. Please, do not protest, for it is the only way! Have no fear for myself or my sons. I possess skills you know not of and beforetime have traveled many leagues in woodlands alone and safe. This time I have my sons who are fine swordsmen. The Lord be with you and with us."

Within the hour, a company of twelve souls left Foix, escorted by a score of Legionary. In an amazing twenty-four hours they rode beneath the portcullis of the Fortress of Carcaso. At daybreak, five of this company were not found in their quarters. A thorough search was made in the citadel, but to no avail. Vittoria, Roger, Ramon, András and Leon had simply vanished, although their mounts were found in the fortress stables.

CHAPTER 27
NEW LIVES

"It is clear as morning that you have grown to love her and surely she adores you! Yet, It is too soon for both of you to live in such a place as this."

Ruith

It is one thing to travel the many leagues from the Woodlands of Ruith to Londinium without the protection of a host of Imperial guardsmen. It was quite another to traverse the *many hundreds of leagues* from Foix back to that forest. Additionally, the second journey would require the crossing of Oceanus Britannicus and never, throughout the immense distance, could their identity be detected.

As she had been called Vittoria for so many years and as she loved being the namesake of so wondrous a Beldam, she thought of herself yet by that name.

The foremost consideration was that they needed to quickly get beyond the reach of the men sent to kill them. But within the vast confines of the Empire how could they escape from the tentacles of the conspirators in the Roman Senate? Even Antonius Pius evidently felt powerless to help her or more likely he simply did not care. Before his demise, Hadrian condemned a number of senators to death. Not only did Antonius pardon them but he pledged that no senator should be executed while he was emperor. Certainly, this encouraged Vittoria's enemies to be more aggressive in the pursuit of her life.

When Vittoria first learned of her extremity, it came into her mind that the only sure place of refuge was the woodland of Ruith. Also, she felt assured that by fleeing Carcaso in the middle of the night, suddenly and without being seen, her family and friends would not be held responsible for her disappearance. That required leaving their horses, for always the stables were well guarded in the great fortress, and she thought it should be easier to disappear into the countryside afoot rather than mounted. As a young maiden, she could easily put leagues behind her. Now, though agile, Vittoria had not the stamina of her youth.

Vittoria knew of the ruins of a Roman fortress twelve leagues north of Carcaso, where there was not so much as a cottage within two leagues of the crumbling castrum. Lucius had taken her there when they were first wed, for it was ruggedly beautiful and offered shelter for an encampment. It was to this unsure haven that she led her four sons, requiring three days, for several times they espied riders and had to hide until they could safely advance. For provisions, they carried dried fish and grain, sufficient for ten days sustenance.

Ruins of the Castrum

Taking rest in the shelter of the old fortification, Vittoria said to her sons, "Glad I am that your sire has made men of you! Life is earnest and what is requisite is seldom expected. I thought we should live in Chateau de Foix until you were all married and I should there enjoy the children you should bring into the world, as have your brothers and sisters before you. It is troubling to think they do not even know what has happened to us! I quickly wrote a missive, explaining briefly our sudden departure and that we had far to travel. Also, I wrote that they must not try to follow us but see to their own lives, and trust in heaven. They will learn soon enough of my enemies. Thankfully, the village of Foix is unlike any other, for there every man is a skilled defender and expert with a sword. It would be a serious mistake for our foes to attempt any mischief in Foix. Nonetheless, I do not believe this will happen, for the villagers live so peacefully and the manner of our leaving should not bring suspicion upon them.

The youngest asked, "Mama, this is a grand adventure! To us it is nothing, but you are old and cannot continue as you have. Surely there is some place you know nearby where you can rest in a warm cottage."

"Leon," she answered, "what is that you say? Hah! I am old? Though my hair is grey I am fit and much stronger than you think! I have traveled before in the forest, alone, for many leagues and did your sire not tell you how I once fought off an assassin! Have no worries for me!"

Roger smiled as he said, "Father did tell me some of your adventures when we rode together. I was astounded! Yet, you were then a young maiden and, as I recall, were wounded and nearly died—only saved, he said, by grandmama Blanche. Still, we see that you are strong and have made this first refuge easily. Now tell us, mama, how far is there yet to travel?"

She was quiet for a time, thinking. Then answered, "It is far, very far. Think of it as if you were traversing from Foix to Carcaso again. In the time we've been gone you should now just be reaching the portico of the chateau! We have hardly begun! The distance, Roger, is *many* hundreds of leagues and this cannot be done afoot. We have, as yet, eluded our pursuers and have fought no battles. We cannot hope such fortunes will continue if we stay afoot. Despite the assassins, there are thieves and murderers along the roads. I traveled Gaul safely before only because I was in the company of the Emperor with his hosts of Legionary!"

András replied, "Then how then can such a journey be made?"

Ramon interjected, "We have our swords, but that is all. We must secure mounts, shields and armor. Mother, have no fear, you have knights for sons who shall willing give their lives for yours!"

Vittoria answered, "Ramon, András, Roger, Leon, indeed I know you are valiant men. Nonetheless, I do not want you to die for me, but live! There is a way but it must be done humbly, avoiding conflict if at all possible. The Olt River is less than thirty leagues distant from this castrum. It flows west and a bit north to Burdigala,[1] the 'Pearl of Aquitaine,' on the coast of the great West Oceanus. On the Olt, we will 'acquire' a small boat and this unseen, leaving silver in its stead as compensation to its owner. Rowing and sailing with the current, it will take us less than a week to reach the sea, and always we must be attentive, ready to fight as a last resort. Burdigala is an important Roman port. Certainly, we can find a merchant captain whose ship is available for hire. We shall tell him that our purpose is to immediately sail to Britannia to fetch a load of tin. I secured this," and she removed from her satchel an Imperial order, which she had hastily copied from an old dispatch of Hadrian's before they left the chateau. "Although it will not withstand expert scrutiny, yet it may suffice when we set also a bag of silver before him."

---

1. The Olt is now known as the Lot River and Burdigala is now Boudreaux.

András said, "It is a good plan! Nonetheless, what if he questions your parchment? Or, forbid, suppose he has already received contrary directions from Rome? I do not think this time our enemies will rely only on furtive assassins, for before you were protected by Hadrian and had many friends in high places. He is gone! Hence, the vipers will strike more boldly. Who knows that we alluded not only the agents of the conspirators but the conspirators themselves? Perhaps Roman senators have already come to the Narbonensis and in losing their prey in Carcaso have already sent dispatches to every port and city in Gaul! Did we not *see* riders? Soon, every person of importance in such places will be looking for Vittoria de Foix and her sons! Surely our foes in the senate will pay a great fortune for your capture or death! Our sire once said that the ferocity of evil unloosed is like a windswept fire. Its scorching flames may reach Burdigala before we arrive, for mounted couriers can easily outpace a small craft that meanders with the current of the Olt!"

Ramon replied, "Brother, this Imperial order is but a ruse, to provide a reasonable purpose for so great a voyage. We carry sufficient gold to buy a captain's silence and to make his profit, for our cargo of tin shall never be loaded aboard his ship—once we are in Britannia, he will never see us more! Hence, when we first arrive in Burdigala we must covertly approach the armory, bribe a sentry and secure the accruements of our station. Then wearing vestments of our knighthood and, if possible, securing mounts, we shall approach this sea captain, not afoot, but as a proper escort of a dame of wealth possessing an Imperial order."

"Yes!" Exclaimed Leon, the youngest son who had only been made an equestrian the year before. "We should have rode from Carcaso clad in steel! Having failed to do so, we must attempt to do as Ramon suggests! Then what sea captain would dare oppose four strong knights?"

Roger laughed as he answered, "What captain would dare

oppose four knights? I say one that has two score Legionary at his command! We left Carcaso afoot and without armor to avoid detection and we must take care in Burdigala for the same reason!"

The prince and princess had always encouraged their children to think for themselves and to thoroughly discuss a matter. Hence, Vittoria had been silent, listening to her sons. Then she said quietly, "I only meant to answer András' question, 'How can such a journey be made?' As we cannot continue afoot, let us carefully make our way to the Olt River and to Burdigala, as I have suggested. However, your concerns and recommendations are well said. András, you have spoken most wisely and conditions are likely as you say. Roger, you are also right! Never can we be impetuous and act with bravado, although Ramon and Leon, you are as brave as your words!

"Now hear me. I am not only the mother of four sons, but I am Princess Vittoria de Foix. As the Prince is no more, I am your sovereign, the commander of four of my knights, sworn to obey my word. Is it not so?"

"Yes," they answered together.

She continued, "Then we shall do generally as I have said, for we know not what lies ahead. We may be caught in an unforeseen circumstance and all will change. Nonetheless, so long as I am able to direct our doings, do as I say. If this cannot be done, act decisively, according to your own wisdom and the inspiration given you of God. Remember, words are weak when action is requisite. Now, *I do need rest*, as Leon has said. We shall camp fireless. Two of you will take the first guard and two the second. We shall leave here an hour before dawn." So saying, the princess laid her head upon the grass, with only a wool blanket for a covering and fell immediately asleep.

Before they quit their camp in the morning, they knelt in prayer. At his mother's request, Roger was appointed their common voice. He said, "Oh, Almighty Father, thy power is omnipotent, thy sight endless, thy blessings boundless. We who journey far do so with great purpose. According to thy will, we live our lives. Only a little while has passed since we enjoyed a splendid home with our sire to lead us, surrounded by the host of our family. Now he is gone to the world of spirits and we are here in this wilderness. We pray that our chateau will yet continue as a sanctuary for our kin and that the Village Foix will likewise be safe from oppression. Blessed we are that mother lives, our queen. May we be obedient to her will, for surely her desire is only to obey thee. Protect us as we traverse this forest and as we swiftly ride upon the Olt. Then, when we attain the coast of the sea, let us covertly acquire the use of a ship and sail to Britannia. May it not be required of us to shed blood. Nonetheless, if such is to be, may we take life mournfully, for precious is breath. In these few words we petition thee for so great a blessing, yet as thou didst command the creation of all things by the hand of thy Son, and it was so, then may our petition be granted, if it is according to thy will. Hence, send forth thy servant, we beseech thee, that we secure safe passage to the land of the sacred woodlands. In the Lord's name. Amen."

Since the time her children were small, Vittoria had taught them how to approach the Divine Throne. Then she had listened daily to their prayers. Yet, never did she suppose that her ears would hear such a supplication of faith. Leon asked his older brother, "Roger, what did you mean when you said, 'Send forth thy servant?'"

Roger replied, "Is that what I said? Well, I suppose I meant our mother. If ever there was a servant of heaven, it is she!"

In three days the company of five safely reached the banks of the River Olt. Fortuitously, they espied a small boat, fitted with two oars and a sail that was let down. Looking around they could see no one about. They left twice the value of the vessel in silver on the rock where it was tied and at once began their voyage downstream. Not only was the current propitious but also the breeze that, except for when the Olt doubled back in its windings, blew at their backs.

Along the tributaries they found cresson[2] in abundance. One evening, as they approached the confluence of the Olt and the great Garumna River,[3] they espied an alcove in the hills above the riverbanks. In a bend of this shallow cave, they chanced a fire and made soup of cresson and grain. It was a most nourishing repast and revived their spirits considerably.

Not having traveled in this region of Gaul before, Vittoria was surprised when they soon sailed into the outlying region of Burdigala, for the western sea was yet twenty-five leagues distant! This she learned from a lone dame who washed clothes along the shore. The Garumna River had become as wide as a lake and great ships were seen in the distance. Obviously, the major port of the city was in the deep waters of the river and not in a coastal bay, as Vittoria had supposed. Immediately new dangers came to mind as she saw the expansive Roman colony with its great fortifications. How could they make their way unnoticed through the city and port? Where could she find such a ship as she had envisioned, emptied of cargo and equipped for a long voyage?

They turned their small boat up a small river, a tributary of the Garumna, and hid it along the bank in a copse of trees. It was decided that Ramon should venture alone into the city, to see how they might adapt their plan to the realities at hand. He was to take no action, only observe and return safely. If he were stopped by someone in authority and asked his purpose, Vittoria told him to say that he was a merchant's son from Narbo and was looking for a tradesman of armor and weapons. "As you are a knight, you are expert in finely forged steel and can speak well of such things. Nonetheless, Ramon, beware of saying too much. Some may ask how you arrived in Burdigala, whether you came by land or sea? Where is

---

2. Watercress.
3. Today known as the Garonne River.

your company, your sire? What is his name? To these reply, that until you find what you are looking for, you must keep your own confidences. Smile, laugh even, if they persist, saying this is the first time your sire has trusted you as his agent. Hence, you must guard your tongue!"

He answered, saying, "Mother I shall act well the part I am to play and will return when dusk falls on the morrow."

Nonetheless, that very night Ramon stumbled back into camp, being nearly overcome with exhaustion. After he recovered his breath, he told of the greatness of Burdigala, of its basilicas, forum, amphitheater, its hosts of legionary, of the many ships in its port and of the multitude that traversed its streets. Ramon said he had not so much as asked a single question of anyone, for he was only looking about, hoping to see something that might suggest a solution to their dilemma when he was accosted by a Roman Centurion who asked him his business. Ramon explained, "I answered that I was a merchant's son, hoping to find one who traded in shields. This did not satisfy the commander who retorted, 'A tradesman here at the wharf? Why 'tis in the town market men show their wares! I've been watching you search out our ships and for what purpose? You have the look of a soldier and your blade is a fine piece! Methinks you must bear the stigmata[4] of missio ignominiosa!"[5] He strode toward me aggressively as he shouted for me to remove my vestments."

Vittoria exclaimed, "But there is no mark upon your body! Did he not see this and let you pass?"

Ramon hung his head, saying, "No. I drew my sword! Though the Centurion was no doubt a veteran warrior, he was no match for me. In but three strokes his sword was swept from his hand and with the fourth—well, it will be hard for him to wield a blade again!"

---

4. Tattoo.
5. Dishonorable discharge from the Roman Army.

Vittoria looked at her son aghast. "You did not kill him, did you?"

"Nay. It would not have saved us, for it was yet light and there were legionary nearby who saw him fall. I ran, was pursued and nearly caught. I heard shouts and calls for others to cut me off. Soon it seemed I was chased by the whole of their army! Yet, I was swifter than their swiftest. Passing a bend, when for an instant they could not see me, I dove into the river. I held fast against the bank as my pursuers passed by. There I stayed until well after nightfall, though I heard talking at times. One said, 'Did you see how he worked his sword? 'Twas no common soldier but a knight, perhaps one of the sons of the lady whom we seek.' His companion asked, 'The Princess of Carcaso?' 'Yea,' the first answered. Mother, I believe our case is much worse than it was! I could not have failed more miserably."

Vittoria replied kindly, "Oh Ramon, you are alive! Although you were too eager to fight, yet you fought manfully and with great wit you saved yourself! Still, our lot is precarious indeed! The whole of the town and the river itself will be well guarded this night. At dawn, hundreds will be sent out to search for us and whither shall we flee?"

Roger answered, "They will think we must surely retreat towards the Pyrenees. We must make our way landward, through the city if need be and get beyond Burdigala. Then slowly make our way to the sea and seek another way."

Ramon objected, saying, "Surely if we do as you say, we shall be quickly caught!"

András replied, "It was mother who led us here and she is led of heaven. We must do as Roger says and get beyond this place."

"Leon," said Ramon, "what say you?"

He answered, "All is not lost until it is lost. Let us follow our dame and if it so be that we are taken, then let us fight to the death for her honor. What else is left for us? Is it not written, 'Do not wrong the dead?' Does not our sire even now look down upon us?"

So ended their discourse and the little company quit their camp

and, following Vittoria, made their way into the borders of Burdigala, Yet soon they heard sounds of those who searched for them.
Remaining outside of the city wall, they made their way eastward.
Coming to the River, they saw in the moonlight vessels moving
about unnaturally. "Search boats," said Ramon. Then they traversed
westward until well past the main road and gate, when once again
their advance was frustrated, for scores of soldiers were guarding the
west wall. There was nothing left for them but to enter the forest and
attempt to bypass the city. The woods were extremely dense with
many fallen trees and impassable undergrowth. No trails or traces
could be found. After pressing ahead for an hour and making but
little progress, Ramon said in frustration, "Mother, we can make no
progress until daylight, and perhaps none even then in this maze.
There is no way to get past Burdigala but through its gates. As the
whole of the city is roused because of my blunder, all is hopeless!"

Nonetheless, Vittoria was not looking toward Ramon but away
from him, for the dame heard the sound of rustling branches. Soon
all of her sons heard this as well and looked steadily in that direction. The dim form of a tall man became barely visible. He seemed to
hold no weapon and they stood very still, watching. When he drew
near, the man spoke, saying, "Have no fear, but follow me closely.
Say nothing." Then he turned about and waited for them in the open
field.

Ramon was about to object, but his mother stopped him. "Say
nothing—no, not a word until danger is past." Then she silently
made her way through the copse until she stood near the tall man,
looking intently at him. Obedient to their mother, they too turned
about. At a steady pace, the man walked through the field to the
main road leading to Burdigala, followed by Vittoria and her sons.
They were astonished, for their mother acted as if she knew the man
and had full confidence in him. The main gate was open but heavily
guarded. Nonetheless, the sentries said nothing as they approached;

not even the soldier's eyes followed their movements. It was as if they entered the town unseen, yet they strode plainly in torch light. Soldiers were searching everywhere. Still the tall man and his charges walked among them undisturbed. Straightway he came to the quay and to a great ship, then across a plank to its deck, followed by the astonished sons and their mother. Sailors stood expectantly at their posts. The mysterious man addressed the captain of the ship and said unassumingly, "Here are my friends. Make way this very night. You shall not be hindered. Sail north, west of the continent and traverse Oceanus Britannicus eastbound, then north again up the east coast of Britannia, well beyond Londinium and nigh to Linnuis, where my friends will quit your ship and make payment."

The captain replied, "Master, it shall be done."

As he turned about, Vittoria said to the tall man, "Thank you, for you have saved us! Are you the messenger spoken of by Ruith?"

He smiled as he answered, "Yes, and I am also the servant Roger spoke of in his petition."

Without further word he stepped upon the plank as if to return to the quay, but they saw him only for a moment more. Though the dock was easily seen in the gray of starlight, yet he seemed to vanish before reaching it.

WITH WINDS predominately from the southwest, the clement voyage to the northeast coast of Britannia was three weeks in length. Vittoria and her four sons kept to themselves as did the crew, each preparing their meals from the common stores of grain and netted fish. The princess spoke with the captain every few days, asking their position relative to the shoreline, which was seldom beyond sight. He was most cordial but never did he ask their names or the purpose of their journey. When at last he set anchor in the natural harbor of the Abus Estuary, he told Vittoria, "A strang'r nor mor ple'sant voy'ge I n'er sail'd. I'm a seaman of m' word an' have deliver'd ya safe. Some ten t' twenty leagues west be Linnuis—I canna say fer certa'n. Neith'r me nor m' men will speak 'f ye." He then named a sum, which gold Vittoria set in his hands and the company of five were rowed ashore.

As they walked west, Vittoria began to recognize the countryside and before nightfall they left the main road, turning into the fabled woodlands. Two hours after the sun was set, they came upon the beautiful cottage. Ruith, now old, being four score and five years of age, was so very happy to see her dear friend and to meet Vittoria's sons. The old Beldam had grown very feeble, although she was still strong in faith. She said, "The Lord is ever giving of grace. I had so grown to love and depend upon you, Esta, those many years ago, that when you left I found it very hard, very hard indeed. Nonetheless, I always knew you would return before my time was come to leave these woods and this life—even when my sight and strength began to fail. Now here you are, come back to us, truly a beautiful mother, for you've brought four fine sons with you."

Another woman, not nearly as old as Ruith, came up to Vittoria and embraced her, saying, "Do you remember me? Oh, surely not, for it has been so long and I am changed!"

Vittoria exclaimed, "Oh yes, *Efa!* You are Efa, my fellow servant and companion when we were both young maidens! You look so well, tell me what has become of you?"

Efa answered, "I married and bore two children, but me husband —well, though we saved him aforetime—he was good to us 'till he began to yearn fer his old life. Me two sons left wit' their sire and I sadly saw them n'er again. Still, me service with Ruith is me happiness."

Before their arrival, only Efa and a little maid remained to assist Ruith, although most every bed in the cottage was given to the care of those who suffered. Hence, all were exceptionally glad with the coming of Vittoria and her strong sons.

One sufferer was a servant girl, named Isabel, who refused to worship the pagan goddess Ashtoreth. Discovered praying, her mistress nearly tore the gown off the virgin's back, whipping mercilessly, cursing, commanding Isabel to deny "her Christ." Isabel did not yield. Her beaten and senseless body was carried beyond the village by a strong oaf and thrown down a ravine, left for dead. Somehow, Isabel did not die and was startled from unconsciousness by the cold of a bitter night. Having heard stories of the "Beldam witch," a feared "specter" who lived in the forest beyond the summit springs, the girl had but one thought: to find this woman. Somehow, Isabel rose to her knees and crawled up the slope of the abyss, then staggering to her feet miraculously made her way to the old cottage —and this only a few days before Vittoria's coming.

Still clinging precariously to life, it was Ramon who strengthened the maiden's desire to live. Faintly, almost inaudibly, she told him her tale, saying she grieved to die so young. He held the cup of his mother's ambrosia to her quivering lips and said she had not come this far, nor struggled so desperately, just to parish. Ramon kissed her forehead, as he gently wiped tears from her eyes, whispering fervently, "Isabel, your life is preserved for a grand purpose. Soon you *will* understand! You are not common, not just a lowly peasant; in the Lord's eyes you are his fair daughter, beautiful even in this great distress, more glorious than any other demoiselle for you would not deny Him!"

When Isabel fell into the deep sleep induced by the aromatic nectar, Ramon did not leave her bedside. Every few hours he helped his dame change the poultices on her yet bleeding skin until the oozing ceased and her flesh began to mend. The ambrosia, together with the prayers of all who were then in the cottage, had the same effect upon Isabel as it had many years before upon Vittoria, when she was known as Esta and had been wounded by the Zealot. When the servant maiden awoke days later, she was amazed, for never had she felt better! The yawning slashes that had flayed her back were nearly mended and could hardly be seen or felt! The superficial cuts about her face, hands, torso and legs were entirely healed and her skin was as soft as a babe's.

As she stood upon her feet, Isabel saw that she was dressed in a clean soft gown, with her hair neatly braided. Ramon said to her, "Vittoria, my mother, bathed and dressed you. Efa, knowing you would soon awaken, cleaned, combed and braided the tresses of your lovely hair." Taking her by the hand, Ramon led Isabel to a mirror and said sincerely, "Look upon your reflection. Have you ever seen a more beautiful maiden than she who looks back at you?"

Isabel saw herself and she was even as Ramon had said. She exclaimed, "How is it done? That cannot be me!" Then tears filled her eyes and Isabel began to weep for joy.

During this time, Ramon's brothers had been engaged in helping Ruith, Vittoria, Efa and the young maid serve others in the cottage. Isabel began working with them and was immediately loved, for she was kind, cheerful and sang wonderfully. The four strong men built an additional room at the end of the timeworn hallway and soon put the out buildings, the orchard and fields in order.

Enchanted Garden

Seeing her cottage and farm renewed and happiness permeating the very air of the woodland, Ruith asked her old friend, her sons and Isabel to sit with her in the garden near the front door of the cottage while Efa and the maid worked inside. Ruith said, "Vittoria, *Esta,* I thank the Lord of All that I have lived to see you come home to our Eden, to this miraculous little heaven of healing. Roger, Leon, András, Ramon and Isabel, how I love you as well and I wish to give you counsel before I die."

Hearing this, Isabel startled and exclaimed, "Oh, our Beldam, our Beautiful Mother, you cannot leave us! For so long, in the village, I heard your name defamed by those who vilify all that is good. But I also heard whispers, for none dared speak these things aloud, that you were an angel of mercy, a worker of Divine will, your woods a refuge. Forgive me, for the evil spoken of you frightened me and I dared not come hither—until I was beaten nigh unto death. I remember you taking me into your arms and your home. Never had I felt such love! Straightway you became the mother I never had. Oh, how I have loved helping you, serving those, who like my former self, are in desperate need."

Ruith replied, "Isabel, I will teach you plainly what few understand, things I have been taught by messengers of heaven—some of Glastonbury and one other, whose blessing enabled this remarkable retreat—and I was taught by an angel maiden when she was known as Esta."

She smiled as she continued, "God gives to each of us according to our desires, whither good or ill, whither for lightness or darkness, joy or sorrow—that which we desire is ultimately ours. Now Isabel, I perceive that which you most desire cannot be obtained in this little woodland. Oh that I had counseled Efa aright when she became a dame." Ruith looked at Ramon and said, "Although I have not heard you speak your affections aloud, it is clear as morning that you have grown to love Isabel and surely she loves and adores you! Think not of how you should fare together in my cottage. It is too soon for both of you to live in such a place as this. Take those who would go with you, your Isabel, those who are healed and your brothers who desire, and traverse the Fosse Way to Glastonbury where other Christians gather. Be their defenders as you journey, for you are knights! Then marry Isabel and raise a good family and hold to the truth!"

Leon interjected enthusiastically, "I will go with you." Then turning toward his mother, added, "Though I will miss you greatly!"

Ramon replied as he took Isabel's hand in his, "Beldam, you see into our hearts. With mother's blessing we *shall* leave this woodland but before we go there is much I desire to understand! You tell us to hold to the truth. Before coming here, I thought I knew much but soon realized I know so little! I would ask you, most noble lady, as I am an eyewitness to your forest, how is it possible? The weather here is clement while storms rage immediately beyond the crossroads. Outside there is inhumanity, life is bartered for profit or power, while within this wood and cottage life is precious and held invaluable. I am told that even in Glastonbury nature abides its seasons and good and evil may act their parts according to the agency of each person. How is it so different here? No wonder the villagers of surrounding towns fear this woodland, for how can they understand it?"

Ruith answered, "All that is, is because of His plan. In this realm, on this earth, He has allowed opposing forces. In mortality we grow strong by overcoming fierce foes. This does not excuse those who take the wrong path. 'There must needs be offenses, but woe to him by whom the offense cometh.' As your own dame has lived in the outer world and in it has reared a goodly legacy, so must you."

The Beldam continued, "There are three archetypes of countries, worlds or places and each has its own inhabitants. The highest is the Celestial, the throne of the Almighty Father and His Son, as also they are the highest of Men. He would that all his children become like unto Himself and inherit His Seat of Omnipotent Power. When earthly men are most believing, God's will is that they build temples to Him, embassies of His heavenly kingdom here upon the earth. As these holy edifices are of the Celestial order they are fitting for His abode when He comes to us. Those who are striving to be like him are worthy also to enter the holy temples and receive His comforting presence. Sadly, these divine edifices are no more but will one day be restored to us.

"The second archetype are the Acadian gardens, remnants of Eden, terrestrial paradises upon the islands of the sea, or along the ocean's shore or in the midst of majestic mountains. When women and men honor the creation and its Creators and live goodly lives, even though they as yet abide not the higher laws, they are citizens of this glorious realm.

"The third archetype are as burning deserts, void of fountains and verdure, as far removed as is possible from the country of God's dwelling. Many are the inhabitants of this telestial[6] place and great and spacious are their buildings. Seeking to imitate the Celestial in form but not in substance, they embellish their basilicas with precious woods, stones, metals and jewels, even calling their buildings temples. In like manner they adorn their bodies, making them appear splendid, yet there is no light in them. Women and men of this order grow unnatural groves or usurp His forests and offer virtue and even life as a sacrifice to their devil gods, for they will *not* honor the true God, the Father and His Son, who are One in purpose.

"While mortal life is lived, women and men may choose the order of their belief. They may *change*, rise or fall, according to their desires."

Isabel asked, "This woodland then, is of the second order?"

"Yes," Ruith answered.

"Yet many a wilderness paradise has been overrun by the third

---

6. Telos, as far removed as possible.

archetype, is it not so?" asked András. "What keeps this forest and cottage so inviolate that even the seasons are tempered and delicious fruit is harvested when winter is without?"

She replied, "It is what I most desired it to be! *As He may change a person so may he change a place, according to His desire.* Yet I was truly amazed when heaven granted my desire and *changed* this small tract of woods alone. So great is the Druidic evil in the lands beyond this that a check was placed upon my forest and it became a refuge from the rites of hell. He may change whatever he likes! The greatest change is the raising of the dead in the last days and most especially when raised to the glory of the Celestial. *Yet, as He may change a place so may he change a body,* or transfigure it that the seasons of the earth and even centuries of time have no effect upon it. Such is *not* the final change of the resurrection to perfect immortality.

"Thousands have been given this temporary, though blessed, change; it is written that the people of Enoch, women and men alike, were transfigured and led to a terrestrial paradise. Also, Paul admonished, 'Be not forgetful to entertain strangers, for thereby some have entertained angels unawares.'[7] He spoke not of spirits, but of those whose bodies are changed, who may appear in their translated or transfigured glory or as mere mortals, so as not to give knowledge to those who have yet to learn the power of faith. I grow old and my mortal nature is unchanged, for I will soon die. Yet I have lived many years in this Eden and know of the wonders and goodness of our all-powerful God."

Each stooped to embrace Ruith who remained seated. She said she did not want to rise but look upon her flowers and hear the singing of birds perched on nearby branches. After a time, all left to perform their duties, save for Vittoria, who sat on the ground at the feet of her old mentor, holding her hand. Quietly she asked, "Ruith,

---

7. Hebrews 13:2

may I keep your cottage and forest when you are gone? So long as I live, I shall not leave it, save to fetch those who suffer and bring them back."

The Beldam did not answer, but for a little while pressed more firmly the hand that held hers. Then her hold relaxed and there was a quiet sigh as the breath of life softly escaped her lips.

ONLY ROGER and Efa stayed with Vittoria. Ramon, Isabel, András, Leon, the little maid and seven others left the cottage and traveled the Roman Road, the Fosse Way, to the Isles of Summerland. The adventure of that journey and the many which followed shall not be told in this chronicle, save that all of her sons found wives who bore Vittoria many grandchildren. Hence her posterity grew in Cordoba, Foix and in the southern realms of Britannia.

Esta known still as Vittoria

CHAPTER 28
FAREWELLS

"Do you not know of the others, those who come to me while I sleep?"

Vittoria

Village near Linnuis

Only one kindly old man rested in the woodland cottage and he was not a victim of Druidic rites. Rather, he left the near village on his own accord, desiring to see for himself whether or not the enchanted forest was ruled by Bel's wench or by a beautiful matron. Long had he heard the frightful tales of those who had ventured beyond the bloody altar at the summit springs. There were so many who said they saw *her* that it seemed only reasonable that a witch did indeed haunt the place. Yet, like Isabel, he also heard the infrequent stories of those who said the Beldam was a godly healer, possessing exceptional grace and goodness.

The aged man had never indulged in the carnal rites of the groves or tasted of the elixir brewed in the pagan cauldron, where the ashes and bones of Ceosan were boiled with strong ale. He knew he was near the end of his days and felt a strong compulsion to venture into the forbidden land. Never given to fear, yet he was not so bold as to confront the village overpriest. In former days, he possessed inordinate strength and was known to never give way to coercion, having bested many a man with his fists or his staff. Hence, as he did not overtly challenge Druidism, the sorcerers and enchantresses let him be.

This man reasoned that if the Beldam were a witch and killed him, he would lose little—for having lost his manly power life had become odious to him. If on the other hand, the Beldam proved to be a kind and beautiful dame, he hoped there was something she could do for him. He laughed at this thought, soliloquizing, "There's naught wrong wit' me but age, an' whoever had a potion or cure fer liv'n too long?" So he quit his solitary stone house and made his way past the crossroads of the summit to the wooded hills beyond. No one inquired where he was going. Nor thereafter did anyone search for him when he did not return.

Not knowing where the cottage was, the old man followed an innate sense or feeling and was delighted when he found it. Sitting on a chair in a magnificent flower garden fronting the home, he saw a lovely woman of age, not so old as was he, but one who had lived three score and ten years. Vittoria greeted him warmly, saying, "Welcome, good friend! You must have walked far and are in need of food and rest."

He returned her salutation, saying, "Hallo there! Ye must be t' Beldam! My, I've had t' finest walk of me life this day! Never did I know these woods surpassed all a'thers hereabouts. An' ye be no witch but a bless'd màter,[1] fer yer countenance is bright as morn!"

Roger, who was nearby picking herbs, helped the old man inside, for he was truly weary from his long walk. Efa set before him a warm bowl of soup, bread spread with thick butter and mashed fruit, delicious cheese and the sweetest spring water he had ever tasted. Then Vittoria, Efa, Roger and their guest gathered round the hearth and pleasantly conversed.

He remarked, "'Tis a large cottage fer but t' three of ye!"

Efa answered, "Sometimes we have many here and at other times, like now, we wait."

"Wait fer what?" He asked.

Efa replied, "For those to come who need our help. We are glad you came!"

Vittoria had been listening carefully to the old man's reminiscing's. "Yes," she added, "and as you've no family left in the village, why not stay with us for as long as you like, perhaps for the remainder of your days? Although we have not power to prolong them, we shall help you make the most of what heaven allows. I

---

1. Mother.

perceive there is much you would like to know regarding the life that follows this. Please stay here, learn and prepare—for one is never too old to make ready for a grand journey."

"Aye!" he exclaimed, "th't would be fine, save I've no coin t' pay ye!"

"None is required," said Roger. "Here you can eat and drink, live and be loved! Like the air you breath, there is no cost to you, save that you act aright."

He answered humbly, "Mayhap I think I've died already an this be heaven!"

The old man proved to be as teachable as a child, yet he was not impetuous or selfish. Readily he joined their daily study of the sacred codices and soon believed wholeheartedly in the one true Lord.

"Mama," said Roger, "for a season we've had no one to care for but our aged friend. Always I ride the near roads and the greensward of the summit springs and no one I've found of late, except to bury. Did not you and Ruith traverse afar to find those in need of succor?"

"Yes," his dame replied, "but we were then much younger and we had others to leave in the cottage. Although Efa and I are yet strong, we are now not strong enough to venture beyond our woods."

Roger exclaimed, "Am I not an Eques? Should I not ride in the strength of my knighthood and seek those in need? This is what I must do: I shall ride up the Ermine Way[2] to Eboracum.[3] There I will do business, expending but a small portion of our silver. I should like

---

2. The Roman Road from Londinium (London) to Linnuis (Lincoln) to Eboracum (York).

3. Eboracum was the Roman seat of military government in northern Britannia, now known as York.

to purchase vestments befitting my equestrian class: a helmet to cover my head down to my shoulders, coats of mail for myself and mount, a brass shield and a new sword, for I have blunted mine hacking trails in these woods. I will not ally myself to the Legion in Eboracum, but will ride where I feel led. Surely, I will bring hither those whom heaven would have you heal!"

Vittoria asked her son, "What if a Roman general asks your lineage, asks for proofs of your station?"

Roger answered forthrightly, "I am no fugitive, but the son of Prince Lucius! I fought for Rome with my sire and witnessed his death near the Danube. This I will plainly declare and have yet the signet ring of my station. If I am asked about my dame, I will tell only that after I left Carcaso with my brothers and my mother, our family was scattered. I will say that you fled to an unknown wilderness, intent on living the rest of your life in solitude. If I am asked what is my business and why I need armor and weapons, I will answer, 'I am a Prince, an Eques, heir to the rights of my sire, answerable only to the Emperor! As he has not called me to his service, I will do as I please. My equestrian class is entitled to trade. I am a publicani[4] and deal in arms, seeking out mountain smiths to find those who forge fine steel.' When asked why then do I need to buy steel fashioned in Eboracum, I will say, 'For my defense until I find that which I seek.'"

Vittoria embraced her son, saying, "Roger, be wiser than was Ramon when he pretended to be a buyer of arms and armor in Burdigala." At this, they both laughed and the next morning he left mounted to ride the Ermine Way.

As he rode alone and carried but a sword, Roger was accosted by robbers and once shed blood before he safely arrived in Eboracum. He had no difficulty in buying that which he sought. As foreseen, the

---

4. A Roman citizen legally free to engage in commerce.

commander of the fortress did ask who he was that he should possess such things. When he answered as he said he would, the commander showed Roger great deference, for he had been to Carcaso and knew his sire, the Prince. He then gave Roger an attestation of his rank and station on parchment and encouraged him in his pursuits, saying he would buy whatever fine arms he was able to obtain.

While riding back toward Linnuis, Roger fortuitously stopped to abide the night in a mountain hamlet. There a clever Druidic priest had made himself overlord. The man was greatly feared but not by the son of Prince Lucius. Roger had just dismounted before the door of the village inn, when this despotic priest demanded his possessions. Later Roger learned that seldom did wayfarers come to that hamlet, for the wicked overpriest was known abroad—unless, that is, the travelers were a guard of legionary. These were shown deference and afforded obsequious hospitality. Thus, Roman officers did not know of the man's murderous thievery.

The Druid lord repeated his demand, "No one rides alone into my village, though he be dressed as a Roman knight, for a true eques would know better than to do so! See, even while you were yet upon your steed, I set my guardsmen round about you. I command that you deliver your horse, equipage, arms and armor to me. Do this and swear obeisance to me as your lord and you shall surely live! Otherwise you shall . . ."

He ceased to speak, for in an instant Roger unsheathed his sword and thrust it into the man's belly so swiftly that it was almost unseen. With a quick twisting motion, he withdrew the bloody blade. In unbelief, the man starred at his own gore before he fell forward without so much as a groan. Roger knew where each guardsman stood. Listening for the meaning of each slight sound, he did not turn himself about, but heard only their hasty retreat.

The villagers were jubilant at the death of their tyrant and welcomed the knight as if he were a kindred son. Because of the parchment of attestation, they recognized Roger as one in authority. He stayed with them for several days, sent their sorcerers fleeing and helped the villagers choose a wise chieftain. Then it was that he learned of their smith and the skill he possessed in forging steel. Hence, Roger truly became a tradesman, for the weapons he purchased there he sold for a considerable profit in Eboracum. Returning he shared the gain and in this manner the village soon became prosperous. Whenever he traveled in their country, serving foremost his mother's purposes, he would abide with them and not to obtain steel alone. There was in the hamlet a flaxen-haired damsel of exceptional goodness, named Aénor, whose affection soon became the greatest desire of Roger's heart.

Three years passed and in that time he carried many a poor sufferer to his dame's woodland, on his horse or laid upon a cart. The virgin whom he loved soon learned the true reason for his travels, not because he told her, rather the fame of his rescues reached her ears. For stories multiplied of a young eques who distained Druidic rites and sometimes, though alone, disrupted their bloody rituals, saving victim's lives. If already wounded, he bore them away, be they man or woman, aged or young, to the Beldam's cottage near Linnuis.

When at last Aénor was confident enough of their love to ask Roger of these things, he confessed that the knight errant was himself. To his surprise she vowed to help him. In this way, Aénor's home became a second sanctuary until such time as the sufferers could be moved to his dame's woodlands.

Roger told all these things to his mother, who one day wisely said to him, "As with your brothers and sisters before, you must now look to your own life. There will always be those in need and heaven will continue to help me when you are gone. Because of you, far fewer are the heathen sacrifices hereabouts for you have caused a great dread among the Druids. Take Aénor as your wife and abide with her kin, for they love you. Continue to prosper her village in your trade and raise worthy sons and daughters in this northern land."

"Oh mama," Roger said compassionately, "how can I leave you alone? You are growing old and have need of my help!"

Vittoria answered him, "Have you forgotten how blessed is my forest? I will never suffer for want of food or the warmth of a radiant hearth. Also, my dear son, my years are many and I feel that soon I shall be *changed*. When my time comes, I must be alone. Please don't ask me why, but trust in my wisdom. Not even Efa can remain now in my cottage."

Roger looked at his mother bewildered and said, "Oh, it cannot be! You want me to take Efa to my new home in the mountain hamlet and leave you truly alone, alone to face a death that you feel is shortly to come? Oh, mama, this cannot be!"

Vittoria smiled brightly and replied, "Ah, and I thought Ramon was my only son given to dramatics!" She laughed as she took Roger's hands in hers, saying, "When was I ever alone? Do you not know that your dear sire is close—closer to me than ever before? Do you not know of the others, those who come to me while I sleep? Have you not heard their soft voices? These are my beloved dead, and truly they live!"

Roger answered, "Often *I do feel* the presence of sacred beings in your cottage. I know that what you say *is*! Yet I cannot bear to think of your form lying still, perhaps by the hearth or in your garden and there is no one here . . . I mean no one who may bury your body! Listen, mama, I shall never be far from you. Allow me to at least return each fortnight and confirm that all is well. Perhaps years may pass before you die. Would you not that I bring my own wife and your grandchildren to see you, that you might cherish them? If then, someday, I find you in that deep and lasting sleep, then I will lay you to rest beneath the sod in this holy place."

Vittoria answered, now with tears in her eyes, "Oh, how I have missed my own. How I love your brothers and sisters, their children and now their children's children! How I long to see my nieces and nephews and their little ones. Soon you will have a family and they too I will love! For this long time, I have lived without the embrace of so many I love! Why is this so, when that which I have most desired is to be a mother to my own and to those who would have me be a mother to them? This last desire has been granted in abundance, here in this cottage! Yet the former blessing is denied me, but I think only for a moment. Long is man's time to man! Age brings a remembrance of time as it really exists. According to this truth, all of life is but a few hours[5] of reckoning to God and those who live with him. I believe that one *time* soon, in as little as two of the Lord's days,[6] our family will be united forever. Then I shall embrace all of those who are mine!"

Roger replied, "Mama, when you speak of such things, it seems .. . well I try to understand, but it is like trying to comprehend eternity. To me forever seems forever distant!"

"When you grow older," Vittoria answered, "you will remember more of your forgotten past and so will begin to understand more of your distant future. That is according to the Lord's plan. He wants you to be vested in the all-important present."

Roger replied, "Ah, but there you go again, mama. Already we are speaking of impossible things and yet you have not answered my question. Allow me, please, that I may return to this woodland each fortnight and see that you are well."

She answered, "Nay, my son. You must trust that I am well. As with your brothers, leave me. Take Efa to your new home. Tell your

---

5. A day to God is a 1,000 years to man. 1,000/24 hours in a day = 41.7 mortal years, which equals 1 hour of Celestial time.
6. Two of the Lord's days equals two thousand years according to man's reckoning.

wife of me and your children too, as they grow. Tell them how much I love them!" She embraced Roger and whispered, "Last night I dreamed a dream. Vittoria, my great grandmama, stood at my bedside and spoke to me. I will tell you her words that you may not be distressed in your leaving. 'Daughter,' said the Lady of White, 'send Roger, your son, and Efa, your friend, away from this cottage. That which will shortly come upon you can only *be* if you abide alone.'"

Vittoria held his face in her hands and looked into his eyes, saying, "Now you must go on the morrow and you must not return again to this cottage or these woods, unless you are *called* to do so. Always be true to the truth. Remember that 'Life is timeless.' Our parting is brief, how ephemeral[7] you cannot yet understand. When again we are united, you shall *know*."

Efa and Roger wept when they left the Beldam's cottage. Efa could not be comforted until they reached the mountain hamlet and she met Roger's betrothed. That very day, the virgin Aénor was wed to him and she became a princess in the House of Lucius and Vittoria de Foix. Then was Efa happy again, although she thought such a thing could never be when living in the outside world beyond the enchanted woodland.

What was more remarkable is that Efa, despite her years, came to love an older villager, one whose unfaithful mate had been led away by the Druid despot in years gone by. They too were wed and his children learned that Efa was dear to them and they called her their own beautiful mother. Roger's wife also became a beloved mother. Aénor bore him fourteen children, raising twelve, for two died when young.

However, these blessings came about years after Roger and Efa

---

7. "Beginning and ending the same day." Oxford English Dictionary.

had left Vittoria alone in the woodlands of Linnuis. And now we must return to that time and learn what befell the Beldam.

CHAPTER 29

RECKONING

"What of the aged dame who bid us come?"
"Oh," she answered happily, "that was how I looked before I was made
young, and that is how I am now seen until you pass through my gate.
Those who travel without, even the good, can scarcely believe the true
nature of life and see according to their belief. Hence, they see me as I was,
and some see me not at all! Twice our bodies are young and only once are
we old, for when we attain our second youth then is the death of age."

The Beldam, from The Knights of the Argoat

It was a rare thing for a senator to visit Eboracum. Before the witnesses of his arrival learned that the aged but illustrious dignitary was a senator, they thought the Emperor himself had come to their fortress city, so great was his entourage. The powerful man, Senator Impius Paetus, had sailed from Rome to the northeast coast of Britannia and up the Usa River[1] to Eboracum aboard a magnificent vessel, escorted by two warships for a singular purpose.

It is often said that love and hate are but two edges of the same sword. This lie is advanced by those who say they once loved only to excuse their terrible vindictiveness after their shallow affections have been offended. Those who love truly wade silently through affliction while those who feel themselves wronged, despite the truth of the matter, strike back as furiously as a Vipera berus[2] in venomous hatred. Also, as love begets blessed forgiveness with commensurate healing, especially over time, hate sires a vendetta so terrible that the thirst for vengeance grows more monstrous with the passing of years.

When Esta was a beautiful young maiden in the employ of Calvus and was a valuable asset to his senatorial clients, a considerable number of the august assembly of 600 became enamored with her and some were overcome with lust for the innocent virgin. Only the watchful care given without her knowledge by Arrian and more especially by the Emperor himself saved Esta from untold sorrows. One senator of tremendous wealth and power was this Senator Impius Paetus. Impius confessed to his friends, "never had I really loved a woman until my eyes distantly swept over the exquisite form of the Maiden of Massilia!" He then attempted to initiate his imaginations, planning his conquest at dinners and festivals but was continually thwarted, even by Calvus.

Then Esta quit the Advocatus to advance the plans of Hadrian. Soon she became a serious threat to the senator's designs, for Impius was man who fostered war in every aspect of his life. Long before she knew of the plots against her life, he was their chief architect. It mattered not that Esta had become Vittoria and had lived many

1. Today known as the River Ouse, which is still navigable to York.
2. The Roman name for the only poisonous snake in Britannia, the Adder.

years in Foix without again challenging his avarice, he was foremost among those who again sought to have her killed. Only the coming of Arrian, Diocles, Michela and Calvus to Foix had saved her—for the senator arrived in Carcaso the very morning after she had vanished from the fortress.

Years again had passed when the senator, now an old but yet able man, learned of the reemergence of Sir Roger de Foix in Eboracum. Although this news was already dated when it came to his ears, it roused again his animosity to an awful frenzy.

For a month the senator waited impatiently in Eboracum for news from his spies. Of Roger, he was told he lived with his bride in a mountain hamlet and was indeed a tradesman in weapons. No one in the village had ever seen Roger's mother and Impius' spies were certain this was not a ruse. Roger was highly praised by the Roman garrison and as Impius had no interest in the young man's life, the senator's agents did not intrude further into the knight's affairs. Then word came from Linnuis to the senator of one called "The Beldam of the Woodlands," an avowed enemy of the Druids who was feared by their boldest sorcerers. As he thought on this possibility a voice whispered in his mind, "Yes, it is she!"

Senator Impius Paetus in Rome

"How grateful I am," Vittoria said aloud but to herself alone, "that I can still find the way to my garden and sit among fragrant flowers! It is such a glorious day!" The Beldam moved cautiously from her narrow porch down the two steps to the well-worn path, for her sight was dim. Since the leaving of Roger and Efa, she had become feeble. Sometimes she would slip lightly into sleep while seated in the garden among the living creatures of her world, the flora and fauna. Or she would nod off in the kitchen, waiting for simmering oats. Nonetheless, Vittoria ate only a bite or two before giving the remainder of her porridge to the squirrels and other small creatures who attended her daily, waiting for this delicious repast. Though Vittoria always arose at first light, she also loved to rest by the hearth, which seemed never to fail for want of fire.

Often she was lonely but never for long. When melancholy enveloped Vittoria, she closed her eyes and spoke to Lucius. He seemed so near that she could almost feel his hand in hers. Or thinking of Roger, she laughed and asked him to tell her again of his adventures on the Ermine Way. It seemed so real to her that she marveled that he was not actually sitting across the table. She loved to remember Señor Mateo and his always present humor. One by one, Vittoria visited loved ones from the past. One moment she recognized that she was a very old woman living alone in a fabled cottage. The next instant it seemed she was a very young demoiselle playing in the warm waters off the coast of Massilia with dear Naomi. As the days passed, she wondered at her solitude and for what purpose it was given.

The Beldam's Garden

THE OLD SENATOR said to his most trusted aide, "Esta, or Vittoria, or whatever she calls herself, is that sorceress called the Beldam by the villagers near Linnuis. Were it not for her, the wealth I possessed when a young man would have been immeasurable and surely I would have become the Emperor of Rome! I do not doubt that she is indeed an enchantress! How else," Impius said wretchedly, "could she have won the chaste affections of Hadrian and though only a miserable woman could have become his voice!"

The aide replied, "Perhaps she used her wiles on Hadrian, for no woman is above such!"

"Hah!" laughed the senator. "Well do I know that it was Esta's rebuffs rather than carnal submissions that gave her power over men. No! The maiden I knew would have died before allowing any man to touch her silken skin. Yet, the Emperor loved and protected her. So did Arrian and that miserable traitor, Calvus!"

Again, the aide spoke, "Well master, you have succeeded despite the frustrations she has given you!"

"Succeeded?" He spat the word as foam fell from his lips. "Were it not for Esta I would have *bought* the throne! I would have swayed my foes by persuasions they could not have resisted and had power over every man's life!"

Wisely the aide was quiet for a time while the heat dissipated slowly from the senator's red face. Then he said, "Master, what will you do now that you have found your nemesis?"

Impius muttered, "We must move quietly, without notice, that no word of our coming reaches her ears! I can no longer ride mounted. Buy a small one-horse carriage with a comfortable rear seat where I may sit or lay as it suits me. Here." He gave the aide a map written on parchment, showing the Ermine Way, wayside inns, Linnuis and the village to the east of the town. An X marked the spring summit at the crossroads. He continued, "The commander of Eboracum has assured me he has cleared the Ermine Way of robbers and that we may safely travel to the south, saying it is a most beautiful journey. I told him our purpose is just that, to enjoy the countryside of the lands he protects. He, of course, offered an escort, which I refused, saying soldiery would obstruct the peace I sought. I obtained this map from the agent I sent to Linnuis. As you can see, it marks all that is needed to prosper my venture."

"It is sufficient," said the aide. "What will you do when you find her?"

The man laughed as he replied, "Why, what will I do? I will watch *you* strangle this Beldam! Yet, do it not speedily, for I know you can break a man's neck as quick as a boy can wring a chicken. No, squeeze slowly. Suffocate Esta by degrees that I may watch her twist and jerk in agony, striving for breath that cannot be had!"

The aide smiled, for this charge was pleasing to his devil mind.

Vittoria found it too difficult to make her way to her old chair in the garden. Hence, she placed a woolen blanket and pillow upon the cottage porch. Sitting atop the two stairs, she fed again the small creatures that chirped their gratitude for her porridge. Then she lay back carefully on the pillow on the small wooden portico, for the day was warm and she needed no covering. Her eyelids were heavy and soon the old dame fell into deep sleep.

First, Vittoria dreamed of her son Lucius and Esta, his wife, their children and their children's children playing happily in Cordoba. Then she saw Cécilia, Jourdain, Felicia and Esclarmonde, each with their companions and posterity, living life worthily in Foix. Then a beautiful *spirit* greeted Vittoria and for a moment, only a moment, the Beldam was puzzled. "Ah!" she exclaimed, "You are my lovely

Phillipa! When you died in my arms you were but a child! Look how beautiful you are! Look how beautiful you will grow to be, for I have been promised I will one day raise you from the childhood of your death!"

Phillipa answered, "Yes mama. I am your own and long for that age."

The scene shifted to the Summerlands and she envisioned Ramon, András and Leon, each with pretty wives, daughters, sons— her own grandchildren and great grandchildren, some who frolicked upon the Tor while others studied in the abbey founded in Glaston- bury. Then at last she saw Roger with his dame and their new born son, living in a new home in a mountainous region that would one day be known as Selgovae.

Vittoria marveled, for they were so many! Then she heard her great grandmother's voice, saying, "My daughter, already your chil- dren are more than a hundred! Save for our precious Phillipa, all live yet in mortality. Succeeding generations of your seed shall number more than a thousand thousand! Can you count the blossoms in your garden—in your woods? Those who bloom in your lineage shall be greater than these. My child, could anything be more wonderful?"

"Nay!" said the old woman.

"Look again!" said the matriarch. "In but three centuries of man's time see those of your blood! Numerous are your daughters and sons in Britannia, Caledonia, Armorica[3], Gaul, Germania, and Hispania."

Vittoria looked and beheld each person born in her lineage. She marveled, for as she gazed upon each face, she knew their names and perceived their strengths and their failings. Nor was she shown these things in haste, for there was time given to see each soul. Some of her posterity were born propitiously in regal wealth and others in

---

3. Brittany

common poverty. Some were hale and hearty while many were sorely afflicted, even unto early death. Yet each individual was blessed with that Light which must be possessed to live mortality aright, according to the measure of truth given for their era.

As she looked upon their faces, she remembered the blessings of certain of her descendants and the warnings given them. "Ah," to one Vittoria exclaimed, "you who will be known as Mariana! What challenges you will confront and how sad shall be your life until your last daughter is born to you. How can I help you?" Then she saw one of her sons of the same era as Mariana, hundreds of years in the future, one who would be sacrificed upon the very greensward that was near her woodland cottage. "Oh no!" she cried out. "Dunn, you are to be made a Ceosan! My Lord, what can I do?"

Vittoria wept and not for these alone. Then her great grandmama again spoke to her. "Did you not desire to be a beautiful mother? There is no greater joy than this and also no greater burden. Yet sorrows will be overcome as you continue to strive for your children's sake."

"I will! I will!" said Vittoria sincerely.

"Then, what is it that you desire?" asked the voice.

Vittoria answered, "Oh, that I should be a Beldam to my seed so long as they are born upon this earth."

Said the spirit of the great lady, "Know that if this is attained, *whatever is needful will be yours to give.*"

"Master," said the aide with a shaking voice, "let us leave this forbidding place. Never have I seen such a loathsome wood! Do you not smell the stench of death!"

"Yes, I smell it too!" said the old senator. "It will pass. Certainly it is but the carcass of some beast left to rot. Press on, man, it cannot be far! If my wane legs carry me, surely such a warrior as you can persevere!"

"But these bogs grip my legs more fiercely, for I am much heavier than you! It is so cold." Nonetheless, he persisted in following the man who had well rewarded the evil he had done for him. How many times had he murdered? He could not remember—at least he could not until entering this foul woodland. For now he clearly saw in his mind each life he had taken. He had heard of waking nightmares but had thought such things foolishness, imaginings of a demented soul. Yet in truth, he *heard* voices coming from the earth and recognized many. His victims were known to him, for they were collogues of his master and more, *for he had killed Impius' own dame, a woman as foul as was her son.* "Oh, do you not hear them?" he remonstrated, "They know! Nothing is hid!"

"Silence!" said the senator. "Was this Beldam not said to be a sorceress? As we are in her forest, she must have access to our thoughts. The voices we hear are nothing but our own fears! When she is dead then all this misery will cease and this woodland shall be as any other. Surely there is food, ale and a warm fire waiting for us in her cottage. After you have killed Esta we shall eat, drink and take our rest in the comfort of her dwelling. You will see, it is but stone and thatch and will warm our bodies as well as any house."

It took much longer for the two intruders to reach the place, many hours more than others who had walked the same way. Nonetheless, they *did* find the beautiful cottage. Yet, they saw only a forlorn lodge, seemingly deserted and still as a necropolis. Flowers bloomed along the pathway, but they saw not the living flora nor did they hear the trill of the songbird, for everything *appeared to them* as lifeless. Stealthily, the two men made their way to the front of the Beldam's home.

"What is that?" exclaimed the aide, pointing to the porch.

The senator looked but did not believe his own eyes. "What? It cannot be!" He took a few paces more and stared down upon a woman, lying still and silent upon the planks of the portico. Deluded, he saw not Vittoria sleeping; rather she seemed to be a corpse, a woman he had murdered by the hand of his aide. To his mind, her fixed visage was horrific, as if she were the slain mistress of a demon, Bel's dame, though he knew ever contorted feature of her face. "Impossible!" he exclaimed. Yet his mind was incapable of seeing what in reality was before him. So long had Impius espoused lies that the truth had become incomprehensible. Impius rubbed his eyes and looked again upon the reposed form lying on the Beldam's porch, but he did not see the beautiful aged woman he had made his foe. Rather in her stead he still saw a lifeless carcass whose face was that of his own stricken mother!

All his life Impius had been a destroyer, even of she who had given him mortal life. Although the copious blood he had spilled had long cried from the bowels of the earth for vengeance, the numerous spirits he had severed from their bodies now flew at him! The ghastly apparitions, the ultimate terrors, surrounded him, their ethereal limbs outstretched struggling to seize him! He heard their desperate wailing and then raised his own stifled voice in chorus with the dead, gnashing his teeth, screaming, *"No! No! It must not be! I am a senator of Rome! This cannot happen to me! I am a god!"*

The old senator turned and ran, stumbled, fell and pled for his aide to help him, help him escape from the horrors of their own doing. Hours later, trembling, he was laid in the back of his carriage and taken to the village inn. There was no physician to attend him and no matron would go near the withered man, for his aspect was dreadful. Nonetheless, the overpriest was summoned and when he arrived the aide told the sorcerer what had befallen his master. Hence, the Druids were again assured that the woodland was accursed.

Left alone in a solitary room, Senator Impius Paetus, the persecutor of Vittoria, died before the rising of the sun. As for his aide, he became known as the Madman of Eboracum, a street beggar who ran when none pursued and pled continually to the air.

As the cool of evening approached, Vittoria awoke from a wonderous sleep. Though earlier she was slightly disturbed, she thought it of no account. She did not know that an old enemy had glowered over her and seeing his worst fear had fled. Embers near the hearth still glowed and she wondered at this. How long had it been since she added wood to the fire? The great woodpile seemed undiminished. No matter, there was warmth and peace in her home.

The Beldam said to herself, "Why am I still so sleepy? Have I not slept upon the porch for hours? Oh, do you remember, Vittoria what you saw in your dream? Yes, oh yes! How can I rest, there is so much I must do!"

Nonetheless, the old woman laid down upon her bed and looked about her cottage, then laughed a little, saying, "My eyes are so weak! Better it is to see in dreams, for then all is clear." She fell asleep again, filled with a strange happiness.

The rays of the early sun streamed through the open windows of the old cottage. Vittoria sat up, stretched and rose easily to her feet. The day was so beautiful and she felt so alive. She looked out a window upon the woods, seeing clearly, effortlessly. A hart grazed on grass just beyond a flowered hedgerow. A family of hares looked up at her and resumed eating roots she had dug for them days before. Songbirds sang to the morning sun, as they always did in her forest. Everything looked as it had for years—wonderous but somehow altered. Something was so different. What was changed?

Then Vittoria looked down at her hands. They were smooth. She felt her face, touched her eyes, then ran to a mirror. Her reflection was that of a beautiful young maiden! *She picked up a cup and felt it solidly, poured spring water into it and drank.* It was so refreshing!

Like the blessed Woodlands of Ruith, Vittoria herself was changed, her body miraculously renewed, transfigured for a great purpose and empowered for greater adventures than ever she had lived before!

NEARLY THREE CENTURIES were come and gone in the world of men while but seven hours of celestial time had passed for the Beldam. Now she understood time as it was before. Always was Vittoria needed but seldom was she seen as she really was. Most often the angel came to mortals unaware of her *nearly* exalted station. However, in great extremities the matriarch intervened in truly inexplicable, otherworldly ways.

A daughter of hers, born an Anglian near Linnuis, a descendant of ten generations, was to be a victim of a deadly conspiracy and yet it was not Nerienda's time to die. Her assassin was not her enemy, but a British peasant who was compelled by a despot to kill Nerienda to save his own wife and children. This, as is told in the Fifth Annal of these chronicles:

> *Near the trail there was a sea cliff that towered fifteen rods*
> *above a foaming alcove. Known to the villagers as the*
> *Point of Paol, the walls of the escarpment were*
> *concave, so that if a stone were dropped the rock*
> *would not bounce down the face, but would fall*

*straightway to the brine below. Nerienda ran to the
ledge, thirty strides distant, then looked back at the
others on the trail.*

*What Nerienda saw, she glimpsed only for an instant.
Running hard toward her on the soft grass, so that she
had not heard his footsteps, was the strange Briton.
His eyes and aspect were wild, deranged—his
weapons his outstretched hands. In the blink of an eye
he seized the princess and by the power of momentum,
swept her and himself of the precipice!*

*All had been a blur as Nerienda tumbled from the top of
the cliff. Vehemently she tore the assailant's hands
from about her waist and tried to right herself, as she
had done many times in her youth, when jumping
from a high waterfall near Linnuis. Still, all was
confusion—sky rolling into crags, into sea, into sky.
Why could she not do it? Then she realized the frantic
Briton had caught hold of her foot. She kicked with
her might, but the effort only seemed to intensify the
horrible whirling. Suddenly, Nerienda slammed
against him and in the next instant struck the
foaming sea. Only three seconds had elapsed, though
she'd fallen from a height thirty times greater than
her stature. She sank deep into the frothing, brackish
water, stunned, unable to move, yet she could see. Her
cape, ripped from her body, was floating toward the
surface. The light above was growing faint. She could
feel herself growing cold and hoped the bitter chill
would numb her terrible agony.*

*Then came the repeal—not that time was undone or the
pain un-suffered. She was lifted much faster than she
had fallen—caught up by a silent wind. The hurt*

began to fade and paralysis was effortlessly swept away.

That she was saved unnaturally seemed then quite natural to her.

"Why grandmother, this is like it used to be!" Nerienda said with delight. Though she did not understand how this was possible, neither was Nerienda confused.

The angelic dame replied, "Look down upon the Argoat, the meadow lands, the sea, the familiar world you trod. Yet I am beside you in the sunlit sky. Nerienda, do you dream?"

"Nay, I am awake," she answered.

"Only less asleep," said the beautiful mother. "Nonetheless, strive to forget not. That you still are is because you have kept more than others. Think back when we spoke of the Angels-Tear. To the people of your village the flowers were mute, yet you heard their soft voices. To believe in that which is true has far greater power than accepting the demands of man's reason. Faith is conforming the mind to the will of the spirit, for there, veiled, resides ageless memories of what was, the help of what is, and the knowledge of what may be."

The damsel asked, "What may be?"

"See," said the guide, "below you is a woodland glen near the trail to Trégor. Rest unseen in the warm shade I give you. Recover, for that is my blessing. Eat of fruit out of season, for until they are come it is your meat and drink. Do right, my daughter, and we will journey again together."

"When?" The question was a plea.

The seraph answered, "When, through you, others we love

are come—when Father's purpose in you is done—
when you dream you are old."
Suddenly, the maiden was no longer in the air but stood in
a lush valley. Though the vernal equinox had yet to
pass, the dell was a marvel, for in it grew a fragrant
orchard, rich in color, abundant in ripe pomes, grapes
and nuts. "Who shall find me here?" asked Nerienda.
The Beldam answered, "Three knights."

As this chronicle is not Nerienda's but Vittoria's story, no more will be told of the Anglian maiden, only that her life was preserved for a great purpose by Vittoria, a mother who loved her dearly.

Many codices could be written and some stories have been told about Vittoria's deeds after she was young again. Nonetheless, we must be careful lest too much is disclosed, for mortality is meant to be a veiled existence. Still only a fool lives for this *time* only. Our temporal existence is but an hour or two of a single day in the life of the angels. Remember, remember, "Life is timeless."

The Angel by Thayer

CHAPTER 30

EPILOGUE AND LAST ADVENTURE

"Beloved, now are we the sons of God, and it doth not yet appear what we shall be . . ."

John

❧

As the story of Vittoria, who first was known as Esta, comes to an end, the reader is undoubtedly left with questions. What of her reunion with loved ones, especially with her dear husband, Prince Lucius? That she became a guardian angelic mother has been told. Nonetheless, there can be no ageless motherhood without ageless fatherhood.

The beautiful painting *The Angel* by Thayer was chosen because of the lady's expressive countenance; although a seraph, she is in a reflective moment, *sorrowful.* Is such a thing possible? Can a being of a high station *feel* incredible sadness? The answer is yes! In truth, the more refined a person is, the greater is their capacity to feel godly emotions.

The highest example of this was the Lord's response to the death of Lazarus. When Jesus saw how Mary and Martha grievously mourned for the loss of their brother, he did not summarily dismiss their suffering, telling the women to take courage for it would all be made right in the end. No, for the Lord possesses perfect empathy. A wonderful man had died and although Christ knew what would shortly transpire, yet the death of his friend had broken the hearts of his sisters and also had a profound effect upon his own. When he was shown the lifeless body of Lazarus, it is written: "Jesus wept."[1]

Yet the mien of Thayer's angel might convey more than sorrow, seeming to express *longing, yearning, missing.*

There are certain immutable rites that are requisite for exaltation in the Celestial Kingdom of Heaven. To Peter and the Twelve were given the keys of this authority, for whatever they bound or sealed upon the earth was likewise sealed or bound in heaven.[2] This power continued on the earth only so long as apostles lived and ministered in mortality. As one died, another was appointed in their stead until all were killed. This immeasurable loss was foretold in holy writ,[3] but it was also prophesied that before Christ's Second Coming there would be a marvelous "restitution of all things."[4]

As Esta was born in that era of loss following the deaths of the key-holders, she was not able to receive the vital[5] rite of baptism. Nonetheless she looked forward to the day when she would indeed receive this saving ordinance, even if it should be after her mortal life. She had read Paul's promise, "Else what shall they do which are

---

1. John 11:35
2. Matthew 18:18 "Whatsoever ye shall bind on earth shall be bound in heaven."
3. 2 Thessalonians 2:1-3
4. Acts 3:19-21
5. John 3:3

baptized for the dead, if the dead rise not at all? Why are they then baptized for the dead?"[6]

Likewise, Vittoria had covenanted with Lucius to be his wife only *until death*, for again they lived in a time when the apostolic sealing power was lost to the world and there was no one that could perform the sacred rite that could bind their marriage eternally. Yet, their love was endless and they lived in the hope that someday their union could be made to last forever.

In our story, when Vittoria was "changed," passing from mortality to a relatively rare transfigured state, it would be likely that she was allowed to greet loved ones who had passed from this life. Seeing her deceased father, mother, grandmother and great grandmother would have been joyous! What of seeing Lucius again? *The reunion with her earthly husband could not be complete nor all she desired, for they were no longer wed!* "Til death do us part" is true of all earthly alliances. Hence, they could not have the close companionship of a true marriage until their earthly marriage was transformed by God through his apostolic servants. Vittoria understood that this blessing, like true baptism, would be part of the restitution or restoration of all things. Although she had become an angel, yet Vittoria *longed* for the day when she would be more and more especially, when she should be forever bound to Lucius.

When and how should this be realized? The narrative states that Vittoria was "nearly exalted." *Nearly* is far from entirely! It is like almost reaching a destination, you are not there until you are completely there.

More than eighteen hundred years have passed since the setting of Vittoria's story. In that time, in reality, countless disembodied individuals have been waiting for the restoration of apostolic authority to the earth. Peter said that the return of living apostles

---

6. 1 Corinthians 15:29

would be a sign that the Second Coming of the Savior was soon to follow. After the restoration, how are the saving rites to be ministered for the living as well as the dead? As Ruith explained to Isabel and Ramon, this is why holy temples are built at God's command.

When nations build foreign embassies in distant lands, the ground beneath these buildings is considered the very soil of the far countries they represent. Likewise, a true temple of God is a Celestial Embassy, wholly separate from the surrounding world. When a person enters a dedicated Temple of the Most High God they become a citizen of the Far Country of Heaven and are given the opportunity to be endowed with the knowledge and power to one day return to their homeland and inherit all the blessings of their Father and His Only Begotten Son. They may also solemnize vicarious rites for their ancestors who, through no fault of their own, like Esta, were unable to receive the saving rituals during their mortal lives.

There are Christians who believe otherwise, who misinterpret a certain saying of the Lord: "For *in* the resurrection they neither marry, nor are given in marriage."[7] This is comparable to saying one cannot obtain forgiveness in the resurrection. Forgiveness must be obtained *in advance* of the judgement of the resurrection. This is done by exercising faith, repentance, being truly baptized and receiving the Gift of the Holy Spirit—and this all must be accomplished prior to the reuniting of our spirits with our bodies. So also, if an eternal marriage is to be realized, the wife and husband must be sealed by apostolic authority, according to the Law of God, *before* they rise from the dead and are judged.

Accompanying the promised restitution of all things is a turning of the hearts and minds of children to their mothers and fathers, no matter how distant their ancestry and an equal turning of the hearts

---

7. Matthew 22:30

and minds of parents, no matter how far descended, to their children.[8]

In our story, the "changed" Vittoria was called to be a glorified *Ministering Angel* to her descendants. Known as the Beldam, she played a vital role in the book *The Knights of The Argoat*, although Vittoria's history and how she became what she was, would not be told until the writing of this work.

To be a ministering servant is to do for others what they cannot do for themselves. In this life we are commanded to do all we can to live aright and accomplish our life's mission. Nonetheless, when we have done all that we can do and are yet in peril, we are saved by the grace of our Lord. Often this saving is done by His agents sent to help us, both seen and unseen, lest we are destroyed. In this manner, a heroine in our storyline, Nerienda, was wondrously saved by her ancestral mother from an early death when she fell from a sea cliff.

However, *there is a reciprocal obligation that rests upon mortal descendants*, a calling as sure as Ancestral Deliverers. This calling is to be *Ministering Deliverers of our Progenitors*. That is, to seek out ancestors who lived and died before apostolic power was restored to the earth, or those who in life did not understand these truths. These *ministering deliverers* are able to enter the temples and vicariously perform vital rites for those who cannot act for themselves. Hence, the living are to be submersed in holy baptismal fonts on behalf of their dead and kneel also at eternal marriage altars for kindred ancestors. Only those spirit persons who accept these ordinances, through faith in Christ, having been taught His gospel in the world

---

8. Malachi 4:5 "Behold, I will send you Elijah the prophet before the coming of the great and dreadful day of the LORD: And he shall turn the heart of the fathers to the children, and the heart of the children to their fathers, lest I come and smite the earth with a curse."

of spirits, are then delivered in the last judgement that attends the resurrection of the just.

Like Vittoria in our story, there are multitudes of the deceased that wait for this saving work to be done. They long to be discovered by a descendant no matter how distant. However, what if the record of their life is undiscoverable? Many lived in times and places where earthly histories were poorly kept or have since been lost. Therefore, in the Father's plan, the final judgement and resurrection will be at the *end* of the Millennium. During this thousand-year period of peace, ushered in by Christ's Second Coming, all things will be gathered together, those of heaven combined with the rightful things of the earth.[9] Thus, during the Millennium, not one person will be overlooked. As truth is taught to those who did not receive it during life,[10] so also no one will be deprived of saving ordinances. All will be found; they may choose to accept truth or reject it and also accept vital rites, or reject them, for God is no respecter of persons.

An ancient mother may become an angel to a daughter and a daughter may become an angel to a mother far removed. As Vittoria rescued Nerienda, a daughter of ten generations, so must ancestors be lifted by their children's children to the last day. It is written that *during* the Millennium, "Then shall the *angels* be crowned with the glory of his might, and the saints shall be filled with his glory and receive their inheritance and be made equal with him."

There are many who are angels, who are nearly exalted, as was Vittoria in the story of Esta, who lack but one thing: the ministering of a deliverer, that is, a son or daughter, to act on their behalf in the Temple of God. When this is done, they shall finally reach their destination in the resurrection, crowned with the glory of His might and receive their inheritance as a daughter or son of the Eternal

---

9. Ephesians 1:10
10. 1 Peter 3:18-19

Father. As John wrote: "To him that overcometh will I grant to sit with me in my throne, even as I also overcame, and am set down with my Father in his throne."[11]

In the story of the Beldam, what does the Enchanted Woodlands near Linnuis represent? Paul speaks of three realms. The first two he names directly, the Celestial and the Terrestrial,[12] but the last dominion is unnamed in most translations of the Epistle of Corinthians. Yet, there are *two* terrestrial types, or two earthly variants: earth during the era of the Garden of Eden, that is, earth *before* The Fall— and the present earth, that is, earth *after* The Fall. The word "telestial" is used to denote this fallen realm, for the present earth is "Telos" or "Tellus," the end abode, that which is the farthest from God's dwelling place.

In the terrestrial life of Eden there was no animosity, not even between man and beast. It was a magnificent garden, unhindered by briars, all seasons were seasons of fruitfulness, unmarred by inclement weather. As part of the restitution of all things, the terrestrial glory of Eden will encompass the entire world. As the Lord descends to inaugurate His peaceful reign, he will first cleanse the earth of all that is telestial or wicked. Those who remain will be transfigured, or changed so as not to suffer in the flesh. Vittoria's "change" was symbolic of this existence. Hence, the Beldam's Enchanted Woods was a small archetype of the terrestrial realm, but not a perfect representation of the Millennial Kingdom. The forest of the Beldam repelled evil whereas the new Eden will be entirely free of malevolence.

That we might transform the melancholy aspect of Thayer's angel, we must foretell the future and write one last adventure in the story of Vittoria.

---

11. Revelation 3:21
12. 1 Corinthians 15:40-42

THE FRAGMENTED FACE of the world has been transformed. No more are there continents and many islands, but the earth is as it was in the days before Peleg,[13] before it was divided. There are no deserts unfit for habitation; all the land is so pleasing to the eye that a description of its glory could not be written entirely before it *was*.

There are no terrors, no raging torrents, no wars of man or nature. Pestilence is a long-forgotten memory. A small boy waits upon a hole in the ground where soon appears a viper from its pit and the two play with one another.[14] No child suffers harm; all grow old until their one hundredth year,[15] when she or he becomes young again, in an instant, and shall thereafter live in the excellence of youth, forever. There are no carnivores, for the wolf, the bear and lion graze on lush meadow grass with their friends, the ox and lamb.[16]

The inhabitants of the earth multiply and joyously build houses, never to be wasted; they plant vineyards and orchards, whose fruit never fails. Throughout the breadth and length of the land there is no weeping.[17]

The sun, moon and stars are of a different order, for there is a new heaven[18] of brilliance that has not been seen since Eden fell, for the earth has left the outer reaches of the galaxy and is restored to orbit the paradisical regions of heaven.

The power of prayer is greatly magnified, for even before entreaty is made or else while the supplicant is yet speaking, God answers the

---

13. Genesis 10:25
14. Isaiah 11:8
15. Isaiah 65: 20
16. Isaiah 65:25
17. Isaiah 65:19
18. Isaiah 65: 17

petition.[19] Every person knows the King who rules their happiness. As the waters cover the sea, so the knowledge of Him envelopes the hearts and minds of his people.[20]

Of all the buildings that are built upon all the face of the earth, the most glorious are the holy temples and they number in the thousands. One of these sacred edifices stands on land that in days past was known as Foix. Kneeling at the altar of this temple is a mortal man and a mortal woman, far removed descendants of Prince Lucius and Princess Vittoria de Foix. Through miraculous means they have "discovered" these royal progenitors who lived mortal lives of excellence and honored the light given them of heaven.

For centuries, Vittoria and Lucius continued to serve their family and their God, learning in the *other* world, teaching, ministering, saving, *waiting, longing* for the day when they would be eternally sealed to each other and receive all the promises given to the patriarchs and matriarchs of old, blessings far, far greater than dominions in Foix, Carcaso, or even the glorious Empire of Rome—for by this sealing in this temple, this day, by the power of their Redeemer, Vittoria and Lucius shall inherit thrones, kingdoms, principalities, and powers, dominions, all heights and depths, never again to be separated, wed to each other forever!

A minister of the Almighty, having received his office by apostolic authority, calls the mortal man and woman by their names, stating that they are living proxies for Lucius and Vittoria de Foix. He then proceeds to give the greatest of all blessings! Many are the witnesses to this regal ceremony, both virtuous mortals and righteous spirits, for it is a joyous celebratory rite performed in the age of the miraculous Millennium. Among those present are Vittoria's papa and

---

19. Isaiah 65:24
20. Isaiah 11:9

mama, her la maire mama[21] and reiremenina,[22] her righteous name-sake, the first Christian Vittoria, also Diocles, the compassionate and valiant charioteer, with Michela, his angelic songstress, who for over two millennia has lifted her voice only in virtue and in praise of heaven, Naomi, Esta's faithful childhood friend, with her husband Ophelos and her goodly sire, Eitan, and her sainted mama, in whose beautiful likeness the Jewish maiden was formed. Also attending are Vittoria's cherished los avis,[23] Maros and Eponi, for all that Naomi promised the Galatians in life has come to pass. Señor Mateo, with his daughter, the second Esta, and her husband, the second Lucius, Phillipa, who died when young, Roger and his beloved Aénor, Ramon with his adored Isabel, indeed all of their children with their companions and many of their friends who learned the truth from them have come to share in the joy of this eternal rite.

Princess Nerienda and Sir Dunn of the Argoat and also others of their posterity witness the *two* who stand in the hallowed room, whose every hope and aspiration is now realized. Vittoria and Lucius know that those who kneel on their behalf at the altar are doing a wondrous thing they cannot do for themselves. It is according to the irrevocable plan of the Father that they should be served by their seed in similitude of their own service to them. The vicarious eternal marriage rite is completed! Lucius and Vittoria embrace and feel such love as eye has not seen nor entered into the heart of man!

IT IS the dawning of a new age and the coming of the heavenly

---

21. Grandmother in Occitan.
22. Great grandmother in Occitan.
23. Grandparents in Occitan.

"country"[24] spoken of by Paul, where all promises made by Heavenly Father to his children are at last realized. It is done! No more are Vittoria and Lucius angels possessing only spirits, for they are raised from the dead, receiving their bodies again, their physical forms perfected and brilliantly Celestialized in the Resurrection of the Just! They are Burning Ones! Their coronation is glorious as The Prince and Princess are crowned and enthroned with an everlasting inheritance, raised to the utmost station of existence, having become like[25] unto The Savior of All, The Messiah, He Who Burns with Omnipotent Power more resplendent than the greatest stars of the galaxy.

Queen Vittoria and King Lucius, together with their kin and other valiant devotees[26] of the Son of the Almighty, now embark upon unimaginable adventures, governing dominions whose grandeur far exceeds the might, wealth and beauty of the greatest earthly realms. That story cannot yet be written but most assuredly, someday, it will be!

The End.

---

24. Hebrew 11:13-16

25. 1 John 3:2 "Beloved, now are we the sons of God, and it doth not yet appear what we shall be: but we know that, when he shall appear, we shall be like him; for we shall see him as he is.

26. Revelations 3:21 "To him that *overcometh will I grant to sit with me in my throne, even as I also overcame, and am set down with my Father in his throne."

www.ingramcontent.com/pod-product-compliance
Lightning Source LLC
Chambersburg PA
CBHW070148120726
47909CB00001B/30